Praise for

The Foundling

A *Real Simple* Best Book of 2022 ★ A *Washington Post* Notable
Work of Fiction ★ A *Kirkus Reviews* Summer Book Club Pick ★
A Women's National Book Association Great Group Reads
Selection ★ Featured in *Lit Hub*'s Best Reviewed Books List

"Leary is such a virtuoso. . . . *The Foundling* arrests us precisely because
its antagonist comes cloaked in the good intentions of progressive social
reform. . . . Book clubs, uncork your bottles."

—*The New York Times*

"The word 'timely' is often used to describe novels that appear at a resonant
historical moment. But when it comes to the regulation of women's bodies
and the criminalization of sex and reproductive practices, it's hard to pick a
time when a novel like Ann Leary's *The Foundling* wouldn't speak to where
we are. Leary's novel is ultimately a hopeful one. . . . [She] is optimistic that
reason will prevail."

—*Los Angeles Times*

"An irresistible teenage narrator and the jaw-dropping caper she pulls off
make this novel a kick."

—*People*

"This eye-opening novel, based in part on Leary's family history, looks at
the outrageous ways our society has sought to control women."

—*Real Simple* (Top Pick for Historical Fiction)

"A fascinating, unsettling, page-turning story inspired by the little-known and horrifying practice of eugenics in 1920s America."

—Lisa Genova, *New York Times* bestselling author of *Still Alice* and *Remember*

"*The Foundling* is a gripping account of the ways big, structural decisions can change the intimate lives of ordinary people. Deeply empathetic to its characters with a sense of awe for the ironies of history, Ann Leary explores the complicated ties of community for those who have none, in a world determined to punish the most vulnerable. Through it all, her characters never lose their sense of humanity or sight of what it means to care for one another."

—Kaitlyn Greenidge, author of *Libertie*

"Leary's latest is a stunning tale of corruption, compassion, and hope, and includes one of the best endings I've read in ages. She's reached back in history and uncovered a shockingly true story, one that resonates strongly today. Full of jaw-dropping twists and intriguing characters—you won't be able to put it down."

—Fiona Davis, *New York Times* bestselling author of *The Magnolia Palace*

MARYSUE
RUCCI
BOOKS

The Foundling

A NOVEL

Ann Leary

MARYSUE RUCCI BOOKS

New York   London   Toronto   Sydney   New Delhi

MARYSUE
RUCCI
BOOKS

SCRIBNER

Marysue Rucci Books/Scribner
An Imprint of Simon & Schuster
1230 Avenue of the Americas
New York, NY 10020

First Marysue Rucci Books/Scribner trade paperback edition April 2023

MARYSUE RUCCI BOOKS/SCRIBNER and colophon are trademarks of Simon & Schuster, Inc.

SCRIBNER and colophon are trademarks of The Gale Group, Inc., used under license by Simon & Schuster, Inc.

For information about special discounts for bulk purchases, please contact Simon & Schuster Special Sales at 1-866-506-1949 or business@simonandschuster.com.

The Simon & Schuster Speakers Bureau can bring authors to your live event. For more information or to book an event, contact the Simon & Schuster Speakers Bureau at 1-866-248-3049 or visit our website at www.simonspeakers.com.

Interior design by Kathryn A. Kenney-Peterson

Manufactured in the United States of America

1   3   5   7   9   10   8   6   4   2

Library of Congress Cataloging-in-Publication Data has been applied for.

ISBN 978-1-9821-2038-2
ISBN 978-1-9821-2039-9 (pbk)
ISBN 978-1-9821-2040-5 (ebook)

*Dedicated to Meg and Paul
and to the memory of our grandmother Mary*

Author's Note

WHEN I began researching my family's genealogy about ten years ago, I wanted to learn how my maternal grandmother became an orphan. I never did find that out; there's no record of her birth or childhood homes. But I did find her in a 1930s federal census record. She was seventeen years old and working as a stenographer in a large Pennsylvania institution called the Laurelton State Village for Feeble-Minded Women of Childbearing Age. My grandmother is dead, and as far as I know she never spoke to anybody about her time working there. I was curious about the off-putting name of the place, so I decided to do a little research. I'm still obsessed with what I discovered.

Laurelton State Village was not a training school for young women with intellectual disabilities, as I had presumed. During the years my grandmother worked there, it was a eugenics asylum, one of many in this country. Its primary mission was to segregate girls and women who were "mentally or morally defective" so that they would not produce future "defectives."

During the first decades of the twentieth century, if a young woman was arrested in a speakeasy or had a child out of wedlock; if she was a lesbian or worked as a prostitute, she was often diagnosed as being mentally defective. These were criminal behaviors at that time, and criminality had become intertwined with widely held theories about the heritability of mental illnesses and intellectual disabilities. Thousands of women, who would certainly test within the normal and above-normal range of intelligence today, were labeled "feebleminded." They were sterilized and/or imprisoned because of eugenics laws. Some were as young as twelve years old when they were committed to homes for the feebleminded. They wouldn't be released until they'd reached menopause.

At Laurelton State Village, the "feebleminded girls" cleared many acres of forestland, labored in crop fields, mucked up after the livestock herds, and did almost all the cooking, cleaning, and other duties related to maintaining the large institution. Many were hired out to work in nearby homes and businesses. Their salaries were paid to the asylum, not the women.

At the helm of this successful public institution was a fascinating superintendent named Dr. Mary Wolfe. Dr. Wolfe had earned a medical degree when few women went to college. She was one of our nation's first female psychiatrists, an outspoken leader of the women's suffrage movement of the 1910s, and a brilliant public speaker. She was an early feminist, a crusader for women's civil rights, and an advocate for the health and welfare of women. At first glance, it was easy for me to see why my grandmother would want to work for such an intelligent, modern-thinking woman.

Then I delved a little deeper. What I learned was the inspiration for *The Foundling*. Having said that, *The Foundling* is a work of fiction. All characters and events are products of my imagination.

I want to add that this novel contains language and attitudes about race, sexuality, and intellectual disabilities that were prevalent in early-twentieth-century America but are certainly offensive by today's standards. The words *feebleminded, moron, imbecile,* and *idiot* were clinical terms at that time. They were used by doctors and psychologists to classify a substantial percentage of the population deemed mentally and/or morally unfit. An example of how these words were used can be found in the following quote. It was written by another celebrated feminist, a champion of women's reproductive rights, and also, like many other progressives of her era, an avid eugenicist.

> Every feeble-minded girl or woman of the hereditary type, especially of the moron class, should be segregated during the reproductive period. Otherwise, she is almost certain to bear imbecile children, who in turn are just as certain to breed other defectives.
> —Margaret Sanger, *The Pivot of Civilization*, 1922

Thank you for reading *The Foundling*.

Ann Leary
October 2021

The Foundling

Part One

One

I'VE been told that my mother had a wonderful sense of humor. Also that she was pretty. But most people recall her wit first, and her easy laughter, and because of this I've always had a better sense of how she felt than how she looked. She must have been happy most of the time if she found so many funny things to say and to laugh about. She died when I was an infant, so I have no memory of her. After I moved to my aunt Kate's house, I'd hear her talking with friends about my mother and me, usually in hushed tones after I'd just left the room.

"She's a somber little thing," somebody would say. Or "She's so shy; she certainly hasn't Louisa's high spirits."

That was my mother—Louisa. Apparently, there was a sparkle in her eye. My uncle Teddy said this about her once, and when I asked him where the sparkle was—what part of the eye, he laughed and gave me a wink. When I asked him again, he told me to shut my trap.

I didn't inherit my mother's high spirits or her sparkly eye, but she did leave me a very nice lady's suitcase. It had been a wedding gift from a wealthy distant cousin. I never saw it until the day Father came for me at St. Catherine's Orphan Asylum. He gave Mother Beatrice no notice, just showed up one afternoon in the summer of 1922, when I was twelve. He arrived in a borrowed black Packard, and when he strode out to the courtyard, where my friends and I were playing, he called out, "Which one of you is Mary?"

At least five of us raised our hands—it was a Catholic orphanage, after all. But I felt, as he smiled vaguely at each of us in turn, like he'd reached inside me and crushed my heart with his hand. I hadn't seen him in almost a year, but I recognized him instantly. I'd grown a bit; I think that's why he didn't know me at first.

"What about Edel . . . or Trudy?" he said. "We called our girl Trudy when she was a baby. Trudy Engle."

I was too thrilled to remain hurt. As soon as I stepped forward, he said, "Well, there you are," and pulled me close. I felt the strange smoothness of his freshly shaved jaw during that brief moment when he pressed his face against my forehead. He used to have rough whiskers when Uncle Teddy took me to visit him up at the lumber mill.

He told me to pack my clothes—he was moving me in with Aunt Kate. The laughter and taunts from some of the older girls when he reminded them of my original name were like blanks fired from a pistol. They were like the loud *pop-pop-pop* from a clown's dummy pistol in the circus that came to Scranton every summer. The circus had a free night for "Foundlings and Other Unfortunates." We all screamed and clung to one another when we were little and heard that clown's gun the first time, but the next year and the years after, we didn't even flinch. We fought over peanuts and candy in the stands while the clown did those same old tired gags. The elephant never left its tent on foundling night—sometimes the acrobats took the night off too. We were left with that dumb clown and a dog act, and who cared about them? We got free bags of goodies. Similarly, who cared about those girls calling me that stupid nickname? I had a father; they didn't. He was taking me away. They were staying there at the home.

"Well c'mon, let's get your things," Father said. He was carrying the lovely white suitcase that had once belonged to my very own mother.

"She hasn't many *things*," Mother Beatrice scolded when we were in the long, low-ceilinged dormitory hall. "Certainly not enough to fill a large suitcase like that, Mr. Engle. I don't know what a girl would do with such an expensive-looking piece of luggage. If you'd given us more notice, we'd have gladly packed her essentials in a parcel as we do for our half-orphans who are lucky enough to have family to go to."

A few of my friends—Dorothy, Marge, Mary Hempel, Little Mary—they'd all followed us inside, and now they gaped at Father like he was a film star—it wasn't every day a real father showed up at St. Cat's. I realized that I was gazing up at him the way they were, more like an awestruck fan than a daughter. I moved closer to him, and I even thought for a moment that I should hold his hand—the way daughters did with their fathers in the movies. But he accidently jabbed me in the shoulder when he tossed the suitcase on the bed, then he pulled a hand-kerchief from his vest to wipe his forehead. It was so hot up there in the ward on summer days you could barely breathe sometimes.

Mother Beatrice was busy examining my mother's suitcase, and that really bugged me. It was my mother's, why did she have to touch every inch of it? Finally, she turned the two brass clasps in front, flipped up the top and whispered, "Oh my."

The other girls and I crowded around to see the inside, which was lined entirely with pink satin. Mother Beatrice tentatively lifted a thin panel, revealing a lower compartment. This was also lined in pink. It was padded, like a pillow, and decorated with little hand-stitched ovals.

"Oh, this is very nice," Mother Beatrice said, her bony fingers flit-ting, spiderlike, across the pink lining and in and out of the pockets. "A place for everything and everything in its place, very nice, though hardly useful for a little girl—now what's this?"

She yanked at a thin strap that was dangling from one of the pock-ets. Out sprang a lady's garter. It was attached to a sheer silk stocking that swept across Mother Bea's throat, and had it been a snake the nun couldn't have screamed louder nor tossed it farther from her. I thought I'd suffocate it was so hard not to laugh. Father was unable to restrain himself. He chuckled and winked at us girls as we giggled into our hands.

"Goodness *me*," Mother Beatrice whispered, staring at the items on the floor. She was blushing to the very edges of her habit. Father leaned over to pick up the stocking and the garter. He wasn't laughing anymore. He carefully folded the stocking and tucked it and the garter into a pocket in his jacket.

"This was my wife's suitcase," he said quietly. "I didn't know there was anything left in it. She only used it once. On our honeymoon."

"Yes, yes, of course," said the nun, clearly flustered, her face still beet red. She crossed herself. Then she closed her eyes, resting one of her hands on the suitcase. The girls and I bowed our heads and lowered our eyelids slightly, but we watched her the way we watched all nuns who prayed—as keen and alert as hunting dogs. We were looking for our mothers' angels (I never saw mine, but I always looked because there were older girls who said they saw their mothers floating above the nuns whenever they prayed). When Sister crossed herself again, I packed up my flannel drawers, woolen leggings, and other items with the help of Dorothy and the others.

My departure from Scranton and my aunt Kate's house, five years later, was almost as abrupt and unexpected as my departure from St. Catherine's had been. One hot spring morning, I was standing in a stinking, crowded trolley, silently cursing the broken-down truck that was blocking its tracks. The next day, I was being chauffeured through town in a gleaming limousine, resisting the urge to wave imperiously at all the common folk stepping over littered gutters and gawking at us as we rolled past.

The day of the stalled trolley, I was late, so I decided to leap from its platform, and at that exact moment it finally lurched forward. I stumbled to the filthy curb, tearing one of my new stockings. I was supposed to meet my teacher, Mrs. Pierson, at a lecture downtown. She wanted to introduce me to her friend—a visiting doctor, who might have a job opportunity for me. I sprinted the five remaining blocks to the YWCA, only to find that the heavy doors to the main hall were closed; the program had already begun.

"My dear, what happened?" Mrs. Pierson whispered, as I sidled into the seat that she'd saved next to her. I began whispering explanations, but she interrupted me with a gentle squeeze of her gloved hand and a smile of pardon. She jutted her chin toward the speaker at the front of the auditorium to indicate that I should direct my attention there.

"Is that Dr. Vogel?" I whispered.

I'd never met a female doctor before, but the stout, dour matron at the podium was exactly what I'd expected one to look like. As I'd tiptoed down the center aisle just moments before, she'd paused dramatically to shoot me a disapproving glare before continuing her speech.

"Oh, dear me, no," Mrs. Pierson responded. "That's Mrs. Danforth—Judge Danforth's wife." She squeezed my hand again, which allowed me to relax a little.

Mrs. Danforth announced, "Finally, I'd like to thank all the ladies from the Woman's Christian Temperance Union for organizing today's lecture and luncheon. Now then—a few words about our distinguished guest—Dr. Agnes Vogel. As many of you know, Dr. Vogel was an outspoken advocate for women's suffrage and served as one of the leaders of the Pennsylvania Red Cross during the war. One of the first women in this country to earn a medical degree in psychiatry, Dr. Vogel is the founder and superintendent of Nettleton State Village for Feebleminded Women of Childbearing Age. We are honored to have her here today to tell us all about Nettleton Village, whose mission is to protect our commonwealth's most vulnerable young women. So, please, do let's give a warm welcome to Dr. Vogel."

I joined in the applause and craned my neck to see over the hats in front of me. I knew Mrs. Pierson was at least forty and that she and Dr. Vogel had attended college together, but the woman approaching the stage looked younger. Unlike the ladies in the audience, who wore linen day dresses or tailored suits—tall, slender Dr. Vogel wore a silk dress with a smartly muted floral print and a chic dropped waist. When she reached the podium, she touched the cheek of her hostess with her own, then turned to face us. No, this elegant woman with the sleek blond bob and fine, aristocratic features wasn't what I'd imagined a female doctor to look like at all.

"Good morning," Dr. Vogel said, smiling out at us. "I recognize many faces here from the Red Cross and our other war efforts, and it's wonderful to be among such fine friends again."

I settled back into my seat and examined the ladderlike run in my stocking. I wasn't really interested in the lecture. It was 1927. Why carry on about women's suffrage now that women had the right to vote? Why maintain temperance clubs, years after liquor had been prohibited and everybody drank anyway? I came to meet Dr. Vogel because I needed a job. Mrs. Pierson taught shorthand, typing, and stenography at the business school I'd attended for the past year, and she told me I was her youngest and most promising student. When she learned that her friend Dr. Agnes Vogel needed a new secretary, she recommended me; the timing was perfect, as Dr. Vogel was engaged to speak in Scranton that week. Mrs. Pierson had insisted that I come and hear the speech, so, after straightening out the stocking, I gazed back up at the stage with what I hoped was an interested expression.

Dr. Vogel was explaining that army examiners during the war had been surprised that so many American men were unfit to serve because they suffered from mental defects. "My research as a psychiatrist, and the research of my colleagues, have revealed that the incidence of feeble-mindedness is equal, if not greater, among girls and women, and it is this population—that of the female unfortunate—who poses the greatest threat to our society."

Dr. Vogel paused, peered over her spectacles, and scanned the rows.

"I just want to make sure there are no gentlemen present." Seemingly satisfied, she said, "I prefer ladies-only groups like this because I can discuss delicate social issues that might cause embarrassment in an audience of mixed company."

I wasn't the only one in my row who leaned forward to better hear this too-embarrassing-for-mixed-company business.

"We're all adults here, so I'm able to say something we all know to be true and that is this: No normal woman will choose to have intimate relations with a man who has the mind of a small child. But it is a sad fact—and ladies, we know it's a fact—that there are many otherwise honorable men who will have illicit relations with a certain type of young woman, regardless of her mental limitations or suitability as a potential mother. I trust you're familiar with the type of girl I'm referring to. You've seen her slinking in and out of bawdy houses and illegal drinking establishments, right here, in your fine city of Scranton. At first glance, she may seem normal enough—in fact, she's often quite pretty. Until you see her again, a few years later, ruined and destitute, begging for handouts, surrounded by her own diseased and illegitimate children. This poor, mentally deficient girl, often unwittingly lured into a criminal lifestyle by the most evil of men, is the type we make every effort to segregate and care for, *before* she has children, not just for her safekeeping, but, most important, for the safekeeping of our communities."

Dr. Vogel went on to describe all the modern facilities at the Village, as she called it, and the progressive programs she had instituted. The girls at the Village—they sang, they cooked, they planted, they learned. I tried to hide my yawns. Finally, the doctor's voice changed to that promising bright tone people often use just before the end of a speech, and I perked up again.

"Yes, we've made great progress at the Village, but we need your help," she said. "We have more than six hundred residents and almost as many on our waiting list. In order to accommodate them all, we require at least three additional buildings. Therefore, I've requested government aid to assist with construction costs. If you have concerns about such an allocation of your family's hard-earned tax dollars, I urge you to consider a case recently publicized by the Public Charities Association of Pennsylvania; a case that concerns two feebleminded women—sisters actually—from a large family of Lithuanian immigrants. These two women have passed their inherited mental defects on to their *twenty-seven* feebleminded, illegitimate, and delinquent children. Yes, we now have twenty-seven additional mental defectives who are being looked after by the commonwealth, and who, in turn, are beginning to produce a third generation of future paupers and criminals. Imagine if we had, instead, provided a safe haven for the two vulnerable sisters during their childbearing years. We'd have prevented the births of scores of unfortunates whose future diseases, degradation, and crime will be our burdens to suffer as well. I hope that you believe, as I do, that preventative work should be at the cornerstone of all charity endeavors. I implore you to take full advantage of our hard-won fight for the vote, my dear ladies, and urge your legislators to support funds for the expansion of Nettleton State Village."

After the enthusiastic applause, I followed Mrs. Pierson to the front of the hall, where the doctor was surrounded by a clutch of admiring women. I was now thoroughly awed by Dr. Vogel. I had no idea there was a place where girls with slow minds could be sent for their safekeeping. It was true that girls of this type were preyed upon by men. I'd seen it myself, now that there were speakeasies scattered all over Scranton. The girls I saw coming and going from these places didn't appear to be normal—some were drunk in the daytime. I hadn't considered the possibility that they were producing children in the numbers the doctor had just revealed, but of course they would be, if their minds weren't right—if they couldn't understand the most basic moral principles.

There were plenty of new businesses opening in and around Scranton, but few of the positions I'd seen advertised were available to women. My plan was to work as a secretary until I'd saved enough to go to college. Mrs. Pierson had urged me to pursue this. "With a college degree, your opportunities are vast," she'd explained. "Why, you might become a schoolteacher or a legal secretary."

It would be a cold day in hell before I'd become a schoolteacher. I was never fond of children, but a legal secretary! If I had a job like that, I could live and work in an exciting city like Chicago or New York. Unfortunately, Nettleton State Village appeared to be in the middle of nowhere, halfway across the state—I'd stopped at the library the day before to look in an atlas and was dismayed to see how rural and remote the area seemed. But now that I'd heard the doctor's speech, I was desperate to work for her. I'd never met a woman who was doing important work. A woman who *ran* something, not a silly old women's temperance club, but—what had she said? Why, she was a cornerstone! Dr. Vogel's work was one of the very *cornerstones* of the state's civic endeavors.

When Dr. Vogel's many well-wishers finally stepped away, Mrs. Pierson introduced us.

"So, you're Miss Engle, the star pupil, eh?" the doctor said, as she shook my hand.

"Yes, how do you do, Dr. Vogel?" I said.

"Aggie, your speech was just marvelous," Mrs. Pierson said. "Now, I know I've already told you this, but Miss Engle is the fastest typist I've ever trained and a whiz at shorthand."

My face grew hot as I said, "Oh . . . you're too kind, Mrs. Pierson, really."

After a moment of strained silence, I noticed Mrs. Pierson was giving me a look and I managed to stammer, "Dr. Vogel . . . well, gosh, I'd be grateful to be considered for the position. That is . . . if you're still seeking a secretary or . . . anybody . . . to work there, for you."

"Yes, we're in desperate need of a secretary," Dr. Vogel said, "and I'm in a bind. Let's walk as we talk, shall we? Must we go to this dreadful luncheon, Thelma?"

"Oh, Aggie," Mrs. Pierson said with a bemused smile. "We'll leave before dessert."

"Fine," said the doctor. "Now, Miss Engle, I'd normally want you to come for an interview and a typing test, but the girl who left is getting married and gave no notice. She won't get a recommendation from me, not that she'll need one."

I had to trot a little to keep up with the doctor's sweeping strides toward the entrance of the auditorium.

"She's marrying. Some local farm boy, I'm told," Dr. Vogel said. She stopped and looked me over. "I don't like hiring girls who are too pretty. As soon as they've been trained, they leave to get married. Well—you're certainly not *too* pretty."

"Oh, why, thank you," I gushed before I'd fully heard her words, and then, probably because my cheeks were now flaming, Dr. Vogel touched my wrist and said, "Of course, you're far from plain, my dear."

"No, not at all . . . I mean, rather, how very nice of you," I managed. And I wondered, then, what happened to the composed, pretty—perhaps even *too* pretty—girl who, little more than an hour ago, had patted her newly coiffed hair, applied just the right amount of lip rouge, and composed clever little speeches of introduction for this very moment. I had imagined a number of conversational opportunities in which I might show my intellect and industriousness before we strolled out of the auditorium together, Dr. Vogel and I, arms linked, already discussing my future promotions.

I'd expected the doctor to be frumpish, manly, and old. I imagined I'd be a breath of fresh air. Instead, Dr. Vogel was glamorous and lovely and smelled faintly of lavender. I smelled like a gymnasium. The fresh linen dress that I'd so carefully ironed that morning had wilted and died in the trolley, and now it hung clammily against my thin frame. My normally curly brown hair had become a sort of spongy, frizzy mass from the humidity, and it coiled around the edges of my hat like damp poodle fur. One of my stockings was virtually shredded, and I didn't seem able to handle my end of this very basic conversation.

But Dr. Vogel was looking at her watch, not at my dress or stockings. She flashed me another smile and said, "I trust Thelma implicitly. You're hired, Miss Engle. Today is Thursday, will you be able to start Monday morning?"

"Certainly," I said, trying to contain my excitement. A job! I had a real job!

"There's a train to Harrisburg. I'll have to send my driver there to collect you on Sunday, which is tricky—that's when he drives me to town to attend church, and that's the wrong direction. You don't think you could leave tomorrow morning, do you? I'm staying with Thelma tonight and plan to leave promptly at eight in the morning. You could ride to Nettleton in my automobile with me. It would save you the train fare and me the bother of arranging your transportation on Sunday."

Leave tomorrow? I hadn't expected to be hired there at the auditorium, and I certainly hadn't planned to pack up everything I owned and move halfway across the state the very next day. But this was the opportunity I'd been praying for. I could finally leave Aunt Kate's house and support myself. I might even be able to start saving for college.

"Well, Miss Engle?" Dr. Vogel pressed.

"Yes, that'll be fine, ma'am," I said. "Thank you, Dr. Vogel, I promise I won't disappoint you."

"Good. Thelma, dear, let's go to this luncheon. See you in the morning, Miss Engle; Mrs. Pierson will give my driver your address."

"Doctor . . . oh, one more thing," I said.

Dr. Vogel and Mrs. Pierson turned and smiled at me.

"About my salary?"

Dr. Vogel lost her smile.

After what felt like a long, appalled silence, Mrs. Pierson giggled nervously and said, "My dear, I'm sure you'll be adequately compensated."

"Yes," I said. "I'm sorry if I seem impertinent, Dr. Vogel, it's just that Mrs. Pierson taught us to agree on terms before starting a job. And I will be moving rather far away."

"Of course," said Dr. Vogel. "You're quite right. I'm not sure of the exact wage—we have a clerk who keeps track of these details. But I believe we paid the previous girl fifteen dollars a week, and she came to us with experience. You look quite young. How old are you?"

"I'm eighteen, Dr. Vogel." Well, I would be eighteen in a few weeks.

"She's very bright, Aggie," Mrs. Pierson said.

Dr. Vogel removed her spectacles and, after pulling a handkerchief from her sleeve, slowly polished the lenses, never taking her eyes off me. I was about to blurt out an apology—for what, I didn't know—when the doctor said, "Fine. I'll pay you the same salary that your predecessor received. Now, Thelma, the sooner we get to this luncheon, the sooner we can leave."

"I've wonderful news, Auntie!" I trilled, all la-de-da, all singsong, when I arrived home. I'd rehearsed this on the way back and had decided I might be able to ward off my aunt Kate's ire with the right enthusiasm. I'd tell her I was her burden no more. I'd been offered a job. A *paying* job—I'd make that clear, since I did have a sort of job at my aunt's. I cleaned and ran errands for her and her adult son, Daniel, to help defray the costs of my room and board, which she reminded me of regularly. Yes, why wouldn't she be thrilled to have my room back? It was just a matter of presentation.

"Auntie?" I called.

An hour later, I was finally alone in my room. I leaned against the door and heard my cousin Daniel's horrible old felted slippers shuffling past my room and down the carpeted stairs. He hadn't left his room during the verbal flogging I'd endured but had no doubt derived great pleasure in listening to every word. Now Aunt Kate's plump, pink man-child was going to join Mama for coffee and a loud inventory of my numerous trespasses.

Who cared? Tomorrow, I was leaving.

I opened my dresser and as I placed my clothes in little piles on the bed, I wondered where I would lodge at the asylum and if I'd have a roommate. I'd made my own slips and drawers from cheap cotton remnants. I had nothing fancy, and I worried that I might share a room with an older, worldlier girl—perhaps a nurse or a secretary who'd been to college. Somebody smart, with silk stockings and lace underthings.

Then I remembered my mother's suitcase. It seemed less enormous when I pulled it from where it had been stored under my bed all those years. Of course, it would appear smaller. I was taller now. But when I dusted it off, I learned something else about my mother. She had an understanding of what made one thing finer than another. She must have had very good taste, because it was a beautifully made suitcase. The soft leather on the outside was ivory colored; it wasn't white, as I'd remembered. That would have been garish. No, it was ivory—almost cream. She'd obviously treasured it, my mother, because why else would Father have saved it instead of tossing it out with all her other belongings? It was probably the nicest thing she ever had, and now it was mine, and no matter where I went, whoever saw me carrying it would assume that I was like my mother. And why shouldn't I act like my mother too, now that I was moving to a new place where people didn't think I was somber or shy? I would arrive with my mother's easy laugh, a sparkle in my eye, and when people saw my fine suitcase, they'd have to wonder what kind of lovely things I had inside.

Two

I HOPED my aunt would stay in her room the next morning, but when I lugged my suitcase downstairs, she was waiting for me.

"I should never have let you go to that night school," she said.

I turned to the mirror and tucked my hair inside my rain hat.

"And why couldn't you find secretarial work here in Scranton? Why do you want to work in a nuthouse in the middle of nowhere? Do you have any idea what evils go on in places like that? I'll give you a week there—you'll come crawling back begging, but I'll not have you."

"No, Auntie, dear, it's not an insane asylum." I stopped fussing with my hair and turned to her. I couldn't let her think that I was going to a place like that. "It's more of a school, or a hospital, really. It's very modern. It's for girls who are—well, slow. _Feebleminded_, is what the doctor said, when I met her yesterday."

"Feebleminded, are they? Well you should fit in quite well, Mary Engle."

Outside, I didn't mind that it was pouring rain. I couldn't stand another minute in my aunt's presence. I stood next to the road, suspecting that she was scowling down at me from the upstairs window, and I pulled my rain hat lower to shield my face from her view. When I saw the long, gleaming automobile turn onto the block and roll slowly toward me, I hoped she was spying, because I'd never seen anything like it. It was a Cadillac limousine, painted a color I'd seen described in a magazine as café au lait. It had black trim, silver fittings, and was driven by a uniformed chauffeur. The car came to a stop at the curb in front of me, and when I lifted my suitcase the tall driver jumped out and took it from me.

"Thank you," I said. He grumbled something in reply. I walked around to the passenger side but was unsure where I should sit. Dr. Vogel was seated in the spacious back seat, reading a newspaper. There was a glass partition separating the driver's compartment from the passenger's. I thought I should ride up front with the driver but wasn't sure. Did Dr. Vogel want my companionship for the ride? Would she consider it unseemly for her new stenographer to jump into the front seat next to a man she'd just met? But surely, I was an employee—I should ride with the other employee. . . .

"Whatta ya waitin' for? Hop in," the chauffeur said in a surprisingly youthful voice, and I saw that he was probably no older than me. His muscular build and suntanned face and hands revealed that he spent more time working outdoors than he did driving the doctor in her glamorous automobile. I thought I might ask him where I should sit, but before I could, he griped, "Oh, I get it," and yanked the front passenger door open for me. "I'm expected to open yer door for you like yer the queen of Siam, I guess."

I slid into the front seat and turned to smile a hello at my new boss. Dr. Vogel was engrossed in her newspaper. The boy jumped back into the driver's seat, and we were off. I was tickled to see that nosy Mrs. Hanover from next door had chosen that moment to venture out into the rain to collect her morning newspaper. She spent hours each day gossiping with my aunt and all our neighbors; now she'd seen a uniformed chauffeur help me into a limousine. Three little neighborhood boys came running to see who was in the long motorcar, and as we drove off, the boys recognized me and waved. I gave them a little wave and thought, happily, *goodbye, grimy little boys; goodbye, dirty old town.*

The driver took a wrong turn, and I realized he was heading back toward downtown Scranton.

"The state road's the other way," I whispered.

This inspired him to execute a series of sharp stomps on the brake pedal, causing the car to stagger so violently that my hat flew off and the contents of my purse spilled around my feet.

Dr. Vogel cried out something that sounded like, "TURK."

"Sorry, ma'am," the driver called back to her.

"Just take a left at the next street, another left at the very next corner and we'll be back on the main road," I whispered. I glanced back and saw Dr. Vogel shaking her head and rearranging her papers.

On the way out of town we passed Dr. Van Dyke's house, where my friend Dorothy lived and worked as a housekeeper. I felt a sudden pang of loneliness at the sight of the house, knowing Dory was inside and not knowing when I'd see her again. She had no idea I was leaving town. I hadn't been able to call her and Marge the night before, though I had wanted to. Dorothy wasn't allowed to take calls in the evenings at the Van Dykes'. Marge lived in a rooming house near the garment factory and had no telephone. I'd write to them once I was settled.

Soon we'd left Scranton behind and were motoring through the Pennsylvania countryside. We drove mile after mile past what looked like the same muddy pastures, the same forlorn cattle all huddled together against the rain, which was now a steady torrent. Dr. Vogel smoked one cigarette after the other in the back seat. At one point, I opened my purse and removed my own packet of cigarettes, but when I went to tap one of them out, I heard the driver clear his throat. He was frowning and shaking his head ever so slightly. I tucked the cigarettes back into my bag. The kid wasn't so bad after all. We drove on. I became aware of a troubling sound coming from the car's engine and asked the boy if he heard it. He just smirked and shook his head.

"I'm familiar with automobiles," I informed him. "I learned to drive when I was very young. There's a strange sound, I hear it."

He grinned broadly and jerked his head to indicate that I should look behind me. Dr. Vogel was asleep. She'd tucked her slender legs under her skirt and rested her cheek against a little silk embroidered pillow. This sweet, childlike pose made her loud snoring quite comical.

The driver said, "Yup, sure sounds like a motor."

I couldn't help but smile. I'd always thought only large men snored like that.

"I'm Charlie Durkin," the boy offered with a quick glance my way. He really wasn't that bad-looking; he had blue eyes, a strong chin and I could see wisps of sandy-colored hair poking out from beneath the brim of his cap.

"How do you do? I'm Mary Engle."

"I know. Doc Vogel told me yer name."

"Oh."

"Ever been out near Union County before?" Charlie said after a few minutes.

"No, I'm afraid I haven't had the opportunity. Until now."

"You'll like it, I guess. It's a heck of a lot prettier than Scranton. More peaceful. Looks like a painting, the scenery around there, lotta people say. We're not near a big town like you're used to though."

"No? What do you do for fun—I mean when you're not working?" I asked with a yawn.

"Wouldn't *you* like to know," he said, turning to wink at me, and I realized he actually thought I was flirting with him.

"I beg your pardon!" I scowled at the road ahead, but from the corner of my eye saw that he was still leering at me.

"Watch the road," I grumbled, and then I repeated the words in a shout as he swerved right off the road and into a shallow, muddy ditch. We were all thrown forward when the car slammed to a crashing halt and Dr. Vogel called from the back seat, "What is it? What's happened?"

"Sorry, ma'am, we skidded a little 'cause of the wet road," Charlie replied.

He put the car in reverse, but the wheels just spun in the mud. He thrust it into first gear and tried going forward. The rear wheels sent a fountain of mud up over the back of the car, but it didn't budge.

Dr. Vogel opened a sliding window in the partition and said, in a calm, breezy tone, "Durk—do get out and see what the problem is. This is a government-owned vehicle. If there's a scratch on it, I'll skin you alive. I'll see that you reimburse the state of Pennsylvania for every penny it costs to repair it."

Charlie leaped from the car and stomped around in the mud, looking at the wheels.

I edged over to the driver's seat, lowered the window, and called out, "I'll drive, Charlie, you push."

Charlie nodded and ran around to the back of the car.

I called out again, "It's the front wheels that lack traction, go around front and I'll try backing out."

"You'll never budge her none goin' backaways," he called. "I just tried. Put her in first gear."

Very well.

I shifted to first gear, stepped lightly on the accelerator, and gazed into the rearview as a thick spray of mud knocked Charlie to the roadside. I leaned out the window again, and said, "If you'll go around to the front, I think we'll have better luck."

He trudged around to the front of the car, and when I put the car into reverse, he gave it a half-hearted little shove.

"Run it over," Dr. Vogel said, her pleasant tone still wonderfully at odds with her words. "The poor creature, hopelessly unfit to carry out the simplest task. Just run it over—put it out of its misery, Miss Engle, it's the merciful thing to do."

What a relief—my new boss had a sense of humor!

"Charlie," I said, leaning out the window and trying not to smile, "sit on the hood, I think the extra weight will give us the traction we need."

Charlie climbed up on the hood, I stepped lightly on the gas pedal, and the car edged backward. When it was on the road again, I slid over to the passenger side. Charlie opened the door and flung his sodden coat and hat on the floor in front of me. I whipped my legs away to keep my stockings from getting soaked.

"Good Lord, Durk, *be more careful*," said Dr. Vogel. "You drive like an epileptic under the best conditions; Miss Engle, come sit back here with me where it's dry."

Cobalt blue. That was the color of the interior. Fine things had colors with evocative names—I knew this from reading *Vogue, McCall's,* and other magazines. Common things were tan, blue, or white, but fine things were eggshell, cobalt, café au lait, ivory, or cream. The bench seat in the passenger compartment was upholstered in cobalt-blue velvet. The ceilings, doors, and floors were all lined in leather of a deeper shade. Midnight. It was probably midnight blue. The seat was wide, but I pressed myself against my armrest in order to not impose on Dr. Vogel any more than was necessary.

We rode in silence for some time. I thought the doctor was reading her magazine, but when I glanced at her, she'd removed her reading glasses and was watching me. She was hatless now, and the way her golden hair framed her face reminded me of those auras in old paintings of saints—it must have been the way the sun was coming through the window behind her. She had few wrinkles for a woman with such fair skin, just tiny little lines that appeared at the corners of her gray-blue eyes when she smiled.

"We've only about another hour. Thelma packed us some ham sandwiches, do help yourself, dear." Dr. Vogel said, pointing at a basket near my feet.

"How kind of Mrs. Pierson," I said. "I'm not hungry just now, but that was ever so thoughtful of her." I straightened my spine and shoulders. The doctor's erect seated posture made me aware of my terrible slouching habit.

"She's very proud of you, Miss Engle."

I smiled at the doctor. Her returning smile and the soft intensity of her eyes had a mysteriously playful quality that made me think Dr. Vogel was no spinster—she'd probably had many sexual adventures with men, and that strange, sudden thought made me blush and look back at my gloved hands on my lap.

"She says you lost your mother when you were an infant and you lived for a time in an orphan home?" Dr. Vogel had shifted so she was facing me.

I looked up at her again, and said, "Yes, ma'am."

"Which one was it? I'm familiar with many of the homes; we receive referrals from some."

"St. Catherine's Orphan Asylum," I said. And then I added, as my aunt and others always did when referring to the place, "It's the order of the German sisters—for boys and girls who have German parents, or at least had them at one time."

"Oh yes, I know of it," Dr. Vogel said with a little nod of approval. "Thelma said you must have received an exemplary academic education there. She told me what an avid reader you are and that you seemed to live in the library when not in school."

"I do like to read, and I think the nuns were good teachers," I said. "I skipped two years when I transferred to public school."

"Too bad they admit only those of the Roman faith to your orphan home," Dr. Vogel said, turning to watch a train that was streaking past us on a nearby railroad track.

"They admit non-Catholics," I said. "In fact, my family is Presbyterian. Some of the children come from Protestant homes. Of course, we all received our christening and catechism there, and we're Catholic now—from the perspective of the Church."

"What about from *your* perspective, dear?" Dr. Vogel said, her attention on me again.

"I still attend Mass," I confessed. "It's familiar to me."

"It's what you've been taught, but it's not who you are. Who you were when you were born, who your parents were, where they came from, your stock and lineage are what determines who you really are, and who you're going to be. Mary Engle is a fine German name."

"Thank you. Actually, Mary isn't the name my mother chose. It's the name the sisters gave me when I was baptized. My Christian name—the one my mother gave me—I guess it wasn't Christian enough for the sisters."

"And what name is that?" Dr. Vogel asked.

I just shook my head, cheeks burning.

"Come, dear, what is it?" Dr. Vogel said, giving me a playful little nudge with her elbow.

"It's embarrassing. My mother named me after a childhood friend—a German girl."

Dr. Vogel said. "Now I'm curious. Please tell me."

"It's . . . Edeltraud," I said, adding hastily, "It's a common name in Germany, but, of course, I know it's odd." I braced myself for the inevitable outburst of laughter. I could hear the faint jeers of little children, nasty little bastard orphan children calling, "Little Trout! Little Trout!"

The doctor didn't laugh. She looked thoughtfully at me for a moment, then said, "I don't think I've heard the name before. I wonder if there's an English version. Edith maybe."

"Our German teacher, Sister Maria, told me that *edel* means 'noble.' *Traud* means . . . oh, I can't recall."

"Perhaps it's related to the word *trud*; it means 'truth' in German, I believe," Dr. Vogel said.

"Well, in *truth*, it's a horrible name to give an American baby. I know my mother meant for me to be called Trudy—before she died. But nobody ever did call me that, you see, because the nuns changed it."

I didn't mention that in my dreams about my mother, she called me Trudy, still.

"And your father? Did he die in the war?"

"No. My father died just two years ago. I was already living with my aunt then. Father ran a big lumbering operation in Upstate New York. They had an influenza outbreak that winter, quite a few of the men died."

"Oh, I'm terribly sorry, my dear, I assumed you never knew your parents, growing up in the home."

"I didn't know my mother." I smoothed my skirt and continued. "Since my father lived and worked in the lumber camps, of course I couldn't live with him. I lived at St. Catherine's until I was twelve. He paid the sisters to keep me there. Rather like a boarding school."

"You were a half-orphan, then."

"Precisely."

"Your father was right not to allow you near those camps and all the drunk men. Full of foreigners, those camps, very dangerous indeed for a child. It sounds as if you had a caring father, Mary."

"Yes," I said. "I did."

Dr. Vogel tilted her head slightly so she could look directly at me again. She seemed to be waiting for me to say more. But I had nothing else to say. Finally, she patted my arm and turned her attention back to her magazine.

"I'm glad you'll have the weekend to get settled," she said, thumbing through the pages. "At present you and Miss Finch, my secretary, are housed in with the Goodwins. Mr. Goodwin manages our farm."

"Miss Finch is your secretary? I thought I was to be . . ."

"No, you'll be working as Miss Hartley's secretary. She's the assistant superintendent. She's more involved with the daily management of the residents. I'm on the road much of the year giving talks similar to the one I gave yesterday in Scranton."

"I see."

"Have you any questions about Nettleton?" Dr. Vogel said, closing her magazine, and turning her full attention back to me.

"I do worry about—well, I haven't been around many of the—

feebleminded. I knew one, the son of the janitor at St. Catherine's. They called him a Mongolian. He was too noisy to sit still for Mass, so Mr. Sullivan, the janitor, waited until the service was over to bring him inside. And Father blessed the boy every week, just like a normal child."

"Yes, as well he should have. We are all God's creatures," Dr. Vogel said.

"I just worry that I might be overwhelmed being amongst so many . . ."

I didn't know how to finish my thought—I had almost said, *freaks.* I remembered the Sullivan child's odd smiles and grimaces. His senseless laughter when the priest dabbed holy water on his forehead. Once, when Father Linden had bent over to pat his head, the boy had grabbed the priest's white frock in his little hand and yanked on it. When he let go, his hand had left a greasy smudge there, and Father Linden gave the boy's ear a sharp blow. I was afraid of the child, we all were. It was hard to imagine living at a place with hundreds of grown women who looked and behaved like the janitor's boy.

"Don't worry," Dr. Vogel said. "We have very few true idiots. Very few imbeciles, for that matter. Most of the girls are morons."

Dr. Vogel must have seen my confusion as she continued. "Today, the feebleminded are categorized into three distinct groups based on tests that calibrate intelligence. IQ tests. The average person has an IQ of one hundred. People who score between seventy and one hundred have a lower mentality but are still, more or less, normal. Those who score between fifty and seventy are classified as morons—they look quite normal, though they have the minds of children between the ages of eight to twelve years. Most of our girls at Nettleton are in this category. They were sent to us because they've exhibited morally delinquent behavior. Our asylum was created specifically to house this type, as they pose the greatest threat to their communities."

"I see," I said, recalling Dr. Vogel's lecture.

"You'll be given an employee handbook," Dr. Vogel said. "You won't be attending to the residents but will live in their community, as we all do. I urge you to be very cautious when interacting with the residents, some are quite cunning and manipulative, despite their intellectual deficits. But remember, the girls are not to be blamed for their condition. They were dealt a very unfortunate hand from the moment of their conception, and we are mindful of this and treat them with utmost care and compassion. Helping others enriches one's soul, Miss Engle, you'll see."

"Yes, of course, it must," I said.

The doctor opened her magazine again. I gazed out my window. The day was almost over. The roadside farms had disappeared, replaced by walls of dense forest, and for at least half an hour, we hadn't passed a single dwelling. Charlie finally slowed the automobile. Then he turned off the main road and onto a narrower lane where he came to a stop. Ahead was an immense wrought-iron gate that blocked the drive. Next to the gate was a stone gatehouse. A short, stocky older man jumped out, waved at us, and limped over to the gate. He unlocked a large padlock that fastened the gate to a post with a thick chain. Then he pushed the gate to the side so that we could drive through. As we passed, Charlie leaned out his window and said, "See you in a few, Pop."

The man nodded and smiled vacantly, squinting to see who was in the back seat with Dr. Vogel. I resisted the impulse to wave like a child. As we rolled past, I saw that the road ahead was bordered on each side by dense forest. I turned and saw the man swinging the gate back across the road. It met the post with the resounding clang of iron against iron.

I was seized then with a sick feeling. It was the same sick longing I felt when I left St. Catherine's with my father, years before. A gate had closed behind me that day as well. I'd been excited to leave the orphanage, but my joy had evaporated the minute we'd pulled out of the driveway. I kept turning around and waving, but Dorothy, Marge, and the others had gone back to the courtyard. In an hour the dinner bell would ring and they'd be sitting at the long dining tables without me. I realized then that I was in a motorcar with a stranger—my own father. All my friends, the Sisters, and Mother Beatrice, would have prayers at six, supper at six fifteen, followed by evening studies. Washroom visits, final prayers, and bedtimes were all at set times that were as reliable and familiar as my own pulse. But where would I be at those times? I felt, that afternoon with my father, and again, with Dr. Vogel, like I had been carelessly forgotten by the world. I felt like a balloon that had been allowed to fly away but now longed for the familiar pull of gravity.

"You'll not spend another night under this roof." My aunt had meant what she said. It was just that morning; it seemed like long ago.

Dusk was settling in, but I could still faintly see the road ahead. I had imagined the asylum would be surrounded by acres of manicured green lawns where the residents would stroll with their attendants. I had expected a wide-open place, not these dark woods. The narrow, rutted road twisted, snakelike, around huge boulders and stony ledges. The trees on either side were thick-trunked and already heavy with summer leaves, though it was still only May. I thought I saw a figure in the woods. Then another. I saw shadowy, feminine shapes slipping through the dense foliage; distorted, idiotic girlish faces peering from behind the centuries-old tree trunks.

"Drop me at my house first, please, Charlie, then take Miss Engle on up to the Goodwins'," Dr. Vogel said.

Her words jerked my frightful imagination to a brisk halt. There were no ghostly figures lurking in the forest. We were just traveling along an ordinary wooded road.

"Yes, ma'am," Charlie called back, turning onto another road.

"The Goodwins are expecting you, Miss Engle. I sent a wire yesterday. Oh, one other thing. You'll want to attend Catholic Mass on Sunday, I presume."

"Yes, ma'am."

"Well, since you seem to know how to handle an automobile, you may drive me to Clayburg on Sundays. I spend the day in town with my mother. You may go to Mass with Mrs. Nolan, our new day nurse. She's a widow. She's complained that the bus to town doesn't leave early enough for her to make it to the service at the Catholic Church. After church, you'll have Mrs. Nolan as a companion for the afternoon. I usually don't return to the Village until after supper."

"Oh, that sounds nice," I lied. In fact, the idea of spending one of my two days off in the company of some old widowed nurse sounded dreadful.

"Yes, did you hear that, Mr. Durkin? You'll have your Sundays off now. That will be reflected in your paycheck."

I wanted to ask if the added duty of driving the doctor would be reflected in my own wages, but I knew the answer. Dr. Vogel had just told me that she was doing me a favor in allowing me to drive to Clayburg to attend Mass.

I heard the sudden baying of what sounded like packs of hounds. The car was approaching a massive stone manor house that was lit up with gas lanterns. A large, brown shepherd-type dog and two smaller black terriers flew at the car, barking maniacally, and Dr. Vogel leaned out the window and called to them. "Hello, Lancaster, you rascal. Hello, Trixie, off there, OFF! You'll scratch the car, Peg."

Charlie stopped the car, jumped out, and opened the back door. The small dogs leaped inside, climbing all over Dr. Vogel and me. I sat very still as I'd been taught by the nuns.

"They're less likely to tear into you if you keep still," Sister Rosemary warned us girls whenever dogs approached. Dr. Vogel was moving though. She was rollicking back and forth with glee as the animals jumped on her. I was astonished to see her laughing as they licked at her pretty face with their horrible tongues.

"Get off, get off now," Dr. Vogel finally insisted. The dogs tumbled out of the car, and Dr. Vogel followed them.

"Good night, Dr. Vogel," I called. But the doctor appeared not to have heard. She was trotting up the massive stone steps that led to the grand front door. Her dogs bounced along beside her, their tails wagging, and their jaws snapping at the air with joy.

"Is it far to the Goodwin house, Charlie?" I asked, leaning forward and speaking through the little window. Charlie was backing up the enormous automobile, a task that seemed to require all of his concentration. When we were heading back the way we had come, I said, a little louder, "I'd hate to get lost out here in these woods. Is it much farther?"

Charlie calmly reached back and slid the window shut. Our brief friendship was over; it had been terminated the minute I moved to the back seat with Dr. Vogel. I realized now that the dope thought in doing so I'd broken ranks with him and tried to butter up the boss. I wanted to explain. After all, it was *he* who had thrown his wet things at me.

"Charlie?" I said in a friendly tone.

I kept trying to catch his eye in the rearview mirror so I could give him a little smile. It was dark now, and the woods were so close. Charlie was the only person I knew. I tapped the glass. He stared straight ahead.

Who cares? I thought. *Who cares what he thinks?*

"Charlie?" I said again, this time louder. I gave the window another knock.

Charlie drove on in silence.

Three

WHEN we finally stopped, we were in front of a ramshackle farm-house on an otherwise abandoned dirt road.

"But . . . this can't be the place I'm going to live," I said. The doctor had made Nettleton Village sound like a modern hospital campus in her speech. I'd imagined a gleaming glass-and-steel residence hall for employees, not an old clapboard house with a sagging roof.

"Yup. This here's the Goodwins'," Charlie said. "Guess it's not a fancy city house like you're used to. But Betty keeps it nice; I sure wouldn't want her to hear you say a thing like that about her home."

"Charlie, of course, I'd never. And my aunt lives in an old row house. It's not *fancy*."

A young man ducked his head into Charlie's open window. He grinned, first at Charlie, then at me. "You must be Miss Engle, we been waiting for ya," he said. He snatched Charlie's chauffeur's cap and put it on his own head, backward. "I'm Hal."

Hal appeared to be in his early twenties. He had a sun-bronzed face and neck, a thick head of reddish-brown hair, and a friendly smile. "We expected you hours ago, Durk—you get old Vogel lost again or what?"

Charlie grabbed his hat back, cursing under his breath. I heard him mutter that he wished *somebody* would get lost.

Hal said, still chuckling, "What're you so worked up about? Come on in, Betty made her meat loaf special for you."

"Nah," Charlie said. "Pop wants me home."

Hal came around to help me with my things. When I was out of the car, Charlie sped off so fast that dirt and bits of gravel flew from the tires and peppered my legs like shrapnel.

"What's eating old Durk? I wonder," Hal said.

Betty Goodwin was waiting for us on the front porch. She had a small child on her hip. She was young, pretty, and quite pregnant, with round cheeks and freckles that disappeared every few seconds when she blushed.

"My wife, Betty! And this is Harry," Hal said, tickling first the tot's little tummy, then Betty's very round one. The child and Betty giggled, and when Betty swatted at Hal's hand, I saw that her front teeth were quite crooked. I later wondered if her self-consciousness about her teeth made her appear shyer than she actually was, because she tended to look down and cover her lips with her hand whenever she spoke or laughed.

"Come in, Miss Engle," she said, her cheeks blushing and blanching, her fingers dancing across her lips. "Come right on in, and we'll get you settled."

"Please, do call me Mary," I said, following her through the door and into a small, tidy front parlor room.

"Miss Engle—Mary, I mean—come have a look," Hal said. He gestured toward a closed door at the bottom of the staircase. "It's all new, go on—after you!"

"Why, thank you," I said, entering what I thought would be my bedroom. Hal followed me, switched on a light, and I found that we were jammed inside a tiny room containing a sink, toilet, and small washtub. This "water closet" had been a coat closet until just six months prior, when, Hal informed me, "Old Vogel finally run the electrical line out." Hal turned on one of the spigots in the sink, and when the water gushed from the spout, he looked at me as if he'd just performed a minor miracle.

"Well, gosh that's swell!" I said, after a moment of floundering for the appropriate response. I was aware that some rural areas still lacked electricity and indoor plumbing, but I'd grown up with these luxuries; even at St. Cat's we'd had cold running water and indoor toilets.

Little Harry squeezed his way into the room by crawling between my legs. He tugged on his father's pants leg, grunting and pointing at the toilet.

"Oh, excuse me," I said, trying to back out of the room. "I'll go so he can . . ."

"Nah, he still ain't trained, but watch this!"

Hal lifted Harry so he could reach the chain that hung from the water tank near the ceiling. Harry pulled it with his little hands, then he squealed with delight as the water disappeared down the toilet bowl. Hal hooted and playfully nudged me with his elbow. I summoned a polite little laugh. I've never found children as entertaining as some people. Nor toilets, for that matter. Now Betty stuck her head inside, and for a brief, terrible moment, I thought she'd rushed over to join the fun, but she just wanted to tell Hal it was Harry's bedtime.

"It sure is nice to be able to use a thing like that inside, finally," Hal said, letting the child pull the chain one more time. I was trying to back out of the room, but we were all packed in there so tight.

"The other buildings here at the Village—they're newer. They've been wired and plumbed for years," Hal said. "'Course, I still use the old crapper out back if I . . ."

"Oh Hal, for heaven's sake," Betty said, her plump fingers flying to her lips. "Let me show you your room. It's upstairs. Your roommate—Gladys—I'm 'fraid she left it untidy; she goes to her family on weekends, Miss Engle."

"Please, I'm begging you! Call me Mary."

Betty's meat loaf was delicious, and so were her buttery mashed potatoes, braised carrots, freshly baked rolls, and warm cherry pie. She and Hal didn't sit at the table with me as I dined. They'd had their supper earlier. Hal sat in a chair next to the kitchen stove. He smoked a pipe and smiled at me whenever I looked his way. Betty hovered over me, asking if I'd like salt or pepper. Another roll? Fresh coffee? More pie? I felt self-conscious at first, eating at their table with them watching me like that, but the Goodwins were so kind and cheery, I soon found myself engaged in easy conversation with them. They'd lived there in the house for five years, I learned. Hal was in charge of all the farming operations at Nettleton Village. They'd grown up in nearby Shamokin and had known each other all their lives. Betty apologized, again, for the state of my bedroom. She'd had to clear my roommate's clothing and other items from my bed so I could put my suitcase on it.

"I wish it weren't in such a sorry state, the first time you see it and all. We told Gladys yesterday that you was coming. Why couldn't she pick up her things before running off?"

"That's Gladys for you," Hal said, with a bemused smile. "Just does what she pleases, never a care about nobody but her."

"Don't worry, it's fine," I said. "I'm sure she was anxious to get on with her weekend plans."

I imagined this devil-may-care Gladys preparing, at that very moment, for a night out on the town—wherever she was. Probably Harrisburg or Philadelphia. I saw her shimmying into a slim evening dress, taking a final pass at her pretty face in front of a mirror and dashing out to a car filled with the old college gang.

I imagined her on Sunday, struggling to find something nice to say to me.

"You've such a sensible hairstyle, Mary, it looks ever so easy to take care of." Or, "You make your dresses yourself? Why, aren't you clever. I wish Mother had taken the time to teach me to sew."

I was, therefore, relieved when I was finally alone in our room and discovered an entirely different Gladys than the one I'd imagined. It's not snooping if everything is thrown around the room. I didn't have to poke around and open bureau drawers to get a sense of my roommate. I'm not saying I didn't; my point is, I didn't *have to*. Gladys wore cheap perfume, dime-store jewelry, and scuffed old shoes. She made her own clothes, but it looked like she didn't have the most stylish patterns available to her out here in the country, and she didn't concern herself with little details like straight seams or matching buttons. I flipped through a trashy romance magazine I'd found on the floor near my bed before tossing it over to hers.

I opened my suitcase and, again, admired the pink lining within. But now I noticed a faint odor that I hadn't detected the day before. It smelled strongly of leather, which shouldn't have been surprising: it was a leather suitcase. But there was something else, something musty and unpleasantly familiar. I realized what it was—that leathery smell mixed with a musky, sweaty odor. They were old-man smells. How odd, that foul smell, in there with all the pink loveliness. I lowered my head and tentatively sniffed again. Yes, if you poured whiskey into the suitcase, it would smell just like old Uncle Teddy.

I found a box of violet-scented talcum powder on the floor next to my phantom roommate's disheveled bed. I sprinkled a little of it into the suitcase. I sniffed the air and then poured out such a great cloud of powder that everything I owned looked like it was coated with sugar. There. Now I could unpack.

Four

June 24, 1927

Dearest Marge,

I'm typing this on official stationery just to show you how very important I am! Yes, I work for the Commonwealth of Pennsylvania, as it says on the top of this page.

My aunt forwarded your kind note, I'm sorry I wasn't able to call before I left. I was hired on a Thursday and left the next morning, so I didn't have time to say goodbye to anybody. I also apologize for not writing sooner, Margie. I can't believe I've been here almost three weeks. Now that I'm settled in and accustomed to the routine, I'll have more time to write.

I had to smile when I read that Auntie told you I work at a "grim lunatic asylum." Nettleton State Village is very modern, the buildings and grounds designed by an architect who's famous for something called the "cottage plan." The residents live in modern dormitories, surrounded by gardens and lawns. The office area in which I sit at this moment has windows that start near the floor and run almost up to the ceiling. The atmosphere is quite the opposite of "grim"!

And the residents are not insane, Margie. They're unfortunate girls with low intelligence. Our superintendent, Dr. Agnes Vogel, is a most remarkable woman. I'll enclose a newspaper clipping that describes her work in the new field of "eugenics"

Before I could finish typing the sentence, Gladys jumped up from her desk opposite mine, and said, "C'mon, Mary, lunchtime, I'm starving."

I yanked the page from the typewriter and folded it in half.

"Why so sneaky?" she said, looming over my desk. "You writing to your sweetie? Lemme see."

"Quiet, she's inside," I whispered. "It's just a letter to a friend. I finished her typing already."

"Rule number nine hundred and ninety-nine," Gladys murmured. "Employees must never engage in personal correspondence during office hours. Those that do will be hung at dawn."

I tucked the letter to Marge into my purse and grabbed a pile of typed correspondence from the edge of my desk. As I thumbed through the letters, Gladys said, "C'mon, I want to get there before the barn crowd."

"Go ahead. I'll catch up after I give these to her."

"Nah, I'll wait, just hurry up." Gladys leaned back against my desk, pulled an emery board from her purse, and began filing her nails.

I knocked on the door next to my desk.

"COME IN!" Miss Hartley shouted with such unexpected volume and immediacy that Gladys's nail file flew from her startled hands. We stood for a moment, frozen in silent hysteria, avoiding each other's eyes in order to stifle our laughter. Then I took a deep breath, pushed the door open, and went inside.

Miss Hartley was standing near the door, having obviously eavesdropped on us. She was a short, wiry woman with thin lips and dark hollows under her eyes. Her hair was white and so sparse that stripes of her shiny scalp lay like evenly plowed furrows between the strands that she somehow secured into a desperate little knot at the back of her head. She wore gray suits with near Victorian-length skirts, starched white blouses, and jackets cut in a square, military style.

"I have the morning's letters, Miss Hartley. If you'd like me to wait for you to sign them, I can leave them with the mail clerk on my way to the dining hall."

"No, no, that won't do. I'll check for any mistakes and you can take them to the mail room after your lunch."

"As you wish," I said, knowing there were no mistakes. "I'm off to lunch, then."

She responded with a dismissive wave, frowning down at the letters.

Gladys and I trotted down the front steps of the administrative building and what a day it was! A warm breeze shifted big, frothy white clouds this way and that, and the air carried the countryside aromas I'd grown to love—lilacs in bloom, freshly mown grass, pine trees, and, that day, the musky fragrance of rich loam being tilled in a nearby crop field.

The administrative building stood at the head of a long expanse of lawn known as "the Green"; the dining hall was at the opposite end. As Gladys and I started across a stone path that bisected the lawn, she linked her arm with mine and said, "Did I tell you Hammy says he'll be taking over his pop's milk route next year? That's when we're gonna marry, me and Ham. He didn't ask Mama yet, 'cause he wants to be able to say he's got the income from the milk route, see?"

"Yes," I said. "I believe you mentioned that yesterday." *And the day before. And the day before that.* Because I shared my bedroom and office with Gladys, and because she never shut up, I knew Hamish "Hammy" Van Sutter more intimately than I'd known any man, and I'd never laid eyes on him.

Several groups of residents—or "inmates," as they were more commonly called—were also on their way to the dining hall, and we had to step aside to make room for them. These girls had just hiked up from the lower crop fields. They wore the khaki-colored work coveralls of the "outdoor girls." Two young women in matching navy dresses—the uniform for paid attendants—walked some distance behind them, shouting out reminders to stop running, stop pushing, and to stay off the grass.

We passed the stone-clad residence halls that stood on either side of the green. There were four of these dormitories—each five stories tall and wider than most apartment buildings in Scranton. I was still drafting the letter to Marge in my mind, describing the place, and I gazed at each of them anew. Except for the bars on the windows, these buildings might easily have been mistaken for modern college dormitories—if you squinted your eyes a little, as I was doing. It did seem odd to hear them called "cottages," though, considering their large size and utilitarian design. And even more incongruously, it seemed to me, they were named after flowers: Rose Cottage and Hollyhock Cottage occupied one long side of the rectangular green. Marigold and Lilac Cottages faced them from the opposite side. Almost seven hundred girls were housed in these four enormous "cottages." There was a fifth dormitory, called, simply, Building Five. It was not visible from the green. It was slightly smaller and was used, occasionally, for detention purposes for unruly inmates.

"We gotta get out of there early today, I can't bear the stench of them dairy girls when I'm trying to eat," Gladys said, tugging at my elbow.

Inside the large dining hall, I saw that some of the "indoor girls" were already having lunch. They were responsible for all the cleaning, laundry, cooking, and sewing for the asylum. The highly coveted indoor jobs were given to inmates with the best behavior and most pleasant attitudes. There was another, much smaller group of indoor girls, consisting of the most profoundly afflicted—the "idiots," as they were classified in their patient records, also filing in from a side door.

Sophie, a childhood friend of Gladys's, was one of the few hired attendants who looked after all the indoor girls on weekdays. Some of the more-capable inmates were supposed to tend to the idiots, and now I saw the usual shoving and slapping as they moved these slower girls toward a table. Though Sophie's job was to manage all the indoor girls, she paid no attention to anything they were doing. She rushed over to join us at one of the staff tables, completely oblivious to the misbehavior of some of her charges. The first time I saw the residents being rough with the more helpless among them, I'd brought the shoving and slapping to Sophie's attention. She and Gladys had looked at me like I had two heads.

"You gotta move 'em along somehow," Sophie had explained. "They're as dumb as rocks, most of 'em."

The Nettleton employee handbook spelled out the rules of the asylum, and I'd studied mine carefully during my first days there.

"*In the management of residents,*" the rules stated, "*all employees must observe an attitude of kindness and understanding. Threats, taunts, or other kinds of abuse are expressly forbidden. A blow, kick, or any other kind of physical punishment inflicted on a resident will be immediately followed by the dismissal of the person so offending. Any resident observed mistreating another shall be reported to the assistant superintendent immediately.*"

Now I realized how naive I'd been when I read those words. Everything had sounded so disciplined and orderly then. It was true that I didn't have a lot of contact with the residents, but I saw enough to know that most employees didn't show a lot of kindness toward them. They tended to shout at them most of the time, and, in addition to the forbidden blows, kicks, and taunts, I'd also witnessed pinches, hair pulling, and even an elbow to the jaw dealt by one attendant to an overly rambunctious young woman. The problem seemed to be that some of the inmates had trouble obeying the rules, due to their mental afflictions, and there were so many of them and surprisingly few hired workers. The attendants were clearly overwhelmed. And the caregivers of the most severely defective inmates were, themselves, inmates. The more feebleminded were cared for by the less feebleminded.

But what I'd observed wasn't much worse than the discipline my friends and I had received at St. Cat's, and our caretakers had been educated nuns, not simple country girls like the attendants here. I also knew the inmates were far better off now than they had been before being placed at Nettleton Village. I'd read several articles written by Dr. Vogel about the condition of the girls when they'd first arrived. Some had been living in almshouses and were ill and malnourished. Others were working as prostitutes and arrived with social diseases and, in many cases, signs of physical abuse.

After two or three weeks, a wonderful transformation takes place for almost every new resident at Nettleton Village, Dr. Vogel wrote. *The restorative power of clean living and physical exercise cannot be overstated. I recently saw a young girl returning from one of our orchards. Her eyes shone, and her skin glowed with health. She carried a basket filled with apples that she had just picked and that would later be served to her in a pie. It was hard to believe she was the same fearful and sickly waif that I'd admitted just three weeks prior.*

The table where Gladys, Sophie, and I sat now was next to a large window with an expansive view of the distant hills. Soon, other staff joined us—two attendants, the head laundress, and one of the switchboard operators. When we were all seated, an "indoor girl" filled our water glasses, while two others brought us platters of ham and vegetables and a basket of freshly baked bread.

Gladys and the others liked to finish their lunch and be out of the dining hall before the "dairy girls" showed up. These were the inmates who tended the large dairy herd. They were supposed to remove their filthy coveralls and wash up before lunch, but they only did this when Dr. Vogel was there. When she was off on one of her lecturing tours, as she was now, their attendant—a rough older woman named Cloris—brought them up to the dining hall straight from the barns. Cloris said that by the time the girls changed, the food was always cold. This annoyed the staff, but Cloris was rather brutish and nobody said anything to her about the overwhelming stench of cow manure that wafted into the dining hall with her girls.

Unfortunately, the first time I saw the dairy girls, I'd thought they were boys. Gladys and Sophie still teased me about this and had been calling them "Mary's boys" ever since. The dairy girls usually arrived around one forty-five, but that afternoon, they came early.

We'd just started eating when Sophie groaned, "Oh no, Mary, your boyfriends are here."

This sent her and Gladys into gales of laughter. I responded to this stale joke with my usual silence. What was so funny, anyway? The dairy girls did look like boys until one was close to them. They wore grayish men's coveralls that were probably once white, and men's work boots that were caked with dried manure. Some wore scarves over their hair, but a few had decided to finish off the men's outfits with tattered newsboy caps that they wore at jaunty angles on their heads.

There was a sudden, loud skirmish as the dairy girls crowded into the hall that day. One of them had stomped on the foot of another, and now they were all shoving and shouting.

Cloris, who was leading the way, wheeled about and hollered, "GIRLS, CUT THE SHENANIGANS, WILL YAS?"

The inmates stopped their childish scuffling, and I saw that the one in front had a little smirk, her cap pulled down low over one eye. When they were almost in front of our table, the girl tipped her cap back off her forehead and said to her friend, "That'll teach her to cut in line, the fat, old—"

She stopped talking when she saw me. I froze with my fork midway to my mouth and stared up at her in wonder. When I saw her equally surprised expression, my heart beat so hard beneath my blouse I thought others might be able to see it. It had been years, but I'd know that face anywhere. It was Lillian Faust; we grew up together at St. Catherine's.

I lowered my fork. I almost said her name, but there was something in her gaze that told me not to. Her fleeting look of disbelief was eclipsed by something darker. She seemed to look right through me, as if I were invisible. I'd seen that look before. Sister Rosemary called it her "cold-fish stare." (*Give me yer cold-fish stare one more time, Lillian Faust, and I'll knock you from here to the next county.*) Lillian cast it first upon me, and then the others at the table. There was something daring and contemptuous in her gaze. A few blond ringlets had escaped her cap, and she pushed them away from her eyes with the back of one of her grimy hands. I was amazed that she was still so very pretty, even all unwashed, and dressed the way she was.

Gladys and Sophie stifled their theatrical choking and turned back to their meals. But I kept watching her as she walked, single file now with the others, to the far end of the hall. I was glad that she hadn't acknowledged me. But why hadn't she? And what was she doing here? Why was she wearing the patients' coveralls instead of the navy uniforms worn by the attendants? Lillian was always a troublemaker at St. Cat's—very obstinate and defiant, but I'd thought her rather bright. Certainly not feebleminded.

On our way back to the office building, I asked Gladys if some of the dairy girls were hired workers, rather than inmates.

"Cloris is hired," Gladys said.

"But what about the others?"

"They're all inmates, 'cept Cloris. They're supposed to be dangerous, some of the dairy girls," Gladys said. Then she pulled me close and whispered, "Dr. Vogel wrote in a letter about one of 'em that she was *oversexed*. I think she worked as a prostitute in Pittsburgh or something. And she's not the only one like that in the dairy. Vogel says heavy work like shoveling manure and hauling water and milk is good for 'em, so they're too tired to cause trouble at the end of the day. *They have minds like beasts, you have to tire 'em out*, Vogel says. *Or they get all . . .* lusty."

"Oh, Gladys, for heaven's sake," I said. She'd doubled over with laughter at the word *lusty*, and I had to wait for her to compose herself before we entered the office building.

There were many letters to type that afternoon, and I was glad for the distraction. It was surprising and upsetting to learn that Lillian Faust was an inmate here. We weren't close friends when we were small—she was two years older—but I'd been a little afraid of Lillian back then. We all were. Now I knew why. There was apparently something wrong with her.

I focused on my typing. Some of the letters I typed each day were related to the business of running the institution—requests for supplies at reduced rates and reports to the state welfare commissioner. But the bulk of Miss Hartley's daily correspondence had to do with residents or prospective residents. I'd found these interactions intriguing at first, but they no longer held much interest; they were so repetitive.

Many letters were from relatives of mentally defective girls from all over Pennsylvania, begging to have them admitted. These queries tended to come from men—husbands and uncles of mentally defective girls. That day's letters were typical:

My wife Edna is slow in the head, I think she would do better living at Nettleton.

My stepdaughter, she's off, she ain't never been right, and now she's taken to telling lies about me to my family.

There was a stock reply that Miss Hartley had me send to these requests. Nettleton Village was over capacity; there were no beds available at present. The girl's name would be placed on a waiting list.

The other letters pertained to girls who were already inmates, and these typically came from mothers and sisters, such as the one I read now from poor Mrs. McManus—Hilly's mother. Mrs. McManus wrote, in her usual childish block print:

Dear Miss Hartley,

Can you please tell me the reasin for keeping my letters from being red by my Hilly? I wrote three times this month and two times before and I never get a reply. I never say nothing in my letters that should keep them from being red by her. And I should like to know when she is coming home. Any person can tell there's nothing wrong with her. I need her home to help me with the childrin, I am a poor widow if you didn't know. She did her time at the work farm in Muncy. One year is the sentence for her crime. She did not do that crime neither, but she done her time and now, two years later, she is still not home. Please tell me when can my Hilly come home to me and I will look after her all the time so she wont get in no more trouble.

From Mrs. Angela McManus

I typed Miss Hartley's response.

My dear Mrs. McManus,

I believe you are confused as to the reason Hilly was sent to us. Hilly is not here because of things she has done but because she is unable to keep from doing these things. I must disagree with your claim that there is nothing wrong with her. In fact, she has the thinking ability of an eight-year-old, according to physicians who examined her at Muncy prison, and our examination here has confirmed that. I have no doubt that if Hilly were released to your supervision, she would add to your burden rather than ease it, by presenting you with more fatherless children. When Hilly is at an age when she is no longer able to bear children, she will be paroled, but not before that time. Your letters suggesting to Hilly that she will be coming home soon only interfere with the wonderful progress she has been making in adapting herself to the community here.

Additionally, her happiness is not served by your reports of troubles involving your home, your financial woes and idle gossip about Hilly in your community. It is much better for Hilly if you try to write of happier things. Correspondence of that nature will be passed on to Hilly. If you have concerns about Hilly that are of a different nature, please feel free to address those concerns in correspondence addressed to me.

Very truly yours,
Miss Eleanor Hartley, Asst. Supt.

I removed the letter and placed it on top of Hilly's file. The file, like all the residents' files, had an index card attached to the outside, with a short description of the patient. Hilly's read:

```
HILLY MCMANUS
16 years old.
Mental age: Eight years and four months.
Single. Walks, talks. American. Protestant.
Moron. Physically heathy and attractive. Reads
and writes some. Immoral behavior. Promiscuity.
Has one illegitimate child. Suggestible, easily
frustrated, confused, and impulsive. Transferred
from Muncy, where she served her sentence for
prostitution.
```

I put a fresh page in my typewriter and turned to my dictation pad.

My dear Mrs. Flannery,

In response to your letter of June 2, I am happy to report that you are correct. As you heard from Lucy herself, she is now spending several days each week working outside the Village. Because Lucy has made remarkable progress in recent months, she was selected to be part of the group known with great admiration among prominent local families as "Dr. Vogel's Girls." Lucy is working as a maid in the home of one of the members of our board of directors. The skills she learned here at the Village have enabled her to find herself thus employed.

As to your question about her compensation, her employer does pay for Lucy's services, but her wages are paid to Nettleton State Village. We are a public institution, as you well know, and Pennsylvania tax-payers have spent far more to keep Lucy here than she is earning as a domestic servant. It's only fair that the commonwealth receives some compensation for the hours of training that have gone into preparing Lucy for this opportunity.

I trust you will take heart in the knowledge that Lucy and some of the other girls who are on work trials outside the Village are on their way to being paroled for holidays and other visits to their families—this is a transition period for them, and I'm happy to report that Lucy's employer is quite pleased with her services. Hopefully, she will be able to begin home visits with you some time next year.

Please feel free to send me any further inquiries you might have on this or any other matters relating to Lucy.

Very truly yours,
Miss Eleanor Hartley, Asst. Supt

I finished my typing almost an hour before it was time to leave the office. If I brought the letters in to Miss Hartley, she'd make me do busywork like organizing files. No, the thing to do was to keep typing. I couldn't finish my letter to Marge; Miss Hartley would notice the crease where I'd folded it and she'd ask me about it. Instead, I placed a fresh piece of stationery in my typewriter and squinted at my pad so that it looked like I was continuing with official correspondence.

Dearest Sister Rosemary,

I was so very pleased to receive your response to my letter. Boston sounds like a lovely city. I'm happy to hear that your nephew's family is well. How nice it must be for you to have them so close. Is Dorchester far from where you live in the retirement convent? Six children! I'm sure you must love to visit with all your young nieces and nephews.

You asked whether I attend Mass on Sundays, here at Nettleton Village. I do, indeed. I go to St. Peter's Church in Clayburg, which is the nearest town. The priest is Father Joseph Doheny. Dr. Vogel spends every Sunday in town with her folks, so even if I were of a mind to skip Mass on a Sunday, I wouldn't be able to, as she relies upon me to drive her.

Do you ever hear from Lillian Faust? I've often wondered what became of her. I know you keep in touch with many of the girls.

Thank you so much for your kind letter and your prayers. I remember you in my prayers always.

With warmest regards, Mary Engle

Five

AFTER supper that evening, Hal lingered in the kitchen with Betty and me, instead of heading off to bed as he usually did. Tomorrow was his day off. Gladys had gone home as she did every Friday, little Harry was in bed, so it was just the three of us. Hal filled his pipe with tobacco, and when Betty held a match to it, he smiled and placed his hand on the back of her thigh. I looked away.

"So, Mary, how's old Hartley treating you these days?" Hal asked.

"Not bad," I said. "You know her—Miss Personality."

I'd been muddling all evening about whether or not I should mention Lillian to the Goodwins. Hal had brought up the subject of work, so I continued, in a casual tone: "But, now that you mention it, something odd did happen today . . . here, let me help you, Betty."

Betty had brought a basket of clean laundry in from the clothesline, and now it was piled on the table. She gave me a grateful smile as I began sorting through it with her. "Well?" she said. "What happened, Mare?"

"I thought I saw somebody I knew from Scranton. In the dining hall." I pressed one of Harry's undershirts flat, then folded it into a little square.

"Oh yeah?" said Hal, puffing away on his pipe. "She an indoor attendant? I didn't know we got a new girl in."

"No. She's . . . well, she's an inmate."

"An inmate?" Betty said, her hands freezing mid-fold.

"What do you mean you *thought* you saw this girl you know?" Hal said.

Their alarm made me cautious. I moved the items I'd folded over to Betty's folded pile and said, "What I meant was—I'm not certain I know the girl. She looks a little like someone from the orphan home where I grew up. But I haven't seen her in years, so . . . I might be mistaken."

"Well, whatever you do, don't let Hartley or Vogel hear you *might* know any of the inmates." Hal said. "Not if you want to stay here. They'll let you go if they find that out, they don't usually keep staff who know girls from outside."

I buttoned one of Hal's work shirts. "Maybe that's why she pretended she didn't know me. Or, like I said, she probably wasn't pretending— she probably wasn't the girl I'm thinking of at all. The girl I knew, we were just kids, of course, but I don't remember her being feebleminded; she wouldn't have been at St. Cat's if she were, I'm sure."

"You were mistaken, then." said Betty. "The girls here, they all have minds like children, right, Hal? There were born that way."

Hal just shrugged. "She coulda had an accident. A few inmates got brain damage from accidents, falls, car wrecks—that kind of thing. They weren't all born mental defectives."

"Oh," I said. "I hadn't considered that."

Lillian didn't look like she'd been injured in that way. But I'm no doctor.

Hal watched us fold for a few minutes. Then he said, "This girl you saw, Mary, she an indoor girl, or what?"

"No, she's one of the dairy girls," I said. I glanced up at him. "Lillian is the name of the girl I knew. She's very pretty."

He took a puff from his pipe, but he held it for an extra beat when I said the name *Lillian*. I caught it. Then he leaned back and blew the smoke above him in lazy, wafting smoke rings. He tapped the pipe's contents into the ashtray and said, "Yeah, I'm sure you were mistaken about the girl, Mary, but I wouldn't say nothing about it to Hartley . . . or anyone else, neither."

After I said good night and went upstairs, I decided to finish my letter to Marge. Now that I was on my bed, writing by hand, I found myself being more candid. I explained that although the institution's practices were modern and scientific, it was situated in a rather remote, very rural part of the state.

Believe it or not, Marge, some of the other workers here seem to think I'm a sophisticated city girl. Paris, London, New York, Scranton—they're all the same to the folks here.

I explained that, fortunately, the nearby village of Clayburg was home to the prestigious Berneston University. Its presence provided cultural offerings to the area—at least that's what I'd been told. But it was summer, and the town was quiet on Sundays when I went there for church. I didn't mention Lillian. I didn't want Marge spreading rumors. I'd wait until I knew more. But I did admit that my weekends were a little lonely.

I'm sure I'm the only employee who counts the hours until Monday morning, I wrote.

I put the letter aside when the room grew too dark to finish. The only lamp was next to Gladys's bed. I didn't want to get out of my warm bed to turn it on. Instead, I pulled my quilt up over my chest and listened to the music from the radio downstairs.

I knew Betty and Hal were dancing—that's what they did on Friday nights. I'd barged in on them on the way to the bathroom during my first weekend there. They didn't seem the least bit self-conscious when I'd wandered into the parlor that night, though they were dancing very close. I'd almost knocked over a small table in my embarrassed rush back up the stairs. I'd chided myself for my prudishness later. Betty and Hal were married, why shouldn't they dance in their own house? Still, I didn't like to intrude upon their privacy, and after that, I stayed in my bedroom after dinner on weekends and listened to their music from there.

"Stardust." "Moonglow." "Shine on, Harvest Moon." The romantic melodies drifted up through the old floorboards beneath my bed, and they had a muffled, faraway quality that made me sad for some reason.

I took my rosary from where I kept it tucked beneath my pillow. My lips formed the words of my Our Fathers and Hail Marys, and I felt less alone. I asked God, as I did every night, to bless Father, Aunt Kate, my poor dead mother, Dorothy, Marge—the usual crowd. That night, because Lillian had made me think about St. Cat's, I added: "Heavenly father, bless dear Sister Rosemary and Lillian Faust."

When we were little girls, after lessons and before prayers, Sister Rosemary, the night matron, read aloud to us. She sat in a lumpy old upholstered armchair in front of the stove, often with a colicky infant or two on her wide lap. We never grew tired of hearing the same few books owned by the orphanage. *David Copperfield, Five Little Peppers, Pollyanna*—there were one or two others, and for the rest of my life, when I reread these stories, all the characters spoke with Sister Rosemary's thick Irish brogue.

One hot summer night, when I was around six or seven, Lillian Faust returned to the ward with a plaster cast on her arm. She'd fallen out of the giant elm in the courtyard that afternoon and had been taken to the hospital. Now, her eyes were still puffy and red from crying, but as we crowded around her, she proudly showed off her cast like it was a trophy.

Sister Rosemary had been reading to us while giving a baby her bottle. She put down the book and said, "I hear you were acting the fool again, Lillian, playing in a tree, have you no brain in that thick head of yours?"

"It was the boys' fault, Sister," Lillian said, perching on the arm of the nun's chair. "Willie from the boy's ward, he dared me to jump. He already did it, so I had to, see? They were calling me chicken."

"Chicken?" Sister scoffed. "It's better to be chicken for a minute than dead for the rest of your life." She shifted the baby so she could examine Lillian's cast. "A broken arm—you're lucky it wasn't yer neck. That's yer foundling luck, there, Lil, sure."

Lillian was one of the few "foundlings" at St. Cat's. She'd been left at the home as a newborn, her parents unknown. Foundlings are blessed with good fortune, all of them, according to Sister Rosemary. She said we could ask anybody in Ireland if we didn't believe her.

"I knew a girl, back home, little Deirdre Murphy," Sister said, poking Lillian's cast here and there. "She decided to climb way up high in a tree, herself. If only she'd just a broken arm to show for it."

I, and the thirty or so other girls in our dorm, scrambled over. There was the usual pushing and shoving as we tried to find the best places to sit on the threadbare rug—the spots closest to Sister's chair. Lillian managed to wedge herself next to the baby on Sister's wide lap, and she smiled down at us from that coveted spot, ignoring Sister's cries of "ACH, Lillian, you're too big now. Off. Get off before I break your other arm now."

"What happened to the girl, Sister?" Lillian asked, once the nun stopped swatting at her. "Did she have to go to the hospital like me?"

"No, she hadn't your dumb luck, I'm sorry to say."

I've often wondered—do all children have a morbid fascination with the pain, suffering, and misery of other children? Or just orphans? It was beyond fascination with us; we had ghoulish, bloodthirsty little imaginations, and that night we peppered the nun with our usual prompts.

"Did she break her neck?"

"Did she smash her head on a rock when she landed?"

"Did the fall make her brain come out of her ears like your cousin, Sister?"

"No, it wasn't the fall that did her in," Sister Rosemary said sadly.

We waited, wide-eyed and breathless, as she carefully adjusted the drowsy baby's little blanket.

"That would have been more merciful, sure." She sighed. "My heart still aches for her poor ma. She was never the same after that, Mrs. Murphy. But who would be? She saw it all from the window of the house. Poor little Deirdre dropped out of the tree, and in the blink of an eye, a bull—a *monster* of a bull—came charging out of nowhere, black and raging, his eyes as red as the embers in this stove here beside me—and he was on her."

The baby was asleep. Sister gently tilted the swaddled bundle up against her shoulder and continued. "The tree, it was in the dairy field, you see girls, and the bull didn't belong in with the cows, but there he was just the same, nobody knows why or how he got in, but he plucked Deirdre Murphy up off the ground, plucked her right up with his horns, and tossed her this way and that like a rag doll."

The baby made little mewling sounds. Sister said, "Ah, there, my little one, there, there, my sweet. . . . *Lillian Faust—you wake her up; I'll knock you dead; don't test me now.*"

Lillian, who loved babies, had been kissing the back of the infant's little head. Now she slid down off the chair so Sister would finish telling the story.

"The bull, girls," Sister continued, "there's a devil of a creature. After all—think about it now, what does a bull eat to sustain itself?"

She scanned our puzzled faces. Finally, a small voice said, "Children?"

"CHILDREN! Good Lord, no, Edith. Bulls eat grass, don't they? Hay and grass. That's all they eat. That's my point. They don't kill to *survive* like lions or tigers, no. They kill . . . for *sport*."

She let that sink in for a moment, then added, "Well, by the time the men had run the beast off, it was too late for Deirdre. She's in heaven with Jesus our savior now, may God bless her soul for eternity."

We did the sign of the cross with Sister and sat in stunned silence. After what was either a short nap or a long silent prayer, Sister opened her eyes and said, "Now, I hope that'll serve as a lesson to you all."

A little girl offered, in a thin, wavering voice, "I'll never climb a tree, Sister. Never."

"Yes, there's that too, but the lesson I meant is to never wander into a field of cows unless you know where the bull is keeping himself."

We lived in a small city. I, for one, had never seen a field of cows. I prayed that I never would.

"But, girls, it wasn't the bull's fault, not entirely, no," Sister said, and now she had that hushed, lilting tone we loved—the voice she used when telling us things she shouldn't.

She glanced at the door. You could hear a pin drop.

"She was cursed-like, poor Deirdre," Sister continued, in a near whisper. "The whole Murphy family had the curse on it. The grandfather, Jimmy Murphy, he's the one who interfered with the fairy fort when he was a child. . . . Sure you remember I told you about him."

We remembered all right. We begged her to tell us again.

Sister Rosemary didn't teach any classes, she only had night duty, and we'd all heard Mother Bea admonish her for telling us stories about fairies, ghosts and other "pagan nonsense." But we knew Sister's stories weren't nonsense—every word was true. She was an ordained nun, and she swore to the heavenly father they were true.

"May God strike me dead if I'm telling a lie," she said. Often.

And she wasn't talking about strangers, they were people she'd known personally who'd been skewered on fence posts, dragged behind runaway pony carts, drowned, trampled, scalded, smothered, or otherwise destroyed because they'd upset a fairy or banshee. Oh, she'd seen plenty of dark magic back home, Sister Rosemary had.

On the other hand, she once saw an angel with her very own eyes. There were angels who watched over us all, even if we couldn't see them. Sister Rosemary saw her own dead mother's angel when she was a little girl. It's what had made her decide to become a nun.

How we loved Sister Rosemary.

After I left the orphanage, I had trouble sleeping in Kate's cold, silent house, knowing that in a steamy, crowded ward across town, softly whispered stories of angels and mothers drifted from cot to cot long after Sister Rosemary had dozed off in her chair.

Of course, now I knew the nun's stories were silly; Mother Bea was right, they were superstitious nonsense. But I wondered if seeing me had caused Lillian to reminisce about St. Cat's as well. She'd been an unruly child, and some of the stricter nuns had dealt with her harshly, but she was a favorite of Sister Rosemary. I wondered if being mentally deficient was a sort of blessing for Lillian. Did she think about dear, befuddled Sister Rosemary as often as I did? If she thought about her, did she find it hard to keep her tears inside, where they belonged, like I did?

Six

WHEN I set off for the doctor's house that Sunday morning, I wondered if a priest ever came to Nettleton Village to offer Mass to Catholic inmates like Lillian. I knew there was a Sunday chapel service for inmates and employees—a Presbyterian minister conducted it. The only other Catholic employee I was aware of was the nurse Dr. Vogel had told me would accompany me to church in Clayburg. I'd never met Mrs. Nolan, but every Sunday, when I arrived at the doctor's house, I expected to find her waiting for me. And, to my immense relief, every Sunday, the nurse had canceled at the last moment. One week she had a sick patient to look after, the next, she was spending the day with a visiting relation. After that, Dr. Vogel stopped explaining why she wasn't joining us, and I didn't ask. I was glad I didn't have to spend my Sundays with some old widowed nurse.

I'd just turned onto the main asylum road when I heard an automobile approaching from behind. Charlie Durkin was bringing Dr. Vogel's Cadillac up from the old carriage shed, as he did each Sunday, but when I turned, I saw he had a girl seated next to him. Charlie slowed down as they pulled alongside, and the girl said, "Miss Engle! Hop in!"

Goofy Charlie had a girlfriend? How was that possible? They seemed to be having themselves a jolly little Sunday morning joyride in Dr. Vogel's car. When Charlie stopped the car and I reached for the rear door, I realized she looked familiar, this girl. The chic, chin-length black hair and the big doe eyes—she looked more like a flapper from the movies than the farmers' daughters who made up most of the Nettleton staff. And I was certain I'd seen her before.

"Charlie, for heaven's sake," the girl said. "Get out and let Miss Engle drive—that way you won't have to walk so far back home."

"Doc likes me to bring her 'round myself, Bert," Charlie said. "She'll skin me alive."

"Nonsense, hop out now, you'll make your folks late for church. I'll explain to Dr. Vogel. Come, Miss Engle, you drive, I'm so thrilled to finally meet you."

Charlie said goodbye to the girl, ignoring me, as usual. In fact, my presence seemed to unnerve him to such a degree that when he jumped out, he forgot to put the brake on, and the enormous automobile began to roll forward with no driver. The girl laughed, but I was quite frantic, as the road sloped more severely ahead. I trotted alongside, crying out, "The brake! Step on the brake!"

Instead of trying the brake, the girl managed to lean over and grab my hand. She shouted, still laughing, that she didn't know which was the brake pedal. She was remarkably strong and pulled me aboard with very little effort. By the time I stopped the car, I, too, was laughing.

"That was—exciting," I said, gasping for breath. I wiped my forehead with the back of my gloved hand. Then I closed the door and eased the car into gear. "I'm sorry, am I to drive you to the doctor's residence, Miss . . ."

"Yes, please, I'm Roberta . . . Bertie Nolan," she said.

"How do you do," I said, turning into the doctor's driveway. "I'm Mary Engle—oh, I guess you knew that. Do you work at the doctor's residence, Miss Nolan?"

"Oh, please, call me Bertie. No, I work in the infirmary. I'm going to Mass with you today in Clayburg, if you don't mind."

Now I turned to stare at my passenger. "But? Are you the nurse? Yes! *Mrs. Nolan!* I thought—I hope you don't think I'm rude, but, well, I pictured you older for some reason."

"Yes, I know, *the widow Nolan.* It does evoke a type, doesn't it? I'm so looking forward to getting to know you. May I call you Mary?"

"Of course."

"Look, there she is," Bertie said. "Did you ever think you'd work for such a fascinating woman, Mary?"

"No," I said truthfully. "I didn't know women like Dr. Vogel existed."

She was standing in front of her massive house, in a splendid Sunday dress and the most divine cloche hat. Two uniformed housemaids stood, sentry-like, on either side of her—one holding several parcels, the other holding leashes attached to two small black terriers. When I parked, the maid with the terriers opened the door to the rear compartment, and Dr. Vogel climbed in.

Dr. Vogel's maids were French, and though I didn't understand the clipped French words that Dr. Vogel used with them, their intent was clear enough. *Idiot* was the same word in French, apparently. I'd learned that Dr. Vogel was sometimes grouchy in the morning.

"Au revoir, mademoiselles," she said to the maids, once she was settled. Then, in a high-pitched, cheery tone that most people use for small children, she sang to her dogs, "Come, girls, hop up on Mama's lap! Upsy dupsy, now. Goooood girls."

When I turned to make sure that the doctor, dogs, and packages were all safely situated, Dr. Vogel sighed, "Well? What are we waiting for? You're five minutes late, Miss Engle."

I sputtered an apology, even though I knew we were several minutes early.

"Oh, Doctor," Bertie said, "I'm terribly sorry, it's all my fault." She turned and reached through the open window of the glass partition to pet the dogs. "I made poor Charlie Durkin wait for me at the carriage house, and I'm afraid I overslept. Now, I always get these two darlings confused, is this Trixie or Peg?"

Bertie's chirpiness worked. Dr. Vogel was happy to be steered toward her favorite topic of conversation—her Scotch terriers. Trixie was the trimmer one, the doctor explained; Peg was more stout. Peg was usually quite fit but had produced a litter just three months prior. They were a superior litter, from a long line of outstanding Scotties that the doctor had bred herself.

"Yes, my Peg was recently judged the best Scotch bitch in all of Pennsylvania," Dr. Vogel boasted.

"How wonderful! But poor Mrs. McLaughlin—she must have taken it awfully hard," Bertie replied casually, still stroking the muzzle of one of the dogs.

My pulse quickened. Had Bertie just referred to a woman as a bitch in front of Dr. Vogel? I winced. Dr. Vogel was so refined, she was sure to take offense. Instead, I heard Dr. Vogel laugh uproariously.

"*Mrs. Nolan!* You should be ashamed of yourself! And on your way to church!"

Bertie turned and faced the front, giving me a little wink.

"Mrs. McLaughlin is the head ward matron, Miss Engle. You might not have had the occasion to meet her yet," Dr. Vogel said, still chuckling. Then, her voice grew more serious. "One of our best employees, I might add."

"Oh yes, Mary," Bertie said soberly. "You'll be very impressed when you meet Mrs. McLaughlin. An outstanding woman. Yes."

The drive to Clayburg took less than an hour. I parked the long vehicle in the usual spot in front of Dr. Vogel's mother's house. Bertie and I jumped out to help the doctor with her packages but were thwarted by a nervous maid who insisted on carrying all the parcels herself.

"I'll take the girls," Dr. Vogel said, taking the dogs' leashes from Bertie. "Now, Miss Engle, my brother and his family will be arriving soon, as well as some other guests. I'd like them to be able to park here, in front of the house. I'm sure you'll find a place closer to church where you may leave my car for the day. I'll be waiting for you at seven o'clock. Please do be prompt."

"Yes, ma'am," I said.

The church was only a few blocks away, but no fewer than five people waved and called out to Bertie along the way. As we drove along Market Street, two young men ran alongside the car until one was actually standing on the running board on Bertie's side.

"Oh, Ralph, get *off*!" Bertie said, laughing and swatting at the man. I was too astonished for words.

"Some rig, Bert!" the man said, ducking his head inside so he could leer at me. His hat blew off, and he jumped off the car to retrieve it.

"Is that fellow—your friend? Shall I stop?" I asked.

"No, goodness no. Keep driving. Don't worry, they just came from the Methodist Church service, those two. They won't be at St. Peter's. There, Mary, why not park there?"

She pointed to a vacant stretch of road just before the church, and I backed the long car into a space between two other cars.

Bertie whistled in admiration. "Where'd you learn to drive so well, kid?"

"My father taught me," I said.

I'd been attending Mass at St. Peter's for almost a month, and I knew a few parishioners by name. I knew Mrs. O'Brien and her daughter, Eileen. And then there was the elderly couple—the Schuberts—I was almost certain that was their name. They always sat in the second pew on the left and—well, that was it. The rest of the congregation was just an assemblage of vaguely familiar people—fellow worshippers I passed solemnly on my way to the altar for Communion or nodded to as I slunk, self-consciously alone, away from the church after Mass.

Bertie, on the other hand, seemed to be on a first-name basis with the entire parish. As we climbed the steps to the church, she returned many friendly greetings, handshakes, and little hugs. I realized, then, that I had, indeed, seen Bertie before. Just the previous week, Bertie had come to church with a young man who looked like he could have been her brother. I remembered them because the boy was so handsome and they both looked so happy as they skipped down the steps when the service ended.

After Mass, Father Doheny stood outside, bidding his flock farewell. He beamed when he saw Bertie and me and said, "So nice to see you on this fine morning, Mrs. Nolan."

"Thank you, Father," Bertie said. "What a thought-provoking sermon. I'm sure you know Miss Engle."

"Yes indeed, Miss Engle, yes," Father Doheny said, but he was smiling at Bertie when he said it.

When we reached the sidewalk, Bertie said, "Come, we're having lunch at the inn at one, but it's only eleven, so, we've plenty of time for a stroll. I must know everything about you. I've been dying to meet you, Mary; I haven't had great luck making friends at the hospital—the other girls are so . . . well they're sweet, aren't they? But—"

"I'm afraid I can't have lunch at the inn," I interrupted, quite flustered. "I only brought money for the offering at church. I have a roll and some cheese that Betty Goodwin packed for me. I'll have that."

"A roll and cheese! You're a riot, kid. We're meeting my friend Brooks for lunch, he teaches at Berneston. He's bringing a friend along for you—I think he must be a student or something. Order up a storm, now, Mary, Brooks is loaded."

I stopped walking and stared down at my scuffed old oxford shoes.

"Oh no, I hadn't planned to do anything like that. I would have worn something nicer, I'd really rather not. You go on. . . . I'll meet you at the doctor's later."

Bertie didn't hear me; she was saying, "Good morning, Mr. Flynn!"

A man wearing a constable's uniform was walking toward us. He removed his hat and replied jovially as he passed, "And good morning to you, Mrs. Nolan."

"I thought you were new around here," I said, glancing back at the cop.

"I moved here . . . I guess about a month ago."

"That's around the time I came. But I hardly know a soul. How do you know so many people?" I asked.

Bertie gave a bored wave to a group of college boys who were calling to her from across the road. "I have a cousin who works here, he's employed at the steel mill. He introduced me to a few friends when I arrived. A friend of my sister's husband runs a dance hall just outside town. I'm from a large family—eight brothers and sisters, loads of cousins. I guess, through family connections, I've made a few friends here in town."

Although Bertie looked younger than some of the college girls we passed, she explained that she was about to turn twenty-nine. She was from Philadelphia and had become a nurse during the war. Her brief marriage was to a boy she'd known all her life. He'd died in Europe not long after their wedding. During and after the war, she'd worked in an army hospital, tending to wounded soldiers. Then she worked at the same Pennsylvania asylum for the insane where Dr. Vogel had once worked. When the day nurse at Nettleton left to get married, somebody recommended Bertie to Dr. Vogel. Dr. Vogel had enticed her to come to Nettleton by offering her an unusually handsome salary, according to Bertie—though, of course, she didn't disclose the amount.

"What about you, Mary?" Bertie said. "Tell me about your folks."

I quickly summarized my early years in the orphan home after my mother's death. "Later I moved in with my aunt. I took a typing course and lucked out when this job opened up."

We walked quietly for a few minutes—if you ever want to stop a conversation dead in its tracks, by the way, just say you grew up in an orphan home. I wondered if I should mention Lillian to Bertie. She did seem like somebody I could trust.

"Hey, maybe you can help me with a little quandary, Bertie," I finally managed.

"I'll try."

"A few days ago, I saw a girl I recognized from the home where I grew up."

"A girl from Scranton? Where? Here in town?"

"No. She's an inmate, actually, at the Village—oh, aren't those darling?" I said, pretending to admire shoes on display in a shop window.

"An inmate! Really? Do you know her well?" Bertie pressed. "Are you friends?"

"Good Lord, no, I haven't seen her in ages," I scoffed. "I wonder how much that white sandal with the little heel costs, do you like it?"

"I'm a nurse, dopey, I won't wear anything white when I'm off the clock. But this girl—did you know she was feebleminded?"

"No, we were just kids, of course." I turned from the window, and we resumed our walk. "I mentioned it to Hal Goodwin, and he said I shouldn't say anything to Hartley or Vogel about it. So I wondered what you think I should do. I mean, later, if they learn that I knew her, will it seem dishonest of me not to have mentioned it?"

After a few quiet moments, Bertie said, "No, I believe Hal's right. When I worked at the state asylum, one of the nurses had a cousin who was admitted. The nurse ended up getting fired."

"Really? Just because she knew the inmate? That doesn't seem fair."

"That wasn't quite it," Bertie said. "Apparently, the nurse was doing favors for the girl. She spread rumors that the cousin's husband sent her there to get a divorce, that she wasn't insane. That's why most asylums don't like staff knowing inmates—it can cause problems. But if you didn't even know the girl well enough to know she's feebleminded, I don't see any reason you should risk your position here. No. I'm not going to lose my new favorite chum the minute I've found her. Never speak of it to anyone, Mary, I forbid it."

A group of leggy, summer-session Berneston girls, in stylish Sunday frocks had crossed the street and were walking in front of us, laughing and talking over one another. I looked down at my plain pale blue dress.

It had white piping on the collar and sleeves, which, I suddenly realized, made it look ridiculously childish. I'd just made it last winter—what could I have been thinking? If only I'd brought some lipstick. That morning, I'd assumed I'd putter around town alone, as usual, after church. Instead, I was about to embark on a double date with the most glamorous woman I'd seen outside of the moving pictures.

Bertie must have sensed my unease as she said, "Now, this fellow Brooks—the one taking us to lunch. He comes across like a real blowhard at first, but he's not so bad. He said he's bringing a student along for you. Whoever it is will be swept right off his feet, Mary, you look swell!"

"Oh, I don't think so," I said, perspiration trickling down my forehead.

"Don't worry, it's a free lunch—you don't ever have to see him again if he's a creep. Oh. There they are."

Up ahead, in front of the inn, were two men. One of them, a dapper-looking fellow in a seersucker suit and straw hat, was waving frantically at us.

"Yes," Bertie groaned. "Brooks is rather pleased with himself, look at that suit. Well, nothing's free in this world; we have to eat don't we, Mary?"

I patted the damp collar on my dress and smiled weakly as the men approached.

"Oh," Bertie said. "That's Jake Enright! You'll like him, Mary."

Jake Enright was tall, lean, and, unlike the meticulously groomed and seersuckered Brooks, he was one of those rare people who manage to be handsome in spite of their best efforts to be otherwise. He wore a rumpled, ill-fitting blazer, and his thick brown hair was slightly mussed. One of the coeds ahead of us called out his name flirtatiously. He tipped his hat and gave her and her friends a broad, easy smile as they passed, causing them all to nearly collapse onto one another with excited giggles.

Why hadn't I brought lipstick?

"So, you grew up in a nunnery, Mary, do continue," Brooks said, after we'd ordered drinks. He'd insisted, as soon as we were seated, that I repeat my boring history that I'd just shared with Bertie.

"No, I didn't spend my entire childhood, there."

"Yes, and for heaven's sake, Brooks, darling, it was a convent school, not a *nunnery*," Bertie said. She gave Brooks a *Do shut up* look, which he missed, as he was squinting at his menu.

"I beg your pardon, Mary—I meant to say *convent*. Now, why did you decide not to become a nun?" he asked, and immediately shouted, "OUCH! That was my bad knee, Bert."

"Did I bump you with my leg?" Bertie said innocently. "So sorry."

"It wasn't that kind of convent," I said. "We weren't preparing to become nuns. It was a—home." Then, afraid that they'd think it was a home for delinquent girls, I added, "It was an orphan home. I was placed there as an infant, after my mother died."

"Oh, I see, yes, yes," said Brooks, and now he was the one who was flustered and embarrassed. "Well, I'm not a Catholic, how the hell should I know about convent homes? Now . . . Scranton, there's a fine town."

"Have you had Sunday lunch here before?" Jake said, kindly stepping in to change the subject.

"No," I said, giving him a grateful smile. "What do you recommend?"

"The sandwiches are all very nice. I also like the onion soup," Bertie said.

"Get the roast beef," said Brooks. "They're very generous with portions here, Mary, you're far too thin."

"Good heavens, Brooks, she is not," Bertie said. "It's very chic to be slender, Mary. You have the perfect shape."

"What do I know about style? I'm just a washed-up old professor of philosophy," said Brooks.

"Yes, yes, we're very impressed, I'm sure," Bertie said, smiling at him.

Brooks took her hand and planted a kiss on it, making Bertie laugh and swat at his head. I was impressed—in fact amazed—at how easy and comfortable Bertie was around these men. She was relaxed and chummy, while I felt like, well, an old nun. Why had I told them about St. Catherine's? From now on I would just tell people that I'd grown up with my aunt.

We had fresh salads, and then, rare roast beef served with enormous popovers that were as light as air, as well as mashed potatoes, carrots, and peas. Brooks taught at Berneston. Jake, I learned, had recently graduated from the college with a degree in journalism. He was from New York City but was spending the summer on campus, working with a professor on an investigation for a newspaper involving a labor dispute at a nearby steel mill. We had dainty little cakes with our coffee. I love food, so I was in heaven, but the best part of the afternoon was yet to come. At some point, I made an offhand remark about not having books available to read. I wasn't always able to get into Clayburg on Saturdays, when the library was open. And even when I did, it wasn't a very big library anyway, and it had a very limited selection of titles.

"But, what do you read?" Jake asked.

"My roommate buys those cheap romance magazines," I said. "And the Goodwins subscribe to the *Farmer's Almanac.* I've actually found those to be quite informative," I said with a chuckle, wondering if Brooks or Jake knew how to cure a sow's "clogged teat," or what to do when a cow's "vessel" comes out while calving. I did, unfortunately.

"Then you must come to Berneston's library. It's open every day, even Sunday. We'll go right after lunch," Brooks said.

"Mary and I can borrow from the school's library?" Bertie said. "You never told me that."

"I don't recall you ever pining for a good read, darling. Yes, of course, Jake and I can check out books under our names. You can return them any time."

And so, after lunch, we wandered over to the college. There were few students on the campus; it was the summer session, Brooks explained, but not many were enrolled in it. We had the library almost entirely to ourselves. It was the most extraordinary library I'd ever seen; I almost cried when I saw the vast rows of books. And I could choose any I wanted, and as many as I wanted.

Jake followed me to the fiction shelves, and we began browsing among the novels there. He asked me who my favorite authors were— a question, I realized, I'd never been asked before.

"Favorites? Why, I don't know. I enjoy so many. I suppose Edith Wharton and Henry James are two favorites. I mean—amongst the more contemporary American authors."

Jake gave a little knowing look as if I'd somehow satisfied a presumption he held about me.

"Also, of course, Upton Sinclair," I added, so he'd know that I was a modern thinker. Then I continued, "D. H Lawrence. Flaubert too."

There. Now he knew that I was no prude, despite all that convent talk at lunch. "What about you, Jake?"

I expected him to bluster on about his reverence for manly authors like Hemingway, Kipling, or Conrad. To my delight, he shared my love for Wharton, Lawrence, and Flaubert, adding to my list E. M. Forster, James Joyce, Thomas Hardy, Virginia Woolf, and F. Scott Fitzgerald. Why, he was a romantic! I exclaimed, with no small amount of blushing, that these too were some of my favorites. It felt so intimate, this discussion, almost as if I'd just shown him a hidden part of my body— a part nobody else had seen.

"What do you recommend I read?" Jake said, giving me a friendly nudge with his shoulder. I wandered along the stacks of books thoughtfully. "What are you in the mood for?" I asked.

"Danger."

"Danger?" I said, laughing. "Jack London danger or supernatural danger?"

"Supernatural," Jake said. "Horrify me."

I was thrilled; I love spooky books. I assumed he'd read *Dracula*, *Frankenstein*, *The Turn of the Screw*. I found Wilkie Collins's *The Moonstone* and asked if he'd read it. He hadn't.

"It's not horrifying, it's just one of those gothic English page-turners," I said. "Now find one for me."

Jake disappeared in the maze of books for several minutes and then returned with *The Monk*, by M. G. Lewis.

"Okay, I'm really not that religious," I protested.

Jake laughed and said, "Don't worry, neither is the book."

Jake and Brooks carried our books back to town and, upon seeing Dr. Vogel's grand vehicle, they insisted on being allowed to sit in it and then each wanted to pretend to drive it. Jake wanted to have a look at the engine, so I helped him figure out how to open the hood while Bertie and Brooks snuggled in the back seat of the car.

"So," Jake said briskly, after he'd marveled at the car's motor, "next

Friday, dinner and dancing. How about it? There's an inn with a good restaurant in Fulton—it's the next town over—and then the four of us can go to Seedy's; it's a great old roadhouse, dance hall kind of place."

"I . . . well, I don't know," I said.

"You don't know?" Jake repeated.

I was staring down at the toes of my shoes but he gently touched my chin with his finger and tilted it up, so I was looking at him.

"I mean, I don't really know very much about you," I said, laughing nervously, and looking away again.

"Well, you know what books I like, I mean, what else do you need to know?" Jake said.

"I'm not quite sure," I said, hating how dull he must have found me. I was eighteen, but had been so sheltered by my strict aunt. I'd never been out on a proper evening date before.

Jake playfully nudged the toe of my shoe with his own. "Come on," he said.

"Well, I'll have to check with Bertie. I mean, what if Bertie doesn't want to go?"

"Bertie's on board, we all discussed it when you disappeared into the poetry annex." Jake said. "It'll be fun."

An hour later, Bertie and I were parked on Dr. Vogel's mother's street. It was half past six. We knew she wouldn't be out until at least seven. I had spent the previous Sunday nights parked, silent and alone, on this very same road. Now we talked nonstop, filling each other in on our lives, laughing at the silly things we and the guys had said and done that day. I hadn't realized how terribly lonely and in need of a real friend I'd been.

"What's it like being a nurse at Nettleton, compared to the state asylum?" I asked.

"The work is certainly easier. The infirmary is rather quiet. There are very few women at Nettleton older than forty, so they're generally a healthy group."

"Weren't you frightened working with lunatics?" I asked.

"No, but it was depressing, Mary. Terribly so. It was crowded. A lot of brutality. I treated victims of horrible violence in the infirmary there. It became a bit too much for me. So here I am, treating healthy girls and young women who have sore throats or sprained ankles. It can be dull at times. We often have days without a single patient."

"Yeah, I can see where that would be a bore," I said. "But, I'm glad that the staff treats the girls here so much better than the girls at the state asylum."

Bertie said, "It wasn't always the staff who abused the girls. The residents at the state asylum were insane—their injuries were often caused by other violent inmates. Many harmed themselves." Bertie closed her eyes and shook her head as if trying to rid it from these bleak memories. "But sometimes brutish members of the male staff did take advantage. . . ."

"I'm glad you aren't there anymore; it sounds awful," I said, not wanting her to go on.

"One thing that I do wonder about, here at the Village," Bertie said, "is what will happen when the girls are older? At the state asylum, many people recovered and were released after a period of time. But there's no cure for being slow. The girls at Nettleton are here until they're in their forties or fifties and no longer fertile. What'll happen to them then? Their parents will have likely died. I don't think enough planning has gone into that. But, that's not my problem—it's hers."

Bertie was pointing to the tall figure standing under a streetlight in front of Mother Vogel's house. She was looking down the street in the opposite direction, in search of us. We tossed our cigarettes out the window, and Bertie sprayed cologne everywhere. Then I pulled the car up to Dr. Vogel and her "girls," who were frolicking at the end of their leashes.

Seven

THE very next afternoon, Bertie appeared at my desk in her nurse's uniform. She was out of breath and I wondered if she'd run all the way from the infirmary just to chat about our plans for the coming weekend. I'd never seen a nurse in the office building before.

"Hi, Bertie," I said, glancing at Hartley's door. Miss Hartley didn't allow social banter at work, but I was desperate to go over our plans. I'd been unable to stop thinking about Jake all day. What did Bertie know about him, really? Had she met anybody he'd dated? Did Bertie think a college boy as handsome and charming as Jake could ever be serious with somebody like me? What should I wear?

But Bertie hadn't come to talk to me. She said a quick hello and went straight to Gladys's desk outside Dr. Vogel's office.

"I need to speak to the doctor," Bertie said.

"She 'specting you?" Gladys asked, barely glancing up from her typewriter.

"No, but it's urgent. It's about one of the girls."

"Lemme tell her you're here," Gladys stood and was about to knock on the doctor's door when she turned and said, "What's the girl's name? So I can tell her."

"Ida," Bertie said quietly. She gave me a sad smile.

Gladys entered the doctor's office and after a brief moment, she beckoned Bertie inside.

A few minutes later, Dr. Vogel opened the door and strode briskly down the hall with Bertie at her heels. Miss Hartley came out of her office. She watched the doctor and nurse disappear down the hall and looked at Gladys for an explanation. Gladys shrugged and returned to her typing.

When Dr. Vogel returned, she gave Miss Hartley's door a brisk knock before thrusting it open and saying, "Where's Charlie Durkin? I need him to take me to town."

"He's just taken the dairy truck up to the service station in Mifflinburg," Hartley said.

Dr. Vogel retrieved her purse from her office, then said, "Miss Engle, the car's out front. You'll drive me."

Dr. Vogel had a strange, pinched expression as we walked to the car, and she was mumbling something that I couldn't quite hear. When I opened the door to the back seat, she said, "No, I'll ride in the front with you. Take me to Merchant's Bank on Market Street, please, Miss Engle."

We didn't speak on the trip to Clayburg. I glanced at the doctor a few times and saw an expression that I hadn't seen before—there was a visible sadness. I parked in front of the bank and jumped out to open Dr. Vogel's door, but she was already out of the vehicle. She clutched my elbow and said, "Come with me, dear."

"Good afternoon, Dr. Vogel," said the young man seated at a desk near the front of the bank's lobby. He stood and gave her a polite little bow. "How may I help you, today?"

"I'm here to see Whitcomb," Dr. Vogel said.

"I don't recall making an appointment with you to meet with Mr. Whitcomb today, let me just look in my agenda."

"I didn't make an appointment," Dr. Vogel said, walking past the clerk's desk and then the row of bank tellers.

The clerk followed us saying, "Now just one minute, please, Dr. Vogel, Mr. Whitcomb is in a meeting."

"Good," said Dr. Vogel, and she threw open the heavy oak door with the shiny brass sign reading: *Mr. James S. Whitcomb III, President.*

I hesitated, but Dr. Vogel gave my elbow a little tug, and I followed her inside, giving an apologetic shrug to the terror-stricken clerk.

Mr. Whitcomb was not in a meeting. He was reclining in his large chair with his feet on his desk, smoking a cigar and reading the newspaper. He was, therefore, quite surprised when we barged in. He struggled to stand, but because he was a very fat man, it was difficult to go from the position of repose to that of a bank president greeting a client. He did manage to right himself, and when his clerk pushed past Dr. Vogel and me, Mr. Whitcomb gave him a sharp look.

"I told the doctor that it would be better if she might make an appointment." said the clerk.

"*No!* Not at all, Cheney, not at all. I'm thrilled to receive dear Dr. Vogel at any time," Whitcomb said with a forced joviality. The clerk nodded and backed out of the room, closing the door behind him.

"So wonderful to see you, Agnes, do sit down," Whitcomb said, gesturing to two leather armchairs that faced his desk. "I don't believe we've met," he said, extending his hand to me.

"Miss Engle is one of our secretaries," Dr. Vogel said, as I shook his hand. She perched on the edge one of the chairs and with a little jerk of her head, indicated that I should sit on the other. Whitcomb repositioned his portly haunches on his own chair and smiled at us.

"What can I do for you today, Agnes? I believe we just sent you a check for the Village Christmas fund a few weeks ago, I do hope it was sufficient."

Dr. Vogel said nothing. Her focus was on the tips of her fingers. She fanned them at arm's length—first one hand, then the other—and frowned at the pretty rose-colored nail varnish, looking for any flaws. Finding none, she turned her attention to a loose thread on her sleeve.

"Or, is this more of a social call? I know Ruth will be thrilled to hear that you came in. We rarely see you these days—you're so busy. Ruth loves reading about your speeches and your travels. She clips everything she sees in the papers and pastes it all into a scrapbook—why, you'd think you were her own sister, she's so proud," Whitcomb said.

"I'm here about Ida," said Dr. Vogel. She leaned back, folded her hands in her lap, and fixed her eyes on him.

"Ida?" Mr. Whitcomb said, with a thoughtful frown. "Is Ida another of your bridge group? I'm not sure I've had the pleasure . . ."

"Oh, I'm quite sure you've had your pleasure," Vogel said breezily.

"I beg your pardon?"

"I'm not surprised you don't know her name. Ida is the girl who's been working as your household maid for much of this year. She's one of our residents at the Village, part of our parole training program."

Mr. Whitcomb's face turned scarlet.

Dr. Vogel stood. She placed her palms on the desk and leaned so close to Whitcomb that their noses almost touched.

"She's the pretty plump thing with red curls, a large bust, and the reasoning skills of a toddler who you raped. More than once."

"I BEG YOUR PARDON!" Whitcomb boomed. He began to stand again but he could not, because Vogel's face was too close. Instead, he pushed himself back in his chair and blinked up at her.

"Yes," the doctor continued, her tone still remarkably calm and measured, despite her assertive posture. "Raped and made pregnant, I examined her myself just an hour ago."

"This is preposterous, Agnes! How dare you come in and accuse me of such filth? In front of this young woman I've never met. I've hardly noticed this—Ida, if that's what she's called. It's Ruth who deals with the girls you send to the house. Like a toddler? Not any of the girls who've worked for us."

"Yes, and who was the girl you had last year? I don't recall her name, but I do remember ordering her confined to Building Five—the house where we send insubordinate residents. She was being punished for refusing to go back to work for you. She's Irish-born. Oh, yes, now I remember. Doreen is her name. She came to us from the Muncy work farm—a former prostitute. The things she said you made her do were too shocking for us to take seriously. We punished her quite severely for lying, even morons can be taught the difference between truth and falsehood. Funny, she'd rather spend a month in a cold room on half rations than go back to you. We thought she'd learned the things she said you made her do during her days in the bawdy houses. I'm a doctor and have never heard of such depraved acts."

Vogel stepped back now, and Whitcomb stood, shakily.

"I will not stand here and let you slander me with this filthy innuendo, Agnes," he said in a low growl.

"This isn't innuendo, *James*, you are a rapist and a moral degenerate of the worst kind, preying on vulnerable and defenseless girls. You might want to phone Ruth before I go to the constable. Mary, go start the car."

I stood, but I couldn't take my eyes off the banker's face. I'd seen Mr. Whitcomb on many occasions during my trips to Clayburg—in the tearoom at the inn or strolling to church on Sunday with his wife's slender arm linked through his. He had a smile for everybody. He was the president of the only bank in town. His wife, Ruth Whitcomb, was one of the bridge group that Dr. Vogel played with every Thursday evening. I had read in true crime magazines about brutes who victimized girls. They were usually hideous, dark-featured fiends who lurked in shadows and, later, gloated over their crimes. Women knew to watch out for these monsters. Now I wondered how many girls knew, as I knew, that there were wolves in sheep's clothing, men like my uncle Teddy—a police officer—and this Mr. Whitcomb. He was a bank president. Nobody ever spoke of the evil committed by "good men" like them.

And no woman I'd known had ever spoken to a man the way Dr. Vogel just spoke to Mr. Whitcomb. Now she was heading for the door, and I rushed ahead to open it for her.

"Agnes, wait. Come back and sit down, please," Mr. Whitcomb pleaded.

Dr. Vogel turned.

"Please, come sit, Agnes. This is all a dreadful misunderstanding, I'm sure."

"Mary, go start the engine so the car is warm for our drive to the courthouse."

I sat in the driver's seat and waited. I hadn't been prepared to witness such a dramatic scene, and now I was exhausted. The bank was about to close. I watched the last-minute customers dashing in to make their deposits. I rested my forehead against the steering wheel, and the smell of its leather casing reminded me of Uncle Teddy. I jerked my head back. Leather and other smells—whiskey, cigars, sweat—they were old-man smells. They were my uncle's smells.

Leather, whiskey, sweat.

When I was very small, Father picked me up each Sunday from St. Catherine's and we'd spend the day with Uncle Teddy, Aunt Kate, and Daniel at the house in Scranton. Around the time I turned eight, Father no longer came to get me. He had become the foreman at a lumber mill up in Hancock, New York, about a two-hour drive from Scranton. After that, Uncle Teddy drove me up to see him. I waited on a bench in the front hall with the other half-orphans after church—Sunday was visiting day. We sat with our ankles crossed and stared down at our hands as the other girls—the full orphans and foundlings—hurled insults at us.

"If my pop was alive, he sure wouldn't keep me here."

"Your mama has a day off from *hooring* and now she wants to see you?"

"Your dad won't come get you. He had to leave the state so they don't 'lectrocute him."

This last was aimed at me. The rumor that my father wasn't able to return to Scranton because he was wanted by the law was consistent, but his crimes varied. He was sometimes a bootlegger or a thief. Other times, a rapist or murderer. I knew they were all lies. There were many foreigners working at the mill now, so Father couldn't leave, even for a few hours. He ran the place. Some of these foreign workers, Uncle Teddy used to tell me, you couldn't turn your back on them, even for a minute. Thieving and brawling was in their blood. They were like animals, most of them.

Father loved my visits. We ate the lunch that Aunt Kate packed for us, and he asked me to say some words in German that the sisters had taught us. It reminded him of his parents, who were born in Germany. I brought him drawings I'd made or little poems I'd written, and he made a big show of admiring them. Uncle Teddy started in with the whiskey and cards from the moment we got to the mill, and by four, when it was time to take me back, he was often walking sideways.

One summer afternoon, Father sat me on his lap in the cab of one of the big lumber trucks and allowed me to steer the truck across an open field. First, he told me to try to keep the rig straight as he stepped on the gas. It didn't take long for me to learn how to keep the enormous, heavy steering wheel steady, no matter the speed. Then I was able to drive us in circles. By the end of that afternoon, he had me driving Teddy's automobile all by myself. The sedan was easy to drive, after that big truck. Father put an old milk crate on the seat for me to lean against—it helped me reach the foot pedals.

The next Sunday, Father let me drive him up and down the mountain roads in Teddy's car. The glass of ale in his hand sloshed all over the place when I forgot to release the clutch or stomped too hard on the brake. It was all great fun, until that afternoon, when I returned to St. Cat's stinking of Father's spilled ale. The Sisters warned Teddy that the next time I smelled of alcohol when I returned, he could just keep me. There were plenty of orphans who needed a bed. But I drove by myself after that—I didn't need Father's help. I drove Teddy's car all over the fields and up and down the roads while the men played cards and drank.

One Sunday, a few weeks later, I asked if I could drive all the way back to Scranton. Father said something about it not being a bad idea, given that Teddy looked a little "tight."

"Nah, I'm fine," Teddy laughed, telling me to scoot over to the passenger side.

I could tell by the way he drove that he was more dizzy than usual from all the whiskey that day. It was very hot and his pungent, oily sweat had seeped out onto his shirt, leaving dark patches on his chest and beneath his arms. He whistled merrily, and every now and then he turned to wink and smile at me. I smiled back, gripping the seat with my hands as the car careened this way and that down the steep mountain road. We hadn't been driving very long when Uncle Teddy suddenly swerved the car onto a little dirt side road. He told me he needed to "use the gents'." I watched him limp off into the woods—he always favored one leg; he'd been injured in the war. A few minutes later, he returned. He asked me if I needed to go. I told him I didn't. Instead of turning the car on and driving, Teddy just leaned back and threw his arm along the seatback behind me.

"You wanna drive?" Teddy asked with a big smile.

Did I ever!

"How about a cuddle for yer uncle, first, eh?" He said, winking at me and tickling my ribs with his thick fingers. I stopped my gleeful giggles when he pulled me roughly onto his lap. He squashed his fat wet lips against my cheek and ear and mouth, leaving slimy wetness all over my face, despite my squirming.

Eventually, he let go of me. He slumped over and seemed to be falling asleep. I was still kicking and swatting at him. I shouted tearfully at him to move over and, amazingly, he did. He was so different than he had been just moments before. He seemed confused. He mumbled something as I maneuvered my way off him so that I was behind the steering wheel. He moved his horrible old haunches along the seat, then slumped his shoulder against the passenger door and began to snore. He didn't wake up until I slammed on the brakes at the bottom of the driveway to St. Cat's. I still wasn't great at stopping, and the car bucked and stalled when I forgot to step on the clutch.

"Hey," he said groggily. "Hey, kid . . ."

I opened the door, but Teddy was now awake, though still dizzy and slurry. He grabbed my wrist in his big hot hand.

"Sweetheart, 'member what I said about your pop. He'll get jealous if he learns we cuddled, he never gets time alone with you, see? And whatever you do, don't tell none of the Sisters—they'll never believe you. I had a girl cousin sent to a nut farm when I was a kid for telling crazy tales about her stepfather, stop pulling away, now, just hear what I'm saying. Yer pop, he'd be angry, see? And he can get mean when he's angry. You don't want him to do something that'll land him in prison, right?"

He shakily reached into his vest pocket. I was staring at the ground. I couldn't look at him, especially at his pants, which were stained from where he'd pressed so hard against my skirt.

"Here, here," Teddy said. He pressed a dollar bill into my hand and shoved me out of the car. I stared at it in disbelief. A whole dollar bill! Sometimes my father would give me a shiny nickel or two. These were immediately swiped by one of the older girls, who always shook down us half-orphans, knowing we might return with candy or coins. But this was a paper bill, the first I'd ever held. I folded it over and over and pressed it into a small, flat rectangle as I walked up the drive to the home.

The door opened, and Sister Eloise stood in the dimly lit hall. "Is that you, Mary Engle? Why, it's almost seven, you've missed your supper. Hurry up, child."

"Yes, Sister," I said. I was tugging at the hem of my skirt as I walked. I had flipped it up and pulled at a stitch until it broke, then shoved the bill into the hem.

"So, the courthouse next, ma'am?" I asked, when the doctor returned to the car.

"The courthouse?" Dr. Vogel said vaguely. She was looking out her window, I couldn't see her face, but her shoulders were slumped, and when she removed a handkerchief from her purse, her hands were trembling.

"Yes, I . . . I thought we were going there to inform the constable—about Mr. Whitcomb."

"No, there's no need, we worked it all out."

"Oh," I said.

I glanced over. Dr. Vogel was shielding her face with one hand while dabbing at her eyes with her handkerchief.

"Ma'am . . . are you okay?"

"Please, just drive." Her voice was trembling now; I realized she was weeping.

The afternoon sun slanted across the road ahead, and it was hard to see where we were going as I steered through Clayburg. Once we were out of town, on the state road, I was able to drive a little faster.

"Miss Engle, do slow down, I've had enough trouble for one day, I don't need a smashed car." Dr. Vogel said, her voice steadier now. She'd removed a compact from her purse and was dabbing powder on her damp, flushed face.

"I'm sorry, ma'am," I said, easing the car into a lower gear.

We drove on in silence for several minutes. Then, Dr. Vogel said, "You're wondering why I'm not reporting Mr. Whitcomb, aren't you, Mary?"

"I'm sure it's not my concern," I said.

"When an innocent girl is so dreadfully mistreated, it should be the concern of every moral person," Dr. Vogel said. "To think, a man—an intelligent man, a family man. To think that a man like that would so horribly abuse a girl like Ida. You don't know Ida, of course, but she's like many of our girls. Very pretty and quite able to carry out simple tasks around the house. But her moral reasoning skills are impaired. She's shown she has little capacity to understand what's right or wrong. In that way, she's almost infantile. Well, I'm to blame for what happened to her. Clearly, she wasn't fit to be sent out, I should have examined her myself instead of listening to Hartley."

The doctor was patting under her eyes with her handkerchief again.

I was stunned. Dr. Vogel was always so assertive and confident, always in control of her emotions.

"Oh, Dr. Vogel, it wasn't your fault, ma'am, how could you have possibly known?"

She flashed me a quick smile when I looked at her and said, "Don't you dare tell anyone you saw me like this, Miss Engle."

"No. Of course not, I would never."

Now the doctor straightened her shoulders, and when she spoke, it was with her usual cool poise. "Did you know I own a pistol, Miss Engle? I'm lucky I never remember where I put it. I might have shot that fat walrus today—shot his puny little cock right off."

"Oh!" I said. *Puny little*—well, it wouldn't do to laugh, but, really.

"How would I have found his little worm under all that blubber? I suppose you could have tried lifting his various laps up with your hands and then I'd have a better chance. Cigarette?"

Dr. Vogel had stuck a cigarette between her lips and held her lovely silver cigarette case open for me.

"Why thank you," I said. "I'm not a habitual smoker, but I do enjoy one—on occasion."

I saw a glimmer of amusement in Dr. Vogel's puffy eyes as she lit my cigarette, and then her own. Why did I lie to the doctor about a trivial thing like smoking? Everyone at the Village talked about how she could tell when people lied; it was part of her training as a psychiatrist. She was able to decipher the thoughts behind people's words. I smoked on my way to work each morning, every time I took a restroom break, and then all evening at the Goodwins'. The only time I didn't smoke was when I was in the office building or when I drove Dr. Vogel. But, so what if I'd fibbed about a thing like that? The cigarette was just the thing to take the edge off.

When we were several miles out of town, Dr. Vogel said, "Some of us actually thought we women were equally franchised when we won the vote, but it's still a man's world, Miss Engle. We have to play by their rules, if we want progress."

I gave her a nod as if I understood.

"The Merchant's Bank is going to finance the new medical building at the Village, with a low interest rate. And the Whitcombs are making a very generous personal donation that will cover much of the initial construction costs. Mr. Whitcomb just decided today; he'll inform the newspaper tomorrow. The board of trustees will be quite pleased."

So, that was it. She'd put *the squeeze* on him, as Uncle Teddy used to say. But what about Ida? I didn't see how the money was supposed to atone for the crime against the girl. She was feebleminded. The banker should be sent to prison. What if he hurt other girls?

"The end very often justifies the means—now that's a fact, Miss Engle, don't let anybody tell you otherwise," Dr. Vogel said. "If I'd reported Whitcomb, there'd be criticism of the Village's very successful work-parole program and much unnecessary scandal. None of it would undo what happened to Ida. In fact, an inquest would only add to her misery. She'd be forced to appear in court to testify about the disgusting things he did. Ida came to us after being arrested as a prostitute when she was sixteen. Any judge would believe Whitcomb's version of events over hers."

I nodded. The doctor was right, of course. Nobody would believe a girl like that.

"Mental and moral weakness in girls like Ida. Men see it. Certain men—they have a predatorial sense for it, rather like lions or cheetahs. I took a safari trip to Africa with my family when I was a girl. Do you know how lions hunt, Miss Engle?"

"I believe," I said, recalling a film reel about Africa I'd seen recently, "they chase herds of deer until they catch one. Or is it elk that they hunt?"

"No. A lion will study a group of antelope, or gazelle—elk don't live in Africa, dear. He'll single out an antelope that's weak or slow. *That's* the one he'll attack. Wild antelope drive the genetically weak, aged, or inferior members away, for the health of the rest of the herd. A defective antelope won't find a mate, its genetic flaws won't pollute the next generation. And, as Mr. Darwin discovered, that's nature's way of ensuring the survival of the most fit of every species. Of course, we're not animals, Miss Engle. No. We're children of God. We must look after our weak and our afflicted, and that's why what happened today is so important. With Whitcomb's donation and the support of the bank, we'll continue to expand. We'll provide a sanctuary for more girls like Ida, and prevent the births of countless others like her."

"But, what about Ida's baby?" I asked, staring numbly at the road ahead. I couldn't help thinking about the weak, mewling newborn, its inherited defects already apparent.

"Ida had a miscarriage today, thank goodness. That's why Mrs. Nolan was so distressed, we hadn't noticed her pregnancy, and we both felt quite sick about that. I didn't see the need to tell Whitcomb that. Of course, we won't send any more girls to his house. Don't worry about the girl, Ida. She's severely limited. I don't think she even remembers what happened with Whitcomb."

I tossed my cigarette out the window. My hands were shaking, but I didn't want the doctor to notice. I gripped the steering wheel firmly, but my eyes were filling. How could any girl not remember something like that? Many of my childhood memories are vague, yet I remember every second I spent alone with Uncle Teddy with dreadful clarity; I'm sure I always will. But Ida had the mind of a toddler. Did she even know what had happened to her?

"Well, look at us, what a pair," Dr. Vogel said, handing me her handkerchief.

"Do you think I made the wrong decision? It's not too late to go back. Slow down, Miss Engle. Perhaps I let my emotions get in the way of logic. Shall we go see the constable?"

I blinked back my tears and squinted at the road ahead. Everything was blurry, and I felt dizzy.

"Pull the car over, Mary," the doctor said. "Let's think this through."

Had she just called me Mary? The doctor had always called me Miss Engle, but, yes, this time she'd said *Mary*. I steered to the roadside and we sat there with the engine idling.

"Shall we go back and speak to the constable, dear? Perhaps we should. I'm too exhausted to think straight," Dr. Vogel said, placing her gloved hand on mine and giving it a gentle squeeze. She let her hand linger there, and I realized she was trembling; she needed comforting as much as I did. I wondered if any of the others at the Village had seen this kinder, more sensitive side of Dr. Vogel. Everyone considered her to be a bit haughty and authoritarian. Now I realized that her lofty, cool attitude toward certain workers and inmates was required of her, but it wasn't her true nature. She ran one of the largest asylums in the state; she had to act stern at times, but it wasn't who she really was.

"No, ma'am, it would be wrong to report this," I said. "The poor girl—Ida, she's safe now. Why add to her misery?"

"You're right, I agree," Dr. Vogel said.

After a moment or two, I put the car in gear, and we were back on the road.

"You know, I've had my eye on you these past weeks, Mary. You remind me of myself when I was your age. Very much so."

I was at a loss for words. How could Dr. Vogel ever have been as awkward and uncertain as me?

"I'm grateful to Thelma for recommending you to me, I wrote her last week, saying so. I see a great future for you here at the Village. What happened to our Ida has never happened before and won't happen again, I do hope it hasn't discouraged you. You mustn't dwell on it. In this work, we must think of the good things we do and not linger on the evil done by others."

"Of course," I said.

"I'm sorry you have to learn about the wretchedness of some men," the doctor continued. "You never had a mother to explain things like this to you. You never had her to take care of you, but you have me now."

Dr. Vogel leaned over and draped her arm lightly across my shoulders. I felt her cool cheek pressed against my forehead for a brief moment. I watched the road disappear beneath the gleaming front of the long automobile as we sped along, and I had the sense that we were flying. I kept the wheel steady in my hands. I dared not breathe. I dared not make a sound.

When we turned onto the Village road, Dr. Vogel shifted back to her side of the seat and studied her face in her mirrored compact, gently dabbing the corners of her eyes where her makeup had smudged. I stopped the car and watched Pop Durkin limp out of the gatehouse to swing the heavy gate open for us. The familiar sights—Pop touching the brim of his cap and nodding as we passed, the roadside ferns, dappled now, with the sun's lingering golden rays, the towering, fragrant pine trees—they brought me back to earth. We were home. Nettleton

Village was my home now, and I realized I'd been happier in the short time I'd lived here than I'd been at any other time in my life.

"Poor old Durkin," Dr. Vogel said, with a soft chuckle, turning to watch him close the gate. "He's been here since we opened this place. I graduated at the top of my class in college and medical school, Mary, I'd been a doctor of psychiatry for seven years, before I was asked to be superintendent here. But I wouldn't be trusted with the vote for another decade and a half. Old Durkin? He never went to school; he can barely read. But he and the rough men who dug this road and cleared this forest, men born in impoverished countries, illiterate, criminal, even feebleminded men—they all lined up on Election Day to cast their ballots. Me? I sat in my office, writing public health dossiers requested of me by legislators that these hordes of ignorant men had elected."

The doctor's words became clipped and terse: "My mother was a suffragist herself, as was her mother before her. My family came to this country one hundred years before it was a nation, yet Italians, Jews, Irishmen, Poles—they marched from the ships that brought them here, straight to the voting booths. Well, most of them stopped at the pubs first, of course. My mother was picketing for the vote with Grandmother, and *men*—foul ignorant men—cursed and spat at them."

"How awful," I said, actually cringing at the thought. I'd spoken only a few words to Dr. Vogel's mother when I drove her to Clayburg on Sundays. Mrs. Vogel was so delicate and refined. "How could any man do such a thing?"

"There's no end to the evil men can do, if given the opportunity," the doctor said grimly.

We were turning onto the road to the main building, and I slowed down.

"I certainly appreciate the work you and so many others did to get the voting act passed," I said, with forced gaiety, trying to lift her spirits. "I can't wait until I'm old enough to vote, I've been looking forward to it for so long."

I hadn't actually thought much about voting until that very moment. My aunt never voted; she believed allowing women to vote doubled the voting power of the "wrong types" of people.

"Yes, Mary, yes, you must," Dr. Vogel said, gazing out her window. She spoke more softly now, apparently lost in some sad thought.

When we were in front of the main building, I slowed the car to a stop.

The doctor gave a weary sigh and said, "I'm glad this day is almost over. Thank you, again, dear, for helping me sort out this ugly business with poor Ida."

I jumped out to open her door for her, as Charlie always did, but she'd already stepped out of the car, and I followed her up the steps.

"I'm sure it goes without saying, Mary," she said, stopping to lean against me for a moment so that she could whisper. "This Ida business is highly confidential. You mustn't share it with anyone, here or elsewhere."

"Of course, Dr. Vogel, you can trust me."

"I know I can," she said, giving my arm a gentle squeeze.

Eight

THE following morning, I was about to begin typing the first letter in Miss Hartley's thick pile of correspondence when Dr. Vogel's office door flew open and Miss Hartley stomped out.

"Gladys, the doctor wishes to speak with you," Miss Hartley said, with more than her usual sharpness, but she wasn't looking at Gladys. She was glaring at me.

And that was the day I was promoted to the position of secretary to Dr. Vogel and Gladys was demoted to the secretary of Miss Hartley. Dr. Vogel told us to swap desks immediately and then asked me to re-type one of several letters that Gladys had botched the day before. Dr. Vogel had been complaining about Gladys's poor secretarial skills ever since I'd arrived, but I didn't think she'd do a thing like this—abruptly demote her and promote me in her place.

When Hartley and Vogel had returned to their offices, I offered Gladys an apologetic smile, but she was hammering away at her typewriter keys, her cheeks and throat mottled with angry red splotches.

I began the first letter:

TO THE BOARD OF TRUSTEES
NETTLETON STATE VILLAGE

Ladies and Gentlemen:

Allow me to begin by expressing my deepest gratitude to you, our governing managers. Nettleton Village is still proving to be one of our country's most modern, efficient, and innovative institutions, and our success would not be possible without your tireless efforts, thoughtful guidance, and generous support. I've enclosed, for your review, a copy of a docu-

ment titled: "*Report to His Honor the Governor of the Commonwealth and to the members of the Senate and the House of Representatives.*" In it, you'll find financial statements and disclosures that account for all receipts and expenditures for the past quarter. Also, please find attached a list of employees, as well as our proposals for expansion next year.

The atmosphere here at the Village remains positive and highly productive, with the comfort, safety, and happiness of our residents always our highest priority. During the last meeting, the question arose as to the education of the residents. As I explained then, it is scientific fact that one cannot be academically educated beyond one's mental ability. Studies of our own residents and their histories have shown us that at least ninety percent have reached their mental level scholastically before arriving here. Because of this, we put a greater emphasis on industrial rather than academic training.

At present we provide a number of group activities that also serve as training opportunities here at the village. They include: sewing, chamber work, cleaning, kitchen, pantry, laundry, fieldwork, dairy, poultry, and light maintenance work such as painting and woodworking.

As always, we are short-staffed. One might assume that the profound idiots require the most supervision and discipline, but, in fact, it is the higher-functioning girls who demand the most guidance from our attendants. Delinquent defectives, for whose segregation our asylum was specifically created, form our largest group. Many of these girls have been out in the world and are restless and resentful after they arrive here and discover that they'll receive no remuneration for their work in the fields or in the laundry. Two years ago, it was decided that Building Five would be dedicated to the housing of the most troublesome cases, and the temporary segregation of some of these girls has increased the health of the entire community. A few days of quiet contemplation on one's own is the best remedy for antisocial behavior.

Some of you have voiced concerns to me about a recent editorial in the <u>Harrisburg Times</u>. The writer is a well-known trafficker in slander—political and otherwise—so I hope those who read his fabrications about "harsh disciplinary methods" here will consider the source. As you know, we don't "strap" the girls or abuse them in any way. The outrageous charge that some girls work as virtual slaves in local *homes and businesses is, of course, absurd. When our more capable girls are suitably trained, we allow them to do light housekeeping work in the homes of respectable members of the community. In fact, several of you who serve on our board have been kind enough to offer this valuable opportunity to our girls by inviting them to work in your own homes and, in some cases, your businesses. Our residents consider it an honor to be chosen to be among the ranks of my employed girls and they ask to be considered for the positions. The wages earned by the girls are paid to the Village and help recover some of the costs of their care. But of course, that was not mentioned in the biased and false news story from the <u>Harrisburg Times</u>.*

If any one of you has questions or concerns about these or other matters relating to Nettleton Village, please feel free to write or call on me at any time.

I look forward to our meeting in December.

> *Submitted with much gratitude,*
> *Dr. Agnes Vogel, Superintendent*

The letters I typed for my new boss were far more interesting than Miss Hartley's dull missives. I was pleased to learn that the case of Ida and the lecherous banker had been an anomaly; I'd heard attendants say exactly what Dr. Vogel had written—girls begged for the opportunity to live and work in the fine homes in Clayburg. They often had their own sleeping quarters, and the work was usually less demanding than their chores at the Village. While Miss Hartley's focus was on the minutia of the daily operations, Dr. Vogel's correspondence revealed that she was concerned with the important, broad scheme of things.

During that first week, I typed letters to the heads of several other institutions for the feebleminded—including one in California and another in Mississippi. I responded to various invitations to social events and sent condolences to a local judge whose wife had died. I also responded to a letter from Senator David Reed of Pennsylvania. In his letter, he'd addressed the doctor by her first name, Agnes! The senator's wife was one of Nettleton's trustees, and Senator Reed wanted Dr. Vogel to know how delighted she was to have been invited to stay at Dr. Vogel's home while attending the next meeting of Nettleton's governing board. She looked forward to it immensely. Also, would Dr. Vogel be so kind as to hold that tea at her mother's as she had promised, for the Women's Republican Club of Union County? Early spring would be an ideal time; he'd like to speak to the good women of Union County about the 1928 election.

Yes, I typed for Dr. Vogel. It would be her honor.

On the Friday of my first week, I typed speeches that Dr. Vogel would give the following week in Pittsburgh and Altoona. When Dr. Vogel read the pages, she made a point of coming out to my desk to compliment me on my work. She asked me if I would please organize her files while she was traveling. "They're an absolute mess," the doctor said, shooting Gladys a quick, exasperated look.

When Dr. Vogel shut herself back in her office, I turned to Gladys.

"What are you and Hammy up to this weekend?" I asked with an eager smile.

She was focused on her Dictaphone and pretended not to hear me. She had spoken to me only when spoken to all week, and even then, her replies were clipped monosyllables. Gladys's ire was a small price to pay for the satisfaction I took in assisting Dr. Vogel. The doctor was a perfectionist and was understandably exasperated by her employees much of the time. Because of Nettleton's location, the population from which it drew its employees was not particularly well educated, especially the younger women, whose greatest aspirations, from what I could glean, were to become the wives of farmers. It was no wonder Dr. Vogel spent so much time deriding the ineptitude of some people she employed. The doctor didn't suffer fools gladly, and she could come across as a tyrant at times. But I'd seen her weep at the misfortune of one of the residents and blame herself for what had happened to her, rather than push the blame on others. That showed her deep compassion as well as her wisdom and strength.

I knew Gladys would get over her resentment in time, but I wish she'd answered me when I'd asked about her weekend plans, because I had plans for once, and I would have enjoyed telling her so—I had a date that night.

We dined at a place called the Fulton Inn. Brooks secured a corner table as soon as we arrived and said something to the waiter about "the usual setup." When the waiter returned, he placed, on the table, a tray containing a soda syphon and four ice-filled glasses. There was also a bowl with sugar cubes and a plate with sliced lemons.

Jake expertly focused the spout of the water bottle so that the fizzy water sprayed into each glass while Bertie squeezed the lemons into them. Then Brooks removed something from his inside jacket pocket and gazed around the restaurant as if he were trying to locate an acquaintance, but I could see that he had passed something to Bertie under the table.

"Oh, look, gang, I've a new ring," Bertie said. She held a long handkerchief in one hand and extended the other so that they could all admire her ring. I actually believed she was showing off her pretty ring and asked her where she had gotten it. Then I saw that Bertie had, in the hand with the long handkerchief, a thin silver flask. She moved the hand with the handkerchief slowly around the tray, concealing her act of pouring a clear liquid into each drinking glass. I looked furtively around the dining room to see if anybody had noticed, but the whole thing took less than a few seconds. Now the flask was nowhere in sight—presumably Bertie had returned it to Brooks. Jake was lighting my cigarette; then he lit his own. I noticed that there were similar "setups" at other tables—trays with ice-filled glasses. Bottles of seltzer, bowls of lemons. Sugar.

We clinked glasses and I sipped my drink. It was strong but sweet. I knew it was gin from the smell—Father and Uncle Teddy sometimes drank gin when I visited. But the sugar and lemon made it very tasty. Gin fizzes! That must be what we were drinking. I'd read about this cocktail in a magazine. I took a small sip, and then another. What a lovely warmth it gave me.

I'd been rendered almost mute with shyness on the entire ride to Fulton. Bertie had ridden in the front seat next to Brooks, and I sat in the back next to Jake. All week, sitting at my typewriter or strolling between home and work, I'd conjured many witticisms with which to delight Bertie, Jake, and Brooks during our ride to town, on what would be my first real date. I was going to tell Jake how perfectly naughty he'd been for giving me *The Monk*, which was just *too* racy, and then I'd lean in to whisper in his ear that I couldn't put it down. Bertie would probably beg me to do my imitation of Miss Hartley for the boys (it had made her cry with laughter when I'd done it for her the previous weekend). I'd crack wise about the silliness of some of the local girls who worked at the Village, and say things like, *You said it, mister!* or *And how!* when others made a point. But once I actually found myself in the middle of the scene I'd so carefully scripted, I forgot all my lines and sat, lips pursed and ramrod straight, next to Jake. He, on the other hand, seemed perfectly at ease.

"Cigarette?" he said, once he'd settled in beside me.

"Why, yes, thank you, Jake," I said, taking one from the packet he offered. He lit mine, then his own, and immediately started teasing Bertie about the headscarf she was wearing. It was a wide white silk band that gathered above her forehead like a turban and was adorned, in front, with a dazzling rhinestone-studded pin. I thought it quite splendid—it was very much in vogue—but Jake laughed at it the moment she sat down and asked her what had happened to her "nut."

"I beg your pardon!" Bertie said in a mock-scolding tone.

Jake leaned forward and plucked at the back of the scarf. "What's with the bandage here? Caught a stray bullet? Kicked by a horse?"

Bertie turned around and swatted at him, laughing in spite of herself. "It's not a bandage, and you know it."

Jake turned to me and said solemnly, "Do they expect her brain to return to normal? I'm no doctor, but it's clearly hopeless. . . ."

Bertie slapped his knee. "You've no sense of style, Jake Enright. Brooks, how do you like my headscarf?"

"Very chic, darling," Brooks said, without glancing at it.

"See?" Bertie said, smiling and batting her eyelashes at Jake. She turned back around to face the front and snuggled closer to Brooks. Jake elbowed me gently, and when I looked at him, he frowned at Bertie's headscarf and gave me a look that said, "Don't you agree?"

And instantly, I realized that the scarf was the stupidest thing I'd ever seen. It did look like a bandage, especially from the back, where we were seated. It looked just like the head bandages on pictures of men returning from war—how had I thought it stylish for even a minute?

When Brooks parked at the inn, I reached for the door handle, but

Jake placed his hand gently on my wrist. He jogged around the back so that he could open my door. Then he offered his hand. As I took it, I felt the confidence of his grip and realized he'd helped countless girls step out of cars like this.

Now I welcomed the newfound ease the gin fizz afforded me in conversing with Jake and the others. But when I noticed I was drinking my second cocktail faster than the others, I set my glass down. I knew what happened when people overdid it. I finished the delicious roast chicken and laughed at the funny story Brooks was telling about a prank he and some classmates had pulled during his college days. It was a very funny story; Brooks wasn't so bad after all.

"Oh, Mary, I can't believe I haven't asked you yet," said Bertie. "Is it true you're working for old Vogel now?"

"Yes," I said. "When did you hear?"

"Just yesterday," Bertie said. "That's great news for you, kid. I hope you got a nice pay raise too. Sorry, boys, we'll stop talking shop now."

A raise. I hadn't received a raise, in fact, the thought hadn't occurred to me until now.

"No, not at all, what's all this about?" Jake asked.

"I received a sort of a promotion," I said.

Why hadn't I asked about a raise?

"*Sort of* a promotion." Bertie laughed. "She's the secretary to the superintendent of our institution. Really, she's going to be running the whole place now, seeing as how Dr. Vogel is away on speaking tours much of the year."

"Well, that's wonderful news, congratulations, Mary," said Brooks.

"Yes," Jake said. "Well done!"

"Why, thank you!" I said, sipping my drink again.

"I want to hear more about your institution," Jake said. "It's for women who are insane?"

"Yes—rather, no," I said. "The inmates are women, but they're not really insane. Of course, they're not really normal either. They're— well, Bertie, you're the nurse, you explain."

"Not much to explain, really," Bertie said. "The place is exactly what it calls itself. It's for feebleminded women of childbearing age— young adult women who have mental defects."

"But doesn't that mean they're insane?" Brooks asked.

"No, not the same thing at all. Our residents have low intelligence," said Bertie. "People who are insane have a brain illness. They probably had normal intelligence at one time but now their brain is afflicted—rather like yours, dear."

For, now, Brooks was making a face mimicking an imbecile and pretending to eat his napkin.

Bertie said, "Anyway, Jake, the feebleminded don't have a brain illness, they have brain . . . lack. Usually they inherited their defects from parents."

"Brain illness. Brain lack. They're idiots," Brooks said. Now he was holding his glass under the table and was carelessly pouring the gin into it straight from the flask. "Why don't we just call a spade a spade, right, Mary?"

He brought the glass from beneath the table and, after an exaggerated nod at a matronly woman who was walking past the table and glaring at him, he drank its contents in one quick gulp.

"I wonder if Jake and I would be accepted at your village," Brooks slurred. "We're quite stupid."

I adopted a snooty affect and said, "No, my good man, I'm afraid you're not quite up to our standards at Nettleton Village. We're very exclusive, aren't we Bertie? Only the profoundly stupid are allowed in."

"Quite so," Bertie said. "Might I recommend the Mifflinburg Village for Slightly Dim-Witted Professors? I hear it's lovely this time of year."

Brooks leaned over to nuzzle Bertie's throat.

"But, what's this *childbearing* business?" Jake asked.

"Oh, well, it's quite simple really. You see . . ." I paused to take another sip of my drink and started giggling at my own joke before I'd finished saying it. "When a man and a woman truly love each other, they will often choose to marry. Then, within a year or two . . ."

"Look who's come out of her shell." Bertie laughed.

Jake was grinning, but he persisted. "Seriously, though, are there no older feebleminded women? No feebleminded children who receive treatment there?"

Bertie said, "It's not really a place one goes for treatment. It's just a place to confine these girls so they can't have children. They're from poor homes, mostly, Jake. They can barely take care of themselves, let alone any children they might have."

"It's one of those eugenic-cist places, Jake-o," Brooks interjected. "It's just like Bryn Mawr, but for the Juke and Kallikak set. Now who's ready for another drink?"

"No, Brooks," Bertie said. "Let's wait. We've still got the drive to Seedy's; let's not get lit."

"Waiter! Waiter! CHECK PLEASE!" Brooks roared, making Bertie wince and then frown and shake her head in exasperation at Jake and me. I had a long drink of water. No more alcohol.

Jake said, "I've read about these places. I was surprised when I learned there was one in this area."

"I know, who would think it—such a modern institution in a backwater place like this," I said. "My boss, Dr. Vogel, is actually quite a fascinating person."

"What kind of medicine does he practice, this *Dr. Vogel*?" Brooks said, slurring. "Imagine that cozy arrangement, huh, Jake? A doctor in charge of all those dumb Doras. Some spiffy setup if you ask me. Where the hell's that waiter?"

I said, smiling at Bertie, "Oh, I don't really think Dr. Vogel views the residents in the way you're suggesting."

"Like hell he doesn't! You should see what old Dr. Handsy is up to when the office door is closed," Brooks said. "I'd put money on his being a full-blown pervert."

"Oh yeah?" Bertie said, with delight.

"How much?" I said.

We'd said these responses too gleefully, and now Brooks knew we had something on him.

"Okay, what gives?" Brooks asked. Then he lowered his voice and leaned in toward us. "You mean . . . he's a pansy?"

"His name is Agnes, dopey!" Bertie said. "The superintendent is Dr. Agnes Vogel. She's a woman. Went to medical school and all that. Let's get out of here—I'm sick of talking about work. Let's go freshen up, Mary."

In the powder room, as we touched up our makeup, Bertie said, "You're a riot, Mary. I can tell Jake's really taken with you."

"Really? You think so," I said. "I'm afraid he thinks I'm sort of . . . I don't know. He's so interesting. I think I must bore him."

"No. He's charmed! I can tell. He's very choosy about girls, from what I know about him. I guess with those dimples he can afford to be. If he were closer to my age, I'd have already . . ." Bertie paused and glanced at me in the mirror. "Well, kid, just keep your wits about you. He's young, but he's seen a bit more of the world than you have."

"I will. I'm feeling a little dizzy from the drinks," I admitted.

"Oh, do be careful—who knows where Brooks gets his bathtub gin. Don't have any more. Wait until we get to the dance hall. They have near beer there."

The roadhouse where we went to dance had a sign outside that called it *The Fairlawn Inn*, but everybody called it Seedy's. It was several miles out of town, and the parking lot was almost full when we arrived. It was not a fancy place, but once inside, it was clear that it was popular with the summer students from Berneston University. The girls had slim, stylish dresses, and the boys wore rumpled linen suits like Jake's. There was a band playing modern swing music, and as soon as we entered, Brooks dragged Bertie off into the crowd on the dance floor.

Jake seemed to know quite a few people, and he introduced me to a small crowd that immediately surrounded us as we entered. "Hello, Iris, Gene! Allow me to introduce Mary Engle," he said.

I began stammering my greetings, but he put his arm around me and swept me onto the dance floor, saying, "Shall we?"

"Okay," I said, having no choice but to follow his lead. "I'm sorry, but I'm terrible at the new dances; I can't do them at all, I'm afraid." Jake laughed and said that he was a terrible dancer too, but the dance floor was so crowded, nobody could move anyway. After struggling through a few numbers, we joined Bertie and Brooks at a table.

"I want to learn the black bottom," Bertie announced. "Look at that pretty girl doing the shimmy there. Jake? Do you know her? She keeps looking at you."

"She's not looking at me," Jake said, without even glancing at the girl.

"Why don't you ever go to the dining hall on Wednesday nights, Mary?" Bertie said. "The girls have dancing that night, and a few are real pros at all the new steps."

"The attendants can dance?" I said, trying to imagine Gladys or any of the other attendants doing anything other than clog dancing to country reels.

"No. The inmates. Lots of them worked in clubs before coming to us. A girl taught my roommate and me how to one-step last week."

"The *inmates*?" Jake said. "Do you mean to say that the—what did you call them—not brain-damaged, but brain-*lacking* inmates are serving as dance teachers?" He wasn't even trying to hide the sarcasm in his tone. "They sound very coordinated for imbeciles."

"Some of the girls are quite physically healthy and athletic, as a matter of fact," Bertie said. Jake looked like he was about to ask Bertie something else, but Brooks dragged her back out onto the dance floor.

We sat, quietly, for a few moments, watching them. Then, Jake said, "I'd sure like to see you again, Mary. How about it?"

Still feeling the effect of the gin, I surprised myself by saying, "I'd like that too."

"Next weekend, then? Maybe lunch on Sunday?"

"Sure. Will you be with Brooks? We'll all meet after church again?"

"Sure, what time is church over?" Jake asked.

"Ours ends at eleven o'clock. What about yours?" I asked.

"My what?"

"Your church, what time is your service over?"

Jake wasn't drunk, but he wasn't sober either. He and Brooks had passed their flask back and forth on the ride to Seedy's. Now he gave me an amused half smile and said, "I don't go to church."

"I see. I suppose you're an atheist, then?" I said, regretting the words before they were even out of my mouth. Oh, that roguish smile of his— I hadn't fully appreciated how handsome he really was until now. Why did I have to sound like such a puritan? It made perfect sense that he'd be an atheist. He was spending the summer helping a professor write about a strike at a local mill. He was probably a communist too. The idea thrilled me. Imagine what Aunt Kate would think.

"I don't know if I'm an atheist, I just wasn't raised in a religious family," Jake said. "But even if I were, I wouldn't be going to church on Sunday. I'd be going to a synagogue tomorrow."

"A synagogue?"

"The closest temple is in Harrisburg, my grandmother was careful to research this for me."

"So, do you mean . . . you're a . . ."

"Jew. Yup," Jake said, grinning broadly.

We'd been leaning across the table to talk over the loud music, but now I drew back a little so that I could look at him anew. "I would never have known. I mean, you don't really look like a Jew, do you?"

I saw a change in Jake's expression. It was very subtle, but I saw it. His grin faded a little, and he narrowed his eyes for a second and looked into mine with a more studious regard. I let out a little scoffing laugh and averted my gaze. He had misunderstood me. I certainly had nothing against Jews. I was surprised, that was all. I was about to tell him that, but he wasn't looking at me anymore. He was watching the girl who'd been shimmying so provocatively. When the band started a new song, Jake jumped up, cut in, and danced off with the girl.

How rude! He hadn't even asked me to excuse him—he'd just left me there, all alone. Clearly, he'd taken offense at my remark. But what had I said? I hadn't said anything insulting. I certainly wasn't prejudiced like my aunt or some of the sisters at St. Cat's, who said very unkind things about Jews. As a matter of fact, I couldn't wait to inform Jake that I'd read many books and essays written by Jewish authors whom I admired greatly. I scanned the crowded dance floor for any sign of Bertie and Brooks, but they were nowhere to be seen. This was a disaster. I wished I'd never come. And Jake had lied. He was a great dancer, now that he was with a partner who knew what she was doing.

After the song ended, Jake plopped himself back down in the chair next to me. He offered me a cigarette, but I declined, frostily. I mean, who did he think he was, leaving me stranded like that? As he lit his own cigarette, I turned to ask him that very question, but he offered me an apologetic and irresistibly charming smile. My anger evaporated instantly. Those dimples! I did feel I needed to explain, so I said, "I hope you understand—well, I didn't mean any offense, Jake. The thing is, we haven't many Jews in Scranton."

"Oh? My uncle and aunt live there with my four cousins. So that makes, at least . . ." He pretended to be counting on his fingers, "I think—six!"

"But I mean, the Jewish people I've known, except for Mr. Oppenheimer who owns the dry goods store—most of the other Jews in Scranton are from places like Russia, I think. They have the strange accents and wear—you know—the foreign costumes that the Jewish people wear, all in black. And some of the men have the long beards and don't speak English. So, that's what I meant when I said you don't look like one. I mean—it's rather like Brooks assuming I was going to become a nun, just because I'm Catholic. . . ."

Instead of allowing me to flounder on, making things worse, Jake said, "My dear Mary, it's fine. If I had a penny for every time somebody made a remark like that, I'd be rich. Don't think about it anymore." More than happy to change the subject, I asked if he planned to write more stories like the one he was researching that summer about the labor dispute at the mill. I needed to lean in close again; the music was so loud.

"Yes, I'm interested in labor problems. Any social issues, really. I'm now quite curious about your work," he said, also leaning in.

"Oh yeah?" I said. It was nice of him to feign interest in my boring occupation as a stenographer.

"Sure. I've heard of your boss. Dr. Vogel. That's a big name in Clayburg. A friend pointed her out to me once in town—she's quite attractive. I'm sure Brooks has seen her, he just can't wrap his mind around the idea that such a beautiful lady might also be highly educated as well. I loved the way you and Bertie teased him about her at dinner."

I laughed. Poor sodden Brooks.

"What's she like?" Jake asked. "Tell me about her."

"I don't know that I should talk about her, really. She's my employer. I do have great admiration for her."

"Yeah? Whatta ya admire most?"

"Oh, I don't know. I suppose her intelligence and her accomplishments. She was the only female in her class at medical school. She's close to many powerful political people in this state and elsewhere. She worked hard to get us women the vote, and now she works tirelessly to help so many girls.

"Poor girls, right?"

"Yes, precisely."

"But she's paid an awful lot for her work, right? I heard she lives in a house as big as the governor's mansion."

"Of course she's paid well. She's a doctor, running a large institution, one of the only in the state that actually makes a profit some years. Why shouldn't she be compensated for her work like any other doctor?"

"Who's saying she shouldn't? But does she help rich girls and women who are feebleminded as well?"

"I'm sure rich feebleminded women have family who can take care of them."

"And are they allowed to marry and have children?"

"Who?"

"The rich morons!" Jake laughed.

I laughed at this too. "How am I supposed to know, Jake? I don't know anything about rich people and their problems."

"And who sends the girls there? A doctor? A judge?"

"Some are sent from jails after they fail some intelligence test, but others are sent by their families—very often, sadly, their own husbands send them. It's a terrible burden to care for the feebleminded, there's a long waiting list."

"Their husbands, huh?" Jake was watching me rather intensely again, the way he had earlier. He was studying me. It was almost as if he was trying to figure out if I was *on the level,* as Uncle Teddy used to say. Finally, he said, "It reminds me of that nursery rhyme. You know— Peter, Peter, pumpkin eater?"

I just shrugged, trying to think of something clever—something an experienced dater like Bertie might say in response. I was fidgeting with a matchbook pretending I was reading an ad on it, but Jake gently took it from me. He held both my hands in his and leaned in so close that his lips were almost touching the side of my face and I felt his warm breath tickling my ear. Then he whispered, in a low singsong voice, " 'Peter, Peter, pumpkin eater . . . He had a wife and he couldn't keep her. . . .' "

His lips grazed my cheek. I thought I'd faint, my heart pounded so.

" 'He puts her in a pumpkin shell . . .' " Now Jake turned slightly and pressed his lips to mine—it was a real kiss, my first romantic kiss, ever. I wanted to kiss him a little more, a little longer, maybe. I also thought that I should resist, but before I could weigh these options, he moved his lips back to my ear and whispered, " 'and there . . . he kept her . . . very well.' "

His cheek stayed pressed to mine. His breath filled my ear with warm little puffs of air, and I bit my lip to keep from giggling; it tickled so wonderfully.

"WE LEAVE YOU KIDS FOR FIVE MINUTES!" Brooks roared as he and Bertie took their chairs again.

Jake led me back onto the dance floor. Now the band was playing a slow, bluesy number, and Jake held me so close that it was easy to move with him, and I felt his cheek against mine again. It had to be the liquor that made me so light-headed and relaxed that I was able to sway so easily, my body pressed to his. He had a young man's body—lean and muscular, not fat and gelatinous like foul old Uncle Teddy. And Jake smelled nothing like what I had come to think of as man smells, though he was perspiring like me and everybody else in the club. This time, when he pressed his lips to mine, I kissed him back, and we seemed to float through the air, the two of us, just like the song. It felt as if we weren't on a crowded dance floor—it felt like we were the only ones there.

Brooks was so drunk by the time we left Seedy's that he could barely walk to the car. After a short tussle about who should drive, Jake bundled him into the back seat, where he fell asleep before we'd even finished situating ourselves in the front. Jake drove, I sat in the middle, and Bertie sat next to me.

"That's it," Bertie said to Jake. "Tell Brooks to lose my number."

Jake laughed, "Oh, come on, Bert. Don't be mean."

"I'm serious. Why didn't your friend George ever call me after that time we all had supper?"

"He thought you were hot on Brooks," Jake said.

"Well, now I'm cool on Brooks."

From the back came a loud stuttering snore followed by an incoherent muttering.

"Frigid, actually," Bertie said. "Tell George to give me a call sometime, will you, Jake?"

I moved my hand onto the seat beside me and Jake covered it with his. I gazed ahead at the road and smiled.

Part Two

Nine

July 7, 1927

My dear Mary,

I've addressed this to the specified locale rather than the main headquarters, as you so carefully instructed. I hope this dispatch won't be intercepted by enemy forces. How wonderfully treacherous your mailroom sounds with all the spying, letter reading, and whatnot. Shall we devise a code, just in case your "friendly lodgers" are turncoats?

But, in all seriousness, I want to thank you for making my past two weekends so merry, sweet Mary, and now I beg you to come to town for a movie and supper this Saturday. Just you and me? Please say yes. I'll pick you up at the same gate? Around six?

Now, Agent Engle, a coded message—one can never be too cautious.

TIF XBMLT JO CFBVUZ, MJLF UIF OJHIU . . .

J BN ZPVST,
Jake (Kblf)

July 9, 1927

Dear Jake,

A movie and supper sound wonderful, I look forward to it.

And thank you for using such simple cryptography. The key you *provided next to your name was kind but unnecessary. I too learned to write scout's code as a small child, by substituting each letter with the one that follows and was delighted to find Lord Byron's words: "She walks in beauty, like the night."*

Until Saturday, then.
J BN,
Mary

July 18, 1927

Dearest Mary,

I'm sorry I haven't been able to write sooner. I'm busy helping the Van Dykes pack up for their summer home.

Your fellow Jake sounds wonderful. Peter and I are still going steady, though, as I said, I've been busy lately and haven't been able to see him as much as I'd like.

Will write again later this week, once the Van Dykes leave. They're going to Lake George and leaving me here to close up the house. Which means a holiday here for me, until I join them at the end of the month.

Your loving friend, Dory

July 20, 1927

Dear Mary,

God bless you for remembering me in your prayers and for being so faithful with your letter writing. Not many of my girls write as often as you. A few can't be bothered to write a single word. Imagine, not even a card at Christmas to an old invalid Sister who devoted her life to their care.

Yes, Dorchester is quite close to our convent here in South Boston. I visit my nephew Bobby and his family every Sunday. The smaller children—the girls—are lovely. The eldest two, the lads, I'm afraid, are hell-bent, both. They curse on the streets with their friends, I've heard them. Curse and drink, the both of them, and so young.

I'm pleased that you've been able to go to Mass on Sundays, Mary. What about the inmates? Does your Father Doheny come to the asylum to offer Holy Communion to the Catholic unfortunates there? I know the inmates are dull-witted and can't know enough to pray or go to Mass, but God still wants to share His love and offer absolution to them. You said that they attend a chapel service at the asylum on Sundays. I shouldn't be surprised if your boss lady there, the Protestant lady "doctor" doesn't try to convert the girls. I've seen Protestants at that game before. Didn't they offer soup in the famine? My grandfather and many of the good people in Cork would sooner starve in this world knowing they'll find themselves seated next to our Lord for eternity. We'll not find any soupers in heaven when it's our time, Mary Engle. But your idiots can't know what your "doctor" is on about, can they? I'll pray for them, all the poor girls at your asylum there. And I'll pray for you too, of course, Mary.

Yes, I did get a note from Lillian Faust, but it was almost two years ago now. It was a lovely letter, I knew her handwriting at once; she always had a fine fist, my Lillian. She had grand news. She was married and expecting a child, when she wrote. Her husband is a Mr. Henning. Tom Henning, I think it is. It's no wonder that she hasn't had time to write. I'm sure she's quite busy with her young family.

May the Lord bless you, Mary Engle, and keep you always close. I look forward to your next letter.

> Yours in loving fellowship,
> Sister Rosemary

July 29, 1927

Dearest Dory,

Sister Rosemary wrote and told me that Lillian Faust is married to Tom Henning and has a child! Could she possibly mean that vulgar Tom who turned his father's blacksmith shop into that speakeasy? Did you ever hear anything about this? I ask because there's an inmate here who slightly resembles her. Isn't that funny? I only saw her once, weeks ago. It made me wonder what happened to Lillian. I know you and Margie never liked her—she could be so mean at times. I never heard anything about her getting married, did you?

Anyway, I think Sister Rosemary is mistaken about Lillian being married to him, I believe she's becoming even more addled with age. I remember you told me that Sister began confusing the girls with one another after I left.

I've been spending my weekends with Jake. I'll tell you more when I see you, dear Dory, but I'm—well, I quite like him. Will write more when I have time.

Love, Mary

August 2, 1927

Dearest Mary,

I am engaged! Peter has asked me to marry him. I haven't been able to tell anybody here in Scranton—you're the only person who knows— I haven't even told Margie. I don't want my family to find out, as they'll replace me immediately when they hear. We won't be able to afford the wedding until next spring. I do hope you'll be able to come home to Scranton for the wedding!

I did hear a rumor that Lillian worked at Henning's speak, Mary. But not that they were married. I often run into girls from the home, but I can't remember the last time I saw Lillian. I'm not surprised she ended up with a bad character like that. I hate to speak ill of her, I know you got along okay with her, Mary, but she could be so cruel to the rest of us. Lillian never had her head on straight—no good was ever going to come to her. Mother Bea said that all the time.

But just think—Margie and I engaged! Lillian Faust is married and has a child. You're next, Mary, with your new fella!

Much love, Dorothy

Ten

ONE morning, Betty asked if I wouldn't mind stopping at the poultry for some eggs on my way home from work. Hal was going to be haying the fields and wouldn't have time. I enjoyed walking to the poultry or the dining hall for provisions after sitting at my desk all day. Jake and I had been corresponding almost daily, and I used these walks to think of clever things to write to him. I told Betty that I was more than happy to go. But it started drizzling around noon, and by the time I left the office, the air was thick and humid, and I heard the distant rumbling of thunder. In the ten-minute walk from the office to the farm buildings, the rumbling turned into sharp claps of thunder, the sky became slate gray, and lightning lit up the fields.

Every girl on our ward at St. Cat's was terrified of lightning. At the first hint of a storm we'd scurry under our cots, hysterically laughing and crying in turns. Sister Rosemary sought refuge under a table, and from there she comforted us with tales about a cousin back home who was chased across a field and into a church by a bolt of lightning and another whose arm was melted by it when he foolishly stuck his hand out of a window to see if it was raining. So, when the storm broke out in full force that afternoon, I ran blindly through the rain, prayers tumbling from my lips. I ducked into the nearest structure, which was a long, low shed, crossed myself, and closed my eyes.

Hail Mary, full of grace, the Lord is with you. Blessed art thou amongst women . . .

I opened my eyes at *amen* and saw that I was in one of the dairy barns. It was the milking hour. The place was filled with cows and girls and the air was steamy with the heavy aromas of manure, hay, and sweat. The animals stood in a row, facing the center aisle of the long barn, and they stupidly munched their hay, unaware of the danger posed by the storm. Each cow was flanked by a girl who sat on a stool. The girls were as senseless as the cows to the perilous weather outside, and they talked quietly to one another as they milked. A fresh round of thunder shook the barn, and I closed my eyes again.

Our Father, who art in heaven . . .

I crossed myself at the end of this prayer and opened my eyes again, only to notice that one of the girls wasn't milking. She'd rested her cheek against her cow's tan belly, eyes shut, lips moving very slightly. Then, crossing herself, she opened her eyes and looked at me.

It was Lillian Faust. I hadn't seen her since the day, many weeks prior, in the dining hall. This time, I felt giddy with relief when I saw her. She felt it too; I could see that. We knew we were foolish to be saying our dying prayers in a little thunderstorm—but we had to. I was about to step closer to have a word with her when there was another sharp crack of thunder. Lillian cried out, and her frightened cow kicked the milk bucket between her boots. She caught it just before it spilled, but Cloris, who was strolling up and down the barn aisle, saw what happened and shouted, "LILLIAN, for the love of God, ya damn moron, mind what yer doing!"

"Yes, ma'am," Lillian said, stroking the cow and straightening out the bucket. She pressed her cheek back against the animal's side, and after Cloris moved on, she gave me a little wink and a smile. I was quite overwhelmed. I didn't care if there was a rule against knowing inmates; I had to speak to Lillian. I had to know why she was there. I started toward her, but immediately Cloris was in front of me, blocking my path.

"Something you want, miss?"

Lillian had turned her head away. Her furtiveness made me cautious.

"No, thank you. I just came inside to get out of the storm," I said.

Cloris grinned and gave me a slightly rough clap on the shoulder. "Afraid of thunderstorms, huh? You're safe enough in here. It'll pass over in a few minutes."

"Yes, I know," I said. "I just ducked inside on my way to get eggs."

"You're Mary, aren't you? You're living up at Betty and Hal's? I'll give you some cream to take with you. Stop on your way back from the chicken house and I'll have it ready. It'll save Betty the trip in the morning. When's the baby expected anyways?"

"I think in another month or two," I said. I wished Cloris would go away so I could speak to Lillian. But Cloris was pleased to find another employee to chat with. She asked me where I was from, how I liked Nettleton, why I hadn't stopped in at the dairy before. I answered in monosyllables, my mind racing.

"Well, it looks like the rain is over," Cloris said finally, stepping outside.

I followed her to the barn door. Sure enough, there were just some light raindrops falling now. The sky was brighter and there was only the dull, distant murmur of thunder.

"Thank you, Cloris," I said, with a quick glance back inside. Lillian was still looking away.

I hurried to the henhouse and retrieved the eggs. When I returned to the dairy barn, the cows were wandering back out to the fields and the girls were shoveling manure from the stanchions where they had stood. They all wore the matching gray coveralls, but Lillian had worn a dark green cap, and now I couldn't see it.

Cloris brought me the pail filled with cream. It was covered with a square of cheesecloth.

"Stop by, visit anytime you like, Mary," Cloris said. "And do let me know when Mrs. Goodwin has her baby."

"I shall!" I said.

The next day, I told Betty that I noticed we were low on butter. I offered to pick some up on the way home.

"Just you wait right there. I'll see what we have in the cold room," Cloris said, that afternoon. As she marched away, barking orders at the girls, I wandered down the aisle. The late-afternoon sun had been so bright, it was hard to see in the long, dark building, but I moved from one cow to the next, searching the face of each girl.

"Here you are," Cloris said cheerfully. "I've put some cheese in there as well." She'd placed the items in a small wooden crate that she thrust at me.

"Oh, thank you, Cloris," I said. I took another step down the aisle, but Cloris grabbed my arm.

"I wouldn't go in any farther, Mary, you'll spoil your shoes in all the muck."

"Oh, I see," I said, looking down. "I've never been in a dairy barn. I grew up in a town. It's . . . fascinating to me, the way it all works."

"Fascinating?" Cloris laughed. "What's so fascinating about a bunch of cows?"

"Well, the way they all stand there so patiently," I said, continuing with my lie. I couldn't have been less interested in the cows; I was trying to find Lillian. "Do you not have to tether them?"

"Nah, their tits hurt like hell when they're all full up." Cloris said.

"Is that so?" I said. I was squinting down the long aisle, so it took a moment for her words to sink in and in my flush of embarrassment, I stupidly repeated myself, "Is that a fact?"

"Sure, they're happy to eat their hay and get their bags emptied." Cloris turned away and spat something onto the ground. Then she just stood next to me, her hands on her hips, proudly surveying the cows and the girls. There was something soothing about the sound of milk spraying against the tin pails and the gentle munching of the cows. One of the girls at the far end of the building was humming a tune and then a few began singing along with her. I craned my neck to see who was singing.

"Well, give my best to the Goodwins," Cloris said.

The next time I offered to get eggs, I just glanced into the barn as I passed on my way to the henhouse. Cloris had seemed suspicious; I decided it was best to just stroll past. At the poultry shed, I handed the basket to one of the girls. It was always the same pretty, slow-moving girl named Inga who took my basket and went inside to fill it. Usually Inga covered the eggs with the checked cloth that Betty sent along in the basket. This time, there was a white cloth on top, instead of the checked one.

"Where's Mrs. Goodwin's napkin?" I said to Inga. Inga just blinked at me stupidly.

"The cloth. The cloth. It was in the basket? Where—is—it?" I spoke slowly so Inga, clearly an imbecile, might better comprehend me.

"It's there, inside," Inga said quietly. She had a thick foreign accent, but her English was very good. "It's underneath. I put a clean napkin on top for you." Inga looked over her shoulder and then whispered, "It's from Lillian, the cloth on top." Then she hurried back inside.

I waited until I was away from the barns and back on the wooded road before I dared lift the white cloth. I recognized it—it was one of the stiff, starched napkins from the dining hall. On the underside was Lillian's handwriting. She appeared to have used a bit of charcoal to write.

Dearest Mary,

I pray that you are still my friend and that you won't betray me. Please meet me tomorrow night at 11? There should be a moon, I can sneak away. I'll wait at the entrance to the wood road, just behind a stonewall there. Please meet me.

L

Eleven

I SPENT that day and the next, fretting. It was risky and violated all rules, meeting an inmate in the middle of the night when she was supposed to be locked in the dormitory. But I had to meet Lillian. It wasn't just curiosity or nostalgia that motivated me. The truth was, I was still a little afraid of her. She was one of the meanest of the ward bullies, when we were little. I worried she might retaliate if I left her waiting for me in the woods. She might tell an attendant or even Miss Hartley that we'd been wardmates at St. Cat's. And then, who knew what lies she might start spreading? I didn't know who this adult Lillian was, but things had clearly not gone well for her after St. Catherine's. Perhaps she was happy here and just wanted to talk about old times. For all I knew, she found life working on the farm as restorative and healthy as some of the other inmates.

Friday afternoon, I finished my typing early as usual. I hoped Dr. Vogel would ask me to do some filing for her. She kept all the inmates' records in a long row of filing cabinets in her office. I thought I might be able to have a quick glance at Lillian's file, but she had me running errands—delivering the week's checks to the payroll office, collecting purchase orders from the kitchen for next week's supplies. By the time I returned to my desk, it was five and Dr. Vogel's office was locked.

Sneaking out of the Goodwins' house later that night was easy enough. Gladys's brother arrived just after supper to bring her home for the weekend. I went up to my room after helping Betty with the dishes but remained dressed. I sat on my bed, trying to read one of Gladys's silly romance magazines. My mind raced, and I found myself reading the same page over and over again. Finally, the Goodwins turned off their radio, and I heard them climbing the stairs to their room. At ten thirty, I put on a sweater and tiptoed down the hall, carrying my rain boots in my hand. I paused outside the Goodwins' bedroom door. I thought I heard somebody talking, but then realized it was just Hal's loud snoring.

Lillian had been right: there was a full moon. Normally, I couldn't see the clothesline that hung from the house to the tree because it was so dark out there at night. Now I could see all the trees, I could even see the shadows of the trees as I made my way along the quiet road. I passed the Aldwyns' house, where Sophie lived. All the lights were off. Soon I passed the lawn in front of the massive administration building, then the rows of brick dormitories. Lights were out for the residents, and the dorms were silent.

I turned off the main drive and onto the farm road. The unfinished road was deep with mud that sucked at my boots and made me stumble. I moved to the side of the road and stepped quickly along the spongy ground there. I was worried about wolves and bears, worried about gangs of loose violent inmates, worried about Dr. Vogel's dogs, worried that if I arrived after eleven, Lillian would lose her nerve and go back to the dormitory. I ran breathlessly along this stretch, slowing to a walk only when open fields replaced the roadside trees.

There was the enormous moon, hovering over a distant hill, so luminous that I thought I should feel its warm rays on my face. The night sky was all around me again. I saw the silhouettes and then the white faces of cows grazing just a few feet away. They lifted their heads and gazed at me, munching thoughtfully as I passed. A few cows wore bells on neck collars, and the tinkling music they made, the gentle chiming, felt like kind greetings. If the cows were so calm, there couldn't be any predators near. My pulse quickened again when I turned onto the wood road. Wasn't this where Lillian had told me to meet her? She had mentioned a stone wall, but I saw only trees. How I hated those woods! I kept walking until I was at the intersection of the old wood road and the main road. It was such a chilly night. I heard the yip, yip, yipping of something. A fox? A wolf? I thought I heard a rustling in the dead leaves on the roadside.

"Mary," said a hushed voice from the woods behind me.

I spun around and watched Lillian step out from behind a tree a few feet away.

"Quick, let's move back," Lillian said, reaching for my hand. "Vogel goes out on Friday nights, and we need to be off the road if she returns early."

I followed her into the woods. There was no moonlight, only blackness all around. When I hesitated, Lillian gently squeezed my hand, guiding me along.

"Wait, Lillian, be careful, I can't see anything," I said.

Lillian said, "Here, there's a dead tree here. We can sit on it." She sat down, and after I felt around for any snakes or large insects, I sat next to her.

"I don't suppose you have any smokes," Lillian said after a moment of awkward silence.

"Of course I do," I said. I'd brought an extra packet of cigarettes just for her and some chocolate bars. When I handed them to her, I gave her a smile. My eyes were adjusting to the darkness, and I saw that she gave me a little smile in return. She took the cigarettes and the chocolate. She held them in front of her. She just looked at them, her hands trembling, her shoulders shaking, and I realized she was weeping.

"Oh, Lillian," I said, putting my arm around her and squeezing her gently.

Lillian gave me another quick smile. She stuck one of the cigarettes between her lips. I had matches, but I was so nervous that my hands shook as I tried to strike them. Two matches blew out before they reached Lillian's cigarette.

When I lit the next match, Lillian covered my hand with her own and steadied it, until both of our cigarettes were lit. We sat silently, smoking. Lillian was shivering. She wore a thin, short-sleeved resident's uniform—the khaki work dress, and she was barefoot. It had been warm that day, but the night air was cool and damp. Nevertheless, Lillian had wandered into the woods barefoot. The possibility of her having had some kind of head injury rose again in my mind.

"Did you forget your shoes, Lil?" I asked gently.

"Forget? On a night like this? Don't be absurd. They lock them away at night. We can't run away without shoes."

"I see. Well, do you want to wear my sweater?"

"No. I'll just be colder when I take it off. I'll just snuggle in closer to you like we girls used to do when the dorm was so cold at night."

Lillian inched over and pressed against me. I unbuttoned my sweater and draped it across my own shoulders and hers.

"I've been wondering what happened to you, Lil. I mean, since you left St. Cat's. I got a letter from Sister Rosemary—she actually thought you were married and expecting a child. Good old Sister Rosemary, always having her stories confused. I wonder what made her think that?"

"I told her," Lillian whispered. "In a letter."

"Why?"

"Because I *was* married. I *was* expecting a child."

I couldn't help glancing at her hand to see if she was wearing a wedding ring, but she wasn't.

Lillian said, with a soft laugh, "Well, to be honest, I'm not sure I was married yet, but I was certainly expecting when I wrote her, so I think I told her I was."

"Oh," I said. "Did you ever marry?"

"Yes. I married," Lillian said glumly. She frowned at the glowing end of her cigarette before taking another drag.

"And the baby? Is the baby with your husband now?"

"No!" Lillian said, and then she started crying. "I lost her, Mary. I lost my sweet baby girl."

"Oh no, Lillian," I said. "Oh, how sad."

"She was beautiful, Mary, she looked just like her father, Graham."

"Graham?"

"Yes, Graham Carr! He's a musician, he's becoming well-known. Have you heard of him? Graham Carr? The jazz player? He's Rosemary's father."

"No, I don't believe I've heard of him. But Sister thought you'd married Tom Henning."

"I did."

Lillian wasn't making sense. I was at a loss, but she continued. "Mary—we haven't much time; it's very involved, but Graham was in

Europe when I found out I was expecting his child. I couldn't get word to him, he was touring, you see."

"Yes, but—what about Tom Henning?"

"I had to marry him, I had no choice," Lillian said. "I wrote to Graham about the baby, I thought he was still in New York, see, so I wrote him there, hoping he'd ask me to marry him. I didn't hear from him, so, after a while, when I was beginning to get a belly, I panicked. I married Henning. I was working for him, and I knew he was sweet on me."

"You're talking about the Tom Henning who owns the speak?" I asked.

"Yes, you know about Henning's?"

"I think I've heard of it."

What else could I say? Everybody knew about Henning's. It was the kind of place Dr. Vogel spoke about in her lectures, where men took advantage of pretty young girls who didn't know better than to work there. How did Lillian Faust end up working in a terrible place like that?

"Didn't the Sisters try to help you find a job when you left the home, Lil?"

"Sure, they found me a place at the textile mill. I stayed there a few months. I worked fifteen hours, some days, for pennies an hour."

"I know they offer opportunities or better pay, though, after a while, a lot of girls from St. Cat's work there, don't they?"

"Yes. And some of us went to Henning's on our nights off," Lillian said. "I sang with the house band a few times, and Tom hired me. Mary, I earned more there in one night than I earned in a month at the mill. The guys in the band taught me how to really sing. We'd spend all night practicing, long after the place closed. Next day, we'd listen to phonographs of all the best jazz musicians, trying to get their sound. Every two weeks there was a different touring band at the National Hotel, downtown, those were the big acts, you know, and sometimes we went there after Henning's closed up. Our boys played with the boys from these groups and learned from them. I'd sing with them too, when they let me."

"You always did have a lovely singing voice, Lil," I said. "Of course, I've only ever heard you sing hymns."

"I met Ethel Waters, at the National one night, Mary!"

"I'm not sure I know who she is."

"She's a famous singer; you've heard her on the radio. Anyway, I met Graham there when his band was playing with ours, after hours. His group was only in Scranton for two weeks. They went on to Philadelphia, Chicago—so many exciting places. We wrote to each other every day, Graham and me. He's fascinating, Mary, he's traveled all over the world. Not just Europe, but the Far East too. They came back to Scranton on their way to New York. They stayed for a week. That's when he and I—well . . ."

"Yes. I see. Yes."

"And Tom Henning and I had already . . . you know."

"Already . . . what?" I said.

Lillian gave a soft chuckle and nudged me with her elbow. "And I'm supposed to be the one who's slow."

"*Oh!* Well, gee, Lil!" I said, and even though I understood now, all too clearly, I asked, "But, how could you have . . . ? I mean . . . with two different fellas? Before you were even married?"

Lillian said, "Don't judge me, Mary. You had family. I had nobody."

"I'm not judging you, Lillian. I want to know what happened, that's all."

"Everybody drank a lot at the club. We all got stinking one night and Tom got carried away after the others left. It was before Graham came back to town. It was just once. Tom knew I couldn't stand him. He took advantage. And forced me. If I hadn't drunk so much, I could have taken care of myself. It was like a bad dream the next day, I couldn't even remember most of it. But, he felt bad about it, I could tell—he knew the others in the band saw my bruises. He gave me twenty dollars the next day. Told me it was a bonus for the extra hours I'd been putting in. When Graham came back, I stayed downtown the whole time he was there. I stayed in his room. I thought I'd leave with him and his band when they went back to New York."

"But why didn't you?"

"Well, it wasn't his band, he was just the trumpet player. They traveled in a bus—they didn't allow girls. He was going to send for me once he was back in New York. I went back to Tom's place. I told him I'd been staying with a girlfriend those nights I was gone. Later, I told him I was expecting his child. Then—we got married. I was going to leave before the baby came."

She couldn't continue; she was crying hard now. I found an old handkerchief wadded up deep in my coat pocket and handed it to her.

"Lil, I'm so sorry," I said. "But maybe the loss of your baby was a mixed blessing." I squeezed her hand gently. "I mean, she's in heaven now, right? And with you not liking your husband and all."

"No, Mary, my daughter didn't die. I had a healthy baby girl almost two years ago now. She's alive."

"What? But you said . . ."

"They took her from me, Mary. She was born a couple of weeks too early. I was planning to leave with my friend Claire; we were going to New York to find Graham, but my daughter was born earlier than we thought. Tom panicked when I was in labor, and he called a doctor. When she was born, they found out she wasn't Tom's baby, so they called the constable." Lillian was sobbing now.

"How awful," I said, stroking her hair. "Please stop crying, Lil."

Poor Lillian. She was always so tough. Even when she was a little girl, she rarely cried. Now I was teary-eyed too. I hated that she'd had so much unhappiness before arriving here.

"Why didn't you just lie about the baby, Lil?" I said, after I'd had a few minutes to think it all through. "Why did you have to tell Tom it wasn't his baby? He deserved to be double-crossed after what he did to you."

"I didn't tell Tom."

"Then, how did he find out?"

"Well, she's, you know—colored," Lillian sniffed.

"What do you mean?" I asked. "Who's colored?"

"My daughter."

I tried to parse what Lillian was saying, and still couldn't fathom what she meant.

"I thought her father was this Graham fellow. The man you'd hoped to marry," I said.

"Her father is Graham. Graham Carr."

"Lillian, Graham is a Negro? Why didn't you say so? How did it happen? Did he force you?"

She gave a bitter laugh. "*Forced!* That's what the doctor asked. That's what Tom asked. No, he didn't *force* me. The only one who ever forced himself on me was my own husband. I loved Graham. I still do." Now she was sobbing.

"Oh, Lillian, oh dear, I'm so sorry."

"The constable came with a woman who worked for some social agency. They tried to get me to tell the name of Rosemary's father—that's what I called my baby, Mary. I only held her for a few minutes, but I gave her a name. Rosemary. After Sister Rosemary."

"You named your baby—with this . . . this *horn player*—after Sister Rosemary?"

"Yes. They said if I admitted that her father raped me, I wouldn't be arrested for fornication and immoral acts—they had a slew of laws I'd broken. They said I'd committed fraud for allowing Tom to think the baby was his. But if I just told them who raped me it, I wouldn't be arrested."

"Did this Graham fellow come and help you then?"

Lillian tossed her cigarette into the dark and shook her head. "How could he? The doctor sent me here the day after Rosemary was born. I never got a trial before any judge for all the laws they said I'd broken. It was the doctor's idea for me to come here right away. Tom was in such a rage—I think the doctor worried he might kill me. The doctor told Tom that I was surely feebleminded to not understand what the baby's father had done to me. What he'd *done* to me. I've never felt so much love in my life as when I was with Graham."

"Oh, Lillian, you were used by that man. Used by him, horribly. You were loyal and never betrayed his name and look where you are now. Would he have done the same for you? I'll say not. And where is he now?"

"New York."

"Yes, drinking and whoring, no doubt."

"Mary, I don't care what you think about me. But you're wrong about Graham. I don't blame you—the nuns taught us to hate and scorn all dark-skinned people."

"LILLIAN! The Sisters didn't teach us to hate anybody."

"Mary. I'm just saying that you've never been allowed to know anybody like Graham and if you did, you wouldn't say such awful things, but anyway, I don't care what you think about Graham."

"But—do you like it here? Do you want to stay here?"

"Are you out of your damned mind?" Lillian said, almost shouting now.

I told her to hush, but she was quite hysterical. "I've been a prisoner here for two years, Mary, you should see the place we sleep. No hot water, freezing cold in winter, stifling hot in the summer. I'm forced to work here in this stinking, filthy hell until I'm an old lady, how could you even think for a minute I want to stay here?"

"Shhh, Lil, I'm trying to help. I meant to say that I think you might be able to leave here, if that's what you want. If you just give Graham's name to the authorities in Scranton. Say he took advantage of you. You were only, what, sixteen?"

"Seventeen. An adult, by law. Do you know what would happen to Graham if he were accused of raping a white woman?"

"I suppose he'd be sent to a work farm. He'd be no worse off than you are now."

"He'd be lynched, Mary. It happened to that colored man two years ago right outside Scranton. And if they didn't kill him outside, they'd get him once he was sent to prison. Being here is awful. But it's nothing compared to what would happen to a colored man accused of raping a white girl, you know that, Mary. They'd kill him."

I hadn't considered that, but of course, what Lilian was saying was possible. There had been lynchings in Pennsylvania, and I knew one involved a white girl's accusations of rape. Still, this colored horn player was traveling the world, growing rich, maybe, while Lillian was locked here; it just wasn't right.

"Lillian, dear," I said, after several long, silent minutes, "I'm sorry for what's happened to you, truly I am. But I don't know what I can possibly do for you now."

"I want you to find my daughter," Lillian said eagerly. "Rosemary was sent to an orphan asylum for colored children in Scranton, I know that. I want to get her out of there, you've heard the stories about the colored orphanages—they're full of rats. The children aren't taught anything but how to work from the time they're old enough to sit up on their own."

"We saw rats at St. Catherine's," I said. I'd finished my cigarette and was shakily lighting another. "We had to work. We ended up okay."

"I need you to write to my friend Claire," Lillian said. "Claire worked at the club with me. Graham called her when he found out about Rosemary and what happened to me. He was beside himself. Claire wrote to me once, then I never got any more letters. I think old Hartley keeps our mail from us."

She looked at me. "Is that true?"

"What?" I said.

"Do they throw away our letters? Nobody ever writes back to me. Does Hartley or Vogel read our mail?"

"I'm not sure, exactly," I said, looking away. "But—I'd be careful what you write—in the letters."

"That's what I thought. That's why I need your help. Graham wants to get Rosemary from the orphanage and help me get out of here. I want my baby to grow up with a family—she has a father. Like you did, Mary."

Two beams of light slanted across the trees. Lillian and I ducked. We huddled together and watched Dr. Vogel's long Cadillac cruise past. Then all was dark again.

"Lillian," I said, "we have to tell Dr. Vogel you're not really feeble-minded, you just made a few mistakes. She's so busy, she doesn't keep up with all the inmates. I'm sure she'll be very angry to learn that one of the girls here is normal."

"*One* of the girls!" Lillian said. "There's plenty of girls here with stories like mine. Some worse. Ask people you know here about Francine Cotter. Her husband put her here so he could marry somebody else; her family tried to get her out through the court. That was ten years ago, she sleeps in the cot next to mine. The girls in the dairy, we're all normal girls. Unlucky, maybe, but not feebleminded. Vogel knows this."

Just when I thought there was nothing terribly wrong with Lillian, she said a crazy thing like that.

"No," I said. "Lillian, that's just not true."

"If all the girls here had mental defects, who would do all the work? She'd have to pay people," Lillian said.

"But I've seen the patient files. The test scores are in there. I've never seen any girls who scored even close to the normal range. These are scientific tests, Lillian."

"I don't want to argue, I have to leave soon, they check the wards at midnight. Ask your pals who work here about Vogel's friend, the warden up at Muncy."

"Mr. Hargoden? It's no secret he sends feebleminded girls here from the women's prison, you can't expect him to release them back into society."

"No, Mary, he selects healthy, strong but docile girls from poor families to send here from Muncy, not feebleminded girls. The last thing Vogel wants is more slow girls here. Ask around about Myrtle Drupp. She knew a former employee here—an attendant who knew she had a normal mind and tried to help her. She went to court and lost the case. That was eight years ago. She's still here. The worker was fired. That's why I haven't told anybody I know you, and I won't, Mary. Other girls have had families try to get them out through the courts. Nobody has succeeded. Vogel won't let any of us leave; it'll create doubt."

The idea that normal girls were sent here from Muncy—it was ludicrous. The former Muncy girls at the Village had been arrested for prostitution and other crimes. One had committed murder—it was in all the newspapers.

Poor Lillian. If only the Sisters had been able to recognize that something wasn't right with her. They'd punished her for her rebelliousness, but they weren't doctors. They couldn't tell the difference between youthful joie de vivre and an inherited mental affliction. Still, the Sisters should have helped her find work as a servant or a cook for a nice family, once she'd aged out of the home. She shouldn't have been sent off to do industrial work; they knew she had an impulsive, wild streak. Working for a well-to-do, genteel family like Dorothy, living with them and other servants—who knows how things might have turned out for her if she'd been placed in a more suitable environment.

Lillian took my hand and gave it a gentle squeeze. We intertwined our fingers, as we girls all did while walking hand-in-hand around St. Catherine's when we were little. I leaned my head against hers and said, "Lillian, I'm sorry about everything that's happened to you. But I don't know how I can help you, except by trying to get word to Dr. Vogel somehow. Maybe one of the sisters can write to her. Perhaps they'll find a better place for you. Shall I write to Mother Beatrice?"

"No, I want you to write to Claire, she's in touch with Graham," Lillian repeated.

"But Claire worked at the speak with you. You must cut ties with these people—Graham, Claire. All of them. You'll never get out of here if you plan to return to that way of life, don't you see?"

"Nobody will know my plans if you write," Lillian interjected. "Nobody opens *your* mail and reads it. Claire and Graham can write to you. At the Goodwins'."

"How do you know where I live?" I asked, suddenly anxious. I eased my hand out of hers.

"C'mon, Mary. Remember? We knew everything about the nuns at St. Cat's. Where they slept, what kind of families they came from. We even knew who had their monthly and who didn't, on any given day . . ."

"You're comparing me to the Sisters?"

"Well, I suppose I am, yes."

"You think I'm like the nuns who whipped our thighs with straps, who pinched our ears? Slapped us?"

"Mary, dear, no. I don't think that," Lillian said, sounding very tired now. She rubbed her eyes with the palms of her hands. "I need you, Mary, probably more than anybody will ever need you. Understand? I'm not allowed to leave this place until I'm old. And, Mary, I'm still so young. Please do this for me. I'm begging you."

"Oh, Lil, I wish I could," I whispered.

"The Holy Mother—she sent you here to me, Mary," Lillian said, peering into my eyes now and smiling at me through her tears. "That day in the dairy, I was praying to the Blessed Virgin, I begged her to help me. I opened my eyes and there you were. And I realized that's why you were in the dining hall that first day I saw you. I'd been praying for help that morning too. See, Mary? She brought you here. She brought you all the way from Scranton to help me. She *chose* you."

Lillian pressed a small piece of paper into my hand. "This is Claire's address in Scranton. Write to her. Tell her she can send Graham's letters to you. Then you can give them to me."

I thrust the paper back. "I can't do that. I don't know this Claire. What if I get caught? I'm paid very little, I mean, where would I go if I got fired? This is a government institution—I could be arrested for getting involved in something like this."

Lillian sat in stony silence. Then she said in a low, even tone, "You're still the same sniveling little coward you always were, Mary Engle." She'd been gazing up into the dark treetops as she spoke, but now turned to glare defiantly at me.

"Oh?" I said, trying to keep a level voice. "I thought I was your blessed savior sent from on high."

Now my blood was boiling—this was the Lillian I remembered. "Gentle when stroked, fierce when provoked," was how Sister Rosemary described her. But Lillian didn't need much provocation to pivot from sweet to vicious in the blink of an eye. Now I remembered how cruel she could be, and how afraid my friends and I were of her at one time. But we weren't children anymore. Her days as my orphanage bully were over.

"Well, you're still as selfish as ever, Lillian," I continued, still trying to maintain a calm demeanor. "I wasn't sent here to help *you*. I was hired because I spent my evenings in boring old secretarial school instead of larking about in speakeasies and consorting with bad men. I consider myself lucky to be here. I like it here, very much. It's not my fault you happen to be here in different circumstances. I mean—even if I could help, where would you go? Right back to your old lifestyle with this Claire and that jazz player. I've heard about Henning's, Lil, it's not just a regular speak, they've arrested prostitutes there—I read the papers. I won't risk my future because you're too stupid to know right from wrong. Besides, if tables were turned, you'd never stick out your neck for me."

"Yes, I would."

"Never," I shot back, my voice rising. "Besides, the tables would never be turned, I'd never be involved in such a disgusting, sordid thing as this—Lillian, a *colored man* you barely knew . . ."

Lillian slapped my face hard. She was always quick. I never saw it coming, and reflexively, I caught her nose with the back of my hand. We spent a few minutes cursing and striking out at each other just like when we were kids, but I pulled away. What was I doing? I was acting like Lillian. I was acting as if I were a moral degenerate too. I stood and hastily brushed off my skirt.

"Look at you, scrapping just the way you did at St. Cat's, you mutt, you're no better than me." Lillian laughed, but I could hear that she was choking on her tears. "The way you hustled Uncle Teddy, the crooked cop, with *cuddles*. What were you? Nine? Ten? Hustling the old creep for candy money. You're no better."

I was turning to leave, but I stopped and gazed down at her. She looked so pathetic, perched there on the old dead tree with her bare feet. Her fake attempt to laugh at me—it was so childish.

"Don't *ever* speak to me again, Lillian Faust, do you hear me?" I spoke in an attempt at a calm but assertive voice and used simple words—the way the employee handbook instructed us to speak to the inmates. "Don't even look at me the next time our paths cross, understand?"

"If only Dr. Vogel knew. Letting that disgusting old beast get his jollies. For money. It's a miracle you weren't sent here yourself. Imagine if I told Vogel what you did that last time you were in his car. . . ."

I rushed at Lillian—she was still sitting on the log. I kicked at her, I was so blind with rage, I wanted to kick her right in the head, but Lillian grabbed my ankle before I was able to make contact. She grinned up at me, tugging my boot, almost pulling me over.

"Let *go*! I'm warning you now, Lillian, you keep your damn mouth shut. If you ever tell anybody anything about me—"

"What?" Lillian taunted. "What'll you do about it?" She gave my ankle a final sharp twist, then let it go, which made me stagger backward and fall to the ground.

"Thanks for the cigs and the candy, *Little Trout*!" Lillian said. She stood up and headed back into the woods, stepping carefully through the muck and weeds with her bare feet.

I hurried toward the road, trembling with rage. Lillian and her friends made up that cruel nickname when they learned my name was Edeltraud. Long ago, when we were all very small.

"Seems like old times," Lillian called from the woods. "Little Trout!"

Twelve

THE next day, Saturday, Bertie and I took the early-evening bus to Clayburg to see what was playing at the movie house. Jake had been hired by the New York *Daily News* at the end of July, thanks to the reporting he'd done on the strike at the steel mill outside Clayburg. As a cub reporter he sometimes had weekend duty at the city news desk. Bertie, too, was dateless—the Berneston college crowd were all away until September. I was exhausted and depressed. The heat in the bus was stifling and I noticed Bertie was also in a foul mood. Neither of us had spoken a word for the first half of the trip. Finally, I asked if it was the heat that had her so down.

"Yeah, and it was a bad day at work," she said. "I treated three girls from the dairy barn this afternoon—one had severe heat stroke. I thought we'd have to take her to the hospital."

I worried that one of the girls might have been Lillian. I doubted she'd slept much the night before. I hadn't slept at all. Had Lillian already told the other dairy girls about our meeting? Would she tell a nurse or attendant her wild stories—well, they were outright lies—about my uncle when she had the chance? Hadn't she threatened to say something to Dr. Vogel?

"I suppose the more fair-skinned girls have a harder time with sunburns and that kind of thing," I said. Lillian was so fair her nose was always burned and peeling in the summer when we were kids.

Bertie gave a little nod and gazed out her window.

I persisted. "Are they okay now?"

"Who?" Bertie said.

"The girls. The dairy girls who got so sick with the heat today."

"They went back to work. I wouldn't say they're in great shape. Have you been in any of the barns this summer?"

"Of course not, why would I?" I said, perhaps too defensively.

"It's hot in there. Blistering hot. The only water the girls have to drink is pumped from what must be a very old well. It's full of sediment. The girls try not to drink it and they become dehydrated. I've written two notices to Hartley about the water. She told me that if it's good enough for the cows to drink, it's good enough for the girls."

"I suppose that must be true. I know the herd is quite robust," I said, using the exact phrase I'd recently typed in a report from Dr. Vogel to a dairy distributor. *The herd is quite robust*, Dr. Vogel had dictated. That's why she was able to sell the surplus. We produced far more milk than was required here at Nettleton.

"Cows drink out of roadside puddles. Does that mean the girls should do so as well? I sometimes wonder if men in prison camps—men who've murdered and committed real crimes, might receive better treatment than some of the girls here."

"No. I'm sure they don't."

Bertie looked as if she might say something, then changed her mind.

"Bert," I said, after we'd ridden for some time in silence, "does it bother you that Father Doheny only has hours for confession on weekday evenings? I mean, I wonder if he would consider hearing our confessions on Sundays after Mass—since we can't make it on weekdays."

Bertie laughed. She hooked her arm through my elbow and pulled me close. "Oh, you really are a convent girl, Mary Engle. What could you possibly have to confess?"

On Sunday, I dressed for church but left the house before dawn. I cut behind the administration buildings and followed the wooded path through the predawn haze. The air was hot and soupy, though it was not yet five o'clock, and I swatted frantically at cobwebs and mosquitoes. The stones and dead leaves that lined the path were slimy with dew and mold. I stopped at a cluster of trees across from the dairy barn. The darkness had dissolved into a yellowy haze, and I watched the cows begin to congregate behind the long shed across the dirt road. They descended from various corners of the distant fields and walked through a narrow gate into the field that surrounded the barn. There was some jostling at the gate—occasionally two cows tried to proceed through it at once and there was some comical sidestepping with much lowing and complaining from the herd log-jammed behind. Once they'd passed through the gate, for some reason, the cows remained in line and marched single-file along a narrow path they'd worn in the last stretch of field before the barn. They took their time, heads low, bellies swaying. There was no rush—the milkers hadn't arrived. There was a rancid smell from somewhere, the dead-mouse-in-the-wall smell that suddenly reminded me of St. Cat's. Tiny gnats formed a little cloud around my head. Finally, I heard Cloris's rasping bark from down the road.

"Move it. Pick up yer damn feet," she bellowed. And I saw the dairy girls trudging up the dirt road. There was no playful pushing now. They didn't speak or rush like they sometimes did when heading toward the dining hall. Like the cows, they took their time. Soon they were just a few feet from the clump of trees where I hid. I saw the girls' faces—some were as brown as bourbon from the sun. I saw that their arms and legs were still caked with yesterday's dirt. I scanned the group frantically until—there she was. Lillian was near the back of the group. She had tied a limp piece of burlap over her hair like a scarf and her face was sunburned and peeling—I hadn't been able to see that in the dark.

I'd come because I was afraid. I'd half expected to see Lillian talking loudly about me to the dairy girls and all of them, Cloris included, reacting in shock and horror at what she was telling them. But she walked in silence, like the others.

I said a silent urgent prayer for Lillian. She was only a few feet away now. I could see her eyes—they were still vivid blue, though she stared dully ahead. *God bless poor Lillian*, I prayed. *Bless her, dear Jesus. Forgive her heavenly father.*

The girls marched to the barn and I saw Lillian pause before entering it. She stopped just outside the aisle door and craned her neck so that she could squint up at the sun. Then she disappeared into the steamy blackness of the shed.

Thirteen

JAKE finally had a free weekend in early September. He drove up to see me on Saturday, and we decided to go to a place called Valley Lake in nearby Glendale. I'd heard from some of the young attendants that it was a lovely spot.

My coworkers had been correct—Valley Lake was just the place to spend a hot early-autumn afternoon. Jake parked on the dirt road and we walked hand in hand along a sandy area next to the lake where young people frolicked in the water. Jake said he wished he'd brought along his swim trunks. "Maybe next weekend we'll come back here, if I can get the day off again. We can bring our suits. Go for a little swim, if it's warm," he said. "Whatta ya think?"

"Sure," I said. I didn't own a bathing suit. I didn't know how to swim, but I decided not to tell him that. I didn't want to add that to the long list of things Jake knew how to do that I didn't: tennis, skiing, sailing. Jake even knew how to ride horses—he'd learned at a summer camp. But what did it matter? It would likely be too cold next weekend anyway.

We found a nice grassy spot to sit down. It was next to a row of wild rosebushes that were wonderfully fragrant and afforded us a bit of privacy, as it partially blocked us from the view of the swimmers. There was a soft breeze, and I closed my eyes and tilted my head back to take in the sun's warm rays. Jake sat so close that our shoulders touched, and I smiled. I'd missed him so.

"How's it going at the job?" Jake asked. He leaned in and nuzzled my neck.

"Fine," I said, giggling a little. His lips tickled so wonderfully.

"Yeah? No stenographer's strikes I should know about?"

His kissing was getting more playful and pleading, and I turned and kissed him. After a few moments, we were lying side by side. I glanced around but nobody could see us, and then I kissed him long and hard, and felt I might cry for some reason. I'd been so lonely and sad since my meeting with Lillian. I was sad for Lillian's situation, but that wasn't all of it. Lillian had reminded me of feelings I had that I didn't like to remember, the way I'd felt as a child, when I was so lonely and unwanted.

But here I was with Jake. He'd driven hours just to be with me again. He could have been with any number of girls, but here he was with me. I loved feeling his body pressing against mine, loved the thrilling sensation of his hands moving up and down my arms, all along my back. But when he moved one of his hands along my ribs, just under one of my breasts, I gently pulled away, as I always did.

Jake let out an audible sigh and moaned, "Catholic girls."

"No. It's not that, Jake," I said. "It's not that I'm religious. I'm just not stupid."

I tried to snuggle up to him again, but he eased away and sat up. I saw him glance at his wristwatch before squinting irritably out at the lake, and my heart sank. He was bored with me. He knew plenty of girls who were happy to do whatever he wanted to do. Fun girls. Interesting girls from interesting families, not fretful Catholic orphan girls like me.

"Jake," I said, sitting up with purposeful calm, determined to hide my mounting anxiety. "You know where I work. A lot of the girls are there because they made mistakes, I have daily reminders of what happens to them."

"My dear," he said, smiling affably at me now, and offering me a cigarette. "I hadn't intended that we start a family right here in public."

I smiled too as he lit my cigarette, but after he'd lit his own, Jake said, "But what do the girls at Nettleton Village have to do with anything? I thought they're there because they're brain-damaged."

"Yes, they are," I said.

"You just said they're there because they made mistakes."

"Well, some can't help making mistakes, Jake. That's the reason they're there. Look, I don't want to talk about my job. There's a situation there. . . . It's been troubling me. I guess I wasn't entirely honest when I said everything's fine, but I don't want to spend my day off talking about work."

"What situation?" Jake said. "I don't like you to have things that upset you. Tell me what it is."

I surprised myself by blurting out, "I learned, recently, that somebody I grew up with, somebody from the children's home, is living at the Village now. Her name is Lillian."

I was just going to leave it there, but Jake, the born journalist, pressed me for details.

"This Lillian . . . you met when you were little girls?"

"We didn't really *meet*. We were both placed in the home as infants, I don't remember ever not knowing her."

"So, you're the same age?"

I told him that no, Lillian was two years older, and then Jake asked more questions, and before I knew it, I'd shared almost everything about my childhood memories of Lillian.

I explained that we'd always lived in the same ward but weren't friends when we were small. When you're five and seven, the two-year age difference is vast. I told him how Lillian and her sidekicks were always the meanest to the younger girls. I was careful to give her a wide berth, avoiding Lillian and her gang when I could, and enduring their bullying when I couldn't. She and the other girls gave us half-orphans the old shakedown when we returned after visiting our folks, grabbing any coins or sweets from our pockets.

"My uncle and my father, they'd sometimes give me a dollar bill or two," I told Jake, even though Uncle Teddy was the only one who ever gave me paper money. I explained how I hid the bills in the hem of my skirt when I returned.

"At some point, I'd amassed a bit of wealth—almost eleven dollars. I kept it squirreled away in a little hole in my mattress," I said. "Nobody knew about it. Sometimes, when the other girls were out playing in the courtyard, I'd tell one of the Sisters I needed to use the toilet, just so I could sneak up to the ward to look at my money."

Jake was grinning. "I love this," he said. "You should write a book. *Little Orphan Mary!*"

I laughed and bumped his knee with mine. I liked remembering those moments alone in the ward. What a sense of power it gave me to see the bills fanned out on my cot. I had all that, but the other girls, even the meanest of the big girls, had nothing.

"Go on. Tell me more," Jake insisted.

I explained that one day, as I counted the money, I heard the door to the ward fly open and slam against the wall. I frantically gathered the bills and tried to hide them beneath my skirt.

"Whatta you hiding there, Trout?" said a strange, scratchy voice. It was Lillian. I didn't tell Jake about the nickname, but I smiled, recalling Lillian then. She was always so scrappy and tenacious. She stayed back near the door instead of barging over to investigate and I saw that her face was dirty and streaked with tears. She was wiping her cheeks with the backs of her hands and repeated her question. "What is it, Little Trout? You got sweets, or what?"

"She'd had a fight with her friends, that's the only reason she spoke to me," I explained.

"So did she take all your dough?" Jake asked.

"No," I said. "She didn't. She wanted to know where I'd gotten it. But then, instead of taking it, she sat on my bed with me and asked if she could hold it. I let her, and after a while she gave it back. We told each other what we'd like to spend the money on. I told Lillian about the various candies and sweets I planned to buy. Lillian told me I was being—what had she said? Oh, I guess that I was being a baby. I was thinking like a little baby. Normally, she wouldn't give me the time of day. But that day, she helped me come up with schemes. Big schemes."

Lillian pointed out that candy was good for a few seconds, but then it was gone. She suggested that, instead, she and I could run an operation.

"Everyone in the boys' ward was mad for Lillian. She could always find one or more boys to do her bidding. She got them to change the bills for us when they were in town, usually down to nickels and pennies. Then, she offered her chores and my chores to the other girls," I explained.

"When you say, offered . . ."

"Whoever would do it for the least amount, got the job. And Lillian and I spent chore time hiding behind the old outhouse, reading true romance magazines that the boys bought for us in town."

"Fantastic," Jake said, lying back in the grass and smiling up at the sky.

I smiled too, remembering those blissfully idle afternoons with Lillian. She liked me to tell her about my father—about the time he'd spent a week's pay buying Christmas presents for a poor family and another time when he'd rescued a man who was trapped under a fallen tree.

"He looks just like Rudolph Valentino, right?" Lillian would say.

"A little bit. People say he does."

Then we'd mull over various theories we had about Lillian's mother and why she'd been forced to give Lillian up. One possibility was that her mother was an heiress to a vast fortune. She'd been forced to give Lillian up when she was born because she and her lover (Rudy Valentino, before he became famous) weren't married. On the other hand, we thought it quite possible that her mother was the actress Marion Davies. Everybody said Lillian looked just like Marion Davies, so it was certainly possible that she'd had Lillian when she was a teenager, then had to place her at the home so she could go to Hollywood and become famous. We also entertained several scenarios in which Lillian's parents were married and had returned to their country—Scandinavia. A few of the nuns said that Lillian's parents must have been Scandinavian because of her looks. Her parents might have somehow lost Lillian when they were vacationing here in Scranton. We never talked about my mother. Nobody ever talked about my mother to me. She was dead. But we loved to talk about Lillian's mother, because she was probably alive and might even come back to get Lillian someday.

"So, what does Lillian do now?" Jake asked, breaking my nostalgic reverie. "Is she running a bootlegging scheme in Atlantic City? Presiding over a brokerage house or something?"

I tried to smile at the absurdity of this. "No, like I said, she's at Nettleton Village now."

"Good, invite her to join us next weekend, I'd love to meet her."

"No, Jake, I think you misunderstood. She doesn't work at the Village. She's—well she's a resident. An inmate."

By the time I'd finished explaining what I could, the sun had dropped behind the hills across the lake and the heat had let up a little. The swimmers were leaving—many lived and worked on nearby farms.

There were afternoon chores to attend to. Jake was no longer sitting beside me. He was pacing back and forth.

"This just isn't making any sense," he said.

"I know, Jake. It's mind-boggling how she ever got herself tangled up with that horn player."

"Horn player? Who cares about him?" Jake said. "I don't understand why you haven't explained to your boss that she's not mentally defective."

"I told you," I said, squinting up at a passing flock of birds. They were geese. They were Canadian geese, heading south for the coming winter. "I could be let go if they find out I know her, and it's unlikely they'll release her even if I do."

I kept watching the loud, honking birds after they'd passed over us. "Isn't that amazing?" I said, shielding my eyes from the late afternoon sun to get a better look at them. "Their formation, I mean."

"Why wouldn't they release her?" Jake said, not even glancing up. "You said there's a waiting list. Why not give her spot to somebody who needs it?"

"I guess, others have tried to prove they don't belong there—they've never succeeded. Lillian said that Dr. Vogel won't let any inmate go because it might create doubt," I said, glancing at Jake again.

"Doubt about what?"

"Well, if one girl has been confined there, but has somewhat normal intelligence, then, of course, people will wonder about some of the others."

"As they should!" Jake said. He plopped down in front of me, took my hands in his, and offered me a kind but concerned smile. I gave him a little half smile in return.

"Please, Jake, let's talk about something else, I never should have brought any of this up."

"No, Mary," he said. "I'm glad you did. I mean, this confirms my worst suspicions about that place."

"Your *worst suspicions*?" I said, pulling my hands from his. "And what are those exactly?"

"You know how I feel, darling. I don't believe in this whole movement of imprisoning the so-called *feebleminded* when they've committed no crimes."

I placed a cigarette between my lips, and after Jake lit it, I took a puff and lazily blew the smoke up into the air. Then, with a weary tone, I said, "Many of the girls at the Village *have* committed crimes."

"Mary, look, you might as well know. I've heard some, well, unpleasant rumors about your boss."

I gave him an exasperated smile. I'd heard rumors too from various staff. There were so many it was hard to keep track, and each one seemed to contradict the other. Dr. Vogel skimmed money from the asylum; Dr. Vogel personally financed the asylum; she'd had many lovers; she'd never had a lover; she was older than she said; she was younger than she said.

Still, I indulged him. "What *rumors*?"

"She's said to be crooked. I suppose she's no worse than any man would be in her position, but you know the old saying—power corrupts? Absolute power . . ."

I finished with him: "*Corrupts absolutely*? Jake, I can't help feeling defensive—you must think I'm quite horrible to work at a place that you hold in such low regard. You must think me corrupt to work there."

"No," Jake said. "I don't think anything like that, sweetheart." He sat beside me and stroked my cheek. He kissed me. I tried to turn away, but he'd seen that my eyes were filling, and he kissed me again and held me close.

"I'm sorry, my dear," he said, looking at me. "What a jackass I am. This is a tough spot you're in, and here I am making you feel worse. I'm so sorry. I just want to help, you know that, right?"

"Yes, of course," I said. I wished I could tell him that the reason I was teary wasn't because he'd made me feel worse. His kindness and kisses gave me a tremendous sense of relief. He still cared for me, even after I'd revealed some of the ugliness of my childhood: squirreling away money like a beggar; being an outcast among outcasts when I was the target of the ward bullies, before Lillian made me her partner in crime. And now, meeting Lillian here. Jake knew all this, but he wasn't repulsed. No. Here he was, pulling me closer. Kissing me again. Telling me how sorry he was.

Jake said, "I'll help you get Lillian out of there, Mary."

"I told you, it's impossible. There's nothing I—or you—can do. I wish Lillian hadn't made such poor choices, but she did."

"But, darling, you just said it; she made poor choices. That's different from being mentally defective. The girl you described doesn't sound feebleminded, she sounds very smart. She's there until she can't have children. Right? So, we're talking about twenty years locked up, maybe more? For what? Having a baby and lying about the father?"

I eased out of his embrace. What had I been thinking telling Jake about any of it? He was a reporter. His job was to seek out and publish sensational stories. And now that I thought about it, he always asked about my work—we'd never been alone without him asking about some aspect of Nettleton Village or another. I'd thought he was being polite, but now I realized he might well have been prying. What if he planned to write about Nettleton Village? These anxious thoughts replaced the warm feelings I'd had just moments before. I busied myself by searching the contents of my purse for my compact. After I applied fresh lipstick and blotted it with a tissue, I was able to give him an indulgent smile.

"It's not about punishing her, Jake," I said, adopting Dr. Vogel's cool tone that I always admired. "Something *is* wrong with Lillian's mind. I was too young to understand this when we were young, but it's clear now. Look at what's already happened to her. She worked in a place that was more of a bawdy house than a speakeasy. She was so drunk one night that she was raped by one man. Another made her pregnant before she was married. Is that normal? I can't begin to imagine what might happen to her if she were allowed back out on her own again. I think she's safer where she is. The Commonwealth of Pennsylvania thinks she's safer there too."

I closed my purse and said, "So I do resent your attitude, Jake."

"Mary, you're taking this all wrong," Jake said, placing his hand on mine.

"Let's go," I said, shaking off his hand and standing. "I want to be back at the Village before dark."

"Already? I thought we'd have dinner," he said.

"No, I'm tired, I want to go back, and I saw you looking at your watch. I suspect you have more interesting people to spend your Saturday night with."

"What? Mary, stop being like this," Jake said, rising to his feet.

"Really, I'm tired," I said. I started for the car. Jake followed a few steps behind. When I reached, shakily, for the handle on the car's passenger door Jake placed his hand over mine.

"Wait," he said.

I stared at the ground. "What is it?"

He tried to kiss me, but I turned my face away. After a moment, he opened the door for me.

We were quiet for much of the ride back to Nettleton. Finally, I said, "There's more to the story than I've told you, Jake. I can't tell you all of it. About Lillian I mean."

"I know."

"What do you mean? What do you know?"

"I know there's more to the story," Jake said.

I had a moment of panic then. Had I hinted something about Uncle Teddy? No. He couldn't know any of that. But there was more to the story than I'd told Jake. More than I'd even allowed myself to dwell upon for more than a few fleeting seconds since I'd left St. Cat's. It was about Uncle Teddy—about the way I'd "hustled" him, as Lillian had said, that horrible night in the woods. Well, it had actually been Lillian's idea. She was the one who told me I should pour extra whiskey into Uncle Teddy's coffee at the mill—that way he'd be sleepy on the drive all the way home. Too tired for "cuddles." She'd encouraged me to "shake him down" when he was passed out. One evening, I found a huge wad of money in his pocket and took six five-dollar bills. When I'd parked around the corner from the orphanage, I'd mussed up his shirt so he'd think he'd "cuddled" me and that's why he'd given me the extra dough, to quiet his guilt, the way he always did. He was snoring—head back, his jaw hanging stupidly, and the cold stub of a cigar was dangling between his thick knuckles. I took it, placed it between my lips, and lit it. Then I put it back between his fingers and hopped out of the car. Maybe he'd burn his hand, or the cigar would fall and burn him right there on his lap. I couldn't wait to tell Lillian of my mischief.

Lillian had changed something that had made me sick with shame and self-loathing into a sort of game. I sometimes suffered bouts of remorse about it, but Lillian always jollied me out of my blue moods.

"So what if the old stinker likes to rub and slobber on you?" She'd say. She made it seem like it wasn't a big deal at all. Even better, Lillian, the boss of our ward, had made me her best chum. The older girls, who'd once bullied me, were now desperate to ingratiate themselves with me.

But later, after Teddy died and I'd moved in with Aunt Kate, I looked back on that time with angst, which grew into horror as time passed. Why had I let Lillian talk me into such behavior? When had I become numb to the drooling and grinding against my skirt from the hard place in his pants, thinking, instead, of all the money I might show Lillian later? And I hadn't been able to confess my sins; Uncle Teddy said that any priest would lock me away in a detention home for what I'd done with him. My father would probably kill him and then go to the electric chair.

I had been too naive to recognize how my friend's deviant mindset had influenced me. It was a sad fact: Lillian wasn't quite right. I had typed many speeches for Dr. Vogel about girls like Lillian, girls who seemed to have normal intelligence when it came to general learning but had, unfortunately, inherited a moral weakness of the brain. They presented such a grave danger with their manipulative ways—I'd experienced this firsthand.

"I know you, Mary," Jake said. "I do think you're being naive about Vogel, but I know you'll eventually do the right thing."

"I'm naive?" I said with an ironic laugh. "*I'm* being naive? That's a bit much, Jake. I've spent hours listening to you and all your lofty ideas about social problems—labor, the poor, immigrants. But they're just ideas—all conjured up in the comfort of your doting parents' dining room, or in cafés with your writer friends. You think you know everything about poor people, but you've never been poor. You've no idea what it's like to be a girl like Lillian, alone in a dangerous city with no family . . . nothing."

My voice was shaking. Jake pulled the car over and stopped. He put his arms around me and tried pulling me close.

"Mary . . . hey . . ."

I shrugged him off and turned so I could face him. "I've never said Nettleton is a perfect place. Neither was St. Cat's. But I was very well cared for there from the time I was a little baby. I've never had anybody who . . . who . . ." I was about to say *loved me*, but I knew this wasn't true—the Sisters didn't love me. "I've never had anybody who cared a whit about what happened to me except the good Sisters at St. Catherine's."

"I care about you," Jake said. "I love—"

"Where would I have been without the home?" I cut him off in order to spare him from having to say things he didn't mean. "Where would Lillian go if she were to somehow be released from the Village, Jake? I know what she's like. She's always been impulsive. . . ."

I had to stop talking to keep the tears from coming. I allowed Jake to wrap his arms around me.

"Oh, Mary, I'm sorry."

"At least she's safe," I whispered, and now I wept into his shirt as he held me close.

"Of course," Jake whispered as he kissed my hair. "Of course, you're right, my dear, my poor dear."

I pulled away and wiped my eyes with the back of one of my hands. Why had I said all that? The last thing I wanted was Jake's pity.

"It's fine, Jake, let's just go."

Jake tilted my chin up and kissed me. Then he handed me a handkerchief and started the car's engine. I took out my compact, and when I opened it, I had to laugh. What a mess I was. I dabbed at my splotchy face and put on some fresh lipstick.

Jake pulled a rumpled packet from his shirt pocket and shook out his last two cigarettes. He lit both and handed one to me. Then he steered the car back onto the road to Nettleton Village.

Fourteen

I WAS almost trampled by Hal when I returned from work that Wednesday afternoon.

"It's Betty's time, Mary," he said.

"Oh! Are you taking her to the hospital now?"

"No, she doesn't need the hospital; she'll have it at home, just like Harry. Dr. Flanders just stopped by. He said I have time to run over to Shamokin and get Betty's mom. He'll be back in a few hours and see how she's doing. Mary, I hate to ask, but can you help her until I get back?"

"When you say help her—I mean, she's not going to have the baby while you're gone, is she?"

"Lord, no! It takes forever. It took her almost two days after the pains started when Harry was born. I just meant help with Harry. Thanks a heap, Mary."

Inside, I found Betty giving Harry his supper just like it was any ordinary night.

"How are you?" I said, rushing to her side. "Hal said that . . ."

"Aunt Mary!" Harry said. He was seated in his high chair. He held both arms up for a hug and I kissed his head.

"I'm fine!" Betty said. "Now, one more bite, Harry."

As Betty pressed the child's spoon into his little hand, I saw her face tightening. She took a deep breath, then let it out. After a moment, she seemed better.

"A letter arrived for you, Mary. It's from France!" Betty said. "And there's lemonade in the fridge."

"Thanks, Betty. Want me to finish feeding Harry? You look like you need a rest."

"No, I might take you up on that in a little while. But go relax for a while, I'm really fine."

I dashed to the parlor table. A letter from France? I saw a return address on the back of the envelope. It was from Martha Snook, an old friend of mine from St. Catherine's. What a wonderful surprise! I thought she'd moved to Chicago with an aunt. What was she doing in Paris? I opened the letter on my way upstairs to my room.

August 29, 1927

My dear Miss Engle,

I beg your pardon for writing to you in the guise of your friend, Miss Snook. I am Graham Carr. I know that Lillian has explained our dilemma to you. She was able to get a former employee to mail a letter to me and told me that I could safely correspond with you at this address.

Miss Engle, I suspect that you hold me in low regard. You are right, of course. I am fully accountable for the tragic circumstances that have befallen our Lillian. But I am determined to help her. I won't rest until she's been released from the asylum where she has been wrongly committed as a mental defective.

Lillian reported to me that you're angry with her. I beg you to turn the focus of your wrath upon me, Miss Engle, and away from her. I'm a few years older and have seen much more of the world. I should have known better than to engage intimately with Lillian, though I was quite in love with her. I still am, but I know that we can never be together as man and wife. Lillian still has the naive belief that in New York or here in Paris, Negro men and white women marry each other freely. I'm sure you know that's a fantasy, it's not possible in real life. As a white woman and colored man, we would be subjected to hate and potential violence wherever we go in this world.

Miss Engle, I reside in Paris now—my orchestra has a permanent engagement at a popular nightclub here. Many French do have a different attitude toward our race, which we find to be a tremendous relief. I dine in any restaurant, sit where I wish on trains. I live in Montmartre, surrounded by other black artists—poets, writers.

What I want to tell you is that I'm also trying to find a way to help my daughter with Lillian move out of the orphan home and in with my family. I have a friend in Scranton who visited the orphan asylum where our baby is living. This friend was told by one of the ladies in the nursery that a social worker is still keeping close watch on little Rosemary. The mother, he was told, is a poor mentally defective white woman who was raped by a colored man. They don't know my name. If they did, they'd have a warrant out for my arrest and I'd be deported immediately. Lillian has told me that I can trust you, and so I do.

My hope is that Lillian will be released soon. I have connections in New York, she's a very good singer, and there is much work to be had in legitimate venues for a talent such as hers. My sister is willing to adopt Rosemary and raise her with her own children with my financial assistance. Lillian may see her as often as she likes. But we need your help, Miss Engle. Lillian believes that the only way for her to leave is to escape, but I think there's too much risk involved. I was hoping that you might be able to persuade the governors of the asylum to release Lillian. It shouldn't be too difficult to prove that her mind is not defective, since you've known her so long. Lillian asked me to tell you that you may communicate with her through a girl who works as a waitress in the cafeteria there. The girl's name is Myra. If you give her a written message, she can be trusted to give it to Lillian.

I place myself at your mercy, Miss Engle. The address on this envelope is mine, you need only give it to the authorities in Scranton, and I will be arrested and charged with the brutal crime of rape. But that won't help Lillian or our innocent baby. Should you decide not to respond to this letter, I will know that you don't wish to become involved in our plight, and I will understand and respect your decision, of course. You needn't worry that I might continue to write to you. I shall not.

Most sincerely yours, Graham Carr

PS—My telephone number in Paris is M2438. Please ring me anytime, Miss Engle and, of course, reverse the charges.

I read the letter in a state of shock. The audacity of this man in writing to me!

I read it again. Then again.

"The tragic circumstances that have befallen our Lillian . . ."

Our Lillian! As if we were old friends. How dare he?

I began composing a response in my mind. *Dear Mr. Carr:* I would write. No, even better, *My dear sir.*

Yes, why not address him with the same formal and pretentious airs that he'd used in writing me? I knew the girl Myra. She was one of two who waited on the staff table. Now, I frantically tried to recall any clues that Myra might have given that she was onto me and my former ties with Lillian. But Myra had seemed completely unconcerned when she served me and the other staff. In any event, Mr. Carr's writing to me was a grave violation of my privacy, and I would certainly tell him so. If the letter had fallen into the wrong hands, I'd lose my job, and then where would I be? How would that help Lillian?

I thought of various stern replies to the letter. But I didn't have a chance to write them, because Betty came up and knocked on my door. Now she looked quite pale.

"I think, maybe, the baby might come sooner than Doc Flanders said."

"Oh no, let me get Bertie, or Dr. Vogel."

"No. I just called Doc, he's on his way back. I was wondering if you might look after Harry for a while. I think I just need to lie down . . . for a bit."

"Of course!" I said.

I walked Betty to her room, and then I hurried downstairs. Harry was in the parlor, pushing a toy truck around the rug and chatting in his little singsong, gibberish way. I sat on the rocking chair and thought about Graham Carr and Lillian. I touched my breast where his letter was. I'd tucked it into my bra. For some reason, my rage at Graham Carr was turning into something else. There was something comforting about having the secret letter tucked there next to my heart.

I didn't know if I would reply to the letter. I certainly had no intention of collaborating with a man I'd never met. But his letter felt, somehow, precious. He'd loved Lillian, this Graham. That hadn't occurred to me before. I'd thought he'd used her and had abandoned her, but now it was clear that he wanted to help her.

When Dr. Flanders arrived, he said, as he marched up the stairs, "If there's coffee, miss, I wouldn't say no to a cup."

I brought the coffee up to him, and Betty was in a bit of a state. She was on the bed, half sitting up and crying. I told the doctor that his coffee was on the bureau, but he didn't respond. He was fussing about between poor Betty's widespread thighs, and I almost ran into the wall as I fled the room I was so embarrassed.

Harry was crawling up the stairs, and I picked him up and carried him back down. "Let's read, my sweet boy," I said.

In the kitchen, I ladled some stew into a bowl and Harry climbed up onto my lap and opened *The Velveteen Rabbit*. He loved pretending to read, though most of the words were nonsense.

I read to Harry, and tried to sound cheery, but I was worried about Betty's loud moaning from the room above the kitchen. Harry took no notice. He flipped from one page to the next and moved his fingers over the illustrations.

"The fairy!" said Harry. He patted the page with one hand and leaned back against my chest, sucking his thumb.

"Yes!" I said, reading: "'She was quite the loveliest fairy in the whole world. Her dress was of pearl and dew-drops, and there were flowers round her neck and in her hair, and her face was like the most perfect flower of all.'"

I had to stop for a moment. My voice felt constricted. Fairies always reminded me of Sister Rosemary. After I continued with the story, Harry's head began nodding against my chest. He was almost asleep when a sound came from above, startling him. It didn't sound like the cry of a baby at first—it was more like the scream of a stray cat in the night.

"That's your new little brother or sister," I said shakily. I was so happy to hear that the baby had been born; why was I getting all weepy? It must have been the letter from Mr. Carr. Plus, *The Velveteen Rabbit* was a very sad story. It was outright morbid.

"That's your new sweet baby, Harry," I said, but he'd already dozed off again.

Harry's crib was in an alcove in the upstairs hall. I had just put him down and was ducking into my own room when Hal and Betty's mother arrived. They didn't notice me in their excitement to get in to see the new baby, but Hal knocked on my door a little while later.

"Doc Flanders just left, Mary. Come meet Betty's ma and little Eliza!"

In the bedroom, Betty's mother, Mrs. Pendergast, was sitting next to Betty, rocking the swaddled baby in her arms. She smiled at me when we were introduced and pulled back the little blanket so I could see the baby's face.

I saw plenty of babies at St. Catherine's, but little Eliza was exquisite. She looked like an angel. I suppose I was biased. I felt like an aunt to little Harry and now this dear little Eliza.

"Oh, goodness," I gushed. "She's so beautiful." I told them I'd make some fresh coffee for everybody, and Hal followed me down to the kitchen for a quick smoke. He began filling his pipe but paused to place his hand on my shoulder. "Thanks again for helping out earlier, Mary."

I was measuring out the coffee, but when I looked at his face, I saw what smiling from ear to ear really looked like.

"Of course," I said. "Are you hungry, Hal? Do you think Mrs. Pendergast would like something to eat or drink?"

Hal seemed not to have heard me. "I have a daughter, Mary," he said, slowly shaking his head in wonder. His eyes welled up a bit, even though he was still smiling. "I have a little girl."

"Oh, Hal!" I gave him a quick hug to hide the joyful tears that suddenly sprang from my own eyes. "Oh, God bless her! I'm so very happy for you and Betty."

I turned back to the coffeepot, blushing and hastily wiping my eyes with my sleeve. Then, because it had just occurred to me, I said, "Where will Mrs. Pendergast sleep tonight?"

"She'll stay in with Betty. I'll sleep on the couch while she's here."

"Oh, but the couch is so short, you'll never fit."

"It's fine," Hal said.

"I'll stay at Bertie's," I said. "I'm sure Gladys will be happy to stay at Sophie's."

"Nah, Vogel won't like it."

"Vogel will never know." I said. "I'll go find Gladys and Bertie and tell them the plan. How long do you think Mrs. Pendergast will stay?"

"I don't think more than a week or two."

A week or two? I couldn't impose on Bertie for that long. Well, I'd stay there tonight, and we'd sort everything out tomorrow.

I thought I'd find Bertie in the dining hall. It was the night the girls practiced dancing. I could hear the music from the scratchy Victrola from where I stood outside, it was playing so loudly. I saw, through the windowed doors, many girls moving around the floor in pairs, but when I tried to open the doors, they were locked. I knocked but nobody heard me, not even Miss Hartley, who stood just a few feet inside the door, monitoring the dancers with arms crossed.

I walked around to the kitchen entrance. This door was unlocked. It was dark inside, with only a thin shaft of light slanting in from the dining hall. I stood just inside the kitchen doorway and squinted out into the hall for any sign of Bertie. I was also looking for Lillian. I wouldn't go in if Lillian was there.

The Victrola was playing a pretty waltz, and I caught glimpses of the girls—attendants and residents alike—moving past the door in time with the music.

I moved closer so I could see the room more clearly. Some of the residents lacked coordination, but I saw a pair waltz quite gracefully across the floor. One of the waltzers was Lillian. I slunk breathlessly back into the dark kitchen. Then the music stopped.

"Where did we hide the records last week? Are they in the kitchen?" said one of the girls, after a long, silent moment.

Then I heard Lillian's voice. She said, "Hold on, just wait a minute, make sure Hartley's not lingering out there."

"She's not *lingering*, the old toad, she's gone home," said another voice, and then an attendant named Alice stepped into the kitchen and flipped on the light switch.

"*Goodness!* Mary! I had no idea you were in here," Alice said.

"Oh, I just arrived, the other doors were locked," I said, and I wandered, blinking, into the brightly lit dining hall, trying to act very natural. Immediately, Sophie, Gladys, and Bertie were upon me.

"Well?"

"Did she have the baby?"

Lillian was sitting on the other side of the dining room, next to another pretty inmate. I glanced at her, she gave me a quick smile, but I looked away, continuing my account of the birth and about the temporary bed shortage.

"Sure," said Bertie. "You can stay with me."

Gladys agreed to stay at Sophie's, and then she went into the kitchen to help Alice find the records. After a few moments they came back into the room, empty-handed.

"Somebody must've swiped 'em," said Alice.

"Or Hartley found them," said another attendant.

Bertie said, "Let's get Elsie to play, she plays better songs anyway."

I followed Bertie to a table in the corner where three of the lower-grade idiots were seated. One of these was a very young girl. She was rocking back and forth in her seat. Bertie squatted down in front of her, and spoke to her with a friendly smile. I'd noticed this girl before, as well as the older woman who sat next to her. They were always made to sit near the staff table at lunch with the handful of other severely afflicted inmates who needed assistance. This older woman had a habit of laughing and pointing at me whenever she saw me. She had a misshapen forehead and one eye appeared to be blind. Now the woman fixed her seeing eye at me, laughing senselessly.

"I see her, there she is again," the old woman cackled.

"I beg your pardon?" I said.

"Your mama! I seen her before, ain't she yer spittin' image?" Her one seeing eye seemed to be focused on something next to me, but there was nothing there.

"Oh, ain't she purty though, and her face so like yours?" she went on, still looking at the air next to me.

"My mother's dead," I said flatly.

For some reason this struck the old woman as uproariously funny, and Sophie had to come over and give her head a hard shove to make her stop her cackling. I hurried back to the other side of the room.

Bertie sat on the piano bench, and Elsie sat beside her.

"Papa's songs, Elsie," Bertie said. The girl was still rocking, but now she smiled and flapped her hands with excitement. Bertie played a few notes, and then Elsie pushed her aside and began playing a very fast jazzy number.

Alice said to me, "Elsie's pa owned a joint in Pittsburgh. She learned to play colored music there. It was a bad place, you know, for miners and working girls. She sure learned some swell songs though. Hartley don't let her play them none. She says it reminds some of the girls of the saloons too much."

I was astonished. I knew this Elsie couldn't talk. She could barely feed herself. I'd seen other inmates helping her during meals. Now she played like somebody you'd hear on the radio.

"Isn't she something?" Bertie said, now joining us. "She's an *idiot savant*. It's a very rare condition. She's the first I've ever met."

Elsie began playing a jazzy song I recognized. Alice, Sophie, and another attendant asked Lillian and a few of the other dairy girls if they'd teach them some steps.

"The Charleston, Lillian."

"Show us the black bottom, Clara."

"All right, all right, you girls line up and watch us," Lillian said. She and her dance partner, a girl called Deena, moved across the floor doing a very fast Charleston. Abruptly, Lillian stopped and said to Alice, "Wait, what about our cigs?"

Alice reached into the pocket of her apron and brought out a pack that she tossed to Lillian.

"If Hartley catches you out smoking, Lillian, you better say you stole those. Or I'll . . ."

"Oh, shut up," Lillian said, tucking the pack into her bra. Then she took Deena's arm and said, "Watch now, I don't know why it's taking you chumps so damn long to learn this. You need to stay up on the balls of your feet. You're all flatfoots, now watch."

I couldn't believe what I was seeing. It was the old Lillian again. She was the same girl here in the dining hall that she'd been at St. Cat's. She was in charge. Even the paid attendants were deferential toward her once Hartley left.

When Lillian and her partner danced, they looked like their movements were being orchestrated from above, from some kind of invisible puppeteer. Almost as if gravity didn't apply to them. Two more dairy girls started dancing, and one of the girls I'd seen working in the kitchen. The kitchen girl started another dance, and Lillian and the others immediately switched to her dance. Some danced in pairs, others danced side by side, like the flappers in newsreels.

"Come on, Mary," Bertie said, reaching for my hand. "Let's give it a try."

"No, really, I'll just watch," I said, feeling quite shy. Bertie joined an attendant, and they danced along with the others. I tried to avoid looking at Lillian and Deena, but it couldn't be helped. Lillian had quick-stepped Deena over to the area just in front of me. When Lillian saw that I was watching, she pulled Deena close and pressed her cheek against the girl's. I looked away; it was disgraceful, two women, dancing like that, their bodies pressed together; it was unspeakably vulgar. They moved off and then circled back, and this time when they passed, Lillian sadly gazed up at me from beneath those thick eyelashes, and I blushed so hard it hurt.

I worried that if I left, Lillian would know how nervous she'd made me. But what was there to be nervous about, anyway? A girl I knew as a child was a patient at the hospital where I happened to work. The girl was dancing now—it was a form of recreation for the residents. What was wrong with that?

Lillian and Deena stopped dancing, and Lillian began offering tips to the others.

"No, Mrs. Nolan. You need to do the little kick every *other* step," Lillian said to Bertie. She held out her hand, and when Bertie took it, Lillian began dancing with her.

"There, that's better," she said, when Bertie started following her footsteps. After a few minutes, Lillian returned Bertie to her previous partner and, without a word, took my hand and swept me into the group of dancers.

"No . . . no . . . thank you," I stammered.

"Come on, didn't you come here to learn some steps, miss . . . ?" Lillian said.

"Oh, I'm Miss Engle," I mumbled. I was sure that everybody must be staring at us, but when I glanced anxiously about, I saw that the others were concentrating on their dancing. Nobody cared that I had my hand in Lillian's hand. Again. Just like those nights at St. Cat's when all the girls in the ward practiced dancing. I felt Lillian's other hand pressed lightly against the small of my back. There we were twirling this way and that—just like when we were young.

"Mary, I'm sorry," Lillian whispered. "I didn't mean those things I said." Then she said loudly, "That's better, Miss Engle, you're starting to feel the rhythm."

I focused on my feet. I didn't dare look at Lillian's face. My hand was trembling and Lillian squeezed it tighter.

"I didn't mean any of it, Mare," Lillian whispered, still gazing off over my shoulder. "I'd never tell anybody about you and me. Or about your old uncle Fatso. Never. I'm sorry if I worried you. I was desperate, that's all."

"Oh, Lil," I whispered. "I'm sorry too." I quickly wiped my eyes with the back of my hand and Lillian whispered, "Jesus, Trout, quit it, what if somebody sees?" She gently poked my ribs and I giggled in spite of myself.

"I'll help you, Lil," I whispered before I'd had a chance to think.

I moved my hand to my chest—I was going to pass Graham's letter to Lillian when suddenly Elsie stopped playing the fast melody. She began playing a slow, somber piece by Beethoven and all the girls groaned and shouted at her.

"ELSIE!"

"The other music, Elsie!"

"Papa's music."

Lillian let go of me and I felt as if I'd been released from a spell. I watched as she returned to a group of girls I recognized from the dairy and began tossing cigarettes to them.

One of the attendants shouted, "Don't you morons dare light up in here."

"Susan, shut your fat mouth for once. We're leaving, it's too late for us," Lillian said. "You'll all be just going to bed when it's time for us to get up for the first milking." The other dairy girls followed her toward the exit.

Lillian paused as they passed the piano and touched Elsie's head. "Good night, Elsie, dear. Thanks for playing."

Elsie grabbed Lillian's hand and tugged it, making a sound that was like a baby. "Bah bah."

"No, Elsie, next time." Lillian moved her hand through Elsie's hair and said, "Jesus Christ, her hair's full of knots, why isn't anybody helping her?"

"She don't let none of us touch her hair, Lil," said one of the attendants.

"That's because you tie her up to brush it when it gets tangled, I've seen the ward matron rip her hair from her head, she's so rough. I don't know why you all won't cut it short, it'd be so much easier."

Sophie said, "Dr. Vogel says hair that's too short on the inmates frightens visitors."

"What visitors?" Lillian grumbled, sitting down on the piano bench with Elsie. "Okay, just once, Elsie, dear," she said. As soon as Elsie started playing, Lillian began working her fingers very tenderly through the girl's tangled hair, working out the knots. After the first few bars, Lillian sang, softly, *"Pack up all my cares and woes, feeling low, here I go . . . Bye-bye blackbird . . ."*

Elsie crooned along. She didn't use words, but she had perfect pitch and hummed a little bit of harmony, which made Lillian giggle in the middle of her verse. As Lillian and Elsie sang, some of the girls danced and Lillian kept working her fingers, ever so gently, untangling Elsie's hair with the tenderness of a loving mother.

Fifteen

I STAYED at Bertie's that night and the next. Bertie's bed was tiny. I got very little sleep. On Friday morning, I awoke crying out in pain when Bertie flipped over in her sleep and drove her elbow into my side. I decided to just get up and head off to the office. I realized this was an opportunity to do something I'd wanted to do for some time. I would read Lillian's file. I needed to know what was really wrong with her. I was certain I'd find some explanation in her file. Something in the intelligence test would indicate a problem with Lillian's mind that only a doctor would be able to detect. I was glad I hadn't given her the letter from the jazz player. But, if he did have some money saved, perhaps he could afford to pay for her to go to another place.

I let myself into the empty administration building. It was still dark, but I didn't turn on any lights. I kept a key to Dr. Vogel's office in my desk; she often asked me to do things in her office when she was away, but I wasn't allowed to go in and out as I pleased. It was hours before the others would arrive for work, but I still peered up and down the hall as I unlocked Dr. Vogel's door, just to be safe. I stepped inside, closed the door, and raced to the little drawer in Vogel's desk where she kept the file key. I opened the cabinet and started rifling through the drawer with the *F* patients. There was no Faust. I started again, but then I remembered—Lillian was married. Her last name was Henning now.

And, yes, that was the name on her file. I pulled it out and read the admission card attached to the front.

```
LILLIAN HENNING
17 years old.
Mental age: 8 years, five months.
Walks, talks. American. Protestant. Moron.
```

```
Can read and write some. Immoral behavior.
One illegitimate child now in state care.
Physically strong. Mentally childish, obstinate,
and deceitful. Prone to violent behavior.
```

I read the card several times. I opened the file folder but there was nothing else inside.

Mental age: 8 years, five months.

Lillian, like me, had been taught mathematics and science and history. We had all learned basic German—it was the first language of most of the nuns who'd instructed us. We had a visiting French nun once who taught us some basic phrases, and Lillian spent an entire summer arching one eyebrow and breathing, *oui* and *merci* and *je ne sais quoi* in response to everything we said, whether the words applied or not. Lillian had a gift for languages; she'd helped me with my Latin lessons during my last year there.

Walks. Talks.

Lillian was the only girl I knew who could read music. She'd taught herself. The IQ tests were very scientific. How could Lillian's abilities have been reduced to little more than walking and talking? Somebody had made a mistake.

And she'd been labeled "Protestant." Lillian was Catholic. There was no intelligence test in Lillian's file. Yes, somebody had made a terrible mistake. The Protestant girl with the eight-year-old mind wasn't Lillian. She'd been confused with some other girl altogether. Somebody needed to give Lillian the intelligence test. Then they'd know she didn't belong there.

I replaced the file and sat at my desk. My thoughts returned to the night when I'd danced with Lillian. She'd said that she hadn't told anybody that she knew me, and I believed her. It was clear, even before that night, she'd kept our late-night meeting in the woods a secret. I'd been highly vigilant after that night—checking the faces of the dairy girls and the attendants whenever I saw them, but they gave no indication they knew anything about me at all. And, because I'd started looking at the dairy girls so carefully, I couldn't help but notice that most didn't show any outward signs that they were feebleminded.

I'd typed many speeches and letters describing "moral feebleminded-ness." I knew that one could appear to have normal intelligence and still have a morally defective brain. But Lillian, who had every reason to resent me, hadn't betrayed me. She hadn't sought revenge by causing me to lose my job. Lillian was trustworthy. She always had been. She'd hated girls on our ward who tattled on others. She'd let a nun raise as many welts as she pleased on her legs; she wouldn't rat on another to spare herself. She was the only person alive who knew about everything that had happened with Uncle Teddy. And she'd never told anybody. I never really worried that she would. Didn't that speak to a strength, rather than a weakness, of character?

And these other dairy girls. Lillian's claim that the warden of the Muncy state prison sent intelligent, healthy girls to Nettleton had seemed ridiculous at first. But in almost every speech I typed for Dr. Vogel, she boasted about the fact that the asylum was not only self-sustaining, requiring little government financial support for its opera-tions; in recent years, it had actually made a profit. The farm was what had made it such a huge success. The crops yielded enough to feed all the inmates and workers, and the dairy operation had grown substan-tially. Dr. Vogel kept purchasing more cows that now produced far more milk than was needed at the Village. The government purchased the extra milk, butter, and cheese to be used at foundling homes and other institutions. This was why Dr. Vogel's name was in newspaper headlines so frequently. This was what had gotten her the large gov-ernment grants that would expand the Village to twice its size over the next few years. Dr. Vogel had proven that female inmates were just as capable as male inmates when it came to doing heavy farmwork, such as building sheds and barns, and clearing forests. The girls planted crops, tended acres of orchards, maintained the huge herd of cattle, and even operated the new modern dairy machines that processed the cheese and butter. Most important, her staff had been able to train girls with inherited mental defects to do this kind of work. No other asylum had been so successful when it came to the rehabilitation and training of the feebleminded.

Was it possible that Lillian was correct—that the prison warden sent some girls who were mentally and physically fit? Poor girls, like Lillian, without families, who were capable and strong? That would certainly explain why the girls were so efficient and capable at their work.

I jerked myself back from that horrible thought to reality. No. That was certainly a rumor. Dr. Vogel would never admit healthy girls; she had dedicated her life to helping the feebleminded. But I knew one thing: Lillian didn't belong here, and the proof was right there in her file. Nobody had tested her. I contemplated ways I might broach the subject with Dr. Vogel. I could just explain that I'd seen Lillian at the dining hall that night and recognized her from St. Catherine's. If Dr. Vogel looked at her file, she'd see that she hadn't been tested when she was admitted and that whoever had admitted her—Miss Hartley, no doubt—had even gotten her religion wrong.

But then, wouldn't Dr. Vogel want to question Lillian? Dr. Vogel was a psychiatrist; everybody knew psychiatrists could read behind a person's words. She could interpret things that were unsaid. If I told the doctor I knew Lillian, she was bound to question Lillian about that. She could easily get Lillian to unwittingly reveal details about our friendship at St. Catherine's, and about the things we'd done—the dreadful things Lillian had encouraged me to do. And if I were fired, how would that help Lillian? No, the information needed to come from another source.

Soon, the office was bright and bustling; the others had arrived. I had a busy day, but I managed to finish my typing before quitting time. I placed a blank page in my typewriter, then pretended to squint at my shorthand pad as I typed.

Dearest Mother Beatrice,

I'm writing to you with full faith in the wisdom and discretion you've always shared with us, your devoted St. Catherine's girls. Lillian Faust is a resident here at the asylum where I am employed. I won't go into all the details in this letter, but Lillian married a Scranton man named Tom Henning. It was not a happy marriage. I'm sorry to have to report that Mr. Henning is not a reputable man, but in fact runs a speakeasy downtown. He is responsible for Lillian being placed here at the Village.

Nettleton Village is a very good home for girls and women who have mental defects, but I'm afraid that, on account of some mistake, which I don't understand, Lillian has been placed here. Unfortunately, I cannot help her, as there are strict rules regarding employees and their relationships with residents. I was hoping that you might be able to write to the superintendent—Dr. Agnes Vogel. She is my boss, and is entirely unaware that I know Lillian. Perhaps you could tell Dr. Vogel that you know Lillian, that she is not feebleminded, and that you will help her find suitable employment upon her release?

I paused. Lillian was often on the outs with Mother Bea. She was a favorite of Sister Rosemary and a few other nuns, but I worried that Mother Bea would recall Lillian's rebellious nature and not be convinced she didn't belong here.

Then it came to me. I typed on:

Mother Bea, Lillian is not able to attend Mass. They have a Protestant service every Sunday at a chapel here on the grounds, and she must attend that with the others. I go to Mass in town. None of the Catholic residents receive Communion or attend confession, Mother Beatrice. I know that even in prison, Catholic men are allowed visits from priests to receive the blessed sacraments.

Again, I'm relying upon your wisdom and discretion. I need this job. I have no place to go if I am terminated. I look forward to your reply, dear Mother Beatrice.

With loving devotion, Mary Engle

I was preparing to leave, with the letter to Mother Bea tucked in the pile of outgoing mail, when Dr. Vogel asked me to come into her office.

"I understand it's a little crowded over at the Goodwins'. You've been sleeping in the nurses' quarters, eh?" she said, as soon as I sat before her desk.

I knew that Hal hadn't wanted Dr. Vogel to know about this, so I said, "It's the usual excitement that comes with a new baby. I'm sure everything will be back to normal in a day or two."

"I'm afraid that's not what the Goodwins think," Dr. Vogel said with a sigh.

"Oh?" I said.

"Hal Goodwin gave his notice yesterday. He's been angling for a pay raise all year. We simply haven't room in the budget. Now he says that they need more room for their family, so they're planning to leave. They've found a farm to lease near the wife's hometown."

I nodded and maintained a businesslike expression, but her words were like a blow to the gut. I'd felt that I'd become almost a part of the Goodwins' family. Betty and I had grown quite close. Neither had ever mentioned any dissatisfaction with the living arrangements to me.

"They forget that their housing and their meals are a large part of Hal's salary," Dr. Vogel said—her mind-reading ability was always so spooky. "I'm supporting a family of four now, but only one of them works. And they'll no doubt produce more children for the good people of Pennsylvania to support in the years to come."

"So—they're moving?" I asked.

"No, we came to an agreement. I can't let Hal leave. He won't get a pay raise until next year, like everybody else, but I told him that they'll have the whole house just for their family. Betty won't have to cook for you and Sophie anymore, apparently that has become too taxing for her. Her mother can remain as long as she likes. Gladys will move into the Aldwyn house—I know she and the girl Sophie are friends. And you'll move into the superintendent's residence for the time being. Until the staff building is completed."

"I beg your pardon, ma'am," I said. "I'm not sure I understand. Am I to live—in your house?"

"Yes, yes, just temporarily. You may collect your things and move in today. I've had my maids prepare one of the rooms for you. It's one of the downstairs rooms, meant to house staff, really. I don't want you to think you'll be living a luxurious life. No, that won't be the case at all. Now, one more thing, about those invitations . . ."

But I hadn't been thinking about luxuries. I was panic-stricken. I did admire Dr. Vogel, very much so, but she was my boss. I loved being able to leave work and go home to the cozy Goodwin house.

"Miss Engle? Are you listening?" Dr. Vogel said.

"Yes, I'm sorry, ma'am, please go on."

"Never mind, I have two invitations that need replies, but they can wait, it's late.

At the Goodwins', I found Betty, Harry, and Mrs. Pendergast in the front room. Betty was holding her sleeping infant. She acted as if she was thrilled to see me, but I knew now that it was just that—an act. Little Harry ran into my arms.

"Aunt Mary," he said, wrapping his arms around my legs.

I lifted him up, swung him around, and let him cling to me. Oh, why had I let myself grow so fond of this boy? I hid my face in his hair until I was certain my eyes were dry. When I tried to stand him back on the floor, his legs collapsed, and he clung to me.

"Up, up!" he said.

"Somebody wants to be treated like a little baby, again." Betty laughed, patting the baby sleeping against her shoulder.

"Are you feeling better, Betty? You look very well," I said.

"Yes, much better, thank you. Ma, will you please bring Mary and me some coffee? And those sweet rolls you baked too. I want to hear all about the office, I've missed you, Mary. Sit and tell me how you've been."

Mrs. Pendergast went into the kitchen, and I said, "I can't stay long, Dr. Vogel is expecting me before supper. I'll be staying at the superintendent's residence for the time being."

"You're moving into the mansion? Oh no! Mary, why?" Betty's voice had risen sharply, but the baby slumbered on.

"I guess you and Hal have felt a little crowded here with me and Gladys," I said breezily. I squatted down in front of Harry and covered my eyes with my hands.

"Well, only a little . . . since the baby came," Betty said.

"*Peekaboo!*" I said, whipping my hands away from my face. Harry screamed with delight. I laughed and covered my face again.

"But I thought they'd set you up in the nurse's quarters," Betty said.

"I had no idea she'd move you into the mansion. How dreadful. You must stay here. We can make room."

I gave Harry another sudden "Peekaboo." Then, to Betty, I said, "I hardly think living in a mansion will be dreadful. I'll have my own room. Really, Betty, I can't thank you enough; this is such a better arrangement."

Betty looked skeptical. "I don't know. Living with her—she's going to think you're on duty twenty-four hours a day." The baby woke up and immediately began wailing. Mrs. Pendergast had returned with mugs of coffee for us, and she smiled down at her wailing granddaughter.

"She certainly has healthy lungs," I said. "I've never known a baby to cry so much."

Mrs. Pendergast said jovially, "Then you haven't been around many babies, Mary!"

"Actually, I have. We had a nursery at the orphan home, and when we were older, we had to look after them. I don't recall them crying much at all." I thought of them now—the little swaddled bundles, often two or three in each crib. They had an odd way of blinking up at nothing, when they were awake. Their eyes moved this way and that, as if they were searching for something up on the ceiling. I found it unsettling, the way they looked around, then suddenly focused—at nothing. They did make sounds, little mewling or gurgling sounds. But rarely did they bellow like Betty's new baby. I'd been worried that there was something wrong with little Eliza, but, of course, I'd kept that worry to myself.

"Oh, yes, I've heard that's what happens in them places," Mrs. Pendergast said. "Betty, remember Mrs. Henderson? Her little ones came from an orphan home—she bore three still babies, poor dear, and then they adopted from a home. They got five now, and they'll need 'em for that farm of theirs. But Mrs. Henderson said that none of the babies cried much, coming from the home and all."

"But, why?" Betty asked. She had her own baby back at her breast. Its crying had, mercifully, ceased.

"Mrs. Henderson said it's 'cause they learn not to, in the home. Nobody picks 'em up when they cry, so they stop."

I smiled now, in recollection. "Yes!" I said. "The Sisters taught us not to pick them up while they were crying. Otherwise, they'd learn to cry for attention. They'd grow up spoiled and needy."

"Good Lord, Betty, not again!" Mrs. Pendergast said, and now I saw that tears were streaming from Betty's eyes. She was actually sobbing. Right there in front of me and her son.

"Give her to me," Mrs. Pendergast said sternly, holding her arms out for the infant. "It's the baby blues, I always got 'em, too. Give me the babe."

"No, I'm just so sad for the little ones in the home." Betty sniffed. She wiped her eyes with the back of her arm and leaned over and kissed her baby's head. Then she looked up. "Oh, Mary, I just realized, you were one too," Betty said, and now she burst into another fit of sobs.

"One *what*?" I said, suddenly hot in the face. I was so thoroughly embarrassed for Betty that I looked away. I focused on Harry, who was playing on the floor at my feet. Imagine crying like that—a grown woman.

"You were one of the poor lambs at the home, Mary. They wouldn't pick you up, no matter how hard you cried," whimpered Betty.

"Yes," said Mrs. Pendergast. "And now Mary's not a big crybaby, like somebody I know."

Mrs. Pendergast gave me a sad little smile. It rubbed me the wrong way. It seemed that Mrs. Pendergast and Betty pitied me.

"I must get my things and go; I promised I'd be at Dr. Vogel's before supper," I said.

"Mary?" Betty said.

I was already halfway up the stairs, but I stopped.

"Yes?"

"Please come and see us every day, if you can. We'll miss you so," Betty said. She was still weeping. How had I never noticed what a fragile, stupid thing she was?

I said, in a determined, calm voice, "Oh, yes, that reminds me. What about my mail—all the letters from my friends and my family? May I still have them sent here?" I emphasized the word *family* for the benefit of Mrs. Pendergast, who seemed to think I'd been plucked from the reeds in the river Nile like the baby Moses himself.

"Of course. I'll keep all your mail for you."

"Thank you. I'll just grab my things and be out of your way in no time."

Dr. Vogel sent Charlie around to collect me in the car, since it was too cold and too far to walk with my suitcase and other belongings. Hal came home as I was packing and he helped carry my things. I'd only been there five months, but it felt like much longer. Not just because I had many more books and trinkets now—it just surprised me that I'd allowed myself to grow so attached to the Goodwins in such a short time.

"Don't be a stranger, Mare," Hal said, giving my shoulder a friendly pat. "I know Betty's gonna miss you something awful."

"Oh, for heaven's sake, I'm not going far," I said, with a deliberate cheeriness. I knew he was just trying to be nice. I knew he was relieved that I was leaving. "I'll see you and Betty all the time, I'm sure."

Charlie ignored me when I climbed into the seat next to him.

"Hello, Charlie," I said. He grunted a response of some sort as we pulled away from the curb.

"I'm afraid it's going to be somewhat awkward living in the doctor's house," I said. "Of course, I won't see her much, I'm sure. I understand that I'll be staying in staff quarters, quite removed from her rooms." Charlie was one of the more active distributers of employee gossip, and I wanted it to be known that I hadn't been promoted, in any way, above my former position. I was still one of *them*, and certainly not in league with Dr. Vogel or (God forbid) Miss Hartley.

Charlie gave me a little dismissive smirk. What an impudent child he is, I thought. Why had I bothered even trying to engage him in conversation? From now on I would do as Dr. Vogel did—speak to him only when absolutely necessary. Anything else was a waste of breath. I would do the same with most of the other staff. Why bother with them? I was the secretary to Dr. Vogel; I had been promoted to that position because of my hard work and skills. Now I was about to move into her grand residence. Of course, they were bound to be jealous, there was nothing I could do about that.

When we arrived at the doctor's house, Charlie carried my suitcase and a bundle of my books up to the front door, while I carried coats and a box containing my letters and other papers.

Charlie used the heavy brass knocker on the door, and, after a brief moment, a young woman in a maid's uniform opened it. She was a petite blonde—one of the two maids I'd seen on Sundays when I picked up the doctor to go to town.

The two black terriers were yapping and circling us. I stood very still. Charlie gave the maid a quick nod and handed her the books. She just stood there holding them, but she didn't invite us in. Instead, she was giving me the once-over. I smiled at her and waited to be introduced, but Charlie just lifted my suitcase onto his shoulder and shouted at the maid, "WHERE DO WE GO?"

The maid frowned at him. I said, smiling, "How do you do? I'm Mary Engle. I'll be lodging here for a short time. . . ."

"She don't speak no English." Charlie laughed. He pushed his way past the maid into the house. The maid turned and motioned with her hand that I should follow. I tried to ignore the dogs. They didn't bite me, but seemed determined to cause me to trip by circling my feet as I walked. The maid admonished them in French and, amazingly, they moved away from me as I stepped into the small vestibule. We walked through it and into an enormous entrance hall with gleaming white marble floors and oak-paneled walls. A round table was stationed in the center of the hall, and on it stood a large crystal vase filled with long-stemmed white lilies. A magnificent winding staircase arose from the right side of the hall, and when I looked up, I could see the top of the house, three stories above us. It was hard to take in, the vastness and beauty of it all. We followed the maid through the front hall and into a grand living room. Of course, judging by the large scale of the house, I had known that it would be expensively furnished, but I'd imagined that it would have a dark, somber, Victorian design within.

What a lovely surprise, then, to enter the bright, modern living room. Along the far wall were four enormous sets of glass-paned doors, each framed with floor-to-ceiling linen draperies of a muted rose, green, and cream floral pattern. On the opposite wall was a massive fireplace with an elaborately carved marble mantel. The walls of the high-ceilinged room were painted an ivory color that matched the mantel exactly. And the furniture! Lovely antiques, many of them with little hand-painted flowers and vines and all upholstered with luscious patterns of mauve, lilac, and gray.

We passed through the living room into a rather narrow hall with doors on either side. I saw that one door led into what appeared to be a long, formal dining room, and another led to the kitchen. Across from the kitchen was a shorter hall. The maid walked to the end and opened a door. Charlie and I waited while she turned on a light switch inside, then we went into my new bedroom.

Charlie let out a quiet whistle of astonishment.

"Goodness," I said. "My goodness."

Part Three

Sixteen

November 1, 1927

Dearest Jake,

Thank you for sending the article you wrote about Charles Lindbergh! That was quite interesting to read about his plans for future flights.

As you know, I've moved, and that's why I haven't been able to get away the past few weekends, but I've promised a longer letter, so here it is. I now reside in what is called the superintendent's residence. Remember when you told me you'd heard it was a mansion? Well, you were correct. It is. If only I owned a camera, how I'd love to send you photographs so you could hate me as thoroughly as you do Dr. Vogel. I have my very own bedroom with my own private bathroom attached. It's one of the guest bedrooms on the first floor. It's lovely. Dr. Vogel has an enormous bedroom upstairs—it's actually three rooms, including her bathroom. She calls it a "suite." It's just like the hotel suites in the movies. And there are three other bedroom suites upstairs, though none quite as grand as hers.

Dr. Vogel still travels several days a week, and I'm often here with the two maids, Claudette and Florence. Claudette has worked for Dr. Vogel for two years. Florence arrived last winter. Dr. Vogel told me they don't speak English. She speaks to them in French, which drives me mad—as you know I can't stand not knowing everything. Well, as it happens—I'm laughing at myself now as I write this—Dr. Vogel doesn't know everything after all.

I made such a fool of myself, Jake. When the doctor is here, Claudette always serves us our breakfast in the morning room. Yes—the morning room! Not the beautiful, oak-paneled dining room with the long banquet table—that's where we have our dinner. We break our fast in the morning room, if you please, just like Miss Austen's Dashwood sisters. Oh, wait, were they the poor sisters? I do hate Jane Austen. But you get the idea.

That first morning when Dr. Vogel was gone, I sat in the morning room, as I had done all week, but nobody brought me my breakfast. And, dear Jake, I'd become accustomed to being served my breakfast! I wandered into the kitchen and there I found Claudette and Florence in their nightgowns drinking coffee and chatting away in their quiet little French voices. When they saw me they just frowned at me. So I summoned the little bit of French I'd learned in school (and from eavesdropping on the doctor and the girls). I said, "S'il vous plaît, mademoiselles—café?"

To which Claudette said, IN PERFECT ENGLISH, "What are you, a cripple? Get it yourself." She didn't even have a French accent. Then she and Florence repeated the way I had pronounced mademoiselle about twenty times, laughing until they cried. I guess I'm making them sound cruel; if so, I'm not portraying it correctly. I was so flabbergasted by the fact that they spoke English—and so relieved, that I began laughing too. Because, the truth is, I was a little lonely that first week and dreaded sharing the house with the two maids, who were supposed to be French. I wouldn't say we're bosom buddies now, but I think they hate me less, and I like having a shared secret with them. Now they only speak French when the doctor is here, and I pretend I don't know the first thing about them. I've heard the doctor tell her bridge group that the girls are from Paris. In fact, they're from Quebec. Oh dear, it's late, I must end this, but before I do, I'll share something else that I find very amusing. I'm sure I mentioned to you that the doctor was a big anti-saloon leaguer. There are many news clippings about the speeches she gave when she was quite young—one in front of members of congress, all about the evils of alcohol. Well, she may hate saloons, but the doctor likes to partake. She has a lot of wine here—her father had been quite the connoisseur, apparently, so they have plenty of bottles that he collected over his lifetime. She drinks it before dinner, during dinner, and then takes it off to bed with her. Of course, I've never been offered a drop. The doctor imbibes for her health! I always wondered why she was so sleepy on the way back from her mother's house in Clayburg. Apparently, Mrs. Vogel also finds wine to be a health tonic.

As always, if you dare repeat a word of this I will have to kill you in a very slow, painful, and carefully thought-out way.

I do look forward to seeing you next week when the doctor is away, dear Jake. I've missed you.

M

During the first days at the doctor's residence, I spent most of my free time in my room. I loved having such a luxurious bedroom all to myself. I read many books—Dr. Vogel had a wonderful library, and she allowed me to borrow anything I wanted to read. I prefer novels, and Dr. Vogel owned quite a few, but most of the books she collected were about science, botany, zoology, and biology.

I discovered some scholarly books that the doctor had mentioned in letters and speeches. One of these I found on the shelf next to Darwin's *On the Origin of Species*. It was written by Charles Davenport, and was titled *Heredity in Relation to Eugenics*. He'd inscribed it for her: *Aggie, keep up your tireless work, my dear friend, C.* There was a book by Francis Galton, who was a nephew or cousin of Charles Darwin. Apparently, Dr. Vogel had attended a lecture of his when she was a young student. But the books I found most interesting were by Henry H. Goddard. Dr. Vogel had a few of his books which were about criminal imbeciles and the causes of feeblemindedness. One book: *The Kallikak Family: A Study in the Heredity of Feeblemindedness*, I took to my room and read over the course of the next several nights. Jake sometimes made jokes about these Kallikaks when he asked me about the Village, and I chuckled along with him, as if I'd gone to college too; as if I knew what was so funny about these Kallikaks too. I knew a little bit about it—I knew it had to do with eugenics, because Dr. Vogel sometimes referenced the Kallikaks in her speeches. Now I could finally see what all the fuss was about.

Martin Kallikak, according to Goddard's book, was a Revolutionary War soldier who, in a weak, battle-weary moment, spent a night with a barmaid, causing her to become pregnant. The pretty barmaid looked normal, but, unbeknownst to Kallikak, was feebleminded. Kallikak went on to marry a woman with normal intelligence from a good family and had other children with her. Henry Goddard was able to study the descendants of both women who had children with Kallikak. The child born of the barmaid inherited his mother's mental defects and became a career criminal who fathered more feebleminded delinquents who begat more, and so on. Some of the barmaid's descendants ended up in prisons and poorhouses; others were committed to state asylums, all at great cost to their community.

The children and grandchildren of Kallikak's normal wife, on the other hand, were strong, intelligent, and prosperous. Unlike their lazy, thieving, moronic half kin, these legitimate Kallikaks became lawyers, ministers, and doctors who chose wholesome, virtuous wives. These solid pairings produced more honorable, industrious citizens, and— well, there it was. The first Kallikak's one-night dalliance was society's misfortune, but it provided future scholars with valuable evidence regarding the heredity of feeblemindedness and criminality.

Imagine if Mr. Kallikak had never met the feebleminded girl, I'd typed in a recent speech given by Dr. Vogel. *Why do we continue to shoulder the burden of born criminals? A farmer thinks carefully about which bull shall sire his dairy herd and which sow might produce the healthiest piglets. One wouldn't breed a racing stallion to a short-legged, sluggish mare and expect her to produce a stakes winner. Why, then, are we so careless about heredity when it comes to human beings—the species God has chosen above all others. It's our sacred duty to preserve the positive attributes of those who founded this country, and not let our population continue to deteriorate through thoughtless pairings of our best young men and women with inferior stock.*

I'd been unable to get away to see Jake those first weekends at the doctor's residence, but we wrote each other almost daily. We'd actually invented our own version of the scout's code—it was just a matter of adding two extra letters to replace the actual one. It was too time-consuming to write entire letters like this, but we often used it when being sentimental.

L OLVWHO IRU PB KHDUW, LW'V WKHUH ZLWK BRX.

I listen for my heart, but it's there with you, was the most recent code

I'd deciphered from him. It was fun, but I also found it very romantic. Slowly unveiling the meaning made the words all the more meaningful.

I still sent and received my mail from the Goodwins' house, but I sensed a change in Betty and Hal's attitude toward me. They no longer asked me to tell them funny stories about Dr. Vogel or to do my imitation of Miss Hartley's barking commands and comical, stilted walk. They were polite during my brief visits, but our conversations were limited to discussing little Eliza and Harry or the weather.

It wasn't just the Goodwins who seemed to view me in a different light now. I'd sit down at a lunch table and the others would abruptly terminate any discussion they were having. They weren't unkind, just guarded. They knew I lived with Dr. Vogel and presumed I was her spy. It really wasn't much of a concern; I didn't like going to the dining hall anyway. I made a point of having my lunch early every day, gobbling it down and leaving before the dairy girls arrived. I didn't want to see Lillian.

I'd still received no reply from Mother Beatrice, and now I worried that sending the letter had been foolish. It would have been better to wait and speak to the nun in person, perhaps during a future visit to Scranton. What if Mother Beatrice had already contacted Dr. Vogel? Well, I knew the answer to that: Dr. Vogel would interrogate me about the matter, immediately. No, Dr. Vogel didn't know. But surely Lillian had heard that I'd moved into the doctor's residence. What if this had made her anxious about where my allegiance lay? What if she started talking to other inmates or attendants about me?

But as the days passed, I became less anxious about Lillian. If somebody started spreading gossip about me and Lillian, I could deny ever having known her. There was nothing in her file about St. Catherine's. Nothing that might connect us. I just had to be patient—Mother Beatrice would write eventually—she'd be able to advise me. In the meantime, it was best to keep my distance from Lillian and the other dairy girls.

On Wednesday nights, the maids went to Harrisburg and visited cousins there. Claudette would leave us a warm stew or a roasted chicken, and I cleaned up after dinner. The first Wednesday, and then every Wednesday that she wasn't traveling, Dr. Vogel, who enjoyed a little conversation with her medicinal wine, invited me to have a cigarette (or ten) with her in the living room before going to bed.

We never talked about work. Instead, I liked getting Dr. Vogel to talk about herself and her family. She'd been the eldest of three children. She had a younger brother and sister. She showed me her scrapbooks and college yearbook and from these I learned that she'd excelled not only in academics but also at tennis and all field sports in her youth. I was fascinated by Dr. Vogel's childhood—it was exactly the childhood I had imagined for myself if my mother hadn't died and Father had been stinking rich. The Vogels had family dinners together every night and "Mother" always kept the children abreast of current affairs and national politics. Dr. Vogel's father seemed to travel quite a bit. He had some kind of career, but I never understood what it was. He died, suddenly, of a heart attack, while Dr. Vogel was still in grammar school. The doctor mentioned that in passing one night, as we were finishing our dinner.

"I'm very sorry to hear that, Dr. Vogel," I said. "How terribly tragic."

The doctor was on her second or third glass of wine, and she gave a short, bitter laugh.

"It would have been *tragic* if he'd lived another year, he was bleeding Mother dry. My father—well, Mary, he was a handsome scoundrel, there's no other way to describe him. He married Mother for her money, everybody knew it. Had he lived another five years he would have gambled away her last penny. Of course, it wasn't *her* money, once they married. More wine, dear?"

"No, thank you," I said. I never had more than one glass of wine with the doctor, but she always offered to refill my glass before refilling her own.

"By law," Dr. Vogel continued, "the husband still has control of every penny and owns all property in a marriage, even if the wife brought all the money to the marriage, as my mother did. That's why I've never married, and I never will. My mother was a Vreeland, from good Dutch, English stock. Her mother—my grandmother—was a Boston Cabot: Harriet Cabot Woodward. Grandmother went to Seneca

Falls with the real suffragists—Mrs. Stanton, Lucretia Mott, Susan Anthony. Oh, those were tough old birds, Mary, if only we had more like them today. They believed in real social change and thought they'd see it in their lifetime." She gazed sadly down at her glass of wine. "Of course, they didn't."

"No, that's a shame," I said. "Shall I see what Claudette left us for dessert?" Sometimes the doctor got a bit maudlin if she didn't eat enough supper with her wine, and I was trying to jolly her out of an impending gloom.

"Yes, off they went to Seneca Falls," she continued, unaware that I'd spoken. "Gran went with her friends, though she was just a young thing at the time. Oh, how that scandalized her father. Many of the organizers were Quakers, you see. Gran met her husband, Mr. Vreeland, there. Seneca is where the group drafted their list. The *list of sentiments*, they called it. Not demands, Mary. Sentiments. They didn't just seek the right to vote. No. They wanted what men had. They wanted the world."

She was about to light a cigarette and seemed to be waiting for my reaction, so I said, "Yes, people forget that, don't they?"

"These women, men too, they believed married women ought to have access to their own income, and the right to divorce, to have custody of their own children, to own property. And they weren't just in it for themselves. They were abolitionists too. And not just the Quakers, Mary. No. My grandparents were good Protestants, and they believed all American men and women should have equal franchise and liberties. Mother still has a letter Frederick Douglass himself wrote to my grandfather." The doctor paused to sip her wine, then jutted out her chin, proudly. "Grandfather Vreeland was a legal scholar who wrote and published several articles about the evils of slavery, Mary."

"They sound like wonderful people, your grandparents," I said.

I knew who Frederick Douglass was—he was the freed slave who wrote books. I thought it interesting that Dr. Vogel was so proud of her family's connection to a colored man. Just the day before, I'd typed a speech for her about the threat that members of "lesser races" from Asia, Africa, and parts of Europe posed to American society.

This threat to the white or what she sometimes called the "Nordic" race had become a more consistent theme in the doctor's speeches. She told me audiences responded enthusiastically to this topic, especially the garden club and church luncheon crowds, so she talked about it more. She reminded her audiences that *women* were to thank for the Immigration Act of 1924, which restricted immigrants from China, Africa, and, most important, Southern and Eastern European countries. The Europeans who were barred—Jews and Catholics, mostly, the doctor added—without fail, posed the greatest threat to America. There were laws against interracial marriage here, but no laws barring a good Christian American girl from marrying the offspring of mentally defective, inbred foreigners who'd been teeming onto our shores for decades, threatening to destroy, forever, something she called America's *ethnic homogeneity.*

Dr. Vogel meant Italian- and Irish-born people when she spoke of Catholics this way, she didn't mean Catholics like Bertie and me. Italians were known for their violent tendencies and their criminal habits. Father complained about them at the mill. He tried not to hire them; they were too much trouble. Everyone knew that men from Ireland drank too much, their wives too, even. Those were the inferior Catholic people she meant. Similarly, when she said that Jews' inheritable diseases and negative traits were the results of inbreeding, I knew she was talking about the Russian and Slavic Jews who were crowding so many filthy city tenement houses. She wasn't talking about American-born Jews like Jake, though I sometimes worried what the doctor would think if she knew of my involvement with him.

"But we have the vote now, Mary. Thank God," the doctor said.

"Yes," I said, quite pleased by her change in tone.

"Did you ever have any plans to go to college, dear?" Now, Dr. Vogel offered me her easy smile and rapt attention. She had a way of finding my eyes with her gaze that just flooded me with joy. If I looked away, as I often did when I didn't know her as well, she shifted her head, so she could catch my eyes. I'd never had anybody pay such close attention to me. It didn't feel like scrutiny; it felt like there was no end to her interest and kind regard for me, and I no longer looked away when we spoke together like this.

"Sure, college has always been a dream of mine. I'm saving for it— maybe someday," I said, basking in her warm watchfulness.

"But you were a good student, were you not? You have excellent grammar and spelling. Another cigarette, dear?"

"Thank you," I said, taking one from the case she'd passed to me. "I received good grades. Maybe someday I'll be able to afford to take a few college courses."

"Perhaps we can find a way for you to attend classes at Berneston while working here at the Village," Dr. Vogel said, after I'd lit her cigarette and then my own. "I'm a trustee. I'll ask Mr. Langdon, the president, what he thinks. They often work around the schedules of male students who are employed. Why shouldn't they allow you to attend on a part-time basis?"

Was the doctor under the impression I had an inheritance squirreled away someplace?

"Would you like that, Mary?"

"Of course! I'd love that, but I could hardly afford a private university on my salary," I said.

"Well, don't let's worry about that right now. I'll speak to Langdon. We've an annual scholarship in my father's memory, I can certainly suggest an appropriate recipient, if I deem her worthy."

"Oh my goodness," I said, feeling my cheeks turn crimson. What an exciting and astonishing proposition. Imagine, attending Berneston!

Dr. Vogel seemed quite uplifted by this idea. "You know, dear, I've never wanted a husband. But now that I'm getting older, I regret not having a child. I'd love to have a daughter. A clever young thing like you. Everything's changed at Berneston, there are so many more opportunities for the female students. I'd so love for you to be a part of that, my dear."

I couldn't think of anything to say, I was so deeply moved by the doctor's words. More than anything, I was moved by the idea that she thought of me as a sort of daughter. I knew the doctor was tipsy, and it was just musing on her part. She couldn't have known what those words meant to me, a motherless child. I had tears of gratitude in my eyes, but the doctor didn't notice, she was emptying the last drops of wine into her glass.

"Nobody lives forever, Mary Engle. Someday, you might very well take my place here. I can't think of a more promising candidate."

Seventeen

November 16, 1927

My dear Mary,

I love imagining how you look when you read my letters, so I like to write whimsical, funny things. Then I can think about the way your pretty nose crinkles so adorably when you smile, and the way your eyes are so beguiling when you're merry, my dear Mary. But today, I confess, I'm sad. I miss you. I was disappointed when I received your last-minute wire on Friday, canceling our Saturday plans again. It can't be that hard to get away for one afternoon and evening. Bertie wrote me to say that she hasn't seen much of you either. She thinks the doctor has been isolating you from her and your other friends at the Village. You said you won't be able to get away next weekend either, though Vogel will be away. The doctor has turned you into the dogs' governess now? I thought you hated dogs.

My dear, I know we agreed not to speak any more about your employer, but I came across a recent editorial she wrote in the <u>Philadelphia Enquirer</u>. I recognized a tactic she uses—one that many powerful and politically connected people use—to offer people, many people, who feel small or forgotten, a sense of power and belonging. I think often about the day when you and I discussed the sad plight of your friend. I hurt your feelings and it pains me still, to think of my thoughtless remarks. But, in your justifiably angry response, you made assumptions about me that I let go at the time, but that I believe were similarly unfair.

It's true, I did grow up in a loving, middle-class family, which makes me quite fortunate. I am also a Jew and have felt the hatred of others, a hatred that many Jews feel at one time or another in most places on this earth. I was bullied, harassed, and roughed up as a kid, but what hurt far more were times when friends, or at least men whom I considered to be my friends, in college or even still at work, get too drunk and toss out things like "kike" or "Jew bastard." Or worse. Often, they'll try to disguise their barbs as jokes. This doesn't cut me as much as it once did. I'm less likely to take an angry swipe at a guy like this because I've learned that he feels, despite all his bluster—terribly afraid. This kind of guy is afraid of being alone and (I believe I'm quoting somebody, now, I don't recall who), but when one hates a Jew, one is never alone. A man will also find himself in good company hating a Negro, a prostitute, an imbecile, or a pauper.

Dr. Vogel is too refined to use frank, ugly words, but when she writes that America's ethnic heritage is being threatened by "dark, immoral, and criminal types of immigrants," she's trying to shift the blame for crime and poverty in this country from the majority, where, logically, it belongs, to the minority. All people want to feel that they are worthy and that they belong. The doctor's speech offers her audiences something that costs them nothing. She gives them a sense of belonging—superiority, actually—by virtue, simply of their birth, not their deeds. She's very shrewd, I do see why you admire her.

As you know, I'm quite fascinated with not just Nettleton Village, but other places like it. I know some of the inmates there are feebleminded, but we know at least one who is not. Your friend. Lillian. Why is she there? Is it to keep her safe, as you have said? Or is it so that others may feel superior, so that they'll feel less afraid and alone, because they're not like her?

Well, my love, I won't go on. I didn't mean to carry on when I started writing. I'm not sure I'll send this. I'm glad I was able to get these thoughts onto a page. But Mary, my dear, please trust that I don't believe you are like Dr. Vogel. I just hope you can resist any efforts she might make to mold you in her form.

I do look forward to seeing you in two weeks, Mary, I'm coming, wire or no wire.

With much longing, J

November 20, 1927

Dearest Jake,

I'm so very sorry about canceling the past few weeks. I miss you too; I miss you terribly. It's just that this is a busy time for the doctor. She's finishing the last of her speaking engagements before the snow season starts. Soon, I'll have more time available on weekends.

Darling, I must insist you never send another letter like the one I received today. I do trust the Goodwins, but letters get misplaced, some end up in the mailroom. I can't have you risk my livelihood. We'll speak about it all when we meet. I plan to send this from town, so I can respond to some of what you wrote, and I feel that I must.

Dr. Vogel certainly does not hate Jews, she has a number of Jewish colleagues and friends—doctors and civic leaders, whom she corresponds with and visits regularly. I've never heard you talk about feeling hated or even feeling Jewish, for that matter, so I'm quite surprised that you feel attacked so personally by words in a speech that made no reference to Jews at all. Similarly, I've never typed or read anything she's written about hating colored people. It might interest you to know that her grandfather was an outspoken abolitionist and a close friend of Frederick Douglass. Dr. Vogel is very proud of this association.

I don't know what Bertie meant about the doctor isolating me, I see Bertie frequently. We still go to church every Sunday. The fact of the matter is, I've been avoiding Lillian. I'm happy to be able to report to you that I've taken steps to assist her, Jake; you're right, she doesn't belong here. But I don't want to see her until I know more. So that's why I've been keeping myself to the house and the office more. Anyway, dear Jake, please, let's not argue on paper. I want us to write the kind of letters we've always written, about lighter things. So, I'll start now.

Yes, Dr. Vogel has tasked me with looking after her dogs while she travels. The big dog lives outside; he's more of a watchdog. But the little terriers, Peg and Trixie, they've won me over. They're Scotties, and at first, they looked identical to me with their little beards and scornful eyebrows and all their jumping this way and that. I tried to ignore them and kept them out of my room, but my rejection seemed to make me even more attractive to them. They sat at my feet when I ate, they leaped onto my bed before I had a chance to close the door. Peg, the larger of the two, is sweet. Trixie, the other, is rather a genius. Florence has taught her many tricks. She retrieves socks, slippers, books, toys, and—oh dear, I just realized how boring this must be for you. Suffice it to say that now I understand why people keep dogs.

Dear Jake, only two more weeks, and we'll be together again. I look forward to it more than words can say.

Love, Mary

PS—You needn't worry about the doctor "molding me to her form." As you know she's slender and I'm growing quite plump on Claudette's cuisine!

When Dr. Vogel returned from a speaking tour the following Sunday afternoon, I had her correspondence waiting for her in her home office.

"I know this week will be very busy, so I thought I'd bring your letters here in case you want to get a head start," I said, taking the doctor's coat and hat.

"Thank you, Mary," said the doctor. She looked tired. Two news clippings had arrived that week. I knew Dr. Vogel loved reading her own publicity, so I had placed the clippings on the top of the pile of letters. I was walking out of the office when Dr. Vogel said, "Mary! Wait. Did you read this?"

I walked back to the desk and she thrust the clipping at me. It was from my hometown newspaper, the *Scranton Republican*. It read:

FRENCH CHAMPAGNE SOLD BY THE CASE TO PENNSYLVANIA HOSPITALS

October 18, 1927—Despite the Volstead Act, champagne is now selling at $5 a case, but don't rejoice yet, thirsty citizens, because the French wine is not being sold at this astonishingly low figure to the public. Uncle Sam has been selling it exclusively to hospitals for medicinal purposes.

Orders calling for the sale of at least 100 cases of the imported wine were received last month from Federal Judge George H. Filmore of Clayburg. The champagne was seized sometime last year at a wharf near Philadelphia. Hospitals that have received champagne at this figure are: Koser Private Hospital, Sunbury Hospital, and Nettleton State Hospital for the Feebleminded.

Orders were also recently received for the sale of Canadian whiskey at $2 a gallon to the following: Good Samaritan Hospital, 4 cases; JC Blair Memorial Hospital, 1 case; Lewistown Hospital, 2 barrels; and Nettleton State Hospital for the Feebleminded, 6 barrels.

I had already read it. I hadn't thought much of it except that it cast doubt on the doctor's assertion that all the wine and champagne she drank and served was from her father's pre-Prohibition collection and was therefore legal to consume. How many quarts in a whiskey barrel? I had no idea, but it must be quite a lot. And not rotgut bootleggers' stuff either—it was Canadian whiskey. I wondered if Bertie knew where it was kept. Probably locked away in the infirmary someplace until a patient needed it.

"Why the hell do they wait so long before sending the clippings? I'm switching services. For God's sake, this article ran weeks ago."

"Yes, they could be a bit more current," I agreed. "Would you like me to look into other clipping services in the morning?"

"Yes, and, Mary, I need to make some calls this evening. Do be a dear and get my telephone directory from the office, won't you?"

I loved the chummy way the doctor spoke to me when we were at home, and I didn't mind the occasional overflow of my work from the office to my evenings and weekends at the mansion. So off I went to the main building for the phone directory. When I returned to the house, the wonderful aroma of roast beef wafted from the kitchen. Claudette was making our usual Sunday dinner.

"Here you are, ma'am," I said, giving the phone book to the doctor.

"Would you be a dear and ring Judge Filmore? Hopefully you can get through to the town operator. Tell her to connect to his home telephone."

"Of course," I said. I had the operator put me through. After several rings, a woman answered and said, "Filmore residence, who's calling?"

"I have Dr. Agnes Vogel calling for Judge Filmore. Is he in, please?"

"I'm sorry, the judge is preparing to have dinner and is not taking calls at the moment."

Dr. Vogel, who'd had her face pressed so close that our cheeks touched, now snatched the earphone and mouthpiece and said, "This is Dr. Agnes Vogel. I must speak to His Honor immediately. Tell him it's urgent."

I left the room, but I could hear the doctor's portion of the conversation from the hall, and I stayed there, just outside the door so that I could listen. I was awed at the doctor's stern bravado. Filmore was a federal judge!

"Yes, yes, I know it's Sunday, George, it's Sunday here too," Dr. Vogel said. "I'm wondering if you happened to see an article that ran in Scranton about the shipment. *No?* Well, allow me to read it to you."

Dr. Vogel read the article aloud and then there was a long silence.

"Of course it's a big deal. Why? Because I received, just last week, a letter from the Department of Health stating that they would be doing inspections next week. They never inspect in November, they always do them in spring. It made no sense to me—until now."

Another pause.

"Well, I have to have something to show. Yes, I'm positive this is why they're coming. We'll do what we did last time, but I need bottles with more recent stamps. Tell Mack. Okay. Tomorrow then. My best to Edna."

When Dr. Vogel arrived at work the next morning, she told me to leave my typing and come into her office.

"I've an errand I'd like you to run. I'd ask Charlie, but it's quite urgent, and you know how slow he is. I need you to drive over to the home of Mrs. Filmore. She's supplying some extra refreshments for the governor's tea next week, and I need you to pick up some of the boxes. She'll have her hired man load everything into the car and then you can drive it back here."

"Certainly, ma'am," I said, thrilled at the prospect of leaving the office for the morning and driving around in the limo, all alone.

In Clayburg, I was aware of the attention the limousine always drew from people on the streets. I lit a cigarette, tilted my hat at a rakish angle, and decided to pretend I was Greta Garbo herself, and that this was my very own automobile; it wasn't often I got to drive it without the doctor on board.

Judge Filmore lived on the same street as Dr. Vogel's mother. The Filmores' house was, like Mrs. Vogel's house, quite large. When I pulled into the circular driveway, a black man was waiting for me, the collar of his wool coat turned up against the cold. Next to him were at least a dozen large wooden crates.

"Goodness," I said, stepping out of the car. "I don't know if they'll all fit."

"They'll fit, all right," the man grumbled. "We fit more than this the last time."

He opened the trunk of the car and loaded a few crates in there. Then he opened the door to the back passenger compartment and piled the rest of the crates there, on the floor and on the seats. I gazed up at the house and saw that a woman was peering out the window. I was sure it must be Mrs. Filmore, so I gave her a little wave, but the woman stepped away, letting the curtain fall across the window.

When I pulled the car up to the administration building, Dr. Vogel was waiting for me outside, wearing her everyday fur and holding what appeared to be a small vanity case. She hurried into the passenger seat and instructed me to drive around to the back of the medical wing. There was a tall, narrow shed there, with a padlocked door. I'd never noticed it before.

"Well, everything goes in here, we may as well get started," Dr. Vogel said. She took a large ring of keys from her pocket and unlocked the door of the shed. Inside were a few crates similar to the ones that the Filmores' man had loaded into the car.

"These'll have to come out, they need to be in front of the others," Dr. Vogel said, and then I was astonished to see her reaching in and hoisting out one of the large crates herself.

"Oh, here, let me help," I said. I grabbed another crate. It was very heavy, and I could see through the slats that it was filled with quart-size bottles. When we'd removed all four crates, Dr. Vogel opened her vanity case. In it were a bottle of glue and a stack of labels with the *Nettleton State Village* insignia on the top of each. On the labels, the doctor had handwritten: *Hygienic Alcohol* and then had stamped them with that day's date: November 13, 1927.

"Quick, unload the crates from the car, Mary," the doctor said. "We must hurry."

"Shall I see if Charlie is around to lend a hand; there are quite a few here."

"Did I ask you to find Charlie?" the doctor snapped.

"No ma'am," I said, sheepishly.

I opened the back door of the car and took hold of one of the large crates, which was also filled with bottles. I bent my legs at the knees for better leverage. Then with a little grunt, I hauled the crate out of the car with all my might. The crate, as it turned out, weighed very little. The bottles within it were empty, so my enormous effort to hoist it caused the crate to fly out of the car, out of my hands, and soar through the air. It landed with a horrible crash just inches from where the doctor knelt. The sound of all the broken bottles was bad, but worse was the realization that I'd almost killed Dr. Vogel.

"WHAT IN THE HELL ARE YOU DOING, MARY ENGLE?" Dr. Vogel shouted.

"Oh, I'm so very sorry, ma'am, I thought it was full, I . . ."

"Yes, well, don't stand there like a fool, quick, quick, clean it up. Throw all the broken pieces back into the crate. Now we'll have to account for those somehow. Well, put the crate back in the trunk and remove the rest, CAREFULLY! Good Lord."

It took almost two hours, but finally we'd affixed the Nettleton Village labels over each of the labels on the empty bottles. Every bottle in the crates I'd collected from Judge Filmore's residence had been empty. While we were doing this, the Filmores' hired man had pulled up in a pickup truck. He had with him a boy of about twelve, who appeared to be his son. He and the boy removed jugs from the back of the truck, and a small funnel, and wordlessly began filling the empty bottles with a dark liquid. When they'd filled each bottle in a case, they loaded it into the shed. Then they loaded the four original cases in the front and Dr. Vogel locked the shed. The man and the boy climbed back into the truck and drove off, having not said a word to me or the doctor. Dr. Vogel and I returned to the car.

As I steered us back to the main building, Dr. Vogel said, "I do apologize, Mary, for using such harsh language back there."

"Oh, no, I'm the one who's sorry, ma'am. It was my own foolishness."

"I just don't understand why you threw the crate at me—I moved in the nick of time—it just missed my head."

The idea that the doctor thought I had purposely hurled the crate at her head struck me as very funny, for some reason. It took an enormous effort not to laugh. "I certainly didn't mean to throw it, Dr. Vogel. I— I thought it was full, so I was just trying to lift it out. I thought it would be much heavier than it was, so, you know, I gave it my all."

I glanced at Dr. Vogel and saw that she was now amused, recalling the Keystone Kops–like mishap. When Dr. Vogel turned and caught my eye, we both burst out laughing.

"Now, my dear," Dr. Vogel said, dabbing at her eyes with her handkerchief, "I'm sure it goes without saying that this is confidential business."

"Yes, of course I won't say a word," I said.

But I'm no moron. I knew what was going on: my father moved whiskey; my uncle, the cop, was a bootlegger too. But what the doctor was doing wasn't really bootlegging. She wasn't *selling* alcohol. That would have been a felony. She was simply doing a favor. Obviously, Judge Filmore hadn't supplied Nettleton Village the whiskey that had been confiscated, as indicated in the newspaper; he still had it or perhaps he'd given it to friends. The many gallons of liquid we'd poured into the bottles had been odorless—it was probably colored water, but inspectors would only examine the cases in the front of the shed, which held real whiskey. Dr. Vogel probably did favors like this for other important people who were generous to Nettleton Village, as well. And what was wrong with doing favors for influential friends? It was a waste to throw out perfectly good Canadian whiskey. Anybody who read a newspaper knew that prohibition was going to end, probably sooner than later. What was wrong with breaking a law that was hardly even a law anymore?

"It's all completely aboveboard," Dr. Vogel continued. "It's just that sometimes we're sent confiscated alcohol for medicinal purposes. And the Board of Health stops in to inspect all our supplies—they want us to account for all shipments. The judge hadn't sent this new shipment yet. I don't mind helping out Judge Filmore. He'll send the real bottles along soon enough. We just need to show the inspectors something when they come snooping. You understand, dear."

"Of course," I said. I wanted her to stop. It was beneath the doctor to fib like this. It embarrassed me. "There's no need to explain."

I tried not to think about Jake's prejudices. He'd called Dr. Vogel corrupt. While whatever she and the judge were doing with the whiskey was probably not quite "aboveboard," it certainly wouldn't rise to the level of corruption. Dr. Vogel wouldn't involve herself in anything she shouldn't. Jake had never met her, and now I wondered if he'd ever met any people as powerful and influential as some of the people I'd met since I started working for Dr. Vogel. Judges, elected officials—people in power who did important work—certain rules don't apply to them; any intelligent person knows that. These officials were burdened with difficult tasks; they were responsible for the safekeeping and even the betterment of society. They had the means, financially and politically, to enact change and to improve this world, and they did. They were not average citizens. They were held to different standards.

Jake had his heart in the right place, of course, but he would never be in a position comparable to a judge or even Dr. Vogel. He could only observe and offer critiques of powerful people. He'd never had telephone conversations with senators and judges, as I did quite regularly, he'd never read their personal letters. I had. Why would I waste time worrying about his ill-informed ideas when I, at age eighteen, already knew more than he'd ever know about how power and justice really work in this world?

Eighteen

BERTIE and I trotted up the steps to church, arms linked, faces turned away from the wind. It was a frosty November morning. Everybody had gone inside except for a young altar boy who stood in his robes at the top of the stairs.

"Mrs. Nolan?" he said, his teeth chattering in the cold.

"Yes, dear?" Bertie replied, smiling at him.

"Father would like to talk to you and—are you Miss . . . um . . . Miss—"

"This is Miss Engle," Bertie said.

"Yeah, you're the one, Father wants to talk to you both after Mass—if you have the time—I guess."

Bertie shot me a quick glance and said, "Sure. Shall we just wait inside?"

"No, he said for you to go over to the parish house after Mass."

"Very well," said Bertie. We followed the boy into the warm, dark church, dipped our fingers into the holy water, and sidled into a pew near the back. After we knelt and prayed, we waited for the service to begin.

"What do you think he wants?" I whispered under the organ's solemn refrain.

"Father?" Bertie said. "I'll bet you anything he wants us to help with the Christmas decorations or something. Maybe organize a children's program."

"Oh no," I said.

"Everybody thinks women without husbands and children are desperate to toil away our lonely hours laboring for free," Bertie sighed.

"We can't say no, though, can we?" I asked.

"Probably not."

The organ music changed. The priest was approaching the altar. As we stood, Bertie whispered, "But he'll serve us lunch and I hear his cook is supposed to be very good."

Bertie had been right. Father wanted us to have lunch with him. I realized as he welcomed us into his house, that Father Doheny wasn't bad looking, for a priest. He seemed younger than I'd thought. His sermons could be as scolding as any other priest's, but away from the altar, he always had a smile and he was his usual jovial self as he showed us to the dining room.

We made small talk as the serving girl placed bowls of delicious-looking lamb stew before us. I thanked him for his sermon, though in truth, I hadn't paid much attention to it. I'd been trying to come up with excuses not to do any volunteer work for the church during my precious time off. Father waited until the server had left the room and then he said, "Girls, I have something rather delicate to discuss with you."

"Oh?" Bertie said. We looked at each other and then at the priest.

"Yes. Last week, I received a letter from a Sister at one of the Catholic orphanages in Scranton. "

I took a long sip of my water. That way, I didn't have to look at either of them.

"This nun," Father continued, "a Sister Beatrice, had received word from an employee at the Village about Catholic girls being denied religious services. Since you two are the only members of my parish employed at the Village, I thought you might know something about this."

I bit my lip and gave Bertie a quick glance. She had been about to say something but paused when she caught my look. She gave me a quizzical frown, but I turned my attention to my stew.

"Father, I'm . . . sorry," Bertie said, "I don't know any nuns in . . . Where did you say it was from?"

"Scranton. I believe the home was called Saint Catherine's," Father said.

I knew, without looking up, that they were both watching me.

I said quietly, "Father, I wrote the letter. Mother Beatrice is the head of Saint Catherine's Orphan Asylum. I grew up there. And, well, so did one of the inmates at the Village."

Bertie said, "Really, Mary? Oh, but yes, now I think I recall something you said once. . . ."

"I was sure you knew nothing about this, Mrs. Nolan," Father said. "I know you would have spoken to me about this immediately instead of reporting to a member of an outside parish."

"Yes," I said, offering the priest a weak smile. "Bertie had no idea I wrote the letter, Father."

I took another drink of water, aware that I was visibly trembling. Had Father spoken to Dr. Vogel about the letter? Vogel would have known instantly that I wrote it—she knew where I'd grown up. But he couldn't have. Vogel would have been enraged. I'd have been shown the door by now.

"I'm terribly sorry, Father," I continued. "I hope I can explain— Mother Beatrice was—well, almost like a real mother to me and all the girls. I didn't think of it as reporting on the goings-on at the Village or in this parish. I wanted to seek her guidance."

"Well? Who is this Catholic inmate?" he said.

"I don't know her well . . . ," I began, and offered him a brief, semi-truthful version of the story. I said that I'd recognized her soon after arriving here. Later, I'd happened upon the girl's file and noticed that there was no intelligence test in it. So I'd written to Mother Bea to see what she advised.

"But, my dear girl, why didn't you speak to Dr. Vogel about it immediately?" Father Doheny asked.

"I was afraid. I suppose . . . I was selfish, Father." I was too ashamed to look at Bertie, so I stared down at my plate. "I was afraid that I might lose my position here, as Dr. Vogel's secretary."

"But why did the Mother Superior think there were Catholic girls at the Village who were being denied services?" Father Doheny asked.

"I—I thought it would get her attention. I never dreamed she'd reach out to you, Father."

"So, you lied to her?" Father said. "Because Dr. Vogel certainly knows that she must inform me if there are any Catholic girls at the Village. There are no Catholic girls there now. We've had a few in the past, but I know of none residing there currently."

I looked at him now. "Father, the girl I knew, Lillian—she is

Catholic. I don't know about any others, but I was surprised that the label on her file claimed she was Protestant. That's why I wanted to contact Mother Bea. Because if they made that mistake, maybe it's also a mistake that she's at the Village."

Bertie interrupted me. "Father, we have a number of Irish, Italian, and German girls at the Village, so I do believe there are other Catholics amongst the inmates."

Father smiled at this and began spreading a thick layer of butter on one of the warm rolls. "I've no doubt you have Irish girls there. Orange Irish, that is. I've a friend from seminary who's the head of a parish in Belfast and the stories he's told me about some of the Protestant girls there . . ."

"But what about this girl Mary knows, Father?" Bertie persisted.

"Mary," Father said, after giving this some thought. "Didn't you say that your friend had married?"

"Yes?"

"Did she marry a Catholic boy?"

I was certain that Tom Henning wasn't Catholic. He lived not far from my aunt; he would have been in our parish. Now I was embarrassed that I hadn't thought of this. "No, Father. I don't believe he is."

"Well, there you are," Father said, now smiling at Bertie and me. "Since she married outside the faith, she's no longer Catholic. It seems that the girl's record is accurate. And that's why nobody has informed me about any Catholic girls at the Village. Surely this girl attends chapel there at the village on Sundays with the Presbyterian minister. I'll send word back to the Sister at once, Miss Engle."

"Thank you, Father," I said. "And I'm sorry to have troubled you with this. I shouldn't have written the letter. I've told nobody about the girl, Lillian. Not even Bertie knew. If I'd thought Mother Bea was going to involve you, I'd never have written to her."

"On the contrary, dear, I hope that in the future you'll bring anything concerning Catholic girls at the Village to me. I'll ask Aggie Vogel about the girl. If she'd like to return to the true Church and receive Communion, I can make the trip to the Village."

"Thank you, Father, but please, I'd rather you didn't mention this to Dr. Vogel," I said.

"But why not?" Father said. He leaned back so his chair was balanced on its hind legs and peered down at me with a stern expression.

"Because, as I said, I haven't told the doctor I know the girl," I blurted out, thoroughly ashamed. "I should have, of course, but now that some time has passed, it's awkward. There is a rule, I believe, about staff and inmates knowing one another from outside. I made a mistake in not telling Dr. Vogel. I see that now. But if you tell her now, I know she'll fire me . . . and I have no family to return to anymore. I know we're doing the work of the Lord at Nettleton Village and . . . and I would be very ashamed for the doctor to learn of my indiscretion."

Again, Bertie chimed in. "But, Father, I would like to add that I've had my own concerns about some of the girls there. I know I can speak to you in complete confidence and I now understand that I should have come to you with my concerns earlier as well. I do think some of the girls, while they might not have made the smartest choices . . ."

Father chortled something like, "I'll say," as he dove back into his stew.

"Some of the girls," Bertie pressed on, and I shot her a cautionary look. This was going nowhere. Why keep at it? But she persisted. "Father, some are there because they've been cruelly taken advantage of. I don't mean to be indelicate, but sometimes by men who are members of their own families, and I do believe some of those girls have normal minds."

"But then, why are they there?" Father asked, and now he could no longer hide his exasperation. He dabbed at his lips with his napkin and then leaned back so he could frown first at Bertie, then me. "I've read that there are hundreds on the waiting list at Nettleton Village. Surely, if normal girls who've been—exploited, in the dreadful ways you suggest, if these girls had a place to go where they'd be safe from evil men, they'd go to such a place, happily. I must say that I consider those Nettleton girls, if they are, as you say, not afflicted like the others, those *misused* girls are especially fortunate that they've been allowed to live in the sanctuary the Village provides them."

"Yes," I said with a tone of finality. "Of course you're right, Father."

Bertie gave me a defeated look and said, "Father, you're so kind to invite us to lunch and allow us to confess our misgivings to you in this way. Mary was recently lamenting the fact that we're unable to make confession, as we should, since the hours don't work for us. But now, we've confessed together and received your wise counsel. And, though we're not in the sanctity of the confessional booth, I wonder if you'll say a prayer for us, Father, as if we were, and offer us absolution."

The priest was only too happy to do so, and as I bowed my head in prayer, I smiled. Good old Bertie. If the priest had any thoughts of discussing any of this with Dr. Vogel, it was unlikely he'd do so now. Bertie had turned the discussion into a confession. Confessions between parishioners and priests were bound by a sacred trust. He wouldn't mention this discussion outside of the room. I was sure of it.

When we left, we still had hours before it was time to pick up Dr. Vogel. We went straight to the inn and sat in the tearoom. Though we'd just finished lunch, we ordered more coffee and biscuits from the server—Mrs. Malone—who was also the owner. She'd send us away if we ordered nothing on a Sunday afternoon.

When she was out of earshot, Bertie said, "Tell me everything."

It was a relief to finally reveal the truth to her. I confessed a little more to Bertie than I had to Jake. I admitted that Lillian and I were very close friends, by the time I left the home. I told her that Lillian always had a wild streak and that she'd talked me into swiping things and other mischief when we were young. I said I was worried that Lillian might tell Dr. Vogel about some of the things we'd done.

"Who would care about that? You were just a kid, Mary. So what if you stole marbles and gumdrops—that's what kids do."

If Bertie knew the things I'd done, would she even be able to look at me?

"I know you're right," I said, hoping Bertie wouldn't notice how anxious my face must look. "But this summer, when you described the conditions in the barns, I was so worried about her. Her name is Lillian. Did she ever come to the infirmary? She's pretty. Blond hair?"

"Of course!" Bertie smiled now. "Lillian from dance lessons! That's your friend? Mary, she's exactly the type I was trying to tell Father about. You don't need to be a psychiatrist to see that she's normal. In fact, she seems a lot smarter than a few of the hired dimwits who work with us."

"I'm afraid there's a little more to the story. I couldn't tell Father, Bert, it's a bit sordid."

I didn't mention Uncle Teddy, but I told Bertie about Lillian's baby and the musician who'd fathered her child. This, I knew, was the difference between me and Lillian. I was now a responsible adult who made intelligent choices. Lillian, on the other hand, had willfully consorted with a man she hardly knew.

"I've certainly got nothing against colored people, Bert," I added.

Bertie had just lit a cigarette and when she squinted at me through the smoke, it looked like she didn't really understand what I was trying to say. Or, she didn't believe me.

"I mean, she hardly knew the man," I continued. "They weren't even married. I believe it's against the law for them to marry, being of different races and all. So, you see why I'm worried, right, Bert? What if she got out and went back to working in bad places again? What if she carries on with other musicians and people she shouldn't? I mean, Dr. Vogel describes girls like Lillian all the time in her speeches."

Bertie glanced around the room, and then she leaned in close.

"Mary, Vogel says lots of things in her speeches—my aunt just sent me a clipping from a Philly paper," Bertie whispered. "It printed a speech Vogel gave there, filled with lies—describing some inmates as pitiful sex victims, others as dangerous criminals, and all with the reasoning skills of toddlers. You know she exaggerates to raise money. You know Lillian isn't dangerous, Mary. Why should she spend decades toiling on a work farm? That's what Nettleton Village is—since we're being honest, now, it's not much better than a prison. Twenty years is a sentence one gets for grand larceny or murder, not for having sexual relations outside of marriage. We have rights in this country. Even us gals."

"Yes, but there is . . . the baby. And I think it is fraudulent to tell a man that another man's baby is his. And unlawful, probably, right?"

Bertie slowly stubbed out her cigarette in the ashtray. An elderly couple were walking past the table. When they were out of earshot, Bertie said, "Come on, Mary—I know you're young, but you know what's what. You know what options a girl like Lillian has. She could have chosen to earn her living sweating on an assembly line or cleaning hotel bathrooms. But, from what little I've seen of her here, it's obvious that she's attractive and vivacious and you say she has musical gifts as well. I can see why she chose to work in that speakeasy instead of a sweatshop—even if it was a lower place than most. I might have done the same in her shoes."

I opened my purse and rummaged around in it so Bertie couldn't see my eyes welling up. I was hurt by the things Bertie was saying. Hurt and angry. She was insinuating that I was somehow cruel and unkind, when in fact, I'd had Lillian's best interest in mind all along.

"Why do you judge her so harshly, Mare?" Bertie reached over and tried to take my hand in hers.

I pulled away and said, "Why do *you* judge *me*? You don't know Lillian; I do. What else can I do? I stuck out my neck and wrote to Mother Beatrice, I'm lucky Father didn't call Vogel as soon as he received the letter. I'd be out on the street begging."

"I hardly think that would happen." Bertie said archly. "Dr. Vogel is too fond of you, she'll never loosen her hold on you—everybody knows that."

"What do you mean?" I demanded.

"I mean, I never see you anymore. Jake told me he hasn't seen you in weeks. You're too busy trotting around on Vogel's heels like her pet dogs."

I wasn't surprised some of the other employees had turned on me, but I hadn't expected this from Bertie.

"I didn't ask to live there," I said, leaning back and glaring angrily at her. "I'm just doing my damned job." Now her words were really sinking in and I hissed, "Did you compare me to her dogs? How dare you?"

"No, c'mon, kid," Bertie said, softening her tone. "Listen, I'm sorry, I just miss you. But this business with Lillian—you should have come to me. I would have told you not to write that letter. There's nothing any nun can do for her. Lillian's problem is that she's married to her own personal judge and jury. Her husband had her sent here. I saw this all the time at the state asylum—if the husband commits a woman, she's sunk, unless he'll take her back. Do you know somebody who might be able to talk him into saying he thinks she's normal? That it was a misunderstanding? They'll let her go back to him."

"He'd never do that, Bert. Lillian said he wanted to kill her when he saw the baby wasn't his."

"Has she no family at all? Aunts? Uncles."

"No, she was a foundling," I said. Then I added with a sardonic smile, "The Irish nun at the home used to say all foundlings are blessed with good luck, believe it or not."

"Oh, yer Sister Rosemary was it, now?" Bertie replied in a perfect Irish accent. Bertie's parents had grown up near Dublin; we'd had lots of laughs about Irish sayings and superstitions.

I responded with my own attempt at a brogue, "Sure, t'was she. When a baby is left, forgotten-like, the family's sins are forgotten too."

I went back to my normal speaking voice. "It was something like that. Just foolishness."

Mrs. Malone drifted past the table, glowering down at our near-empty teacups. She wanted us to order more or get lost. We took little pretend sips from the cups until she was out of earshot.

"Did you say Lillian was singing in that saloon where she worked?" Bertie asked.

"Yes, she's a lovely singer."

"I might have another idea," Bertie said. "I'm not sure if it'll work but it's less risky."

When I returned to my room that evening, I wrote a note. I wrote it on a small piece of paper—small enough that it could be handed to Myra in the dining hall, without anybody noticing.

Dear Lillian,

This Wednesday when they have dancing, come to the black door next to the terrace where I live now. 8:00. I have a plan.

> *Destroy this.*
> *Your friend, M*

Nineteen

WEDNESDAY arrived, cold and spitting rain. I was typing reports to the governing boards for Dr. Vogel, but my thoughts were on that evening. I worried about meeting Lillian at the doctor's mansion, and I now thoroughly regretted the plan. What could I have been thinking, inviting Lillian to Dr. Vogel's house?

Before I'd written the letter, I'd thought that perhaps we could meet in the woods again. But it was too cold, and now there was snow on the ground. Nobody was ever at the house on Wednesday nights when the doctor was away; it was the maids' night off. But what if Dr. Vogel came home a day early? No, she never did that. I had confirmed with Dr. Vogel's hostess in Pittsburgh that she would stay there until Thursday morning. It would be fine.

When I returned to the doctor's house after work, it was almost dark, though it was only five thirty. Claudette had told me that she'd leave chicken in the oven for me, and I decided I'd wait and share it with Lillian. I turned on the radio and sat at the table, trying to read, trying to keep from worrying. It grew dark, and I switched on a light above the table and looked at the clock. It was only six fifteen; the minutes were dragging.

Finally, when it was almost eight, I removed the chicken from the oven. It was in a heavy covered pot, and when I opened the lid, I saw that Claudette had made me some roasted beets, brussels sprouts, and potatoes. There was also a pie that she'd left out to cool on the counter. I placed two plates on a tray and filled the plates with the chicken and vegetables. I cut two pieces of pie and poured two tall glasses of milk. I carried the tray down the hall and placed it on the dressing table in my room. I'd decided that we should talk in my room. That way, if an employee should stop at the house for some reason or another, they wouldn't find Lillian sitting at the kitchen table. I knew that the residents were served a cold meal of cheese and bread in the evenings and thought it would be nice to surprise Lillian with a warm supper while I explained the plan.

At eight, I stood inside the kitchen door, listening. The rain was coming down hard now and the wind was whistling. Five minutes passed, then ten. Perhaps Lillian hadn't been able to get away. Then, suddenly, I heard it—three gentle knocks on the door. I opened it and saw Lillian standing there, soaked and shivering.

"Quick," I said. "Quick, inside."

Lillian was wearing a man's oversize work boots from the barn. I had her take them off and leave them by the door. She wore no coat, and her thin uniform dress was soaked through.

I led her to my room, and when we were inside, I closed the door.

Lillian gazed, wide-eyed, at the beautifully furnished room.

"I'm just staying here until they finish the employee's lodgings," I said.

"It's lovely, Mary. I've never seen such a beautiful room," Lillian said meekly.

"I have some warm supper for us. See? There on the table. But first, let me give you something dry to wear."

I removed a warm flannel dress from my wardrobe and handed it to Lillian.

"You can change in the bathroom, if you'd like, it's right here."

I opened the door to the bathroom, and Lillian shuffled in, shivering. She looked down at the gleaming white bathtub in wonder.

"Oh, would you like to have a warm bath, Lil?" I said. I'd heard that they still didn't have hot water in the wards.

"Really?" Lillian said. She now had tears in her eyes. "Can I really?"

"Yes. Why not? Here, I'll turn on the water. The water stays hot until the tub is full, can you imagine, Lil? I'll fill it up for you," I chattered on, trying to hide my shame and embarrassment at Lillian's diminished condition. "I have this lovely lavender bath powder too, Lillian. Here, I won't put in too much. Now you get in and soak and . . . and after your bath, we'll eat."

As I fiddled with the faucets, Lillian undressed. I added some more of the lavender powder that made the water all sudsy, and fussed a little with the spigots until the temperature was just right.

I'd seen Lillian undressed many times, of course, but we were just kids then. I thought Lillian might be self-conscious to be seen undressed, now. But, when I turned around, she was just standing there. She was far too thin. Her arms and throat were a mottled brown—like a farmer's skin, tanned like leather from months of working outdoors. But the rest of her—her breasts, the tops of her thighs—was very pale. Too pale. And she had bruises on her arms and legs and a long, recently scabbed-over scar on her shoulder. Her hair was dirty and limp, her fingernails jagged and filthy, her eyes red-rimmed.

"Here," I said briskly. "Lil, take my hand. I'll help you. Just step in. I know it's such a deep tub. I had trouble with it at first too."

When Lillian had settled herself into the tub, I turned to leave so that she could bathe in private, but Lillian said, "Mary, please. Stay with me. I'm afraid."

I said, with forced merriment, "Lillian Faust afraid? I never thought I'd hear that."

Lillian was pressing the palms of her hands against her eyes. Was she crying? "Please?" Lillian whispered. "Please don't leave me alone in here, Mary, dear."

"Sure, Lil," I said. "I'm right here."

I gave Lillian my warm robe and slippers to wear, then put the dinner tray on the bed, and we devoured everything, even most of the pie. When we were finished, we lay back on the bed together, moaning about our full bellies.

"Lillian, you know Mrs. Nolan, right?"

"Sure, the nurse. Oh this bed, Mary. These sheets . . . so soft."

"I know. Now listen, Lil, this is important."

Lillian rolled over onto her side so that we were face-to-face, and I told her that Bertie had organized a Christmas concert with some of the inmates at the request of Dr. Vogel. It would be performed for the trustees at their annual meeting in December. Lillian would sing a solo. Not "Jingle Bells," but "Ave Maria," in Latin. The way we sang the hymn in church at St. Cat's. An inmate as pretty and poised as Lillian singing in perfect Latin would almost certainly raise questions about her from the trustees.

"I want you to be prepared, Lil. I believe Dr. Vogel will want to question you after the concert is over—she's going to want to find out how you came to be here. You must tell her you were raped—that's how you came to have the child."

"No," Lillian said. "I won't say that."

"Listen to me, Lil! I know what happened. But tell her you were raped by a stranger, a violent black man. You never knew the name of the baby's father. See? That way you won't implicate Mr. Carr. I've given this a lot of thought."

"She's Rosemary," Lillian said, pressing her forehead against mine and peering into my eyes. "Don't say 'the baby.' She's my daughter. Her name is Rosemary."

"Yes, well, tell Dr. Vogel that you had Rosemary because you were raped but were afraid to admit that; you feared he'd come back and kill you. And maybe even Rosemary. Say that you lied to protect yourself and the baby. Dr. Vogel is nothing like old Hartley, Lillian. She's very kind and will be quite alarmed to learn that you weren't tested, I'm sure of that. But you must do exactly as I say. Do you promise?"

"Yes, yes, Mary. I will. That's what I'll say. Oh—this bed," Lillian sighed, stretching out across its length. "I'll bet you still pray, Mary Engle. I'll bet you say your prayers here every night, but you don't know that you're already in heaven."

"I do pray, Lil, I've been praying for you."

Lillian squeezed her eyes shut, but tears still leaked from the corners.

"What is it, Lil?" I whispered.

"I'm afraid to have hopes about seeing my Rosemary. I'm afraid I'll die if I'm disappointed again. I'll die if I don't see her, Mary. Do you know that she's two years old now? I wonder if somebody's adopted her."

"But that would be wonderful, wouldn't it? If a nice family adopted her?"

Now the tears really flowed.

"Let's focus on the concert, I think it'll work." I said, with forced gaiety. "You'll sing it in perfect Latin. We'll have the trustees as witnesses, I'll tell Dr. Vogel that I think I know you afterward. Just remember, we barely know each other."

Lillian smiled through her tears.

"I'm too afraid to think about it. I'm afraid to get my hopes up. Let's talk about something else. Tell me about your pop, Mary. Tell me some stories about your father, like you used to do."

"No, Lillian, I haven't any stories. I haven't seen him in years."

A strand of Lillian's damp hair was touching my cheek we were so close. Just like when we were little girls, huddled back then, on a rickety old cot in the ward.

"Tell me some of the old stories, then," Lillian whispered. "Please?"

I reminded Lillian of the time my father lifted an enormous tree that had fallen on one of the workers at the sawmill. He'd lifted it alone. "A man can suddenly have the strength of ten men in a situation like that," I said.

"Yes." Lillian smiled. "It's a miracle. What about the time he secretly left toys for the children whose parents died in the train accident?"

"He dressed up like Santa Claus. He found out the name of the uncle they were staying with. He spent almost a month's pay on their gifts. He didn't get me anything that year for Christmas. But I didn't mind," I whispered.

"No, because you could imagine how happy the children were." Lillian sighed.

"Yes, and I had a father."

"And they had nobody," Lillian whispered.

Lillian took my hand in hers. She kept wiping her eyes with the other hand. She was still teary, but she also smiled.

"Didn't you say he had a tailor who made his suits special? And that he always dressed up special for you on Sundays when you came?"

What was I doing telling silly tales like this? I wasn't a little girl anymore.

"Lillian, dear, I . . . I made up those stories. I made them all up. My father—he never did any of the things I said he did."

"I know," Lillian whispered.

I propped myself up on my elbow and frowned at Lillian.

"You know? What do you mean? Did you always know?"

"No, I believed you when we were kids. I was—I guess I was sort of in love with your pop, even though I'd never met him. I think I was in love with the idea of him. Isn't that funny?"

"Yeah," I said, lying back down again. "I guess I was in love with the idea of him too." We lay there, staring up at the ceiling.

"You were right about Henning's," Lillian whispered. "The place where I worked, it was a bad place, some real rough characters came and went. I heard stories. I had no idea how bad your uncle Ted Engle was, Mary. I knew he was a monster because of what he did to you, but I didn't know some other criminal stuff he and your pop were involved in."

"Lil," I whispered. "I know. Stop talking about them."

Lillian was quiet. I felt her breath against my neck. Then she said, "I'm only talking about it because you felt so guilty about the accident, with your uncle. I know you blamed yourself. You pushed me away after that. You never visited us after you moved to your aunt's. I know it was memories of that day—you thought you killed him, but it was an accident."

"Lillian, enough." Now I was becoming angry. "I said I don't want to talk about that."

"Okay."

But it was too late. I was back in Uncle Teddy's car with him. I no longer smelled Lillian's lavender-scented hair. I smelled his foul sweat, his rancid breath. That was the day he was so drunk he'd passed out with the cigar in his hand—the day I'd taken the six five-dollar bills from his pocket. I'd parked us on the dead-end road around the corner from St. Cat's, where he always dropped me off when we returned from the mill. He was passed out cold. I'd mussed up his shirt. I'd lit his cigar, hoping it would burn his pants. I was just about to get out of the car. I was just about to put the parking brake on when I had an idea. The road sloped, slightly, in the direction the car was facing. At the bottom was a shallow, muddy bog. I imagined Uncle Teddy waking up there hours later and trying to back the car out of that mess. I imagined his curses as he waded out of that swamp in the middle of the night. I put the car in gear, leaped from the driver's seat, and scampered behind a cluster of bushes, thrilled by my own devilry.

But Uncle Teddy must have been awakened by the car's sudden movement. I heard a strange bellow come from the car. I saw the vehicle swerve, sharply. He must have blindly grabbed the steering wheel from where he sat, slumped, on the passenger side. The car jerked to the left, instead of going straight down the sloped road into the mud. One of the front tires rolled up and over a boulder on the road's edge and rocked as if it might turn over. Instead, it righted itself and sped across a narrow strip of weeds, then disappeared down a very steep bank into a ravine on that side of the road. I didn't even know the ravine was there—it was behind a bunch of trees. After a horrible moment, I heard a crash. I heard the smashing of metal and glass. I scampered down the bank, down into the thick woods. I saw the car resting on its side at the bottom of the ravine. A tire still slowly turned, but I couldn't hear Uncle Teddy anymore.

Instead, I heard the shouts of men from the road above. I crept through the weeds and made it back to the home without anybody seeing me. Lillian found me in the old outhouse, hours later. She told me that Uncle had died in the wreck. She helped me clean off the mud. She stopped my tears. She told me that it was an accident, that I wouldn't burn in hell for eternity.

Within a few weeks, my father moved me in with my aunt. I stayed in touch with Marge and Dorothy, but whenever I thought of Lillian, I felt sick with shame, guilt, and, eventually, rage. After all, Lillian was the one who had encouraged me to get Uncle Teddy more liquored up before our rides. She was the one who made me "hustle" him and steal and eventually to cause his death. This is what I thought when I was twelve, and I hadn't allowed myself to reconsider this position until now.

Now it was time to be honest. Lillian had never forced me to do anything. She'd only helped make a nightmare—the rides with Uncle Teddy—more tolerable. She hadn't told me to pull the stunt with the car. I did that. I hadn't planned to kill him. And I was glad that he was dead. That was the truth.

I rolled back so I was facing her again. "I have to confess something to you, Lil. It was because I was so very afraid that I didn't help you sooner. I didn't admit it to myself, until now, but I know, deep down, I was afraid you'd tell Vogel that I murdered my own uncle."

"No, it was an accident—not murder."

"But it was that fear that prevented me from helping you sooner. I convinced myself that you belonged here, but deep down . . . I was afraid. I was afraid of you."

"I know. But enough now, Mary," Lillian said. "Let's not blame ourselves, there are worse people to blame. Now we're sisters again."

I was so tired. "Let's just rest for a few minutes, Lil," I said.

Lillian woke me just before dawn. We'd both dozed off. It was only luck that she happened to wake up while it was still dark.

After I showed her the path back to the "cottages," I hurried about the house, hiding all traces of her. I carried our empty plates back into the kitchen, washed and dried them, and placed them back in the cupboards. I scrubbed every inch of the tub. I made the bed. The bed where we'd nestled together under the covers, just like we'd done when we were little girls—like sisters. How my heart thrilled when I recalled it all now. I was filled with a sense of lightness. I didn't know how heavy my guilt—about my uncle, about Lillian—had weighed on me until now, when it was lifted. And it wasn't just guilt I'd felt toward Lillian; it was a dark, burning anger I'd developed toward her for being here, and causing these guilty feelings. What a relief I felt now. Lillian wasn't defective for helping me find a way to make my uncle's foul behavior less horrible. She just thought it would be a good idea to trick him. Because it would help me. Because he deserved it. And because she was smart.

Dr. Vogel had said that she'd be back in the office sometime Thursday morning, but it was almost three when she finally arrived. I had decided to work through lunch. I didn't think I could face seeing Lillian in her filthy barn gear today. I was famished and exhausted when Dr. Vogel finally arrived, but I managed to greet her with a smile. "Good afternoon, Dr. Vogel," I said, standing to take her coat and hat. "I was starting to worry."

Dr. Vogel said nothing. She just gave me a sad gaze.

"May I take those for you, ma'am?" I asked, still holding my arms out.

The doctor just shook her head. She gave me a strange look. Then she hung her own coat and hat on the coatrack next to my desk, turned, and walked into her office, closing the door behind her.

I glanced over at Gladys.

"Wonder who died?" she whispered.

I sat back down at my desk and placed another page in the type-writer.

The only other time I'd seen the doctor like this was when she learned about what had happened to Ida with the banker, Mr. Whit-comb. Was it possible that Vogel knew about Lillian coming to the house last night? No, that couldn't be it. If she knew, she'd certainly have fired me on the spot. Why, for all I knew, the doctor could have me arrested for allowing a patient into her house. There was no point in trying to read the doctor's mind. Perhaps somebody had died, as Gladys said. The thing to do now was to focus on my work. I had one last letter to type. As always, I read the letter carefully when I finished it. I found several errors. I was so tired and anxious that my mind had wandered. I'd mistyped words, forgotten a few commas and had even left out an entire sentence. I had to type the whole thing again. This time I paid closer attention.

After reading it one more time, just to be sure, I tapped on the doctor's door.

"Come in," Dr. Vogel said.

I found her seated at her desk, examining an accounting ledger. I gently closed the door behind me.

"I have all the typing that you left for me. The letter to the trustees is on top."

Dr. Vogel sat back, removed her eyeglasses, and gazed sadly up at me. I placed the pile of papers on the doctor's desk and then took a little step backward.

"Please sit down, Miss Engle," Dr. Vogel sighed. She had been call-ing me *Mary* for weeks. Now it was Miss Engle again? I sank into the chair across from the doctor's desk.

"Is there something I can do for you, ma'am?" I said after several long, quiet moments.

"Yes, there is something, as a matter of fact," the doctor said, her tone cool and measured. "I wish that you would be honest with me. I wish that you would stop deceiving me. I wish that you'd stop playing me for a fool."

I opened my mouth, but I had no words. It was true, then. The doctor knew about last night. Somebody must have seen Lillian leaving. It was hard to breathe.

"I'm afraid—I don't understand," I said. I looked down as I said it, so the doctor wouldn't be able to see the deceitfulness in my face. I had to come up with an explanation. There was nothing to do but tell the truth about Lillian and last night. "I suppose, you must be referring to my meeting . . . with . . ."

"Meeting? Is that what you call your little liaisons? *Meetings?* It sounds quite a bit more cozy than that, my dear," Dr. Vogel said, and my cheeks burned with shame.

"I can explain," I said. "It's certainly not what you might be imagining."

"Explain? How do you explain choosing to consort with a muckraker of the worst type? Your Jew lover—Jake Enright—is not just a second-rate yellow journalist; he's a known communist, an agitator, and an anarchist. But I'm sure you already know all this."

I felt as if the wind had been knocked out of me. I was relieved that Vogel seemed clueless about Lillian's visit, but the doctor seemed to think I'd been sexually intimate with Jake—that we were actual *lovers.* That I'd fully engaged in immoral sexual acts with him, outside of marriage, like a mental defective.

"I beg your pardon, ma'am, but I think you might have heard some false gossip."

"Oh?" Vogel said. "I suppose you've never heard of Mr. Enright, then?"

"No, I do know Mr. Enright. We've become friends. But we're certainly not lovers." Even saying the word *lovers* made my throat constrict with panic. For now the other words the doctor had used to describe Jake were penetrating. *Muckraker. Communist. Scum. Jew.*

"I haven't seen him in over a week. Before that it had been over a month. We had dinner . . ."

"At the Fulton Inn. Yes, I know. And you were seen dancing with him all summer long at that cheap roadhouse and driving all over the countryside in his convertible."

"Oh, that wasn't his convertible," I said.

There had been a weekend in a convertible, yes, but it wasn't Jake's. At night, how divine it had been, there in his arms, under the stars.

"Excuse me?"

"I beg your pardon, Dr. Vogel, I just—well, that wasn't his convertible."

Your skin is so soft, he'd whispered in my ear. *So very soft, it's like touching air.* His hand was on the inside of my thigh, I remember feeling like I was floating amidst the stars above.

"He'd borrowed the convertible. From a friend," I said quietly. I needed to focus now.

"*Ah!* Well, then," the doctor said, with a sickly sweet smile. "That does put my mind at ease. It wasn't *his* convertible. That changes everything. Your Mr. Enright has engaged in organizing illegal demonstrations at the steel plant, he's published lies about the officers of the company, including my own brother-in-law, who's a partner there, and now he's publishing lies you've told him about Nettleton Village and about me. But he doesn't drive his own convertible. Miss Engle, that positively makes my heart soar."

I had no words.

"Dr. Vogel," I finally managed, "please believe me. I didn't know any of this about Mr. Enright. I know he's a journalist. I did know that he was writing about the steel plant, but I didn't know anything else. I didn't know that your family has any connection to the plant. But even if I had known, he almost never discussed the strike with me. And of course, I'd never talk to him about you."

Dr. Vogel walked around her desk and stood in front of me. I stared down at my shoes. They were fawn-colored pumps that I'd recently bought and still loved to admire. The ankle straps were fastened on each side with clever little pearl-white buttons. I'd bought them because they reminded me of a darling pair the doctor sometimes wore. Today, she wore very chic, but businesslike, navy calfskin oxfords.

"Look at me. Look at me, Mary," Dr. Vogel said.

Of course, the navy shoes are much more sensible for work, I thought, raising my eyes slowly. They perfectly matched her crisp linen skirt and silk blouse.

The doctor took my chin, gently, in her hand and tilted my face toward her. She was trying to draw me in with her gaze.

"Don't lie to me, child," she said softly.

My chin had been grabbed and shaken by nuns, my ears pinched and twisted. I'd been swatted, slapped, spanked, and strapped, many times, like all the children at the orphan asylum. But somehow, the way the doctor so gently cupped my chin in her palm, despite her rightful anger, hurt me more.

"I'm sorry, Dr. Vogel," I whispered.

The doctor gave my cheek a tender stroke as she released me. She turned to her desk and grabbed a newspaper. For a fleeting moment, I thought she might try a different tack by rolling it up and batting me on the head with it. I would have preferred that to her sad disappointment. But Dr. Vogel began reading, and now the anger was returning to her voice:

"'Habeas corpus motions were filed last year for three young women currently imprisoned,'" Vogel paused here to repeat the word for me: "*Imprisoned!* Did you hear that?" She turned back to the paper and continued. "'Currently *imprisoned* at Nettleton State Village. The mother of one girl, Miss Edna Schmidt from Shamokin, testified that Superintendent Vogel had told people that her daughter would never be released, as she was one of the best milkers in the dairy. Judge George Filmore presided over all three cases. Witnesses included family members and friends of the inmates as well as doctors and administrators from Nettleton State Village. In each case, Judge Filmore determined that the girl was, indeed feebleminded and would remain at the village for the duration of her childbearing years.'"

The doctor paused and seemed to be silently reading, then she said, "Oh, here we are—'Judge Filmore, a member of the asylum's board of trustees since its inception, did not recuse himself, as the girls' lawyers had requested. Though he asserted that the court had no conflict of interest in this case, recent reports cast that into question. Last month, Judge Filmore supplied the hospital with large quantities of confiscated Canadian whiskey at a bargain price, to be used for "medicinal" purposes.'"

The doctor folded the paper and tossed it onto her desk. "The word *medicinal* was in quotes."

Now Vogel leveled a very cold gaze at me. "So? What do you have to say?"

"I . . . I didn't know about the three girls," I answered truthfully. "The trials—were last year? Dr. Vogel, of course you know I wasn't here then. And this is the first I've heard of these court cases, so I certainly didn't say anything to Mr. Enright about that."

"Oh, don't be coy with me. I'm talking about these accusations about Judge Filmore and the medicinal alcohol." Vogel was almost whispering now. "You're the only person here who knows about that. Even Hartley doesn't know."

Now I realized why she was so hurt and angry and I leaned in so I could quietly reply. "Oh my goodness. Oh no, Dr. Vogel. I understand how you might think I said something to Mr. Enright, but I'm telling you the truth, ma'am. I never said a word about anything like that to him."

I *was* telling the truth, so it was easy to look the doctor sincerely in the eye now. I continued, "It seems—isn't what he reported quite similar to the other article last month from the Scranton paper?"

"No, it's not similar at all," the doctor said, turning to look out her window. "This story links Judge Filmore to the idiotic hearings last year and the recent medical whiskey supply. And it's written by your Jacob Enright. Again, Miss Engle, I don't like being taken for a fool."

"Dr. Vogel," I said, "I had no idea that your family is in any way connected to the steel mill. And Mr. Enright is certainly not my—my lover. I made his acquaintance when I first moved here and knew very few people. We're friends, that's all. I don't know him . . . that well, I certainly wouldn't *confide* in him."

I was glad the doctor was looking away when I started in with these whoppers. Jake and I wrote each other daily. I'd been lovesick over him from the day we first met. Bertie, Hal, and Betty Goodwin knew that. What if Vogel asked them? It was slowly dawning on me how stupid I'd been about Jake. He'd written a scathing article about my employer, without telling me. What a betrayal. How dare he?

It was true that I hadn't told him about Judge Filmore and the confiscated whiskey. And I didn't know anything about the court cases of the girls who'd tried to leave. But I'd told him something even more incriminating—that at least one inmate, Lillian, was not feebleminded and had been sentenced to Nettleton anyway.

Of course he planned to publish that, I realized, panic seizing me. He'd been back in New York all these weeks, yet suddenly decided to write a critical story about Nettleton Village for the local paper out here? Would the story about Lillian be next?

The doctor sank back into her chair and sadly studied the newspaper again. She had the same forlorn and confused expression she'd had the day we'd gone to confront the lecherous banker, Mr. Whitcomb, about Ida.

I was sick with guilt. How could I have been so naive about Jake? How could I have told him about Lillian? It wasn't Dr. Vogel's fault that Lillian had been sent here, but now I knew that there had been rumors of other girls who might be normal and unlawfully confined here. Dr. Vogel couldn't be expected to know everything about the hundreds of girls here. But, if word got out about Lillian, Dr. Vogel would be blamed. Dr. Vogel had taken me into her home and treated me more as a guest there than an employee. Dr. Vogel told me she felt a motherly affection toward me; she'd trusted me; she'd confided in me. And how had I repaid her? I'd blabbed about something that Hal and Bertie had warned me to keep to myself, something that could potentially cause the doctor serious harm.

I rushed to her side and knelt next to her chair. "Dr. Vogel," I said, and my voice broke. "Oh, please—I'm so very sorry, Dr. Vogel." I buried my face in my hands, so she couldn't see my tears. "I was stupid to become friends with somebody I know so little about. I'm sorry. I'll never forgive myself for my foolishness."

"Oh, Mary," the doctor said, in a soothing tone. I felt her cool hand on my head. She was stroking my hair. I pressed my cheek against the doctor's knee.

"I hope you do believe me. I didn't tell him about the judge or anything like that. But you're right, I should never have trusted him."

"Mary," Dr. Vogel said. "You're young, my dear. But you must grow up now. You must behave like an adult and be mindful always, with whom you choose to associate."

"I know," I said shakily. "And I will." I stood now, and turned away, wiping the tears away with my handkerchief.

"Now, my dear. Let's call it a day. I've my bridge group tonight. Why don't we go home?"

All I wanted to do was crawl into bed when we returned to the house. I was sleep-deprived and anxious. But it was Thursday night—bridge night at Dr. Vogel's. Her first guest, Mrs. Schultz, arrived moments after we did.

"Mary," the doctor said, "do be a dear and entertain Mrs. Schultz while I run upstairs and change."

"Oh now, Agnes," Mrs. Schultz said, "I don't need to be entertained! But, Mary, I just received a letter from my Sally, I look forward to introducing you two when she's home for the holidays. Oh, those Vassar girls—I'm afraid she's fallen in with a rather fast set."

"No, I'm sure that's not true," I said, following Mrs. Schultz into the living room and trying to appear interested in her usual account of her daughter's many dances and many friends and how they snuck off to New York to visit jazz clubs and how lucky Ruth was that she was so pretty, as her grades were just too appalling.

"Oh?" I said, between hidden yawns. And "Is that so?" And "Imagine that."

Soon, another guest, Miss Cloutman, joined us in the living room. "Who's our fourth tonight?" Miss Cloutman asked.

"I'm not sure," Mrs. Schultz said. "I saw Ruth Whitcomb this morning, she won't be here, she and James have tickets to the theater tonight. Oh, Mary, in case I forget. She wanted me to tell Agnes how well the new girl is working out. Do remind me, will you, dear?"

"Certainly," I said. I was about to offer them drinks when her words sunk in. It sounded like she'd said Whitcomb. Mr. Whitcomb was the name of the banker Vogel had confronted.

"I'm sorry, Mrs. Schultz," I said. "Who has a new girl?"

"The Whitcombs. They've had terrible luck with the last couple of girls who've worked for them, I've always had great girls come to me from Agnes. But now they've a new Village girl and she's been very well-behaved, not sullen like the last. Oh, there you are, Agnes! I was just saying, Ruth and James are very pleased with the new girl you sent them."

"So glad," Dr. Vogel said, as she swept into the room. "Now, shall we eat, I'm famished."

"I beg your pardon," I said, my eyes fixed on the doctor. "Mrs. Schultz, do you mean Mr. Whitcomb, the bank manager?"

"Yes," said Mrs. Schultz. "Well, I believe he's actually the president there at the Merchant's Bank."

"The veal!" Dr. Vogel said gaily. "It's going to get cold. Ladies?"

The others headed for the dining room, but I remained sitting, as still as a statue, there on the long velvet sofa. I gazed wordlessly up at the doctor.

"Mary?" Vogel said. Usually, I joined the bridge ladies for supper.

"I'm afraid . . . I'm not feeling well, Doctor," I managed to say. "Will you excuse me?"

"But, my dear, aren't you hungry?" Dr. Vogel asked, and I saw a fleeting look in her eye, an expression I'd never observed on her before. It was fear, but there was something else. She was angry. She maintained her pleasant smile, and I maintained mine.

"I'm truly sorry, Dr. Vogel," I said finally, "but I've the most frightful headache." I was amazed at the steadiness of my voice and my calm demeanor.

"Very well, dear," said the doctor. "Good night."

In my room, I curled up on my bed and tried to avoid any thoughts of Jake or Lillian. To think that, just a few short hours ago, I'd mentally aligned myself against both of them. To think that I'd sobbed like a little baby and begged Dr. Vogel to forgive me.

Dr. Vogel.

She'd sent another girl to live at the home of the foul Mr. Whitcomb. I couldn't imagine what might be happening to the girl, perhaps at that very moment.

If Dr. Vogel would do a thing like that, she was capable of anything. The girls who'd been sent from Muncy prison, and other girls like Lillian, girls with bad luck who'd made bad choices. Docile girls, not all of them feebleminded—she was capable of arranging to have them falsely imprisoned here.

I should have said something right there, in front of the others. They needed to know.

"You're the same coward you always were," Lillian had said that night we met in the woods.

"Better a coward for a minute than dead for the rest of your life," Sister Rosemary used to say. We thought it was funny. *Dead for the rest of your life*—it made no sense. But apparently, I'd absorbed the meaning behind them and made them into my credo. I always believed that heroics were best left to fools and saints.

That was another Sister Rosemary saying.

Part Four

Twenty

WHEN we reached the steps of the church that Sunday, I said to Bertie, "I'm not going in, I'll meet you later."

"What?" Bertie said. "Where are you going?"

I just shrugged. Bertie giggled and nudged me. "On Sunday—how perfectly sinful, I'll say a prayer for you and Jake, but I can't promise anything."

"I'll see you at the car at seven."

"The car? All day? You really are a wicked thing!" Bertie laughed.

"Shhhh!" I said. I ducked to hide my face behind my hat's brim and scurried around the corner. I walked several blocks, then turned into a cluttered alley behind the butcher shop. The rank odor of meat and blood was everywhere, making me gag. I ducked behind a small shed next to the butcher's and startled a pair of rats who disappeared under its rotting foundation. When I finally heard a car approach, I no longer cared who saw me, I ran out to the road.

"Well, good morning, my dear!" Jake said, stopping the car next to me. He started to get out, but I said, "No, stay in the car!"

I opened my own door and dove inside. "Go, go, go!" I said, keeping my head down below window-level. "Drive back the way you came, don't go through town."

"Okay, lovely to see you too, darling." Jake laughed. He pulled the steering wheel into a full rotation, then stepped on the gas. "What's the urgent matter that you referred to so cryptically in your telegram?"

An hour later we were parked on the side of an abandoned dirt road. I was facing Jake, my arms crossed angrily, my back pressed against the door.

"I don't know what else to say but I'm sorry," Jake said. "I guess I should have told you about the article, but I didn't even know if they were going to run the thing. Ike Brown—he's the editor at that stupid local rag—he asked me to write something as a favor. They're short-staffed, and I guess news has been a little slow in this little corner of paradise."

"You never mentioned this *Ike Brown* to me before."

"I'm sure I must have," Jake said.

"No."

"Huh . . . Well, maybe it never came up. I got to know him when we were covering the strike. He knew I was interested in Nettleton Village."

"How? How did he know that?" I demanded.

"Because I told him. You know I'm curious about the place; I've asked you about it many times."

It was true. He often asked me about the Village.

"I guess I thought you were interested in it because I worked there," I said. "Silly me."

"Come on, that was part of it, Mary. But Ike sent me some clippings about the trials last year. He told me that there had been other attempts in previous years—families trying to get girls out. I assumed you didn't know about them—they happened before you moved here. I didn't want to put you in an awkward position by mentioning it to you. That way, you wouldn't have to lie if Vogel asked you about it."

He cocked his head and gave me that charming smile of his, but I wasn't having it.

"So, that's, you know, one of the reasons I didn't tell you," he said, losing the smile.

What a fool I'd been. What a fool he must have thought me, all this time. I wanted to cry, but I carried on in an attempt at a business-like tone: "You must have known it would be bad for me, Jake. Plenty of local people have seen us together. You put me in a very bad spot. I could have been fired. You should have told me you were going to publish the story. I would have told you not to."

"And that's the other reason I didn't tell you," he said, and now he actually had the nerve to laugh and try to give my cheek a little playful pinch.

I was speechless. I pushed him away and stared at him. Then I said,

"What else are you going to write about my job without telling me? Have you already told your pal Ike about Lillian and me? Does he know what a hateful monster you think I am for not helping her?"

Jake lost his smile. "My dear, are you nuts? I would never tell him about that. I'd never write about anything personal, or repeat a word that you've told me in confidence, how could you think I would?"

"Because you've been dishonest from the start, Jake. Why didn't you tell me Dr. Vogel's brother-in-law is one of the owners of the plant? All those weeks you were here and you never told me that."

"There aren't any Vogels associated with the plant as far as I know. I've seen the list of partners, that's public information. I would have noticed if the name Vogel was on there."

I knew that Vogel only had one sister, Elizabeth Vogel Miles.

"Is there a Mr. Miles?" I asked.

"Sure, Stephen Miles. His father started the plant."

"That's Vogel's sister's husband," I said.

"I didn't know that. Darling," he said, looking pleadingly into my eyes, "I would have told you if I knew there was that kind of connection, you have to believe me."

"I don't believe you because you also didn't tell me you knew about the business with Judge Filmore. That's what really got me in hot water because I'm the only one at Nettleton who knows about that, and so of course she thought I told you."

"Knows about what?"

"About the confiscated whiskey and the judge."

"What about it?" Jake said.

"Well, you're the one who wrote the damn thing," I said. "You know about the liquor, everybody knows. It was in the paper last month."

"You just said you're the only one who knows about it."

"I'm the only one who knows how they manage the paperwork and everything." I saw a fleeting, hungry look in his eye, and I realized my blunder.

"Go on!" he said.

"Nothing. Let's go," I said.

"I've heard that the Village goes through all those barrels of whiskey at an astounding rate," Jake said. "And a lot of people wonder why a home for feebleminded and delinquent girls needs any medicinal alcohol. It's not a surgical hospital, after all. And why does a hospital need cases of French champagne?"

"I have no idea, I couldn't possibly be less interested in any of that," I said with a bored shrug.

"Mary, listen," Jake said. Now he wasn't trying to humor me with apologies, he had a serious, urgent tone. "I didn't think you knew anything about the liquor. Which, obviously—you do." He glanced up at the rearview mirror and said, "Who knows you're with me?"

"Just Bertie."

"Okay. Good. Listen, this is serious, Mary. Do you realize how dangerous it would be if we're seen together?"

"Yes, of course. That's why I didn't want to be seen in your car. I'll be fired and I can't leave Nettleton, not yet, anyway."

"Mary, if the doctor and judge are dealing black-market hooch in the quantities I've heard, they're in with some very dangerous people. It wouldn't just be a matter of firing you, they'd need to keep you quiet. They risk jail time—or their necks, if their middlemen are implicated."

"*Black market? Middlemen?*" I scoffed, thinking of Dr. Vogel's polished silver serving trays and the framed portraits of her regal-looking mother and grandparents, posing in front of their Newport summer "cottage." Florence served whiskey sours to the dear bridge ladies and other guests when they arrived and champagne with dinner—always in etched crystal glasses that Dr. Vogel had inherited from her grandmother.

"You've got it all wrong, Jake," I said. "There's nothing like that going on. She just serves it to her friends. Maybe she does a few favors for people who help her raise money for the Village, like the judge. She knows you and I know each other, and I'm still breathing."

"I don't think you're safe staying on there, Mary."

"Anyway, I've said what I came to say. Drop me off where you picked me up, nobody will see us. I'll get lunch with Bertie. You're making a big deal out of nothing."

Now Jake placed his hands on my shoulders. "Mary, look at me. Listen, now. I think you should come with me. Get Bertie or somebody to send you your things."

"Have you lost your mind?" I laughed—it was so preposterous. "Go with you? Where?"

"To New York."

"But I haven't any place to stay. I have very little money saved. I'm not paid well—you know that."

"You'll stay with me."

I stopped laughing. "Oh. I'll stay with you, will I?"

Jake had been looking over his shoulder, squinting back down the deserted road, but now he turned back to me and he looked quite pale.

"Yes, I know—we'll have to get married and—*we will*! We can get married tomorrow." Jake grinned nervously then—he seemed to have astonished himself as much as me with those words. He awkwardly put his arm around my shoulder. He pulled me close, but his embrace felt rough and tense.

"Listen," he continued. "I was gonna tell you anyway. Things are going really well for me at the paper, Mary. I got a little promotion after the Sacco and Vanzetti items I wrote. I'm getting better assignments."

"Why, that's wonderful, Jake," I said, my eyes searching his.

"So, what I'm saying is, I've had a feeling . . . a feeling from the very first . . ." He paused. "Did you see that?"

He was now craning his neck to peer at the deserted road ahead. I saw nothing, but I wasn't really focused. I was slowly digesting the words he'd just spoken. He'd said we would marry. Now he was saying he'd had a feeling from the start. I thought I was the only one who'd felt such a strong sense we were meant to be together. He felt that way too. He loved me too. He'd just asked me to marry him. I was trembling, but I clutched his hand.

"Let's get out of here, I thought I saw something," Jake said. "I'm sure I'm overreacting, but . . . just to be on the safe side."

I gazed out my window as he turned the car around.

Mrs. Jacob Enright. I'd practiced writing it many times. I'd practiced making my married signature seem effortless and it had been, as our surnames were so similar. His was more attractive, of course—*Enright!* So much nicer than Engle.

Mrs. Jacob Enright. It put things in perspective. Someday, I would tell our children about this and it would be a romantic story. Yes, I met your father while working at a hospital. When they were older, I'd tell them about what the place was really like. Maybe even that Lillian—"Aunt Lil"—had once been wrongfully sent there. I scooted over so I could rest my head on Jake's shoulder.

When we were back on the main road, he said, "Now, where were we?"

"You'd mentioned New York," I said.

"Yes! Right. Let's go now."

"Jake, be serious, I can't go now," I said, giving his shoulder a playful nudge.

"I know you still feel loyalty to your boss, especially after what you wrote me about her college offer—I get how you might feel a sort of daughterly affection . . ."

"What?" I pulled away from him. "Affection? For Vogel?"

Jake looked at me.

"I loathe her, Jake. I see her for who she is now."

"Oh yeah?" Jake gave me an astonished grin. "But, then, why go back?"

"I have to get Lillian out." I realized that I hadn't even told Jake about our plan; I'd just hinted about it in a letter.

"Bertie and I, we think we can reveal to the board that Lillian is intelligent without exposing either of us. That way, when I do leave—I'll have to stay on here for a few weeks at least, just to avoid any suspicion that I had anything to do with her escape. But when I do leave, I'll tell Vogel I've been offered an exciting position in New York City. She'll write me a letter of recommendation and that'll help me. I was thinking of moving to New York anyway, but, Jake, are you serious about us starting a life together—in New York?"

"Of course I'm serious, darling. Now listen, this is what you have to do—take the records. Especially the records of the whiskey. But also, the residents' intelligence tests and the wages paid for the girls who're sent out to work as servants. All of it—take the carbon copies if they exist. We have to expose Vogel. You said you hate her—this is the right thing to do. I knew this was big. I've known from the very first that I had to write about Nettleton."

Now he gave a scornful laugh. "Nettleton State Village for Feebleminded Women. *Of Childbearing Age!* I almost forgot that part. The longest name of any establishment I've ever heard of. It made me suspicious from the get-go, Mare. There's starting to be more public doubt about eugenics practices, here and in Europe. Exposés are the thing now, but nobody's written a story about one of the delinquent girl asylums— a work farm like Nettleton Village, where girls are sent—no judge, no jury. Now it's mine to tell."

"Jake, no," I said, my heart racing at the thought. "You must never write or speak another word about it, to anybody."

"Not now," he said, looking away from me with a nervous little laugh. "Of course, not while you're there. I mean later, when you and Lillian are out." He glanced at me. "You know—when we're in New York. We'll get married right away. Later, I'll write something that won't just be read in New York. This is a story for *The Atlantic*. I've always known this would be the story that would make me."

"Oh, I see," I said softly, after I'd had a moment to absorb the fact that this was what he'd always known. It was about the story, not any kind of real love for me.

I remembered that feeling I had when my father came for me at St. Cat's. "Which one of you is called Mary?" he'd asked, looking at me and then at the others, draining my heart dry with his lost, vacant smile.

But I was a child then. I wasn't a child anymore.

Earlier that week, when I'd learned that Dr. Vogel—*dear* Dr. Vogel—had sent another innocent girl to the foul Mr. Whitcomb's, I stopped being a child, finally. I grew up in that moment and saw, not a concerned and caring mother figure, not an idealized role model. I saw the real Dr. Vogel—duplicitous, scheming, and cruel. Now, it appeared that I was finally able to see the real Jake.

"So that's what you were talking about when you said *It was meant to be*, you knew it was meant to be—from the beginning," I said, staring dully out at the road ahead. It surprised me that I didn't feel terribly sad. I didn't feel much of anything. I guess you become less emotional when you finally "wise up," as Uncle Teddy used to say. I realized that until Dr. Vogel finally lifted the veil of my ignorance, I'd had a childishly obscured view of things. I saw the world *as through a glass darkly*—a line from the Bible, I'd always thought poetic.

Now I saw the world as it really was, a place better understood by scientists than priests. I lived on a planet, one of many in the universe. It was inhabited by organisms that passed genetic qualities from generation to generation. God, angels, one's divine destiny—these were fantastical ideas that were conjured by men long before evolutionary science was understood. They were like Sister Rosemary's stories of luck and fairies; they were meant to frighten or entice us, but they weren't real. My heart was just an organ. It had nothing to do with love; it couldn't be crushed by feelings.

I turned back to Jake and said, with a little laugh, because it was funny when you thought about it, "You meant, you knew Nettleton Village would be a great story from the time we met?"

Jake gave a laughing whoop and smacked the steering wheel. "You said it, my sweet Mary!"

I laughed too, and scooched back closer to him, He pulled me tight and kissed my head, and soon I was overcome with giggles. I'd thought he'd meant he knew *he and I* were meant to be. It was really so comical, now that I thought about it. It was like the haplessly crossed wires of communication that happened between people in funny movies.

"Yes, let's do get married, Jake! Won't that be a hoot?" I said, thinking: why not behave as if we were in one of those movies. It really *was* funny how confused I'd been. I was nearly choking with laughter at my earlier foolishness. Yes, why not get married, just for convenience's sake? It would be fun to be married.

Jake was still driving quite fast, but he kept glancing over at me because now I was giggling so hard I had tears streaming from my eyes. "Mary?" he said. "You okay?"

"Of course," I cried gaily. I bit my lip and swung my thigh over his. Then I began kissing his neck, very tenderly, and as I did, I hiked my skirt up just enough so he could glimpse the top of my stocking, just where you could see a bit of my skin there, just below my garter.

The car swerved into the other lane, then back into our own. There was no danger. It was a gray winter Sunday, the road had been deserted for miles. I swung my other leg over, so both of my thighs were draped across his. Now the car swerved right off the road, and came to a jolting, bucking stop. I climbed over so I was straddling his lap and we kissed.

We kissed for a long time. He pulled away, once or twice to glance ahead and then, nervously, up at his rearview mirror.

"Nobody's out here," I whispered breathlessly. I pulled my sweater off over my head, and when I lowered the bra straps down over my shoulders, he stared at my breasts, and stammered, "But darling, what . . . what if . . . somebody drives by?"

"Don't worry so much," I whispered, touching my lips to his ear. "It's an old country road. Besides, the windows . . . they're all fogged now, aren't they?"

A few seconds later, when I began working the buttons on his trousers, he said, breathing heavily, "But . . . are you sure? I haven't any protection or anything. . . . Aren't you afraid?"

"I'm not afraid," I breathed into his ear. "No, I'm not in the least afraid, Jake, no."

It was my first time. Uncle Teddy's "cuddles" always happened through our clothes. I was a child then. But I wasn't a child anymore. This was another thing entirely. As we moved and swayed, Jake looked into my eyes. He was looking at *me,* I gently cradled his face in my hands and kissed his forehead and cheeks and lips.

I thought: this is what they call *passion* in novels.

I thought: this is what the nuns warned us would happen if we "lost control" when we were with boys.

Jake murmured, "I love you, Mary," into my ear, into my breasts, and throat, again and again, and I realized that I hadn't lost control. It was the first time in my life I'd ever felt fully in control. I was a little weepy, because it turned out I wasn't numb after all, and it hurts a little, feeling love and so many other things all at once. It hurts and it feels good too.

I whispered, "I know you do, Jake, I love you, too, my dearest. I love you. I do, Jake. I do."

I felt him deep inside me, I felt him deep inside my heart, and I thought: the heart isn't just an organ and the world isn't just what we see and if love is more than just an idea, the same might be true for God and luck and angels too.

Twenty-One

THERE were eleven members of the Nettleton State Village Board of Trustees, who met on Monday, December 12, 1927. They included several out-of-staters as well as a few illustrious locals such as Judge Filmore and Mr. David Langdon, the current president of Berneston College. I had all necessary documents typed and proofread well in advance, and when everybody had assembled, Dr. Vogel called the meeting to order. I was seated at a little desk to take the minutes of the meeting.

After a short welcoming address, Vogel turned the meeting over to Mr. Alan Hotchkiss, a local attorney who was the president of the board. They approved the doctor's budget for the coming year and reviewed some proposals for construction of a new building.

As I typed away, I thought, happily, *Lillian and I will never see that new building. I'll be Mrs. Enright then. Lillian will be free, finally.*

The next item on the agenda was a proposal for improvements in the four dormitories.

"Those buildings aren't very old, Aggie," Mr. Hotchkiss said. "What needs to be improved?"

"The windows," Dr. Vogel said. "All of them."

"What's wrong with the windows?" asked Mr. Weston, the district's state senator. "Didn't we have Buchman and Sons do all the windows? I'm the one who urged you to give them the contract. I'll have their necks."

"It's not the glass," said Dr. Vogel. "I'm sure you all read about the mischief last spring—attempts by a few of the girls to run off for some fun. We need to replace all the metalwork and latches that secure the windows."

"Oh, I didn't like the recent article about the hearings, Aggie," said Mrs. Reed, the senator's wife. "I thought that business was behind us, but the reporter was repeating the rumors about the girls being normal. And the way he besmirched our Judge Filmore's good name!"

Filmore interjected with a bemused chuckle, "My dear Mrs. Reed, I don't let that sort of thing bother me. It's the nature of my position." Now he took on a more serious expression and said, "But, Agnes, I am concerned about the continued problem of the girls getting out of the buildings. How do they manage it? I know they have limited mental facilities, but it always seems to require some planning that makes one wonder about their mental defects."

Dr. Vogel removed her glasses and sat back in her chair. "I'm glad you brought that up, Your Honor. It's something I address in my talks to social workers and others. When people think of the feebleminded, they usually call to mind a Mongolian idiot. As you know, only a small percentage of the girls here are idiots of that type. Surely, you've seen the girls during your visits—you know that many appear to be quite normal. Most of our girls have the minds of girls between the ages of six and ten. Think of your own girls at age ten, or girls you might know. They may sound intelligent, but their knowledge is, of course, quite limited. And many of our girls are surprisingly clever in their own, very limited way. Nature has a wonderful way of helping all creatures compensate for deficiencies. The blind, for example, often have much better hearing than the sighted. Similarly, some of the girls at Nettleton were born with an elevated sense of cunning."

"How interesting. I've never had it explained to me that way, it makes perfect sense, doesn't it?" Mrs. Howell said. There were many utterances of agreement and wonder from around the table.

I typed away, thinking, *Mrs. Jacob Engle.*

"Yes," said Dr. Vogel. "Many of our girls are highly adept at deceit." She paused to look at me then, jolting me out of my dreamy state.

"The highly manipulative nature of the girls is something we must always bear in mind, here at Nettleton." She seemed to keep her gaze on me a moment too long, before turning back to the others.

It was just my imagination. She wanted to make sure that my full attention was on what I was typing. After our awkward exchange about Ida the previous week, neither of us mentioned it again. In fact, the doctor had praised my efficiency in preparing for this day.

The trustees were served lunch in the dining hall with the residents. Dr. Vogel had arranged that the dairy girls be served sandwiches in the barn, and only the quietest and most presentable girls were there. The rest would eat after the officers had adjourned to the conference room.

When we finished lunch, Dr. Vogel announced, "We've prepared a special holiday presentation for you this year—a choral recital."

Bertie led the chorus into the dining hall. I couldn't look at Lillian. I straightened the papers in front of me as the singers began with "The Holly and the Ivy" and proceeded with three other carols.

Elsie, the savant, wore a pretty velvet frock. Her hair was swept back into a braid that had a red satin ribbon tied into a bow at the end. She was making her guttural little sounds, her little MMMMMMM . . . MMMMMM sounds. She seemed to find the braid and the ribbon quite distracting. She moved her head from side to side so that the ribbon hit her left cheek, then her right cheek and then her left again. Her jaw hung open, and she stared ahead stupidly.

"Friends, allow me to introduce our Miss Elsie," Dr. Vogel announced to the group.

I saw that although several of them smiled indulgently, they seemed uniformly unnerved by Elsie's odd behavior.

"Miss Elsie came to us from a very sad family situation," Dr. Vogel explained. "As you can see, she's a profound idiot. She's unable to talk and functions as a two-year-old in most aspects except for one. After she came to us, we discovered that she has an aptitude for music. She's gifted, as a matter of fact. So we've worked with her, training her to use this gift, and now, I'm proud to present the results of our efforts."

I watched Bertie's expression as Dr. Vogel gave this little introductory speech. Everybody at Nettleton knew that Elsie had learned the piano before she came to the Village. If anything, she had been kept away from the piano, not encouraged to play it. But Bertie smiled kindly at the trustees, revealing no surprise at the doctor's words. Sophie tried to lead Elsie to the piano, but the girl seemed to be overwhelmed by all the people in the room, and she balked. She tried to pull her arm away from Sophie, but Sophie gave it a sharp tug.

Bertie sat at the piano and played the first chords of "Parade of the Wooden Soldiers." This got Elsie's attention. She dragged Sophie to the piano, sat down on the bench, and nudged Bertie aside. She played, at first, with the technical precision of any accomplished pianist. But then she added wonderful flourishes that were so cleverly done that several of the board members gasped with delight. Dr. Vogel had rolled the typed pages of the meeting's agenda into a sort of paper baton, and she used it to merrily tap out the rhythm on her open palm. Up and down the keys Elsie's fingers flew; one barely noticed that her head lolled from side to side in such an odd manner. Dr. Vogel glanced, with pride, at the smiling trustees who were seated around her.

When Elsie finished that song, she started playing one of the ragtime melodies that she loved so much, but Sophie gave her arm a quick jerk and said, "Ice cream, Elsie dear!"

Thrilled by this bribe, Elsie stood. The trustees applauded, but Elsie was oblivious to their enthusiasm. Ice cream. That was all that poor Elsie could think of now.

"And to conclude our program, I trust you will enjoy a solo from our very own . . ." Dr. Vogel glanced down at her notes. "Miss Lillian!"

Bertie sat back at the piano, and Lillian stepped forward. She looked extraordinarily beautiful. She wore the same plain blue dress that the other residents wore, but she'd tied the belt lower on her hips so that it looked like it had the dropped waist that was in fashion. Her blond, wavy hair, which she usually kept hidden beneath that old cap, was washed and combed and framed her face perfectly.

Bertie played the opening bars and Lillian began her solo.

"'Ave Maria. Gratia plena,'" she began.

I was afraid that she'd be too nervous to sing well, but her smooth, soulful voice filled the room, and my arms were suddenly covered with goose bumps.

"'Benedicta tu in mulieribus. Et bendictus,'" Lillian sang, gazing at each of the trustees in turn. She smiled, slightly, but her eyes were brimming with tears.

My heart soared. There! That's exactly what I'd wanted the trustees to witness. Lillian was not just a gifted vocalist; she could sing in Latin. And she had such an understanding of the context of the lyrics that she was moved to tears. She was not a mental defective—anybody could see that. I looked at the row of trustees seated next to me and saw that they were quite moved. It was hard to make out what Dr. Vogel was think-ing. She gazed coolly at Lillian, neither smiling nor frowning.

At the end of the song, Lillian did a little curtsy and the trustees clapped with great enthusiasm. "Brava!" said one. And then they all repeated, "Brava!"

"Thank you, Mrs. Nolan. Thank you, girls!" Dr. Vogel said. "Now, my friends, if you'll follow me . . ."

Bertie led the girls toward the door. As the group passed, one of the trustees, Mrs. Howell, stood and touched Lillian's sleeve.

"My dear," she said, "what a lovely singing voice you have."

"Thank you ever so much," said Lillian with a pleasant smile. I could see the trustees were quite curious about her.

"I'm afraid we must get back to business," Dr. Vogel said. "Ladies? Gentlemen? Shall we adjourn to the meeting room?"

"Just a moment, Aggie, if you don't mind," said Mrs. Howell, "You've done us such a kindness, arranging this musical program. I'd like to ask this fine soloist how long it took her to memorize the Latin lyrics."

"I learned Latin in school when I was quite young," Lillian said, again with an easy eloquence. "How very kind of you to—"

"She was raised in a Catholic orphanage, I believe," Dr. Vogel in-terrupted. "Their religious services are in Latin—all the children mem-orize the phrases."

Bertie was now urging the other girls to proceed to the door, but Lillian remained standing in front of Mrs. Howell.

"She seems to have such an extraordinary command of the words, though," Mrs. Howell continued, but now she spoke to Dr. Vogel as if Lillian weren't there. "It's so surprising from one of the girls here at the Village."

"She has no grasp of the meaning," Dr. Vogel said again, as if Lillian were not a few feet away. "They're like parrots. They can repeat words and phrases beautifully, but there is not the understanding that you or I . . ."

"I beg your pardon, ma'am," Lillian said. "But I read and write Latin with a full understanding of the language."

"Lillian, come, it's time to go," Bertie said. The show was over; it was time to move on. Dr. Vogel was arranging papers on the table before her with a rigid smile.

"Of course, Schubert wrote the song in German," Dr. Vogel said, with a clipped, scoffing laugh. "That's the true version. Well, back to business, I'm afraid."

"Ich spreche Deutsch," Lillian said. Now she addressed Mrs. Howell directly. "I'm fluent in German, ma'am. I received a good education. I know Latin; I'm not a mental defective. Please—do believe me . . . you must."

"MRS. NOLAN!" Dr. Vogel shouted.

Bertie, realizing Lillian's emotional state, tried to take her by the arm, but Lillian twisted away from her grasp and clutched Mrs. Howell's hands in her own. She sank to her knees before her and said, "I can sing the Schubert lyrics as they were written. Ich kann die Schubert text singen!"

"Goodness *gracious*," said Mrs. Howell, whipping her hands away from Lillian and clutching them near her heart. She stared down at Lillian in horror.

"GET HER OUT!" shouted Dr. Vogel. But Lillian began a frantic, off-key a cappella rendition of the song in German, still kneeling in supplication. "'Ave Maria! Jungfrau mild. Erhore einer jungfrau flehen. Aus diesem felsen starr unn wild . . .'"

Dr. Vogel said, through gritted teeth, "Mrs. Nolan, we've a great deal of work to do, Miss Lillian has become too excited. Please take her to the infirmary and see that she is cared for."

"Of course," said Bertie. The other girls had already left, and now Miss Hartley was at Bertie's side. The two women forced Lillian to her feet and hustled her toward the door.

"I'M NOT DEFECTIVE," Lillian screamed. "YOU ARE. YOU ALL ARE!"

No, Lillian, I thought. *No, this isn't the way.*

Dr. Vogel said to the group, with a chuckle, "She's not acting like a defective, is she?"

I tried to catch Lillian's eye. I wanted to get her to stop, but Lillian was focused on Dr. Vogel. "I don't belong here and you know it. I'm normal. I've a normal mind, I'm not the only one—we're NOT IDIOTS—get your hands OFF me, you BITCHES!"

Bertie and Miss Hartley managed to push Lillian through the door with them. Lillian's muffled screams could be heard for several seconds, and then they stopped.

"Good Lord," said Mr. Hotchkiss, after a moment of astonished silence from the entire group.

"Yes, I'm so sorry you had to see that," said Dr. Vogel, "but that's a perfect example of the dangerous type I was describing earlier. This patient appears normal, almost superior, but in fact, her brain is profoundly afflicted. She memorized phrases in foreign languages in order to con people. She's worked in a brothel and has a violent criminal record. Lillian has had at least three illegitimate children, if I recall correctly."

"How absolutely dreadful," said one of the trustees.

Liar, I thought.

"She touched me," said Mrs. Howell, staring down at her hands as if they'd touched a leper. "Did you say she's violent?"

"Yes, you saw for yourself. You saw her aggressive tendencies. But I wouldn't have allowed her to harm you. Her children are wards of the state now. Much more severely afflicted than the mother, I'm afraid, and now the state must pay the price," said Dr. Vogel. "Shall we return to the board room?"

Dr. Vogel had arranged a formal dinner for the members of the board at her house. Claudette and Florence had spent days preparing for it. I wasn't included in the dinner. I was to remain at the office and clear up the conference room after the meetings were over. I did so, hastily, then dashed off to the infirmary to see Lillian.

It had been hours since the disastrous concert. Horrible hours of wondering what to do. I was certain that Miss Hartley had sedated Lillian, then bound her to a bed in the infirmary. Bertie had told me they were required to do this with unruly inmates—she hated the practice. I wondered if Lillian had, in her hysterical or drugged state, told Miss Hartley about collaborating with us. When I got to the infirmary, I found Wilma, the alternate nurse, seated at the front desk.

"Hi, Mary," Wilma said, glancing up from the book she was reading.

I just nodded and ran past her into the sick room to see Lillian. There was nobody in the sick room. There was nobody in the lavatory.

I returned to Wilma's desk and said, "Where is she?"

"Bertie? Where do you think? She's upstairs. Her shift ended an hour ago."

"No, I mean the patient. Didn't you have a patient here? Lillian?"

"Not since I got here." Wilma glanced down at clipboard on the desk. "Nope, nobody in here all day."

I ran upstairs. Bertie had a suitcase on her bed and was tearfully throwing her belongings into it.

"What are you doing? Where's Lillian?" I asked.

"Oh, Mary," Bertie said, and we hugged. Bertie closed the door and pulled me next to her on the bed.

"Where's is she?" I repeated. "I thought Vogel said to sedate her. I thought she'd be here."

"She's in Building Five. That's where Hartley sent her, Mary. Lillian was slapping and kicking us; she was wild. Hartley knocked her in the head with her baton and sort of stunned her. Then, two attendants came over from Building Five. You know—it's where they isolate the women in little rooms, Mary. Not a very nice place. I've had it here. I'm going home."

"But what about Lillian?" I said.

"I'm sorry, Mary, but what can we do now? Nothing. You can't tell Vogel you know her after that spectacle. She'll know we set up that whole charade. I think we should both skedaddle. Come to Philly with me."

Bertie continued shoving blouses and skirts into her suitcase.

"Bertie, stop. You can't go. What about Lillian?" I repeated. "What about me?"

Bertie offered me a sad smile. "I'm sorry about Lillian, kid, I know it's rough. But we tried to help her. You should be proud of that. Come with me to Philly. My folks will let you stay with us until you find work."

"No," I said. "We can still help Lil. I need to send a wire to Jake. There's nobody in the office, I can call it in from there." I started for the door and stopped. "You've been to Harrisburg—where can you get a coffee near the train?"

The Western Union clerk made no effort to hide his annoyance as

I spelled out the telegram. I used the code that Jake and I had devised. "X-U-J-H-Q-W stop," I whispered into the office phone.

Urgent, was what Jake would decode.

I continued whispering, letter by letter, in code, what, I hoped, only he would understand: *Meet me Harrisburg Sunday. 12. I have papers. Diner 2 blocks E of station.*

I did a last-minute tidying up before turning off the office lights. When I returned to the doctor's house, the trustees were still in the dining room and, from the sound of it, having a very merry time. Peals of laughter rose above the chatter every few seconds. I attempted to sneak down the hall to my bedroom but Florence was carrying a tray back to the kitchen and stopped me.

"The doctor said to send you in to them when you get home," she said, nodding toward the dining room.

"I don't want to interrupt—it sounds like they're having such a nice time," I said, trying to ease past her.

"Mary. She said the minute you walk in the door."

"Thanks, Florence," I said.

In the dining room, the guests were seated around the long table. It had been set with all the doctor's finest linens, silver, and china. Claudette was circling the table, pouring "Daddy's" wine into the crystal goblets. Mr. Hotchkiss was the first to notice me when I wandered, shyly, into the room. He stood, and then the others looked my way, the men also rising from their chairs.

"Oh, please," I said. "Don't get up."

"There she is! Come, dear," Dr. Vogel said, waving gaily. She was seated at the head of the table and beckoned me to her side. I sidled next to her, and the doctor reached out and held my hand.

"We were just talking about you, dear," Dr. Vogel said.

"Oh?"

"Yes," said Mrs. Howell. "We were saying what a wonderful job you did organizing everything."

"Thank you, but really, it was nothing," I said. "Just part of my job."

Mr. Langdon, the college president, said, "I told Aggie that I'd like to steal you. We desperately need you in the administration office at Berneston."

"David, I warned you!" Vogel laughed. She gave my hand a little squeeze. "Anyway, you'll soon be seeing enough of our Miss Engle. I think we should tell her now, don't you?"

The guests all voiced their agreement. They were beaming up at me. Dr. Vogel still held my hand in hers, and I felt like little Harry, when he held his mother's hand. And, like Harry, I wanted to shrink behind Dr. Vogel where I could safely peek out at the group from there, but of course I didn't. I just stood there, grinning stupidly.

Mr. Langdon stood and reached into his vest pocket. "Here it is." He removed a pair of spectacles from the same pocket, placed them on his nose, and began:

"'My dear Miss Engle: We, the governing board of Berneston College, are pleased to invite you to join our current freshman class. We hope that you will agree to enroll in the winter semester, which begins on January 10, 1928. We will work with your employer, Dr. Agnes Vogel, to arrange a schedule that allows for you to retain your position at Nettleton Village while attending classes here at Berneston. We look forward to your affirmative response, as we anticipate that you will be a treasured member of the Berneston community. Signed . . .'"

Mr. Langdon peered over his spectacles at me and gave me a benevolent smile.

"Yours truly."

I'd never been comfortable in front of a group, and now to have this incredible offer, tonight. And all this attention focused on me. I thought my buckling knees might give out altogether and I had to lean against the back of Dr. Vogel's chair to steady myself.

"I just—I don't know what to say," I finally stammered.

"I'm sure a thank-you will suffice, my dear," Dr. Vogel said with a kind laugh.

"Yes, of course, thank you so very much, Mr. Langdon. And you too, Dr. Vogel."

Langdon handed me the letter, with an overly ceremonious bow that made several guests applaud. I clutched it to my side. I didn't want to look at it. I didn't want the others to see my hand trembling.

"Have Florence bring in another chair, dear, join us for dessert," said Dr. Vogel.

I looked at the faces around the table. All the smiling faces. All the trust and kindness aimed at me as Florence made her way around the table refilling wineglasses again. The judge, the college president, the governor's wife, the business owners—these were educated people. Good people. They couldn't all be corrupt. They believed in Dr. Vogel.

"Thank you, no," I said, after an awkward moment. "I'm so sorry, but I'm quite exhausted. If you don't mind, I think I'll head off to bed. Will you all excuse me?"

As I slipped out of the room, I heard snippets of the chatter around the table.

"She's so diligent—tomorrow's a workday after all."

And "Did you hear Aggie say she might hire another girl so Miss Engle may enroll full-time?"

"She's receiving a full scholarship, what an opportunity—she hasn't parents, from what I understand."

"I think Aggie has come to see her as more of a daughter than a secretary."

I sat on my bed and smoothed the piece of stationery flat on my lap. It had the lovely Berneston insignia embossed across the top, and I moved my fingertips lightly along the raised letters. There was Mr. Langdon's bold signature in glossy ink on the bottom.

"We are pleased to invite you . . ." it read. They hoped I'd accept their invitation. They believed I would be "treasured" in their community.

The main road from Nettleton passed the tall gates that led to the college, and I always craned my neck to have a look when passing by in a car or bus. You could see the top floors of the library from the front gates. You could see the huge, domed planetarium on the hill at the far end of the large campus. I hadn't been in the planetarium, but I knew it held telescopes so powerful you could see other worlds. You could see stars and planets that most people had never heard of. Most people in this world—they'd live and eventually die and never even know these heavenly galaxies and so many other wondrous things even existed.

Twenty-Two

VERY early the next morning, I unlocked the main door to the office building. Then, fumbling along in the semidarkness, I unlocked Vogel's office. It was at least an hour before dawn. I had a lot to do before the others arrived.

Inside the doctor's office, I closed her shades, turned on her small desk lamp and removed a large ring of keys from the top desk drawer. I knew where everything was. I'd followed the doctor into the office on the day of the whiskey caper, and she had me place the box with the false medicine labels in a tall locked closet next to the filing cabinets. I knew there were other boxes and folders in there as well. Now I quickly tried each key until I found the correct one and opened the closet door.

There it all was. The box of labels and thick folders filled with yellow carbon copies of receipts. Dr. Vogel had carefully recorded each shipment of "medicinal alcohol" that had been received here at the Village. There were hundreds—they dated back to 1920. Unfortunately, there was just the one yellow duplicate sheet of paper for each delivery; the originals had obviously been sent to government authorities. If I removed them it would be obvious the minute the doctor opened the closet. The fat files filled with yellow paper would be empty.

But Dr. Vogel had me type almost everything in duplicate. When I typed a letter, I rolled three pages into the typewriter cartridge: the original, the grey carbon paper, and the slightly yellow page on the bottom. The original type would be transferred via the carbon ink onto the yellow page. Most of the office files were filled with documents on yellow pages. I just needed similar-looking invoices to replace the liquor invoices and I knew just where to find them.

I stuffed the whiskey receipts into a book satchel I'd brought with me. I replaced them with dairy receipts. The dairy receipts were so numerous, nobody would notice that some were missing. They bore the same Nettleton State Village insignia. They looked the same, unless you took the time to read them. If Vogel opened her closet, she'd still see the fat folders filled with copies of receipts. Only if she took the time to review them would she see that the whiskey and wine had turned into milk and butter. I'd be long gone before a new batch of whiskey arrived. She had no reason to check those files until then.

Pale golden stripes appeared on the wall of the doctor's office, faint at first, and then brighter. It was the early rays of sun seeping in through the slats in the doctor's blinds. I stashed the book satchel under my desk in the hall. I often brought a book to read at my desk while I ate lunch; nobody would think that strange.

I looked at the clock. It was only half past seven. There was still time. Dr. Vogel kept a file of all the inmates who were out on work "parole"—girls who worked as live-in servants, laundresses, and cooks for Dr. Vogel's friends. Dr. Vogel billed their employers for their wages. I typed those invoices for her. I gave the checks to Miss Hartley when they arrived.

I opened the file drawer holding the records of the work parole girls. I knew there were currently six, because I typed their invoices and received the checks for their salaries. But what about the new girl who'd been sent to the banker's home? And now that I thought about it, why had I never seen Ida's file?

But there were only the six girls I was familiar with. I pulled out one file. The index card was on it with the girl's name and description:

HARRIET STORRS.
American. Protestant. Moron.

She was working as a laundress at the home of a Clayburg family. Inside her file was a sheet of paper with the heading: COMPENSA-TION RECEIVED. Beneath that was a list of weekly dates with $6.00 next to each. The doctor was open about the fact that the girls weren't directly paid the wages they'd earned. Their wages helped compensate the state for the cost of keeping them here. But where were the files of the others?

I heard footsteps in the corridor. They were getting closer. I shoved the file back into its folder, slammed the cabinet shut and nudged the doctor's door all the way open with the toe of my shoe. When Miss Hartley appeared in the doorway, a second later, I was carefully arranging papers on the doctor's desk.

"Miss Engle?" Miss Hartley said. "My goodness, I thought I was early." She frowned up at the wall clock, then at me.

I said wearily, "I woke up too early and couldn't get back to sleep. We've a busy week ahead of us, so I came in."

I turned my attention to a vase of fresh flowers on the doctor's desk. They were long-stemmed white roses. I pulled a few that were fading, then carefully rearranged the others. Miss Hartley disappeared into her office. I buried my face in the fragrant petals, closed my eyes and inhaled.

That Saturday, I used the phone in the booth at the back of the inn's dining room. I asked the operator to reverse the transatlantic charges. I'd wired ahead, so Graham answered immediately.

"Hello my friend," he said.

"Oh, hello," I said.

We didn't use names. We exchanged quick pleasantries about the weather. Then I said, "Your cousin's trip to New York, it's all arranged."

"On the date you mentioned?" The connection wasn't great, but I could hear that he had a soft but somewhat raspy voice, and I wondered if that came from playing the trumpet.

"Yes. My brother, Jake, he'll drive her there. He has the money you wired. He found a room for her in a lady's hotel. He says it's nice."

"Good. My sister and her husband. They've decided they will adopt the new baby. Please tell my cousin, I know she'll be happy for them."

"Oh, how wonderful," I said.

I heard a faint siren from his end; it was different than the sirens our police cars used: it had a fast, high-low sound that quickly faded away and then was gone. I wondered where he was just then. Was he gazing out a window from his flat in Montmartre? Was he looking out over the rooftops of Paris below? Maybe he was in a phone booth outside a café filled with his friends—fellow musicians, artists, and writers too. Expats, Europeans, black, brown, and white people, all together in a gay French bistro, imagine a place like that. They'd all be dressed to the nines and having drinks, I realized; it was evening there. It would be warm inside, and the women would wear long strands of beads and fur stoles . . .

"My dear?" Graham said. "Did you hear me?"

"I'm sorry," I said. "What did you say?"

"Just that the baby will be home with them soon."

"Oh, yes," I said. "I'll tell her."

Graham began speaking in French, as we'd planned, just in case any nosy local switchboard operators were on. He spoke slowly so I could jot down notes.

Oui, I said, when he paused, *Très bien*, I said.

Later, back in the house, I used an old French-English dictionary the doctor kept in her library.

We arrive NYC the last week of December, booked at Savoy New Year's Eve, and the week following. Please tell her how much I love her, how very happy we'll be when we're together again.

The next day, Bertie and I dropped the doctor at her mother's house, parked the car, and took an early train from Clayburg to Harrisburg. We met Jake at a diner near the train station, to go over everything one last time.

"It has to be on a Wednesday—maids' night off, correct?" Jake asked, after we'd ordered our lunch.

"Yes," I said. "And it has to be this coming Wednesday, Jake. She's been in Building Five for over a week now. It's . . . well . . . you tell him, Bert."

"It's where they put girls who misbehave. I've actually never been inside, but I've had girls sent to me after a few weeks in there. They're not in great shape when they come out. They're locked in small rooms with no furniture, but somehow they manage to break their own fingers and toes. A girl came out missing her front teeth . . . once . . ." Her voice trailed off, and she looked sadly down at her hands on her lap.

I couldn't look at Jake; I felt too ashamed, but I managed to say,

"But . . . it isn't often girls are sent there, right, Bert? And usually, they're disturbed girls. Violent girls. Not girls like Lillian."

"I don't know. . . . I never asked," Bertie said softly. "I'm not proud to admit that. I'm not proud that I looked away. I can't wait to leave that place."

"Let's focus on Wednesday, Bert," Jake said, giving her shoulder a gentle squeeze. "You're confident you'll be able to get her out of the building without anybody seeing you, Mary?"

"Yes, there's a series of underground tunnels," I said. "I've only been in one short passageway, but I found the blueprints in Vogel's office. It's like a maze. I've memorized it. There are mechanical supply rooms down there, a big coal room, a furnace room—there's even a morgue."

"Yeah, I've been in the morgue," Bertie said, taking a sip of tea.

"You have?" I said.

Bertie seemed to have burned her tongue. She set the cup back on its saucer and mumbled, "Mmmm-hmmm."

"Did one of the inmates die since you've been there, Bert?" Jake asked.

"No, not since I've been there, no, let's proceed," Bertie said. "So you'll be able to get her down to the tunnel from Building Five, Mary?"

"All the dormitories have stairs to the tunnels," I said. "I plan to hide the clothes for her trip someplace down there. Nice things. Warm things."

"If the furnace is down there, somebody has to feed it. They might see the clothes," Jake said.

"Take her to the morgue, Mary," said Bertie. "There's no reason for anybody to go in there unless somebody dies. There's a big sink and running water there. She'll need to clean up a little. She can change there. Leave her stuff. I'll go later and grab her old things. I'll toss them in the furnace."

"I'll take back roads until we're out of the county," Jake said, frowning at a map he'd spread out on the table.

I turned to Bertie and whispered, "When were you down there in the morgue?"

"Ida. The . . . still baby." Bertie mouthed the words so Jake wouldn't

hear. She snatched her purse from the seat between us and shakily removed a packet of cigarettes.

But once we got to the part about meeting Jake at the back road to
the mill, we were all giddy with excitement. I would give Dr. Vogel a
Mickey Finn with her wine—knockout juice, there was plenty kept in
the infirmary. Then, when she was sleeping soundly, I'd sneak Lillian
out in the back of the doctor's car, telling Pop Durkin that I was running an important errand. Jake would be waiting at the mill, which was
closed after eight. He'd drive Lillian to New York. Christmas was on
Sunday that year (I'll never forget that Christmas fell on a Sunday in
1927). On Saturday morning, Christmas Eve, Bertie and I would take
the train to Manhattan, and we'd celebrate with Jake and Lillian.

"It's a good plan," Jake said, grinning broadly. "It's a damned good
plan."

"I'll have to leave you all on Christmas morning—I'm going to
Philly to be with my family," Bertie told us.

"Are you coming back Monday night, Bert?" I asked. I planned to
return to the Village on the Monday afternoon after Christmas, since
we were given the day off for the holiday.

"No. I'm not coming back at all."

"Bertie," I cried. "We talked about this. We can't leave right after
Lillian escapes—it looks too suspicious. Plus, you'll never get a letter of
recommendation if you just don't return to work."

"We'll see," Bertie said.

Jake said, "I doubt either of you need worry about recommenda-
tions, once Mary and I carry out our scheme. Speaking of which—don't
you have something for me, Mary?"

I'd almost forgotten. Bertie had asked me on the train why I'd
swapped out my usual purse for a large canvas carryall, and I'd said
that I had some Christmas presents for Jake. Now I opened the bag and
removed stacks of paper that I'd bound with string. I placed them face-
down on the table.

"What? What's all that?" Bertie asked.

"You didn't tell Bert?" Jake said, grabbing the pages and flipping
through them. Bertie leaned across the table and looked at them with
Jake, while I glanced anxiously around.

"It's all there," I said. "Put them away." Jake tucked them into his battered attaché case.

"You got everything?" Jake asked.

"Everything and more," I said.

"Oh, Mary!" Bertie said. "Those receipts! When did you do all this?"

"I've been going to the office early each morning. Vogel told me she thinks I'm angling for a big Christmas bonus." I smiled at Jake and said, "Somebody is going to write a very interesting story, once we get Lillian out safely."

"*Ooooh*, Jake! Do you think Vogel will go to prison?" Bertie said.

"Of course not. She's too well connected," I said.

"We'll see who's loyal to her once the Feds get involved," Jake said. "Are you sure the liquor inventory's in here?"

"Yes," I said. "Everything's there. But not a word, Jake, you promised. You can't mention it to anyone until after Bertie and I leave."

"Where will you live, Mary, once you leave?" Bertie asked.

"My dear, what's with you?" Jake said. "You didn't tell Bertie about that either? We're getting married, Bert!"

Bertie let out a cry of delight and hugged me. Jake and I both tried to hush her—everybody in the diner was looking at us.

"How perfectly wonderful," Bertie said, dabbing at her eyes. "And I take full credit. I introduced you kids after all! So—when's the wedding?"

A waitress stopped at the table to refill our coffee cups. When she left, I said, "We're not really planning a traditional wedding. Too expensive. We'll just go to city hall—you know."

"I found us an apartment downtown, Bert," Jake said, taking my hand in his and kissing it. "It's a small place, but the building has a lot of character. We'll have a little wedding luncheon. Bert, you'll come!"

"You keep describing this place as having a lot of character, Jake," I said. "It's making me nervous."

"It's no palace." Jake laughed. "Some might describe it as a sort of—tenement building."

"Oh, how perfectly charming." I pulled my hand away so I could take a sip of my coffee.

"It's just for now," he said. "It's just until I get another promotion. Once that happens, and you get a good office job, we'll find a nicer place."

A good office job.

Where would I find a position like the one I currently held? Luxurious living quarters, paid tuition at a top private university, and the potential to someday be the head of a large institution? Nowhere. With luck, I'd find a boring old secretarial job. But where, in a big city like New York, would I find a position that promised real opportunities for women? A job where a girl like me could be promoted to the top someday?

Nowhere.

I placed my cup back in its saucer and gazed sadly down at it. Would Jake ever understand how much I was giving up? I could have helped Lillian escape, as we planned, and still have gone on to Berneston University. It was unlikely my involvement with her escape would be discovered if I hadn't stolen all the records for Jake. I could have gone on to become a lawyer or a doctor after Berneston. I turned so I could ask Jake if he'd given even a moment's thought to any of this, but when I did—oh, those damned dimples, there they were.

I threw my arms around his neck and Bertie laughed and said, "Kids! Really, not the time nor place—you're not married yet. Stop! People are watching!"

Twenty-Three

ON Wednesday afternoon, Florence and Claudette rang the office to say they planned to leave for Harrisburg earlier than usual. They were concerned about the weather. So was I. It had started to snow around midday. But by the time I left the office after work, it had stopped. I went to the infirmary on my way back to the doctor's house.

Bertie gave me a small medicine bottle and said, "The top has a little dropper in it. Put two drops in her wine—she won't wake up for hours."

Florence had left a casserole in the oven for Dr. Vogel and me. Bertie's little bottle was in my skirt pocket as I shakily carried the casserole into the dining room. I had to behave as if it were any other Wednesday night. I placed the serving dish on the table, moved toward my usual seat, and froze. The doctor had placed a large, official-looking envelope on top of my plate.

"What?" I whispered, backing away slowly. "What is it?" I was sure it was a warrant for my arrest—the doctor had found out about the missing records in the patient files.

"Well? Open it, Mary," Dr. Vogel insisted. I opened it, removed the papers, and, after a moment, laughed. It was a list of the course offerings at Berneston University.

"You must choose soon, my dear," Dr. Vogel said kindly, "I thought we'd look it over tonight."

We moved our chairs close together and studied the pages as we dined. What a relief to have something to distract me, temporarily, from my dark task. Bertie had told me to wait until at least eight o'clock before giving the doctor the "knockout juice."

"The stuff kicks in fast," she'd said. "Make sure you don't give it too soon. You need to make her think she drank too much. Keep pouring the wine. Then give it to her."

And now we had the perfect excuse to linger at the table after we'd finished eating. There were so many courses to consider: *biology, the history of Western civilization, French literature, art history, music, dance, philosophy.* I asked lots of questions. I refilled the doctor's wineglass.

"I'd love to study art history," I said. "I know that's not the most practical course. But I've always wanted to know more about art; do you think it's silly?"

"Indeed not!" Dr. Vogel replied, all sweet and soft from the wine. "That's what college is for, dear, one must become educated on all the humanities, not just the practical subjects."

It was easy for me to convince the doctor that I was excited about attending Berneston. I turned off the part of my mind that involved Lillian and poor Ida; I shut out all the dark thoughts about my uncertain future. It was like turning off the cold-water faucet in my lovely little bathroom and just letting the warm water run. I wasn't going to be Mary in some shoddy office's stenographer pool. I wasn't going to be plain old Mrs. Enright, the housewife, washing reeking diapers. No, I was going to be Miss Engle, the Berneston coed, seated in an art history class at one of the finest schools in the country. I'd sit in the front row. Or, maybe the second row—I could choose to sit wherever I wanted, but the front row would be best for art history. There were bound to be photographs and films to view.

Yes, it was very simple to act breathlessly exhilarated as I read the course descriptions out loud. When Dr. Vogel wanted to see the description of a biology course, I handed her the page. I had transferred the little medicine bottle from my pocket to the inside of my sleeve. Now, as the doctor squinted at the course description, it was easy to tap one, then two drops into her wineglass as I refilled it. I added one more for good measure—I'd learned from Uncle Teddy that a little more was a good idea. It was simple to watch her sip that wine, and chat with her without any show of guilt or remorse. I mused, dreamily, about taking the freshman literature course.

The doctor's eyelids appeared to be growing heavy. I asked her whether I should join the debate club. The doctor's reply was so slurred, it was hard to understand, but I said, "Yes, I agree. I shall."

When the doctor's chin was nodding against her chest, I was forced out of my reverie and sprang into action. Bertie had warned me, but I wasn't prepared for how fast the drops worked. I had to help the doctor up the stairs to her room. She was giggling and mumbling incoherently the entire way. After she fell across the bed, fully clothed, she began snoring almost immediately. I ran downstairs and poured the remainder of the wine into the sink. Back upstairs I flew, with the empty bottle and the doctor's wineglass from the table. It wasn't unusual for the doctor to take her wine off to bed with her after dinner. I left the empty bottle on its side on the floor, so she would know how she happened to fall asleep fully dressed.

I stood there next to the bed for several moments, listening to the doctor's loud breathing. The light from the chandelier in the hall lit the room with a dim yellow haze. There was no turning back now. I had to kneel to ease open the drawer of the bedside table. The drawer's hinge made a little scraping sound as I pulled it open. I froze. The doctor's face was only inches from my own, but she was still out cold. I reached inside and . . . where was it? I knew the doctor kept her pistol there. The doctor had mentioned it when we'd visited the banker, Mr. Whitcomb, and I'd looked all over the house for it while the doctor was traveling earlier in the week. I'd found it there, in the top drawer of the bedside table. But now all I could feel were handkerchiefs, packets of cigarettes, and papers. I groped frantically and finally realized that what I'd thought was the back of the drawer was actually the muzzle of the pistol itself. It banged loudly against the drawer as I shoved it, and again, I froze. The doctor's snores and snorts continued. I removed the pistol—it was just a backup plan; I hadn't even told Jake about it. It was just in case of emergency. I left the room, careful not to close the door all the way. It always made a loud click when it closed. I ran down to my room, grabbed the bundle I'd packed for Lillian and put on my coat, hat, and gloves. I was able to fit the pistol into one of my coat's deep front pockets.

I looked at the old grandfather clock at the bottom of the stairs. It was almost half past eight. The matron should be at the nurses' party by now. I ran outside and down the front steps of the mansion. The snow had started up again, but now it was a heavy snowfall, rather than the light flurries we'd had earlier in the day. I pulled my hat tighter around my ears.

I had the key to Building Five. I had the key to Lillian's room. It was all going as planned. The matron wasn't at the front desk. I looked around but saw nobody. I heard a woman's loud, mournful wailing from one of the floors above me. Somebody shouted something that sounded like "Rosa," and another female voice shouted something back. I started up the stone staircase, and the wailing and shouts stopped at once. All was still. I knew the residents were listening as I made my way to the third floor, then scurried along the cold, dimly lit corridor. I had the sense there were ears pressed to all the doors that were bolted shut. I found room twenty-four. I put the key in the lock, turned it, and pushed the heavy oak door open.

"Lillian," I whispered, but I was so overwhelmed by the stench in the tiny, windowless room that I thought I might choke. I pulled a hand-kerchief from my pocket and pressed it to my nose as I made my way to the hard bench where somebody lay. "Lillian, is that you? Lil, wake up."

Lillian sat up with a start and cried out, "NO!" flailing about. I covered Lillian's mouth with my hand and pressed her head to my chest. "It's me, Lil. It's Mary. Hush now. We must hurry."

What a horrible smell. It made me gag.

Lillian sobbed and clutched me. "No, no. She'll see us, Mary. She'll hurt us."

"Nobody's here. The matron isn't here, but she'll be back soon, though, Lil, hurry now."

With effort, I led Lillian to the door and looked up and down the corridor. I knew there were dozens of inmates housed in Building Five, but it was dead quiet. I put my hand around Lillian's shoulder and helped her down the hall to the stairwell. I hadn't expected Lillian to be so weak. I practically carried her down the stairs. She'd been in the detention building for only ten days. What had happened to her? And that smell. Now I knew why Bertie had told me to take Lillian to the morgue in the tunnels. There was running water and soap in the morgue. And nobody would look for us there.

When we reached the bottom of the stairs, I guided Lillian through the underground passageways to a door that I'd propped open with a book earlier that day. I nudged Lillian into the room and closed the door behind us. Then I lit a match.

"Oh, Lillian," I said. "Oh, what have they done to you?"

There were four narrow windows up near the ceiling, so I didn't turn on the electric light. I lit a candle and used it to find the washbasin and soap. Lillian had already pulled the filthy gown over her head and thrown it on the floor.

"They don't let you out of your room there, Mary. I had to use a chamber pot. When I shouted at the one—the fat one . . ."

"Shhhh, Lil, never mind, we'll get you all cleaned up."

"She threw it in my face. All the shit and piss and blood in the pot, right in my face. That was days ago, Mary."

"Never mind, Lillian. Mr. Carr is waiting for you in New York, Lil."

"Graham?" Lillian cried. "Graham's waiting?"

"Yes, quick, we have to hurry now."

I led Lillian to the washbasin. "Sorry, Lil, it's cold water." I pushed Lillian's head under the faucet and was horrified to see Lillian turn her face so she could gulp frantically at the water as it poured out.

"Lil, when's the last time you ate or drank?"

Lillian said, "Give me soap—give me something, Mary."

I handed her a bar of soap and we began scrubbing her from head to toe. Then I helped her into the warm woolen dress and coat Bertie had left there earlier that day.

"Where is he?" Lillian kept asking. "Where's Graham?"

"He's in New York. I'm taking you to meet my friend Jake. He'll drive you to New York. You'll be there by morning."

"I can't believe it." Lillian said, hugging me, her face wet with tears.

"Now eat this; I brought you a tin of hot soup. You're so weak, Lil. . . ."

Lillian took the soup from my hands and drank it straight from the container. When she'd finished all the broth, she took the spoon that I handed her and gobbled up all the chicken and vegetables.

After I'd helped her put on warm boots and mittens, I led the way through another dark tunnel until we climbed the stairs into the east wing. This was the office area where I worked. I no longer needed to help Lillian.

She was trotting alongside me, crying, "Hurry, Mary.'

We left the building and ran out into the cold night. It should have been a short jog down the old service road to the vehicle shed, but while we were inside, the snowfall had become even heavier. The wind was blowing it right at us. We leaned together and pushed against the gales until we were at the back door of the long shed. I had unlocked it that afternoon. Now I nudged it open and led Lillian past the farm trucks to Dr. Vogel's automobile. I opened the rear passenger door.

"Get in and lie down on the floor, Lil. I left a blanket there for you—cover yourself with it. Don't make a sound once we start moving."

I tried to push the enormous shed doors open, but it took some effort—a thick layer of snow had accumulated. I managed to open them wide enough for the car, then jumped into the driver's seat and started the engine. I didn't turn on the running lights; somebody might notice. I started backing up, but the long car only made it halfway out before the rear tires began spinning in the snow. I shifted gears and pulled forward into the garage again. Then I shifted back into reverse and pressed the gas pedal to the floor. The car lurched back until we were several feet from the garage and then it fishtailed wildly, almost hitting the doorframe with the front fender.

"Damn!" I cried. When I tapped on the gas pedal, the engine roared but the car's rear tires just skidded in place. I was about to tell Lillian to come steer while I pushed when I thought I saw something in the distance. What was it? It looked like a little flicker of light. Then it was gone. Perhaps it was my imagination. Wait—there it was again.

"Mary?" Lillian whispered from the back. "What's going on?"

"SHHHHH!" I hissed. "I think I see somebody."

The spot of light grew larger, and I saw that it was a flashlight carried by a tall person. The size of its beam grew as it neared. Now I saw another, shorter person was marching alongside. It had to be Vogel and old Hartley. I reached into my deep coat pocket; Dr. Vogel's pistol was there.

It was hard to breathe. My eyes were blurred with tears, and my hands shook. I told Lillian, again, to keep quiet. Of course those drops wouldn't have been enough to keep Vogel down for long—now I wished I'd emptied the entire bottle into her glass. I told Lillian not to worry, took a deep breath, then stepped out of the car.

But it wasn't Dr. Vogel and Miss Hartley. It was Charlie Durkin. Next to him was Cloris, the dairy matron.

"Jeesus Key-rist, Mary Engle, what're ya doin' out in this storm?" Cloris shouted cheerfully.

Charlie, too, seemed more amused than alarmed. I was weak with relief—it was clear that they had no idea an inmate was missing.

"Hello, Charlie . . . Cloris," I said. I pulled my hat down over my forehead a little, hoping to hide that I'd been crying, but Charlie was looking at me strangely.

"Dr. Vogel . . . she needed me to run into town. She . . . there's something I need to get . . ."

"Yer not goin' into town with that boat." Cloris laughed. "Not to-night, yer not. The roads must have three inches already. We came out here to put chains on the tires of the milk truck."

Charlie had already removed some heavy chains from a pile on the floor and was stooped next to one of the wheels on the truck.

"Yup, last year we got hit by a surprise storm and we caught hell for having no way to get the milk to the distributor. That ain't happening this time," Cloris said.

"Pop always knows the weather, Clo," Charlie said. "He says it'll stop snowing in the next hour or two, I still don't see why we need to mess with this."

"I told ya, my cows woudn't leave the milkin' shed tonight and they never make no mistakes about a storm when it's coming. We're getting a blizzard and I ain't gonna watch old Hartley flip her lid tomorrow when we can't take the milk."

Charlie moved a set of chains to the next tire. Cloris took another set of chains and moved to the rear of the truck.

"We'll give you a hand getting the doctor's rig back inside once we get these chains on, Mary," Charlie said. "You're not going to town tonight."

"But, are there no chains for this car?" I asked.

"Chains? On Doc's car?" Charlie said. "You know how much those tires cost? Vogel don't use that car in the snow. I'm surprised she thought you could drive in this. What'd you say you were doing?"

"It's official business. I'm—well, I'm not at liberty to say," I said shakily.

"*Oh!* We beg your pardon!" Cloris said. "She's not *at liberty*, Charlie, didja ever?"

"Official business, huh?" Charlie scoffed. "Doc Vogel run out of liquor again?"

Cloris had been stooped over, checking one of the chains and now she pressed her fists to the small of her back and groaned as she straightened up.

Charlie finished putting chains on the last tire and began walking toward Dr. Vogel's car.

"You get in and steer, Clo. Mary and I'll push her back inside."

"*No*," I said. "I'll do it. Just, I'm fine. Go home."

"You can't leave this fancy heap out in the snow," Cloris said. "We'll put her back inside, and then Charlie can drive you to town in the truck." She began pushing past me toward the driver's door, but I grabbed her arm.

"No," I said. "I'll drive."

Cloris jerked her arm back angrily and said, "I ain't pushin'—you're the moron that backed this rig out in this storm. You're lucky we came when we did, ya spoiled runt."

She moved toward the car door again. I pulled Vogel's pistol from my coat pocket and pointed it shakily at Cloris.

"Don't open the door, I told you not to, now just . . . don't," I stammered.

"JEEE-SUS," Cloris said, staring wild-eyed at the gun.

"Mary, what the hell?" Charlie said. I swerved and aimed the pistol at Charlie, back at Cloris, then at Charlie again.

"Get away . . . both of you," I said, blinking through my tears. "Don't go near that car. Get away, damn it or I swear, I'll shoot you both. Just give me the keys to the truck, Charlie, and then leave. I'll shoot you, I swear I will. . . ."

Cloris waited until I swung the pistol at Charlie for the third time, then she calmly drove her elbow into my ribs. I cried out and dropped the gun. Cloris kicked it over to Charlie.

"Now let's see what you're hidin' in there, ya damn lunatic," Cloris growled, and when she opened the back door, Lillian let out a series of screams.

Cloris scrambled inside, and Lillian's screams became muffled. I rushed over, and when I saw that Cloris had her hand clamped over Lillian's mouth, I yanked at Cloris's coat and grabbed at her hair.

"Let her go! Don't you touch her."

Charlie grabbed me, spun me around, and shook me hard. "Shut up!" he said. "What the hell's going on?"

"OH NO," I heard Cloris saying. "Oh God, it's poor Lil. It's me, Lillian. It's Cloris. I was wonderin' what they did with ya. Oh, what I'd like to do to that beast, Vogel. It's okay, Lil, it's me. It's Cloris."

Charlie let me go, and we looked inside the car. Lillian was hugging Cloris.

"Don't make me go back. They'll kill me, Clo," Lillian said.

"No, you ain't going back in there, Lil, not never," Cloris whispered, stroking Lillian's hair. "Lie down. Lie down, dear, and shut yer trap, or you'll get us all in trouble."

Cloris climbed out of the back and slid into the driver's seat. "Quick!" she said. "Quick, before somebody sees. Push us back inside."

It took several tries, but we were finally able to move the doctor's car back into the garage. Charlie helped Lillian from the car. Then he lifted her in his arms and carried her like a child, all swaddled in the blanket, over to the milk truck. Cloris opened the back door to the truck. I clambered inside and helped Charlie settle Lillian into the large empty cargo area with me. Lillian was no longer crying. "Where's Cloris," she said frantically. "Where is she?"

Cloris leaned inside and said, "I'm here, Lil, now don't be stupid, shut yer trap, I don't wanna say it again,"

"Shhh, Lillian," I said.

"Bring Clo with us, Mary," Lillian said. "She'll help us."

"I'm not goin' with yas," Cloris said. "I need to be back in the ward or the other matron'll wonder. God keep ya safe, Lil."

Cloris turned to go, then stopped. She was rubbing her eye and I thought she might be crying, but when she turned it was to thrust the pistol, handle first, at me.

"Keep this. I don't know where ya got it, but when she's safe, be damn sure ya put it back where it came from. And if my name gets stuck in this mess, I'll find that pistol and shoot ya dead with it, you can count on that." She turned and stomped off into the driving snow.

Charlie closed and latched the doors. Lillian and I were now in complete darkness. Charlie backed the truck out of the garage. The chains seemed to be working. There were no windows, but I felt very little skidding or swaying as we made our way along the service road. Lillian and I huddled against the back wall, facing the rear doors. Now I was the frantic one.

"What if it's a trap, Lil? What if Cloris is calling the police?"

"No," Lillian said. "She wouldn't do that."

"How do you know? She's such a nasty piece of work," I cried.

"Cloris?" Lillian said. "She's not so bad, Mary. It's just a job for her. She hates Vogel. I trust her. But what about Durk? He gives all of us the creeps the way he won't ever look at us, I don't trust him."

"No, Charlie's okay," I said. "If he were going to turn us in, he wouldn't have gone to all that trouble back there, moving you from the car to the truck and all—right?"

"I have no idea," Lillian said.

"It's fine," I said, as bravely as I could manage.

The truck slowed and then stopped.

"What's going on?" Lillian whispered.

"I think we're at the gate. Charlie's dad's the guard. He'll give him a story and get us out onto the road."

The car idled for several long moments, and then I heard the door of the cab open and close. My heart raced. Why was Charlie getting out of the truck? Why didn't he drive us through? Now I realized I'd been wrong about him after all. Charlie just wanted to have us both locked inside the truck so we'd be trapped until the police arrived. Cloris probably removed the bullets from the pistol before giving it back to me.

"Oh God, Lillian, I'm so stupid, I'm such a fool," I cried. Lillian didn't seem to hear me. She was hugging her knees to her chest and was whispering something frantically. I thought she was delirious, but after a few seconds, I was able to make out Lillian's words. I pressed myself closer to Lillian and whispered along.

"'Hail Mary, full of grace . . .'" we prayed together.

The heavy boots of men crunched in the snow just outside.

" 'Blessed art thou . . . ,' " we prayed.

I heard the men shouting but couldn't make out their words through the gusting wind.

" 'Now and at the hour of our death,' " we prayed, and then we started the prayer again and then again. " 'Holy . . . blessed . . . women . . . womb . . . mother.' " The words flowed like our tears—unbidden, constant. " 'Holy Mary, mother of God,' " we whispered. " 'Pray for us sinners, now and . . .' "

The rear door swung open, but we didn't scream. We continued our whispers and averted our eyes as somebody angled a flashlight's glare at us. It was over now. We were together. We might never be together again but we were together now. We held hands beneath the blanket. We prayed to the Blessed Virgin—the holy mother of Jesus, and I thought of Sister Rosemary, as I so often did when I said my prayers. It always soothed me.

Where is Sister right now? I wondered as Charlie climbed inside the truck, his scowling father right behind him.

Is she lonely? Does she ever think about Lillian and me? Is she thinking about us at this very moment? I pressed my head against Lillian's and recalled how warm it had been in the sleeping ward some nights when we'd huddled together this close with the stove still glowing hot and Sister reading to us. I could still smell the wet wool leggings and mittens hanging on the stove. I could hear the lovely creak of Sister's rocking chair on the old floorboards.

"Didja say one of em's Doc Vogel's girl?" old Mr. Durkin grumbled. "I don't have my damn eyeglasses."

"Yeah, Pop. It's Mary, the secretary who lives up at her place. The other's a dairy girl."

I squinted up at the men through my swollen eyelids. Charlie's father tossed a large bundle next to me and then jumped back out of the truck.

"If you ain't back in an hour, I'm lockin' the gate," he said. "I ain't getting sent up the work farm for nobody, not even my own son."

"Okay, Pop," Charlie called after him. Then he said to us, "It's usually a twenty-minute drive, but in this snow, it might be an hour or more. He won't lock me out. Don't worry."

"You'll take us to town?" I asked, weak with relief. He was going to help us after all!

"Town? No, word'll be out soon about a missing girl from the Village. I'm taking her someplace safe till the storm passes."

"No, Charlie, we're meeting a friend over near the mill. He's going to take her to New York."

Charlie was shaking his head no, but then stopped. "Wait, what friend? Was he that fella from the newspaper?"

"He does work for a paper, but not around here. You don't know him, Charlie, his name is Mr. Enright—he's waiting for us at the mill, just outside town."

"No, he ain't. He was arrested there a couple of hours ago. Heard it from my buddy who works there. They arrested him for agitating last summer, they heard he was gonna be around I guess."

"No," I said. "That can't be true."

Charlie said, "Shut up and listen to me now, Mary. We're all gonna get nailed to the wall if we get caught. Yer man Enright got arrested. My friend, Clyde, he knows him. Clyde and some other guys are gonna post his bail tonight if they can get through the snow. 'Cause Enright worked hard trying to help them, I guess, and they feel obliged to him. But if he gets out, he ain't taking nobody nowhere tonight. He's gonna be holed up somewhere safe until the storm passes and then, if he wants to save his neck, he'll go back where he come from."

Charlie jumped down and slammed the cargo door shut. A few seconds later, the truck rolled forward. I listened for the clang of the gate as Pop Durkin closed it behind us, but all I could hear was the fierce howling of the wind.

Lillian said, "Was the old man Durk's father? The gatekeeper?"

"Yup," I said glumly. Everything had gone wrong. We should have postponed the whole scheme when the snow started that afternoon. "I'm sorry, Lil," I said.

"About what?" Lillian said. She threw the blanket off of her and shouted gleefully, "I'm outside. I'm outside the gate! Who knew it could be that easy!" She was laughing and trying to stand. She was trying to peer through the slats on the side of the truck.

"EASY?" I shouted. "Are you out of your damned mind? I threatened to shoot people. My . . . fiancé—he's in jail. Sit down before you fall! Lillian?"

She just stood there, wobbly-legged, peering through the slats at the outside world.

"Do ye want to be dead for the rest of yer life, Lillian Faust?" I said, with my best attempt at Sister Rosemary's Irish accent.

Lillian laughed, plopped herself down next to me, and gave me a hug.

"I'm so happy, Mary," Lillian said. "I'm so very, very happy."

"I should have waited until the storm passed," I moaned.

"No, I couldn't wait any longer. I needed you to come tonight. I prayed you'd come. I was praying to Jesus and the blessed Mother and they sent you to me, Mary."

The drive seemed to take forever. Lillian and I filled each other in as much as we could along the way.

"The man who was going to take me to New York. Did you say you're going to marry him?"

"Yes," I said sadly.

"And he works for a newspaper? He sounds swell, Mary. How did you meet him?"

I told her about Bertie and our weekends and about Jake's trips to the mill, covering the strike.

"I hope Durk was right about his friend getting him, Mary. Clo told us about the goings-on at the mill. She said they got some Pinkerton men out here now from New York. Remember? When your uncle worked for them . . ."

Of course I remembered; it had been in all the newspapers and Teddy had boasted about it for years. The Pinkerton Detective Agency had rounded up every hooligan in New York– every drunk and vagrant who knew how to fight and they'd hauled them to a nearby mine that had been shut down by a strike. They arrived at night when the strikers were dozing. That was the last night of the strike. Twenty men were gravely injured—mostly strikers—but also a few "agitators" and journalists. "Commies," my uncle had called them. Two men had died.

"Oh God," I cried. "What if they've beaten Jake? They might have killed him. It's all my fault."

"No," Lillian said. "Didn't Durk just say his friend is helping him?

It'll be fine, he's probably been released by now." But she didn't sound so sure. We sat silently for a little while.

"Mary," Lillian said, "that was my first time in Building Five. I'd heard about it before, but I was never in there. It's hell."

"I'm so glad you're out, Lil," I said.

"But there's at least thirty girls in there, maybe more," Lillian said. "I was locked up most of the time, but they took me out to clean and do other work. Mary, there's a lady who's been in there almost a year. I heard she was normal when she went in there. Just mouthed off about something to the wrong attendant. She's missing her front teeth now, has an arm that was broken and didn't mend right, and now it's useless. And she used to be normal. Now she's insane. That matron, Olga, she strapped a girl's arms above her head for a week. Miss Hartley knows everything that goes on in there, she has the water turned off for days at a time. There's a young girl in there who's very sick, Mary."

"No, they send sick and injured girls to Bertie Nolan. She sends them off to the hospital if they need it."

"Not if they were hurt by a member of staff, Mary. They don't want anybody to know. You have to help those girls, Mary. There's a few . . . I don't think they're gonna last long."

"Oh, Lil, I can't help everyone."

"You can help them. You can help the girls in Building Five."

"Let's talk about something else, something nice. Let's talk about your Rosemary," I said finally.

"Oh! Have you heard anything about her?"

"Yes. Graham's been communicating with the home." There would be time later to tell Lillian that those communications had been telegraphs to and from Paris.

"You've met Graham?"

"Not yet, but we spoke once by telephone. Rosemary's still there at the home, Lil. But she's not an orphan anymore. Graham pays for them to keep her now. His sister is going to adopt her."

Lillian was beaming. "I can't believe it! How is she? Is she okay?"

"She's very healthy."

"I want to take the train to Scranton as soon as I get to New York, Mary. I want to see Rosemary."

"No! The first place people will look for you is Scranton."

"I have to see her."

"No, Lil. You're going to New York. After enough time has passed, Graham's sister is planning to adopt her, she lives in New York. Then you'll be with her."

"I'm afraid something will happen to her before that. Tell me everything about her. Tell me everything Graham said about her."

"He didn't say much."

"Please," Lillian whispered.

"She's very plump and happy," I began. "She never stops smiling."

"She gets that from him," Lillian said dreamily.

"I think she must be like you too," I continued. "Apparently, she's the favorite of all the workers there." The words came even easier than those I'd made up years ago about my father. Because this time, the words were true. Graham had told me all of this in French when we spoke on the phone. When I translated the words later, some of the ink ran off the page from my tears.

"She'll be three years old next March," Lillian sighed.

"They say she's very smart, Lil, like you. And pretty."

Lillian was wiping her eyes with the back of one hand but with the other, she squeezed my hand tighter.

Lillian said. "I want you to be her godmother, Mary, will you?"

"Why, of course," I said, my voice trembling.

"What else?" Lillian asked. "Tell me more, Mary."

"I don't know much else, Lil."

"Does she have toys to play with? Does she have anything of her very own?"

"Yes," I said, remembering more of what Graham had shared. "She has a little doll Graham bought her. He bought toys for some of the other girls at the home too."

"He's like your pop, Mary."

"No," I said. "He's nothing like my father. He really does send money to the minister to buy toys for the other children, I'm not making this up for you, Lil. He's a good father."

"What else?" Lillian whispered. "Tell me more about my baby."

Twenty-Four

"HOLD on to my jacket," Charlie said. He'd shut off the truck's engine before helping us down, and now it was too dark to see. The snow stung our faces. We clutched the hem of Charlie's thick wool coat and followed him blindly until we saw something ahead. It was a door, painted a light color, and as we got closer we could see the rest of the small cabin. Charlie had the bundle his father had given him thrown over his shoulder, and he lowered it to the ground. He felt around in it until he found a wooden stick with a key attached. He unlocked the door, and then held it open for us.

Inside, he dropped the bundle and turned on his flashlight. The cabin was just the one room. There were a few pieces of furniture covered with large, filthy dustcloths. I pulled on one and exposed a lumpy sofa. Lillian uncovered a table and chairs. A rack holding shotguns and rifles was mounted on one wall. The rear wall of the cabin was stone clad with a large fireplace in the center. Logs were piled high next to it. Charlie immediately began loading the stove with wood. He had no gloves and paused, occasionally, to blow on his hands.

"Charlie, I don't think you should light that. Won't the smoke draw attention?" I said.

"Nobody ever comes out here in winter, 'specially not in a storm like this. Hand me another log."

"Who owns it?" Lillian asked, eagerly passing logs to him.

"Folks from down Harrisburg. Lawyers. Businessmen. They bought a couple hundred acres up here. It's like a hunting club, I guess. They got this cabin and another, up on the hill a ways. Closest farm is on the other side of that hill and nobody can see this place from the road. Not in this storm. My pop knows the farmer who looks after it. We hunt here when the owners ain't around. They never come up here in winter."

Acorn shells and mouse droppings were scattered about the dusty floor. Men's hunting coats and thick woolen trousers hung from pegs next to the gun racks.

"I love it here," Lillian said. She was running her hands over the jackets and then she took one of the shotguns down and began dusting it off with her sleeve.

"Careful, Lil," I said.

"It ain't loaded," Charlie said. He'd just lit the rags he was using as kindling, and now he sat back on his heels and watched as the little flames began to flicker in the hearth.

"I smell men," Lillian said. "This place—it makes me realize how very much I've missed men."

I saw Charlie raise an eyebrow, but he continued to gaze into the fire.

Lillian pressed the sleeve of one of the flannel hunting coats to her cheek.

"Whenever you talked about going to those logging camps with your dad, Mare, I always pictured cabins like this. And I bet they smelled like this. Like old apple cores and tobacco and sweat."

"They were kind of like this, some of those places," I said, shivering at the memory. "Now what's the plan, Charlie? How long can we stay here?"

"*We* can't stay here another minute. We gotta get the truck back. Lillian can wait out the storm till tomorrow morning when the snow's over. I'll come get her after I take the milk to the distributor—the county keeps the main roads cleared now that they got the new motor plow. I'll make up something about the truck needing mechanical work in town. I'll run Lillian down to Harrisburg then. She can catch a train to New York. She can't be seen with your friend from the newspaper, that's for sure."

I wanted to hug him. He made it sound so easy. And it was, really. He'd just drive Lillian to the train in Harrisburg . . .

"Oh," I said. "I almost forgot, Lil! Here's some money." I shoved a thick envelope at her. When Lillian opened it, she said. "Jeez, I can't take all this, Mary."

"Yes, you can. Mr. Carr had it wired to me. It's from him, not me.

His hotel is on the envelope. When you get to Harrisburg, call him if there's time. Have the operator reverse the charges. If you can't manage to call, take a taxi to his hotel when you get to New York. The address is there—on the envelope."

Charlie pointed to the bundle on the floor. "There's a tin with my pop's dinner in there and a canteen full of coffee. He put a blanket in there for you. Some other stuff. Like I said, I'll be here as soon as I can in the morning."

"Thank you, Charlie," Lillian said. "I can never thank you enough."

"Yeah, I know," Charlie said, looking down awkwardly. "We gotta go, Mary."

I pulled a small parcel from my coat pocket and thrust it at Lillian. "Here's something from me, Lil."

"What is it?" she asked. I had wrapped up the little box with paper and tied it up with a red bow.

"It's for you. I was going to give it to you on Christmas Day, but you'll be in New York on Christmas Day. Lil—it's this Sunday. Wait and open it then." Inside were a new set of rosary beads and a medal of St. Christopher, the patron saint of travelers. "Actually, open it, in the morning, when Charlie comes," I said. It would be nice for Lillian to be able to pray to St. Christopher on her way to New York, so she wouldn't feel alone. I meant to give Lillian a quick hug, but once I had my arms around her, we couldn't seem to let go.

"I don't think I'll ever see you again, Mary," Lillian said, sniffling.

"Of course you will, don't be stupid," I said. "I'm going to visit you in New York all the time. I'm going to live there too, remember?"

"We gotta go," Charlie insisted. I gave Lillian one last squeeze, then followed Charlie out to the truck. I looked back at the cabin as we drove away. You couldn't see smoke coming out of the chimney in the storm. You couldn't even see the cabin. Lillian would be fine until the morning.

The journey back took longer than the drive to the cabin; much more snow had fallen. Now that I was seated in the cab with Charlie, I could see how treacherous the driving actually was.

"Careful! Careful now, Charlie, you need to pump the brakes going down this hill or you'll skid again," I said.

"I know what I'm doing."

"But . . ."

"I got us here didn't I?" Charlie snapped, and I realized how un-grateful I must seem.

"Yes, yes you did, of course you did, and thank you, Charlie. I'm just—you know, worried."

"You should be. Vogel's gonna be a monster for the next week or two. They send reporters around whenever a girl gets away."

"They've found all the other girls who tried to get away, right?" I said.

"No," Charlie said. "Where'd you get that idea? Plenty other girls have snuck off and never got caught. Your friend ain't the first one I've helped. My mom, my pop, most of the folks who work at the village have helped a girl at one time or another."

I turned to him in disbelief. "But, I read in a newspaper that every escape was thwarted—they're always found."

"That's 'cause Vogel's uncle owns that newspaper."

"Oh . . . huh," I said. "Why did you and your folks help the other girls? Who were they?"

"Most of 'em were from nearby towns. Vogel and Hartley don't take in local girls anymore, 'cause in the past their folks would give us money to help get them back out. Cloris helped a few girls just 'cause they weren't looking like they'd last another winter. My mom used to be one of the field attendants. She'd help a girl if she looked like she couldn't take the strain no more. But we usually knew somebody who knew their folks."

"Wouldn't Vogel send the police after them? She must have known where they lived."

"No, she don't like to involve the police, because then the newspa-pers that ain't so friendly get onto the story. She'd rather keep it quiet."

After riding in silence for a few minutes, I said, "I didn't know that Cloris—and the others—were so, well, caring. I thought they were a little cruel, some of the workers—to be honest."

Charlie said, "Well, they don't get paid much and the girls can get out of hand. Who are you to judge 'em, anyways? We don't got much of a choice. If you don't come from a farming family, you don't got a lot of options about where to work out here. They can only hire so many at the mill, and nobody hires women. I wouldn't go judging us so quick if I was you."

"I wasn't judging you or the others, Charlie."

"Yes, you were. You've looked down your nose at me from the minute I picked you up in front of your house in Scranton."

"That's not true."

"Thinking you're better than us every minute of every day," he continued. "But you're the one that outta be judged. You lived in a fine house and still came clear out to the middle of the state to help Vogel keep those girls here—girls like your friend, called defective, half of 'em, when they ain't. Kept like criminals until they're old."

"That wasn't my house, Charlie," I interrupted. I couldn't bear to let him go on. "I'm sure you know I lived in an orphan home when I was little. That house belonged to my aunt; she hated me."

"But you coulda worked someplace in Scranton," Charlie said. "That's all I'm sayin'. You didn't have to come out here and be Vogel's sidekick, living in luxury up at her house while your friend . . ."

"I . . . I see how I might have come across," I said to Charlie. "I see how you and some of the others—might've thought I was—putting on airs. I'm sorry."

"Never mind. Who cares? I'm glad your friend is safe."

We were almost at the bend in the road just before the Village gate.

"I don't know if I can explain why I let Lillian stay there for so long, but, of course—I was wrong."

"I said, who cares, Mary. She's safe now."

I thought about how safe I'd felt these past months at Nettleton Village. I'd never had so much confidence in myself and so much hope for my future. And I'd convinced myself, all along, that it was Lillian who was safer there.

"I wonder how long it'll take Vogel to figure out we went to school together, me and Lil. You think she'll have me arrested?" I said.

"No, now you listen, Mary, Doc's gonna be more scared than you if this gets out. Just don't be afraid of her and don't tell her nothing. She can't prove nothing, even if she suspects you or any of us. Pop's going to leave his little lamp on in the gatehouse if they know she's missing. If that happens, everybody'll be out looking. We'll say you came along to help me get a spare chain down in Mifflinburg. If nobody's looking yet, I'll drop you at the drive to her house. You gave her dope, right? She'll never know you were out."

We rounded the bend in the road. "Good," Charlie said. "Light's off."

I breathed a heavy sigh of relief. Nobody even knew Lillian was gone yet.

At the gate, Charlie jumped from the cab and trudged through the snow so he could unlock the chain that held it shut. I scooted over so I could drive the truck through, then moved back over after Charlie closed the gate behind us.

When he was back behind the wheel, Charlie turned to me. For the first time since we'd met, he gave me a genuinely warm smile. I smiled back. We were very tired, but we were very happy. We felt the rare comradery that comes with having attempted something seemingly impossible, and certainly foolish, together. Now we realized at the same quiet, elated moment that we'd actually pulled it off.

Or so I thought until he put the truck in gear and said, "This whole damn mess, it ain't over, you know."

"Yes, of course," I said. "But your dad didn't leave the lamp on. If they haven't figured out she's gone yet, nobody'll know we were even out, right?"

"Yeah," he said. "Well, I'll get her when I take the milk first thing tomorrow. I should be back from Harrisburg by lunch. I'll look for you and let you know that she got to the train safe. Then we can breathe easy."

"Charlie," I said, turning to face him, "I hope you know how much I appreciate everything you've done." But he seemed not to have heard me. He was frowning at the road ahead. A strange look clouded his face.

"Something ain't right," he said. "There's no lights on anywhere. You can see the windows from the cottages when you turn onto this driveway. They never turn off all the lights in the residences."

I looked around. He was right. There wasn't a single light on in any of the buildings.

"Christ, the damn electrical lines must be down 'cause of the snow and wind. Pop coulda left the light on in the gatehouse but—no power. They might know she's gone, there might be searchers out everywhere."

"Oh no, no, no, that can't be possible," I said. We'd just turned onto the drive leading to the doctor's house. Charlie stopped the truck near the steps to the entrance and we both stared up at the house.

"I left the little foyer lamp on, but now it's completely dark," I said, my heart sinking. I wondered how long we'd been gone. It was at least two hours. Maybe three. Charlie's father might have tried to give us a signal that they were searching. Vogel might be up. She might know we'd been out, Charlie and I, out in the storm for hours and now a girl was missing.

We barely breathed as we peered out at the road and the surrounding woods.

"Okay. I still think they don't know she's gone," Charlie said. "There's a steam whistle behind Main. It's for fires and runaways and it wakes up everybody in the whole area—they'd be out with flashlights now if they knew she was gone."

"I'm sure you're right," I said. "Bertie was gonna give that nasty Mrs. Swensen from Building Five the same stuff I gave Vogel. She's probably passed out."

"Well, c'mon, get out quick. Somebody will sound the alarm tonight, who knows when."

I hopped down from the truck.

"Mary," Charlie said. I turned to him, the wind nearly blinding me. "You got us all into this." He was almost shouting now so I could hear over the gusts. "Just don't mess up; we're all on the line. The doctor can't prove nothing, hear?"

I tried to reply, but I was shivering so hard—not from the cold but from fear. I just gave him a little nod and watched him drive off, leaving deep tire tracks behind him. I looked down at my boots. I was leaving footprints. I kicked snow over them. Instead of climbing the snow-covered steps to the front door, I made my way around to the kitchen door, covering my tracks as well as I could along the way. I had keys to all the doors, and after some fumbling, I was able to open the kitchen door and step inside. I sat on the floor to remove my boots, shushing Trixie and Peg, who were greeting me with excited little yips. I carried my boots and tiptoed along in my stockings.

The house was entirely dark, but I made my way to my bedroom by feel. I needed some light. Vogel kept little kerosene lamps in all the rooms—she'd told me that the electricity often went out during storms. I shoved my wet boots under my bed and felt my way along the mattress until I found the bedside table. I moved my fingers over the book I was reading, the little ashtray that I never dared use, and then felt the base of the pretty little glass lantern with the polished brass base. I reached into my pockets for matches, and that's when I felt the gun. It had felt so heavy when I'd taken it from the doctor's bedside drawer, but I'd been carrying it in my pocket for hours and had gotten used to its weight. I'd completely forgotten about it. I had to put it back.

I lit the lantern and carried it out into the hall. The house was heated with coal, but there were always drafts on cold nights like this, and the flame in my lantern flickered and threw twisting shadows that shimmied up and down the walls. Up the winding staircase I went, the flame in my lantern leaning back as if in protest, my shadow towering over me. When I was outside the doctor's room, I placed the lantern on the floor. I gave the door a little nudge but it wouldn't open. Someone had closed it.

I felt a dreadful sinking in my heart. It hurt to breathe. What had happened? Was the doctor awake? If so, I couldn't open the door—not without knocking. The doctor could be walking around naked, for all I knew. And what reason would I give for being there?

But, perhaps a draft had caused the door to shut. I knelt on the floor and listened for any sounds from within. I peered into the little crack beneath the door, but it was dark inside. The doctor wouldn't be walking around in the dark, naked or clothed. A draft had closed the door. I turned the little knob on the lantern and lowered the flame. Then I turned it off completely. There were many windows in the upper hall, but the sky was heavy with clouds from the snowstorm. I couldn't see my own hands. I said a little silent prayer and felt my way up the door to the brass doorknob and turned it until I heard the latch click. I eased the door open, crept inside, then closed it carefully behind me.

All was still. Grateful for the thick carpeting that covered the entire floor of the doctor's room, I crawled along, head down, hands groping ahead of me. I believed I was moving toward the bed, but I should have felt its frame by now. It must be off to the left. I moved that way and then—yes—I was touching the silk bed skirt. I followed it along the foot of the bed and then around to the side where Dr. Vogel slept, the side with the table. I was about to reach up to open the drawer when I realized that the dark room was too silent. The doctor wasn't snoring. Her head had to be within a few feet of my own. I held my breath so that I could hear the doctor's own breathing. Silence.

I'd given her too much of Bertie's knockout juice. I'd killed her. It took several moments, but I finally summoned the nerve to reach up and feel for the doctor's cold arm or face. I felt nothing. The bed's covers were mussed, but the doctor wasn't there. I groped around as much as I could from my kneeling position, then got up and crawled all over the bed. There was nobody in it.

I was about to run for the door when I heard a coughing sound and then a door creaking open. The doctor had been in her bathroom. I scrambled off the bed and backed up into a corner. I couldn't see the doctor, but I could hear the rustling of her skirt as she approached. I pressed my back against the wall. Now the rustling was closer, and I heard the doctor clear her throat again. She was within inches of me. She must have realized the electricity was out when she went to the bathroom. What if she lit her lantern and saw me crouching there?

There was a groaning of bedsprings, a long sigh from the doctor, and, after a few moments, snoring. Now I didn't hesitate. I pulled the drawer open, shoved the gun inside, and closed it. I felt my way along the wall until I touched the doorframe. I opened the door, slipped through, and, as I closed it, I heard the long, eerie scream of an alarm siren somewhere outside. It sounded like the sirens I'd heard watching films about the war in Europe. I started toward the stairs but I heard Dr. Vogel crying out.

"What is it? Who's out there?" Dr. Vogel called out.

"It's me, Doctor, it's Mary," I said. " I think—I think we have an emergency."

Twenty-Five

BY six o'clock in the morning, Vogel had summoned everybody involved in the night's search to her residence. There we stood in her foyer, sleep-deprived, and numb from the hours out in the storm: Miss Hartley, Cloris, Charlie and Pop Durkin, Olga Swensen—the portly matron of Building Five—and me. Hal Goodwin had been roused to help in the early morning hours, along with two other matrons. We stood, wet and shivering there in the doctor's white marble-floored foyer, while the doctor paced back and forth questioning each of us in turn.

"You! Mrs. Swensen!" Vogel said to the frowning matron. I wondered if the others noticed that the doctor was a little unsteady on her feet, still slightly woozy from last night. "How on earth did she get past you?"

"I—I thought I'd go on over to the infirmary to see if they needed anything. The power had gone out, ya see, Doc. And . . . I didn't know . . . if they had a patient. . . ."

I knew that Olga was the monster who'd thrown the contents of Lillian's chamber pot at her. I enjoyed watching her fail so dramatically at lying.

Dr. Vogel now stood face-to-face with Olga, and she said, quietly but sternly, "Do you know what I am?"

"The . . . superintendent? Ma'am?"

"I'm a doctor."

"Yes, of course, Dr. Vogel. Of course you are, yes indeed, ma'am."

"I'm a psychiatrist. I'm trained to discern whether a person is truthful or lying. I know you're thinking of your next lie right now. Be careful what you say next. Why did you leave Building Five last night?"

Olga crumbled immediately. I knew she would—the biggest bullies are always the most cowardly. Tears and snot streamed down her plump, mottled red cheeks as she told Dr. Vogel, in fitful, gasping sobs, that she'd gone to the infirmary for a little Christmas party. Yes, they drank alcohol. Yes, the alcohol was meant for sick patients; she knew that. She ratted out Bertie and the other matrons who were there. It was their idea. She'd only been there for a half an hour. Maybe less.

"Are you saying that you left the girls in Building Five unattended?" Vogel said.

"Yes, Doctor. Yes, ma'am, but they was all locked up and everything."

"What if there'd been a fire? Did you ever think of that? Who would've let them out of their sleeping quarters?"

"I was only planning to go for a few minutes. We always leave 'em locked up in the cells when we take our meals. I told Miss Hartley last year we should have somebody in the building when we're out and she said the girls was fine as long as I made sure they was locked in and all."

"I never said any such thing," Miss Hartley said, her eyes darting from Olga to the doctor, then back to Olga.

"So it's Miss Hartley's fault the girl escaped?" Vogel said to Olga.

"No—I just meant . . . Miss Hartley, you did say . . ."

"Listen to me now," Vogel said to Olga. Then she turned to the rest of us standing with our backs against the foyer's wall. "Listen to me, all of you. I've been told we're in for another day of snow, maybe two. Nobody knows when the phone and power will be restored. If that poor girl is out in this, she's likely dead already and it'll be on all of you, do you hear me? We've never had a girl manage an escape, let alone die trying."

I shot a quick sidelong glance at Charlie. Just last night he'd informed me that many girls had escaped, but now he stood there, stone-faced.

"You'll be held responsible if that girl dies," Vogel continued. "You're as good as murderers, each and every one of you."

This made no sense. Even if a girl had escaped into the woods and died, why would the blame be on the others assembled here? I must have frowned because the doctor snapped, "What is it, Miss Engle? You look upset about something I said."

"No, ma'am. I'm just worried about the missing girl," I said.

"Nobody's to be allowed in or out of the gate, Durkin, understand?" Vogel said to Charlie's father.

"Sheriff Eckers left about an hour ago. He's coming back with some men and some scent hounds," Pop said. "Should I let him in?"

"Yes, of course let him in; he's the sheriff. Use your damned thick head," Vogel said. She was pressing her fingers to her temples. The others were exchanging looks. Dr. Vogel could be stern, but they'd never seen her like this. She continued, her voice rising, "I told Eckers he was wasting his time with the dogs. They'll never find a scent in this snow. What were you thinking, taking the truck out in that storm, Durk?"

I looked at Charlie—he was playing dumb, gazing slack-jawed into the air in front of him. I wanted to smile. I'd underestimated him all this time.

"I needed an extra chain for the truck. One of ours snapped. I couldn't get it back in the shed after going to the supply, snow was blocking the doors," he said.

"I noticed the lights from Charlie's truck after I found out the girl was missing," Olga Swensen offered. "I was on my way here, but he said we should sound the alarm first."

"You should have come to me first, both of you," Vogel said. "We might've found her before she even knew we were looking, but you let her know we were after her."

"Ma'am, I considered that," Charlie said, "but we took the truck over to Building Five, soon as Olga gave me the rundown, and the only tracks in the snow was from Olga's boots. So, I knew then that the girl musta left an hour ago, maybe more, cause her tracks was already covered up. Olga said the girl didn't have no coat or nothing so we were afraid she might die . . . from the cold and all."

Dr. Vogel raised her hand to silence him and closed her eyes in exasperation. She said, quietly: "You were wrong to sound the alarm. I won't say it again, that's what got the sheriff out here and by the end of today, everybody in this county will know a girl walked out. Now—Miss Engle, Miss Hartley, you two stay here, the rest of you, keep searching."

"Dr. Vogel, I got something you need to know," Cloris said, as the others filed out the door.

I tried to give Cloris a warning glare. I knew it. She was going to rat us out.

"Yes? What?"

"My girls was upset this morning during milking. They heard about what happened. The missing girl—Lil—she was real popular with the others and they was all riled and threatenin' to not milk till she's found. They wanna help look."

I was able to breathe normally again. Dr. Vogel frowned at Cloris for a moment as she considered this. Of course it would help to have more searchers.

"No," she said finally. "We can't risk it. What if this is part of a plan? What if they're all trying to get out? I don't want the sheriff's men talking to the girls. Besides, who'll milk? Who'll muck the barns?"

"I just thought I'd tell ya," Cloris said, as she turned to go. "They're a little wild, I just wanted you to know."

"Tell them there's plenty of room in Building Five if they get any ideas!" Vogel said. "Now leave, all of you."

Charlie was halfway down the steps when he called back, "Oh, Mary, I forgot to tell you. I can't deliver that package for you today, 'cause of the storm."

"Yes, I thought that might be the case," I said. I knew he wouldn't be able to get Lillian until the snow stopped. I wondered if he had any news about Jake, but of course I couldn't ask.

"I'll get it to the post office right after I take the milk tomorrow," he said.

When I closed the door, Dr. Vogel said, "What was that Durk said?"

"Oh, I had some Christmas gifts for my aunt. He was supposed to take them to the post office two days ago. He just wanted me to know he'll drop them there tomorrow."

"He'll drop them on his own time. The Commonwealth of Pennsylvania is not paying Charlie Durkin to be your errand boy."

"Of course, you're right, Doctor, I'll tell him when I see him."

I made breakfast while Miss Hartley and Dr. Vogel pored over some large survey maps in the dining room. When the coffee, eggs, and toast were ready, I loaded everything onto a large tray and carried it into the dining room. Claudette made things like this look so easy, but I was sure I would trip and drop everything. I was exhausted, having had no sleep the night before. I managed to make it to the table and I placed the food and coffee in front of the two women.

"There's an old logging road that runs from the coal shed to the back acreage," Vogel was saying. "I haven't been up there in over a year, but there was once a gate, somebody might have met her." She paused and frowned at me.

"Well?" Vogel said. "Aren't you going to eat? Where's your plate?"

"I noticed we don't have much in the pantry or the icebox. Of course, Claudette and Florence usually go to the market today, but who knows when they'll be able to get back in this storm—certainly not before tomorrow. I thought I'd run over to the dining hall and see what they have there for tonight."

Dr. Vogel smiled as she dug into her eggs. "I don't know what I'd do without you, Mary Engle. See that, Hartley? There's a girl who can think straight. We need more Mary Engles around here, she'll be running this place someday, mark my words."

"Is that so?" Miss Hartley said. Then she cleared her throat dramatically and slid a file folder over to the doctor.

Dr. Vogel dabbed at her mouth with her napkin, squinted down at the folder, and said, "Oh, right, I almost forgot. Mary, I asked Miss Hartley to bring me the file on the runaway girl. It turns out, she's from Scranton. In fact, she was raised at St. Catherine's Orphan Asylum. Isn't that where you lived as a child?"

I placed my hand on the table. I had to steady myself. "Yes," I said. "Why do you ask?"

"The girl was named Lillian Henning," Miss Hartley said, flatly. "She was about your age, you must have known her."

And for a brief moment, I felt like we were characters on a film reel that had become jammed, Vogel, Hartley, and me. Frozen in place. They were staring up at me. I gazed, dumbly, down at the file.

"Lillian Henning?" I said finally. "That doesn't sound familiar. May I . . . please look at the file?"

Dr. Vogel nodded and continued eating, but Miss Hartley studied me carefully as I opened the folder. It was just as it was when I'd found it in the office. Nothing but the letter from the doctor. No intelligence test or other information.

"I don't see anything about St. Catherine's here," I said, somewhat relieved. "I see from this letter that she's from Scranton. I'm sorry, but I don't recall a Lillian Henning at St. Cat's." This was true; I'd known a Lillian Faust, not a Lillian Henning.

"I keep an admission journal," Miss Hartley said. "I interview each inmate when she arrives, and I keep those notes in the journal. The missing girl grew up in the same orphan asylum that you grew up in. As soon as the phone lines are back in working order, I'll ring the home and see if they know anything, but we thought you must know her and might have an idea about where she'd try to go."

Why had I written that damned letter to Mother Bea? As soon as they spoke to her, she was bound to tell them that I'd written her. But Charlie had told me it sometimes took weeks before the telephone lines were repaired after a storm; the thing to do now was to remain calm.

"I think I would recognize the name, and I don't," I said, sliding the file folder back to Miss Hartley. "Anyway, I'll head on over to the dining hall now, it looks like the snow's let up a little." I was desperate to end this conversation. I had to speak to Bertie. Had she managed to find the soiled clothes in the morgue and put them in the incinerator as planned? Was there any news about Jake? I was almost out of the room when Miss Hartley called after me, "Lillian Faust was her name when she was a girl."

I stopped. Then I turned slowly back to face them.

"Lillian *Faust*?"

"Yes," Hartley said, with a smug half smile. "Henning was her married name."

"Yes, yes . . . I did know a Lillian Faust," I said meekly. "Do you mean to say that the girl—the missing girl? Is she Lillian Faust?"

"Mary, come sit, you look quite faint," Dr. Vogel said. "This must be very hard to hear, especially since she's still out there in this weather. Oh dear, this must be quite a shock to you."

"No, I'm fine," I said, managing a little sad shrug. "It's just surprising to think that somebody I used to know—to think that she's an inmate here. I didn't know her well. She's an older girl, as I recall, and of course, I left the home so many years ago."

"She was in the choral group that performed for the trustees, Miss Engle," Hartley said. "You were there. You must have noticed her."

I looked up toward the ceiling as if trying to recall a memory. Then I shook my head and said, "Nobody stood out to me. I was twelve when I left the home, Miss Hartley. I look entirely different now than I did then; I imagine she looks nothing like the girl at the home."

"Of course," Dr. Vogel said.

"At least now I have a name to add to my prayers about the missing girl," I said. "If you'll excuse me, I'll run along."

"No, Mary," Dr. Vogel said, placing her fork on her plate and pushing herself away from the table. "You'll stay here with me. You need to rest, I know you didn't sleep much last night. It'll be a long day. Hartley, arrange for the cook to have provisions brought to us. Mary, go lie down, dear, I'll need your help later."

"Yes, ma'am."

"Some Christmas week," Vogel groused, as I was leaving the room. "A fine Christmas this will be if the newspapers hear of this before we find the girl. Now let's see that other map, Hartley."

I was exhausted, but when I collapsed onto the soft bed, I couldn't stop fretting about Lillian in that cold cabin. And now—what if the phones were back in service before I was able to leave? Once Hartley or Vogel spoke to Mother Bea, I would surely be arrested.

But Lillian was out of that wretched cell, and that thought alone soothed me. Lillian would realize, from the ferocity of the storm, that nobody was coming to get her today. She'd use as little firewood as possible; there was plenty to get her though the storm.

I must have dozed for some time because when I awoke, the room was dim. I jumped from my bed and looked outside. The snow had stopped; the afternoon sun was low. I saw that the driveway in front of the mansion had been partially plowed. Good. Soon, Charlie would be able to get Lillian and take her to the train in Harrisburg.

I realized, suddenly, that I had to go with her; I had no choice now. As soon as the phones were back in service, my involvement with Lillian's escape would be known. I had to find Charlie before he went to get Lillian. I'd go with her on the train to New York. Jake would help us. He was probably there by now. He'd know whom we should speak to; he'd know a lawyer who could help me if the doctor took legal action. And once he'd published the article about Dr. Vogel and the judge and the whiskey, nobody would care about my involvement with one missing girl.

I opened my closet and lifted my mother's suitcase down from a shelf at the top. Could it possibly have been less than a year ago when I'd packed it to come here? I was so apprehensive, yet full of hope, then. Now, when I placed the suitcase on the bed, I hardly recognized it. I hadn't used it. It was in the same condition as when I had arrived at the doctor's house, but it looked old and a bit dirty, perched there, on the fine French bed linens. When I opened it, the pink satin lining looked cheap, even in the dim light of the room. I imagined my mother's delight when she'd first opened it; she probably thought it very fancy, the way we girls at St. Cat's had when we saw it. Now I knew the shiny pink satin was too much; it was gaudy and second-rate. It had been poorly sewn as well, some of the stitching was already frayed. And it was far too small to hold all the things I'd accumulated in my time here. New clothes, books, shoes, boxes of letters—mostly from Jake. Well, I would take the letters and the best clothes. Maybe I could get word to Claudette and Florence and they could send me the rest of my things in a week or two.

I was just folding the last blouse I could fit into the case when there was a knock on the door. Dr. Vogel never came to my room or even entered this hall, so I thought maybe Florence or Claudette had returned. But in fact, it was Dr. Vogel. She had Trixie and Peg with her, and they jumped up on my bed and sniffed around my suitcase with much eager excitement.

"Oh, hello, Dr. Vogel," I said, moving to stand in front of the suitcase. "Have you any word about the girl?"

Dr. Vogel was carrying a lantern. She'd obviously had a bath, and she seemed to have regained some of her usual cool composure, but her lantern's flickering flame made me think she was still a little shaky from last night. She set the lantern on my nightstand and swatted at the dogs.

"Off! Down off the bed, girls!" she said, She perched on the side of my bed and looked sadly around the room.

"No, she hasn't been found," Dr. Vogel sighed. "The main roads are still not clear—phones and power are still out." Now her gaze settled on the suitcase behind me. "Are you packing, Mary? Are you going someplace?"

"Yes, well, not today, of course," I said, turning and trying to quickly close the suitcase. "I'm going to New York City on Saturday. Remember? I'm spending Christmas there with a friend. I just thought I'd pack now and get it over with."

The doctor flipped the suitcase lid back open and began poking idly through its contents.

"My dear, I think you're overpacking. All this for two nights? Nothing to wear out for the evening?"

Jake's letters were all tied up in a bundle that I'd stashed at the bottom of the suitcase. I gently scolded the dogs who'd hopped back onto the bed—they gave me an excuse to pull the suitcase away and close it.

"You're right," I said. "I didn't know, really, what to bring. I'm not sure what my friend has planned for us. So, I thought, well, I'd pack for anything."

"I'm sorry, Mary," the doctor said. "But I think you'll have to cancel your trip. Even if the girl—Lillian, from your orphan home in Scranton—is found, I'll need your help. Word is already out about an escapee. There'll be letters to the trustees, the newspapers are bound to plague us. Hartley had an early supper sent to us from the dining hall. Come, eat with me. We'll both need strength—we've some long days ahead of us, Christmas or no Christmas."

"Certainly," I said.

I was fastening the clasps on the suitcase when the doctor said, "I'd leave that thing open until you have time to unpack, it needs airing. It's got a rather stale smell, hasn't it? Next time you plan a trip, I'll give you something much nicer, my dear."

Twenty-Six

"ISN'T it lovely the way the candlelight changes the atmosphere?" Dr. Vogel said, as I sat in my usual spot beside her at the table. "I find it soothing. It reminds me of dinners in our dining room when I was a girl." She poured wine into my glass and then into her own.

"It is pretty, isn't it?" I said, looking around at the candelabras that had been placed around the room. There was a fire in the fireplace, which warmed the room considerably. There were still maps and papers strewn around the table, but the doctor had cleared the places where we sat.

She lifted her glass, as she always did, and I touched its rim with my own.

"Good Lord, Mary, this is a terrible, terrible tragedy, an absolute nightmare," the doctor sighed as she took a sip.

"We can't give up hope," I said. I also took a healthy sip. I was worried about not being able to leave, worried too about Lillian and Jake. I took another sip.

"No," Dr. Vogel said, "we must still hope and pray but we also need to strategize a bit. We have to prepare for the worst. Whether she's found or not, there'll be an inquest. It's just terrible timing, so soon after that nastiness in the papers about the judge and confiscated whiskey."

"Oh?" I said. "How do you mean?" Yes, the room was prettier by candlelight, but it was harder to make out the doctor's expression as she spoke. I scooted my chair a little closer to her. She seemed to think I did this to comfort her, and she placed her hand on mine for a moment and gave it a gentle squeeze of gratitude.

"Bad press, Mary. This is quite bad, but I won't let it cause us any permanent harm. I'll phone my lawyers as soon as the lines open again. Now that I think of it, your trip to New York is impossible. We'll have to meet the lawyers in person, you and I. We can't have nosy switch-board operators listening in. But, Mary, you may rely on me—I'll protect you."

"Protect *me*?" I said.

The doctor was cutting into her ham. When she didn't reply, I wondered if she'd heard me. I was about to repeat the question when she turned to offer me a sympathetic smile. "Why, yes, dear, you're quite involved, unfortunately."

What else had she learned? The phones were still out, so she couldn't have spoken to Mother Bea.

My mouth was very dry. I took a sip of my water. Then, in as steady a voice as I could manage, I said, "Dr. Vogel, as I told you, I didn't really know the girl. I didn't know her at all, not really."

"The girl?" The doctor had turned her attention back to her meal.

"Yes, ma'am. The missing girl. Lillian. I didn't even know she was here. Why would I need to be protected?" Now I was glad for the dimness of the lights, hoping the doctor couldn't see me too clearly as I fumbled for these lies. "I have no idea where she is."

"Mary, what on earth are you carrying on about? Of course you don't know where she is. I'm not talking about the missing girl," Dr. Vogel said. She was looking at me now as if I'd lost my mind completely.

"But you said . . . I'm not sure . . . What were you talking about?"

"I'm talking about the judge and that business with the medicine. Filmore's hired man knows that you and I swapped out the labels and some of the contents of the bottles. It might look, to some, as if we're—well, common bootleggers." The doctor paused to chuckle, briefly, at the absurdity of this.

"But bootlegging is a felony," she went on, pointing her knife at me for emphasis. "Nobody will understand why we weren't following exact protocol that day." She lowered her knife and cut into her ham. "You and I know it was all aboveboard. But we have no way of knowing whom the Judge's colored man or his son might have told. There'll be news stories about the missing girl. I wouldn't be surprised if your man Enright is in town sniffing around like a mongrel already. And that gives the local rags an excuse to pry into that business with the judge again."

Why did she mention Jake? Did she know where he was? Now I reached for my wineglass instead of my water glass and I took a healthy swig.

"I don't think Mr. Enright would have any reason to be up here," I said, after carefully placing my wineglass back on the table. "And, ma'am, I'm not really involved with any of the business with the judge. Or the *medicine*. Not really."

"No, quite right," Vogel said, placing her hand on mine again, and giving me a smile of reassurance. "You're not involved, and you never were. We must stick to that line, Mary. I'll perjure myself in a court of law, if it comes to that. You can rely on me. It's all my fault. I got you into this. I'll handle it."

The doctor refilled her wineglass and my own. Then she pointed to the plate of cold ham and potatoes on the table before me.

"We must eat," she said, jutting out her chin defiantly. "We must remain strong. We have some trying times ahead, but we'll get through this, dear."

I managed to force down a few small bites, but my mind was racing. Jake had all the documents that proved that the doctor and the judge were running large quantities of confiscated whiskey and wine through the Village. It never occurred to me that when it was published, the facts might also implicate me. But those records went back for years; long before I came here. I'd only helped the doctor once.

"I'm to blame for the missing girl too," Dr. Vogel said gloomily. "I gave Hartley too much power, I stopped managing things as carefully as I used to, and this is what happens. That Olga! Leaving the girls unattended so she could go to the infirmary party. I'm shocked at Mrs. Nolan, Mary. Shocked. At the end of the day though, I'm to blame."

"I don't think you'll be blamed," I said. "You weren't blamed when the other girls escaped, right?"

"What other girls?" The doctor said, turning to me, and I immediately realized my mistake. Charlie had told me about the other girls. Vogel had been acting, all along, as if Lillian were the first girl to run away.

"Didn't the newspaper article—the one Mr. Enright wrote—didn't it mention other girls escaping? Or something like that?" I managed, moving my food around my plate.

"No. Certainly not. That was about inmates whose families tried to get them out through the courts." I was focusing on my plate, but I felt the doctor's piercing glare.

"But," I said, summoning the courage to face her again. "I do remember hearing—wasn't there talk in the trustees' meeting about girls escaping?"

"Yes, escaping the *buildings*. Not the grounds. The girls here are too slow to come up with any workable escape plans—you know that. Good Lord, Mary, let's focus on the crisis at hand. The missing girl and the judge." The doctor's voice was calmer now "We haven't time to discuss silly rumors about other girls. I need you to go to the office later tonight. Quietly though, Mary. Make sure nobody sees you. There are records there that you need to bring here to me. Anything to do with the judge and the medicinal whiskey."

I refilled my water glass. It was so hot in there, with the fire going, and my throat was so dry from the salty ham.

"Dr. Vogel," I said, and now I made a point of looking directly into her eyes, so she'd absorb the sincerity of my words. "I don't think we should have the files here. And—I thought you didn't want me to be involved. Wouldn't that be—I mean, if you're planning on hiding or destroying records, wouldn't that make me more involved?"

Dr. Vogel tilted her head and gave me a baffled little smile.

"But you *are* involved, Mary. I'm trying to hide any evidence of that. And while you're there, I need the files of the girls who are out on work parole. There are some that you might not be aware of, you'll find those records in the same closet as the medicine labels."

"Work parole records?" I said, my mind still scrambling about those liquor records. I'd given them to Jake. I'd replaced them with old dairy receipts. I couldn't hand those over to the doctor.

"Yes, work parole," Dr. Vogel said. "I need the records of every girl who has worked outside the Village in recent years. I want to review them. Perhaps they helped this girl who escaped."

"Oh," I said. "*Dr. Vogel's girls*—as they're called."

I looked down at my plate. I'd given those records to Jake too.

There were many other girls out on "work parole." I found their files in a box at the back of that closet. There were dozens. They worked in Clayburg and Lewisburg and Harrisburg. Not just in homes but in factories and other businesses too. Their salaries were paid directly to Dr. Agnes Vogel. They were deposited in her personal bank account. And for some stupid reason, Dr. Vogel kept a record of this. Exactly how much she'd been paid for each inmate's "vocational training parole" and how she was paid. Sometimes cash, sometimes with a personal check.

Dr. Agnes Vogel, I'd thought, as I rifled through the files. *American, Protestant, Moron. Walks, talks, records her own crimes.*

Now I said, "Are you worried people will find out about Ida?"

"I beg your pardon, dear? Ida?" The doctor was pouring what was at least her fourth glass of wine. "The girl who escaped—isn't she called Lillian. Or was it Lila?"

"Lillian, yes, that's the name of the one who ran away, but what about Ida? She worked for Mr. Whitcomb, the bank manager." I was amazed at my calm tone. "Are you worried that somebody might find out about her, and the other girls you sent to work there?"

The doctor took a sip of her wine and said, "Oh, yes. Poor Ida. I've had many hundreds of girls here since we opened the Village, Mary, I can't be expected to remember them all." She sat back, tilted her head to the side, and gazed at me thoughtfully. "Now I remember Ida. That was a sad business. I shouldn't have let you talk me out of going to the police that day, Mary."

I touched my napkin to my lips, and then had to use it to dry my sweaty palms when it was back on my lap.

"I didn't talk you out of going to the police," I said.

"No," Dr. Vogel said, with a little smile and a wink. "Of course not, you must maintain that position and I'll back you up, Mary. Still, I should have gone to the police. Never mind that now, I have the best lawyers in the county, we'll go to them tomorrow. Together. Now, pass me that map, will you, dear?"

"But you sent another girl to the Whitcombs," I said, my anger overpowering my fear. "Mrs. Wallace, from your bridge group, she told me. You heard her."

"Did I?" Dr. Vogel said, squinting down at the map now, with one eye closed. All the wine seemed to have suddenly affected her vision. "I don't . . . I don't quite remember that. Old Hartley decides who goes out to work. I'll have to pay closer attention. Another glass of wine dear?"

I didn't put anything in the doctor's wine that evening, but you wouldn't know it. She finished the bottle we had with dinner, and then she moved on to whiskey. I thought she'd been toying with me, making those implications about my involvement with the judge during dinner and blaming me for what happened with Ida. But now she seemed to have forgotten all about it. She appeared to have full confidence in me, still, and I realized I'd never fully appreciated the enormity of Dr. Vogel's arrogance. How could somebody like me pose any threat to Dr. Vogel? It was inconceivable to her; it wasn't just that she was tipsy. She thought of me, not as a sort of daughter, but as a useful little fool. I had to keep my emotions in check, so I tried not to think about Lillian or Ida or the other girls. Instead, I focused on the survey maps spread out before us.

"What's this?" I said. "Is that a shed or something?" I thought it wouldn't hurt to offer up a red herring or two. I wanted her to forget that earlier idea of having me go get the records from the office.

The doctor leaned across the map with her candle and said that there used to be a shack out in the woods; she had it torn down years ago.

There was a knock on the door.

"It's probably Durk, go let him in," Vogel said. I noticed she was slurring slightly now, from the effects of the wine.

But when I opened the door, it was Sheriff Eckers. "Evening, miss," he said, removing his hat. "Is the doctor still awake? I'd like to tell her where we are with the search."

"Certainly, come in," I said. He followed me into the dining room.

"The sheriff is here, ma'am," I said.

Vogel leveled an angry glare at me. She didn't want the sheriff on the property, let alone in the house. Then she smiled warmly up at Eckers and said carefully, "Hello, Sheriff, any news?"

"No," Eckers said. "We heard a girl was picked up hitchhiking earlier, but she's not one of yours. She'd snuck off to visit a boy at his farm, and the storm caught her by surprise. She was just going home to her family."

"Girls will . . . be girls," Vogel mumbled. "Anything else?"

"No, we're just glad the snow stopped. Tomorrow's going to be a little warmer. Maybe some of this snow will melt and then we might be able to find her." The sheriff frowned down at the hat in his hands and said, "Dr. Vogel—I . . . I don't want to upset you, but I'm afraid we might be looking for a body at this point. I mean, her being so slow in the head and not having the right clothes for the weather and all."

"Of course, I'm aware of that," she said. She turned her face away and appeared to be wiping a tear from her eye with her handkerchief. "One of our matrons was lax in her duties and . . . will be let go from her position." She cleared her throat, to obscure the slurring, then continued. "She'll be fired at once. But, I'm the superintendent. I'm responsible for the welfare of all . . . of all the girls."

She buried her face in her handkerchief. I rushed over and patted her shoulder gently, saying, "No, Dr. Vogel. Nobody is to blame but the girl."

Eckers agreed that the doctor was being too hard on herself.

"We have excellent staff, as you know, Sheriff," Vogel whispered. "That's why—it's why this time—this one time—is the first that such a thing could be here."

I caught the sheriff's quick glance at the doctor's empty glass and then at the bottle on the table.

"Sheriff, thank you for the news," I said. He took my lead and followed me toward the door.

"Good night, Doctor," he called back, but she was dabbing at her eyes again.

I opened the front door, and as the sheriff put his hat on his head, he said, "You're the secretary?"

"Yes, I'm Mary Engle, sir."

"Anything you can tell us about the girl that might help with the search?"

"I didn't know her, Sheriff. I'm not sure how I might be of any help."

"I just mean, do you know if can she talk and all? Can she follow directions or commands or is she too slow?"

I'd almost forgotten how the outside world perceived the girls who were sent to the Village. The sheriff was under the impression that there was a woman wandering around in the snow as senseless and bewildered as a small child.

"Most of the girls here can understand simple commands and also speak, but she's, of course, limited," I said. "That's what has us so concerned. She wouldn't know how to survive in this."

The sheriff looked very sad. He shook his head, and as he turned to leave, he said, "I guess your boss had to take some medicine for her nerves."

I got his meaning. He knew Dr. Vogel wasn't just upset—she was drunk.

"Yes, she did, as a matter of fact." If I knew where Jake was, or whether the records I'd stolen were in safe hands, I could ask the sheriff to protect me. But who would believe anything I said about the whiskey, the girls farmed out to work, salaries lining the doctor's own pockets. I had no proof. The proof was all gone. I'd stolen it.

"Well, I wouldn't be surprised if reporters show up," the sheriff said. "Word is out. You'll be doing her a service to not let her speak to anybody until she's had some sleep. A person—well, they might get the idea she was drinking."

"Of course, Sheriff. I'll watch out for her, but as you said, she's had to take medicine for her nerves. The doctor . . ." I made sure he saw me biting my lip as if I were struggling with this lie. "Dr. Vogel certainly doesn't drink *alcohol*."

He chuckled and gave me a wink. "Yeah, me neither. Never touch the stuff."

I watched him drive slowly off. I was about to go back to the doctor in the dining room when I saw the headlights of the dairy truck approach. I had no coat on, but I scrambled down the snow-covered steps. Charlie was driving. He slowed to a stop and I opened the passenger door.

"Hi, Charlie, the sheriff was just here. . . ."

I was interrupted by a low moaning sound. I saw that there was a heavy blanket covering something on the bench seat next to Charlie.

"Is that—Lillian?" I whispered.

The blanket moved and I saw a man's head poke out. He wore a sheepskin hunter's cap, and his face was smeared with blood and dirt, but I knew instantly who it was.

"Jake! Oh God, what happened to you?" I cried.

"I'm fine, get . . . in," Jake whispered.

"My cousin who works out at the mill—he dropped him at my folks' house. The roads are almost clear," Charlie said. "We gotta get Lillian now. By tomorrow, everybody's going to be watching everything we do."

I ran inside for my coat and hat. It didn't take much to convince the doctor that Charlie needed me to drive to Sunbury with him. That's where the milk distributor was, and he had almost two days of surplus to be transported before the milking tomorrow.

"Suppose he skids off the road or something," I said to the doctor, when she protested. "I'm afraid he might run his mouth off to anybody who might help him—he might talk about the—trouble here. If I'm with him, I can keep an eye on him."

"Okay. But come to me the minute you get back. I might . . . rest . . . but wake me up when you return," Vogel said.

I wanted to run to my room and grab my suitcase. But the doctor was drunk, not unconscious. It was too risky.

I took my hat and coat and squeezed into the truck next to Jake. I thought he had to remain curled up under the blanket to conceal him from view. When we'd left the gates of the Village, I told him he could sit up. He moaned something in reply.

I pulled the blanket back and saw that he was curled with his knees up near his chest, not because he was hiding, but because he was in pain. He held on to his side with one hand; he had a pint of whiskey in the other.

"Jake?" I said. "Are you awake? Can you hear me?"

He nodded and moaned.

"We have to take him to the hospital, right now, Charlie."

"No," Jake whispered. And he seemed to be saying something else, but I couldn't understand him.

"He'll be okay," Charlie said. "He's got a busted rib or two's my guess. Hospital's in the opposite direction from where your friend is. We gotta get her, now or never."

"I'm . . . good," Jake grunted. Now he propped himself up, grimacing and sucking in his breath at this slight movement.

The drive back to the hunting lodge was much quicker than the drive we'd taken—was it two nights ago? No. It was just last night. It felt like a week had passed. I realized it had probably felt longer to poor Lillian, all alone there in the drafty cabin.

As we drove, Jake managed to fill us in on what happened. He'd been waiting for us at the mill when the hired Pinkerton men showed up and started in on him. Fortunately, he'd let a friend know he was there, and he showed up and convinced them to let him go.

"How?" I asked. But Jake seemed to be dozing off. We drove on in silence for a while, and then I said, "Do you think Lil's run out of firewood, Charlie?"

"Dunno."

"There are other things she could burn there to keep warm, right?"

"Yup."

Charlie was exhausted and clearly regretted ever getting himself involved in this. Jake was passed out cold. I busied myself with thoughts of us all arriving in New York tomorrow. I would drive Jake's car; it was hidden in a side road near the mill, he'd told me. We'd get Jake to a hospital to be checked out along the way. Then, later, maybe as soon as New Year's Eve, when Jake and Lil were feeling better, all of us would celebrate. And Graham—he'd be with us too. All of us. Together at last, to ring in the new year.

By the time we arrived at the turn-off to the cabin, I was trembling with excitement. The driveway to the cabin was unplowed, and Charlie had to go slowly through the thick powder. The truck's headlights shone on a stand of pine trees, and then the cabin was visible in the distance. I was thrilled to see smoke spiraling from the chimney.

"She didn't run out of firewood, at least . . ."

"Who the hell is that?" Charlie interrupted.

An old jalopy of a truck was parked near the cabin. It had come from the opposite direction—its tracks in the snow were visible behind it. The engine was running, the headlights on.

Jake stirred and mumbled, "Whas going on?"

"Who did you tell she was here, Charlie?" I cried.

"I didn't tell nobody," he said.

We were still several hundred yards from the cabin. Charlie stopped the truck and turned off the headlights, hoping whoever was in the other truck hadn't noticed us. The other truck was parked in such a way that its headlights illuminated the entire cabin. All the windows were dark. There were no footprints or tracks in the snow. The only indication that somebody was inside was the smoke from the chimney.

"Lillian will be able to hide in there someplace," I whispered.

Jake was now sitting in a hunched position, and he squinted at the cabin. I clutched his hand.

"If they go inside, she'll hide, I'm sure," I said.

"She might be able to sneak out the back," Charlie said. "Maybe she'll see our truck from that side window and sneak out and we can grab her while they're searching inside."

Two men climbed down from the cab of the truck. They both looked elderly and in no rush to get inside. The younger man (who was easily sixty) had a rifle slung casually across his shoulders. He waited while the other lit a cigarette.

"Hold on, now. That's Nate Varnum and his pop," Charlie said. "They're the farmers up the road—they watch this place. I can talk to them, Bud and my dad are cousins. He's a good guy."

Charlie was just about to open the door when the front door of the cabin flew open.

"No, no—what the hell's she doing?" Charlie said.

The other men craned their necks to get a better look at who was coming out of the cabin. Charlie honked the horn, then jumped out of the truck.

"Jesus," said Jake.

"NATE!" Charlie called. "Nate, Bud, it's me—Charlie Durkin. . . ."

The men turned to look at Charlie.

"Look someone's coming out the door," Jake said. "Who's that guy?"

"LILLIAN, NO!" I screamed, but she couldn't hear me. She was wearing oversize men's wool trousers and a hunting coat. Her hair was tucked up into her cap. She looked like a scrappy teenaged boy, like a little hobo, but it was Lillian who came charging out of the cabin. She had a rifle pressed to her cheek, aimed at the two farmers. I knew it was her because of the way she moved her hips when she ran—they were slung low, her knees bent and her toes angled out ever so slightly. Lillian always did a kind of madcap scramble like that when she was particularly excited or joyous about something. When we were playing. When we were little girls.

The first shot shattered the glass of the farmers' truck's windshield. The sound of it echoed across the valley, drowning out my calls to Lillian. The men scrambled back behind their truck. I turned the headlights on and honked the horn.

Now that she was illuminated, I saw that Lillian was grinning triumphantly. She would never return to Nettleton State Village; she'd never let these men take her back there alive.

She cocked the bolt of the rifle and raised it to her cheek again.

I jumped down from the truck and yelled, again, "LILLIAN!"

Lillian turned toward me.

"Mary?" she said.

At least that's what I thought she said. She was too far away, but Lillian said something; I saw her lips moving. She said something, and she was still smiling as she spun very slowly in a sort of backward pirouette, her arms flung wide and the rifle sailing from her as the echo of the farmers' rifles sounded once, then again and again.

Twenty-Seven

AFTER helping the men move Lillian, Jake seemed to have trouble breathing. He needed medical care. Charlie said it was urgent now; he'd almost certainly punctured a lung. The sun had just risen, but the road was still covered with snow, and it took us an hour to get to the hospital.

Jake kissed my teary face before an orderly wheeled him off. The receptionist let Charlie use the telephone to call Dr. Vogel. A lot of what happened that morning is blurry now. I guess I was in shock, but I do recall Charlie's end of the conversation. I was clinging to his jacket and listening, my face pressed to his.

"Yeah, they were taking her on over to the county morgue. No, it's in Northumberland County. I dunno." Charlie frowned and tried to jerk his arm away from my grip, but I hung on tighter. "That's where they said they were taking her," he said. "I didn't know Sunbury's in a different county, neither, but it is. Northumberland's county coroner, he's gonna come out to the Village this week. I guess there's some legal papers. Yeah, Mary's with me, we're coming back now, but it'll take us a while."

We rode back to the Village in silence. The sky had brightened, the wind had died down, and shadows of lingering clouds shifted in dark panels across the flat white fields we passed. We crossed a small bridge that spanned a narrow, partially frozen river. Reeds poked, bone-like, along its icy edges. I saw a cluster of tiny black birds shoot out of a shrub, explode into little frantic spirals, and settle back down into icy branches.

Finally, we turned into the drive to the Village. I blinked, mistily, out at the trees that lined the long, winding driveway. The limbs on the pines hung low, heavy with snow, just like a Christmas scene in a storybook. How frightening the woods had seemed when I'd first arrived last spring. What a timid, stupid thing I was then.

We drove past the pair of farm horses, standing in their frozen field. They raised their heads in unison. One arched its neck and trotted alongside us in the snowdrifts, its tail raised like a flag. The other followed, and I noticed how graceful they seemed. The proud way they tossed their heads and their springy strides made them look more like the gallant Arabian steeds I'd seen in a movie than the tired plow horses I knew them to be. They pranced along the fence line, following the truck to the end of their field, then wheeled around and galloped back the other way.

We turned onto the main drive, and that's when we saw them. Women and girls, all inmates—it looked like a hundred at least—were wading through the snowy field toward us. Some were already in the road. Charlie slowed to a stop, and they surrounded the truck. Their voices rose from all sides of us like a whispered chorus. *Is it true? Is Lillian gone? Is she really dead? What happened to Lillian?*

They'd already heard the sad news. I blinked out at their faces. I realized that I'd avoided looking at the inmates' faces whenever possible, from the very first day I'd arrived at the Village. I watched as one girl did the sign of the cross as we passed. Many had raw, red cheeks that glistened with tears, and some had snot running down over their chapped lips, but I didn't look away. I looked at each girl, and I thought of all the names I'd read on their records: Emma, Diana, Elma, Sarah, Anne, Ingrid, Freda, Miriam. On paper, they'd had no more meaning to me than the crop inventories I'd typed: oats, wheat, beans, corn. Now I looked from one face to the next, and thought, *Are you Diana? Sarah, is that you?*

We finally stopped at the entrance to the main building, where more girls gathered, shivering, their heads bowed in sorrow. Soon the sun would melt the snow on the road. Soon the girls would be back in the long, dark barn, or in the kitchen or the laundry. Later, the cows would emerge from the shed, relieved of their daily burden—the milk that kept coming for calves they'd never known. The girls had come out to mourn their lost friend. I felt God's presence then, as the truck drifted, finally to a stop. I felt it as I never had before.

Hal Goodwin leaned his head inside the truck. He took my hand and helped me out, whispering, "You okay?"

"Yes," I said. Betty Goodwin and Bertie immediately huddled around us.

"Oh, Mary, I'm so very sorry. What a shock," Betty said. "Hal thinks you should come on over to our place right now."

"Yup," Hal said. "Let's go."

Bertie gave me a hug and whispered, "We gotta move quickly now, Hal's going to take us to the train—they know the deal."

"These girls," I said, gazing from one inmate's face to the next. "Hal, do you know which of the girls is Francine Cotter?"

Bertie said, "Mary, listen to us, we need to focus now."

"Francine Cotter had the cot next to Lillian," I said, recalling that night long ago in the woods with Lillian. *Ask people about Francine Cotter*, Lillian had said. Her husband had put her here too.

Dr. Vogel was now at our side. She was still wearing last night's clothes and was more disheveled than I'd ever seen her.

"Thank goodness you and Mr. Durkin found our poor Lillian, Miss Engle. If only you'd have thought to look there sooner."

She was using her loud, public-speaking voice. I saw there were other people, in addition to the staff and inmates, crowding around us. Sheriff Eckers was there and four or five other men. One of the men pulled a camera out from inside his large overcoat. He aimed it at an inmate who looked to be about fourteen years old. She was shivering because she wore only a thin dress and boots in the snow. Her arms and legs were bare.

The sheriff knocked the camera from the man's hand and grumbled, "Show a little respect."

"OUT!" Vogel shouted at them. "Sheriff, I'm not going to ask again, tell these men they're trespassing."

But Sheriff Eckers was looking at another police car that was approaching. When it stopped, Eckers walked over to it. There were other cars behind it, driving slowly, as if in a funeral procession.

"Vultures," Vogel grumbled. "Coming all the way out here just to gape. I'll sue any of you who dares write about this tragedy. Do you hear me?"

Cloris strode toward us with a group of dairy girls at her side.

"Is Lillian in the truck, Mary?" she asked shakily, her eyes red-rimmed.

"No. She's at the morgue, over in Sunbury," Charlie answered for me.

Another photographer jumped out of a car. Men and women emerged, one by one, from other cars. I recognized some of them from town. There was Mrs. Malone—the matron of the inn. I saw the Schuberts from church. Many had newspapers in their gloved hands or tucked up under their arms.

"What's the meaning of this? Why's the gate open?" Vogel demanded. "Sheriff, have these people removed, they're trespassing."

But the sheriff was reading a newspaper that a man handed him. The man gave newspapers to some of the inmates who asked for them as well. He handed me a newspaper too. It was the *Mifflinburg Times*. The headline on the front page read:

RECORDS FROM NETTLETON VILLAGE RAISE QUESTIONS.

Jake didn't tell me he'd already written the article. The plan had been that he was going to wait until I gave my notice. Then I saw that the article wasn't written by Jake; it was by Ike Brown.

I scanned the article and the words, *abuse* and *illegal* and *alcohol*, jumped out at me. Near the end, I read: *An employee of the asylum, concerned about the welfare of the inmates, provided the records to an individual who then passed them on to this newspaper.*

I heard murmurings from some of the people who'd arrived in cars.

Why haven't they proper coats and boots?

I thought they couldn't read.

Cloris said loudly, "Most of the girls here can read and write. This newspaper item here's the gospel truth. I work here. I know it."

Dr. Vogel had read as much as she wanted. Now she rolled her paper up and waved it in the air.

"OUT! All of you, out of here. Sheriff, do your damned job, arrest anyone who won't leave."

"This here's not private property," a man said. He was an elderly man with a woman who appeared to be his wife at his side. "My taxes help pay for this place. You don't have no right to run me off. We had a niece in here, once. Died when she wasn't yet twenty. They said she had an accident, tripped and fell down the stairs, but we always wondered."

Vogel walked briskly toward them. I couldn't see her expression, but it caused the couple to shuffle back a few steps.

"Tell it to a judge. I'll see you in court," Vogel said. Then she turned to the rest of the crowd and shouted, "That goes for all of you. Everybody out."

"Aggie, dear, good gracious what a mess," said a woman's voice.

It was Mrs. Howell, from the board of director's meeting. She wore a fur coat and was accompanied by her husband—a tall, thin, serious-looking man who scowled across the crowd. Dr. Vogel hadn't heard her; she'd moved closer to Sheriff Eckers to hiss threats at him. He was still squinting at his newspaper.

"Mrs. Howell, thank goodness," I said. "I'm Dr. Vogel's secretary."

"Yes, of course, Miss Engle," said Mrs. Howell. "I had Mr. Howell drive me over as soon as we read the article."

Now Vogel was beside us. "Eloise, Stephen," she said to the Howells. "Very glad you're here. Stephen—you're a lawyer, get these people to leave. Tell them we'll sue."

"I don't represent the Village, Aggie, you know that," Mr. Howell said. He was gazing sadly at the girls who shivered in the cold, passing newspapers from one to the other.

Mrs. Howell said, "I've heard from a few others on the board, Aggie, we'll call an emergency session as soon as possible, to see if any of these claims bear any truth at all."

"They most certainly do not," said Vogel.

Bertie took this opportunity to pull me aside. "Mary, c'mon, go get whatever you can and pack up quick—Hal's got his car running and waiting. Hurry, Vogel's distracted."

I couldn't move.

"Now," Bertie said. "Let's go." Hal and Betty huddled close again and urged me to follow them.

"We need to help the girls in Building Five," I whispered. "You've never been in there. These people are here now, this is our chance—they need to see it, or nobody will believe it."

"You can have that reporter write about it," Bertie said.

"No, we need witnesses," I said. "Hal, you know what the girls are like when they leave Building Five. What happened to Lillian—it can't all be for nothing. She wanted me to help the girls in there."

"Mary," Hal said grimly. "You're tired and you ain't thinking right. Listen. Listen to me now." He gave my shoulders a little shake and looked into my eyes. "Keep your mouth shut, it's not just your neck on the chopping block here—think about Bertie, Charlie, Cloris. And now me and Betty. We wanna help you, but this here's serious business now. What happened to Lillian—you could be blamed, you know."

Bertie said, "Think about Jake, Mary. Think about you and Jake, now, don't make a bigger mess. . . ."

"Sheriff Eckers," I said loudly. The sheriff looked at me. Dr. Vogel looked at me too. I heard Hal curse as he turned and stomped away from me.

"There's a problem that needs your attention." I said it before I had a chance to chicken out.

Better a coward for a minute than dead for the rest of your life.

"What kind of problem?" Mrs. Howell asked.

"Mary? What are you carrying on about?" said Dr. Vogel, "Whatever it is, I'm sure it can wait."

"The girls in one of the residence halls, some are in urgent need of help." I looked calmly at Vogel and said, "It's Building Five. The sheriff needs to go right now. There are girls who are very unwell, and . . . and . . . I don't know how they survived the storm, with the power out. The conditions in that building—they're worse even than it says in the newspaper. Worse than I ever knew."

"Mary, you've had a terrible shock," Dr. Vogel said. "You're not making sense. Sheriff, I insist you clear these people out at once. I'll help our Miss Engle."

"Well, Doctor, now I'm told there are people in danger," the sheriff said. "There's already one girl dead today. I'll go over and have a quick look, make sure everybody's okay."

"You most certainly will not," said Dr. Vogel. "That's a women's residence. We don't allow men to just wander in. Do you want me to have you cited for charges of indecency?"

The sheriff looked exhausted.

"I'll go," said Mrs. Howell. "Sheriff, I'm a trustee here at the Village. I'm on the governing board. I can inspect the building, see what the fuss is all about."

"Eloise? No, that's out of the question," said Vogel, using a kinder voice now. "I know you're trying to help, dear, but really."

"This way, Mrs. Howell," I said.

"I'll come along," said Mrs. Malone, the owner of the inn.

"No," said Dr. Vogel. "Now listen to me, all of you. There are women in Building Five who are violently disturbed. Opening the doors to their rooms without trained personnel is inviting disaster. I won't allow such a disturbance. Eloise, all of you. I thank you for your concern, but I must think of your safety."

"Can you not come along to the building, Aggie?" Mrs. Howell said. "Certainly you know how to handle any who misbehave. I do think we'd be quite negligent not to see what Miss Engle is talking about."

"No," said Dr. Vogel. "I will not. I'm calling my attorney, then the county prosecutor, Sheriff. Yes, I'll call your boss. I'll have you fired."

"It'll just take a few minutes," I said to the women. "Please come with me."

Dr. Vogel grabbed my elbow and gave it an angry jerk. "Miss Engle, you'll be discharged from your duties if you take anyone to that building. It's not safe. Your actions and words are giving me some very worrisome ideas, you'll be wise to do as you're told."

"I'll come too," Bertie said cheerily, pretending she hadn't heard the doctor. Cloris and Betty said that they'd be happy to come along as well.

Mrs. Howell looked at her husband. He gave her a sad nod. "Well, there we are, let's get this over with, Miss Engle," she said.

"You're fired, Mary Engle, you too, Mrs. Nolan, Mrs. Goodwin," Dr. Vogel said. "Sheriff, these people are no longer employed by the

Village, please have them removed, I'll not allow them to disturb and harass our residents. ECKERS!"

Cloris led the way. Mrs. Howell, I, and the others followed. The path to the building was shoveled, but it was narrow, and we had to walk single file. When the building loomed before us, I realized that I hadn't seen any of the other residents the night I'd snuck Lillian out of Building Five; they'd been locked in their rooms. What if they were wandering freely around the building, violent and disturbed, as the doctor had described them. What if they attacked us? But Cloris's determined stride gave me confidence. When she tried to open the door to the building, it was locked. She pounded on it.

"Open up, Olga, I've got a lady governor here," said Cloris.

"Oh, well, I'm not exactly a governor . . . ," Mrs. Howell protested.

The door swung open and Olga Swensen, the matron, stood there, speechless.

"We're here to check on the girls," Cloris said. "Follow me, ladies."

"Nobody told me nothing about it," Olga said, crossing her arms and blocking the door. This was the woman who'd thrown the contents of Lillian's bedpan in her face.

"We're telling you now," Cloris said. "We want to see the residents—move over."

We followed Cloris inside. Our eyes took a few seconds to adjust to the dark, but the stench of urine and other human filth crashed over us like a wave. Mrs. Howell cried out, her gloved hands flying to her face. Mrs. Malone pressed a handkerchief to her nose.

Bertie said in a voice that was almost a growl. "This place smells like . . . I don't know what, Olga Swensen. You should be ashamed."

"We do have ventilation problems," Olga muttered.

Our snow blindness was gone. We stood in a small vestibule. There was a desk to the left and behind it, an arched doorway leading to a dark winding staircase. Ahead was a long, dim corridor lined on both sides with solid wooden doors, all closed. There were sliding metal bolts across each door, secured in place with heavy padlocks.

"I'm going to find Dr. Vogel, see what this is all about," Olga said. She reluctantly handed me her heavy key chain. "You're sure she said this is okay?"

"Yes," I said. I took the keys without looking at her.

"The locks—they're numbered, same as the keys," she said as she rushed out the door.

From somewhere above was a loud and intermittent clanging; it sounded like a heavy chain rattling against iron. From another part of the building, a young girl's voice called out, "Maria? Can you hear me? Maria? Maria?" The place had a cold, dank, underground feeling though we'd climbed up several steps to come inside.

We followed Cloris into the corridor. I fumbled with the many keys on the key ring. There was a faint humming on the other side of the first door. I found the key to the numbered padlock. The steel bolt made a loud scraping noise when I slid it to the side, and the humming stopped instantly. The entire building was now as silent as a tomb. We stood there for a moment, we women who'd come to see. We huddled close together in the dim passageway. We barely breathed. We were listening—for what, we didn't know—and then I pushed the heavy door open wide.

A young woman sat on a wooden bench. It was the only thing to sit on besides the floor, and I realized that must be where she slept. She'd been knitting a scarf with some dark strands of wool, but now her needles froze mid-stitch and she peered up at us with a shy, inquisitive smile.

"Hello? I'm sorry, who is it, please?"

We introduced ourselves. She told us her name was Ethel. She stood, to be polite, I suppose, but we urged her to sit. She wore only a thin gown; it was rather see-through, and we didn't want to embarrass her. There was a filthy, overflowing chamber pot on the floor. Water dripped from a leak in the ceiling in one corner.

It took us over an hour, but we met all forty-seven occupants of Building Five. Bertie and Cloris stayed to help move them out of the building, but the rest of us trudged, sadly, back to the main building. Some of the locals were still hanging around. Dr. Vogel stood next to the front door of the main building. She shook her head grimly when she saw us approach. Mrs. Howell refused to look at her as we climbed the steps to stand next to her. From there, Mrs. Howell made a short announcement to the group assembled on the driveway below.

"My name is Eloise Howell. I'm a member of the board of trustees of Nettleton State Village. I'll be calling for an emergency meeting of the board immediately. What I've just witnessed—the condition in which we found the girls and women in one of the buildings, is something . . . Well, it's something I'll never forget." She paused so she could shoot a sidelong look at Dr. Vogel. "It's something that makes me deeply ashamed. What I saw . . . is reminiscent of the dark ages."

Mr. Howell had made his way to us, and now he whispered something to her.

"That's all I'll say about that today," Mrs. Howell said, her voice trembling, "Except that, please, it's time for everybody to go home. We've had a tragedy here. I gather most of you have already heard, an inmate who ran away in the storm has died. Please, let's all go now and pray for her and the other unfortunates here."

As Mr. Howell led her away, the others started back to their cars.

I turned toward the path leading to the superintendent's mansion, but Dr. Vogel stood in front of me.

"Where do you think you're going?" she demanded.

"I'll be quick, I'm just getting my things."

"What *things*? Everything in my house belongs to me. You need to go with the sheriff now. He's been waiting for you. He has questions about your involvement in the death of Lillian Henning."

The sheriff was seated in his car, which was still parked in the driveway. He appeared to be dozing. I took a step in his direction, but Vogel grabbed my wrist.

"Listen to me now," she said. Her voice had lost its angry edge now that it was just the two of us. "I do have compassion for you, Mary. I can't imagine how sick with self-recrimination you'll feel when you realize the magnitude of your errors. The promising future that is no more, college, a career, everything I offered, gone. And for what? I've known there were problems in Building Five. It'll all be sorted out. I'll still be here tomorrow, and the next day, and for years to come. You, on the other hand—a jury will decide where you'll end up, but that won't be the worst of it."

I felt so light-headed, it was hard to focus on her exact words, but I did wonder why she wasn't shivering or hunched against the cold, like I was. She only wore a knit dress and a cardigan. She hadn't even put on proper snow boots before coming outside, Yet, she still carried herself so elegantly. She always had such a regal posture—even now.

The doctor grabbed me by both arms and shook me.

"Mary, are you listening? Do you understand? A woman lost her life because of you. You'll have to live with that, forever."

I realized this might be the last time I ever saw Dr. Vogel. I wanted to look at her face one more time. She was so pretty. You forget how a person really looks, when you see them every day. When you get to really know them. Now I saw all the lovely details that had so thoroughly awed me when I first saw her at the Scranton YWCA. Her high cheekbones; her fine, straight nose; and those gray-blue eyes that were searching my eyes so anxiously now.

"I don't understand why, Mary." Dr Vogel said. My gaze seemed to soften her a little and she offered me a sad smile. "Why, would you so recklessly endanger the life of a helpless resident? And why, after everything I've done for you, would you betray me so horribly?"

The last of the cars had disappeared down the long drive. Eckers was waiting in his cruiser below. The setting sun had managed to bleed through the remaining whisps of a low cloud, and it cast a soft pink haze across the distant fields. The wind that raged just hours ago had died, and the world around us was eerily lucid and calm. I could see the little white puffs of my breath and the doctor's as well. Somewhere, not far off, a branch snapped from a tree, and I heard the soft thud as it landed in the snow.

"I did know Lillian, Dr. Vogel," I said. "She was my friend; she was more than a friend—she was like a sister, actually. That's why I did it."

I did it. I did something for once.

The doctor lost that elegant posture for a brief moment. She took a little stumbling step backward, hugged herself, and whispered, "Well, I've gathered it was something like that. But you never said anything to me. I would have helped her."

"I did it for Ida too. And all the Marys," I added. "There are so many Marys, Dr. Vogel. It was the same at St. Cat's—all the Marys."

I started down the steps. The snow in the shoveled path crunched under my boots as I took one careful step and then another.

Dr. Vogel followed me. "What *Marys*? What are you ranting about, child?"

"Your girls, Dr. Vogel. The names on the inmate roster. It's okay, you can't be expected to remember them all," I said. I stopped at the bottom of the steps to brush strange, sudden tears from my raw cheeks with the back of my mitten. How many times had I read that long inventory of names, without a single thought of the living girls and women stockpiled here? All of them waiting. Not forever. No, they didn't have to stay here forever. Just until they'd shed their last blood of youth. Then they'd be released, one at a time, like caged white doves, free to enjoy the cleansed, better world that awaited us all, someday.

"Listen to me, Mary," Vogel said, her voice attempting a kindlier tone now. I'd started along the path toward the driveway. She took my hand, so I'd stop walking, and she squeezed it tenderly. "You're not well, I see that now. I can fix this. Come home. Come home with me, Mary."

"There are quite a few Annes too," I said, taking another step toward the road. Dr. Vogel followed, and I wondered what Eckers thought of the strange way the two of us were walking, hand in hand like that. Perhaps I reminded him of a little girl leading her mother toward some new and exciting discovery. That's what I felt like, anyway.

"And Elizabeths, Catherines, and Ruths," I said, not wanting her to let go of me just yet, trying to keep her interested. "We have more than a few of those. I think it's lovely to name girls after saints, don't you?"

The shoveled path ended. The doctor had to stop walking; the snow was too deep for her shoes. When she released my hand, I caught my breath because I had a sudden sense of falling, the way one does in a dream, and the blood rushed straight to my heart. I used to have dreams about my mother holding my hand and letting go. When she let go of my hand like this, I fell and couldn't stop falling until I awoke, drenched in fear and sorrow. But this wasn't a dream; I was just leaving another place. The sheriff would take me to a jail cell, and another gate would shut behind me forever. I turned to have a last look at Dr. Vogel. *Agnes* was her first name. She was shivering now. Why hadn't she put on proper boots or gloves? I turned back toward the road, and when I stepped into the deep drift, snow avalanched over the sides of my boots and soaked my stockings.

Agnes wasn't an uncommon name. We had several at the Village. I'd looked at the girls that morning, at last. Some were fair, some darker; some had wrinkles; others still had pimples. They had brown eyes, green, gray, blue. I thought of each face now and forgot about the cold that stabbed my wet toes with each step.

"Which of you is called Rose?" I should have asked them that morning.

Rose Stuart, 14 years old. Reads, writes, Protestant, moron. I'd typed her name on a list of recent admissions. And did any of them know Lucy Sheehan? I should have asked that too. Lucy was my age when she arrived—she walked, talked, and she could read and write too. I'd stolen Lucy's file and given it to Jake. She'd been paroled out to work and returned after a month with a bad limp and a black eye. *Vera Ayers, Frances Schultz, Noreen Hill, Lisa Myers, and Ida Storrs.* I stole their files too. I did that. That had to count for something. I hadn't been a coward, and I wasn't dead. *Sarah, Lilah, Missy, Belle, Charlotte, Susan.* I'd taken their files too.

The sheriff opened the door to the back seat of his sedan. He gave me a sad smile before slamming it shut. As we drove away from the Village, I closed my eyes and thought of the others whose files remained. I thought of each name, so I wouldn't forget.

Twenty-Eight

August 29, 1928

Dearest Sister Rosemary,

Thank you for the lovely prayer card in honor of our wedding, Mr. Enright and I will cherish it always. And, how very kind of your priest there in Boston to say a special Mass in Lillian's memory, please do thank him for me. I'm taking my lunch break at my desk as it's raining out, so I thought I'd write you a quick note now and then a longer one later in the week. In response to your question, the company I work for does manufacture parts for refrigerators, but I don't actually work in the factory—that's in New Jersey. I work in the distribution office here in Manhattan.

I wasn't eating at my desk just because it was raining. Jake and I were trying to save up enough money to move from our one-room basement cold-water apartment to a better place. When the rest of the girls who made up the stenographer's pool hurried off to the lunchroom at noon, I'd unwrapped my sandwich and decided to respond to Sister's most recent letter. It was overdue; she'd written me several weeks before. Her letters were very sad. She was unable to come to terms with Lillian's death and her grief caused me a great deal of angst and guilt. I wanted to be able to alleviate her pain, but of course, I couldn't. I tried to write about happier things. Now I typed: *The people I work with are very nice and I've made a few friends outside of the office as well. My favorite is a girl named Olivia. She lives in our neighborhood. She moved to New York not long after I did.*

Mr. Wilcox, my boss, had returned from lunch. I'd finish my letter later. But as I typed inventories and memos, that afternoon, I thought about how much Sister would like my friend Olivia. She's Catholic, for one. She came here to New York like me and millions of others, with big dreams, her past discarded forever. Olivia found a job, right away, as a coat-check girl at Bonwit Teller, but she's so pretty and vivacious, she was soon promoted to a sales position in the hat department and from there to the dress department, where she works now. She's a talented singer. She's got a few connections in the music business, and she sings at a jazz club downtown when she can. She has very little spare time, but on Sundays, Olivia spends the entire day with her niece, Rosemary. We'd taken little Rosemary to the park just the day before. As we watched her and the other children play, I read Sister's most recent letter out loud.

She was so young, my Lil. No, I never dreamed a thing like that could happen to her. Never. Well, luck will only get us so far. Even a found-ling is a fool to press it, the way Lillian did. She shouldn't have married the man, Henning. He was a Protestant, what did she think would happen. Oh, it grieves me so, dear Mary. I can rest now that you've told me that your Mr. Enright is a good Catholic.

Olivia swatted me and said, "You lied? You said Jake's Catholic?"

"No, she asked me if he was Protestant, and I told her the truth—he's not Protestant."

Olivia just laughed. "Well, he's not," I said. "Anyway, that's about it. She signed off in her usual way—'We'll see our Lillian in heaven when it's our time, Mary.'"

Olivia had been smiling at little Rosemary's antics on the slide, but now she turned to me and said, "Oh no, imagine her shock when she gets to heaven and I'm not there. She'll have to assume I didn't make the cut. I'm at the other place."

This made me laugh. "She might think you're in purgatory. Sure, it's no heaven, but I'm told it's not so bad."

"It's bad," Olivia said, with a wry laugh. "I've been there."

The Varnums, the hunters who'd shot Lillian, were father and son, but they were both old. Neither could see very well without eyeglasses.

They'd fired several shots in their terror at being fired at by Lillian, but, only one bullet had found her. By the time Charlie and I were at Lillian's side, Nate Varnum and his father, Bud, were already kneeling next to her. They were ripping open her jacket and shirt to find where the blood was coming from.

"You saw what happened," Bud cried out to us. "He shot at us first. Dear God, what have we done; he's just a tramp. Why'd he come out shooting like that?"

Nate said, "He's breathing, Pa, maybe it ain't so bad."

The blood seemed to be coming from the right shoulder, which Nate said was good—no vital organs there. We tore her jacket and shirt open to make sure she had no other wounds.

"What's this? What . . . ?" Bud said, rocking back on his heels. We'd just exposed her chest. I had assumed she'd at least be wearing a brassiere, but she wore no undergarments. I learned later that she'd hadn't worn a bra or a slip or stockings since she'd arrived at the Village. Those were luxuries, so none of the girls wore them under their baggy uniforms. Now Lillian's breasts were fully exposed, but I was focused on the nasty, ragged hole in her shoulder. Blood was bubbling out of it.

Nate pulled his shirt off and pressed it to the shoulder wound.

"Oh Jesus," Bud said. "Charlie, run inside and grab a blanket. See if there's whiskey—anything like that. We never thought we'd be shooting at nobody tonight, that's for sure."

I was kneeling next to Lillian. I called her name. Bud said, "Charlie Durkin, is that you—what the hell's going on?"

"She's a girl that run from the Village," Charlie said. Jake had limped over. He knelt beside me and whispered, "Oh no. Oh, Mary."

The men still needed to make sure she had no other wounds. When they turned her to look at her back, I heard Lillian give a soft, low moan.

"Lillian," I cried. "Can you hear me?"

"That's right, miss," Bud Varnum said. "Talk to her, don't let her fade away, LILLAN! YOU HEAR ME, MISSY? Jesus Christ, what have I done?"

"Mary?" Lillian moaned. "Mary?"

"Yes, Lillian, I'm here. I'm right here."

Charlie had run back to the truck and was now driving it toward us.

"Keep talking to her," Nate said. He'd brought some bedsheets from the cabin and was ripping them to make bandages.

"Lillian? Can you hear me?" I said, holding a cloth to her wound to stanch the flow of blood. She was moaning in pain and then she seemed to have fainted.

I helped Nate wrap the sheets around Lillian's chest and shoulder. His father, Bud, squatted next to me.

"We never thought we'd see nobody come charging at us like that girl there, no, we sure didn't."

"You mustn't blame yourself," I whispered.

"Well, you saw it," said Bud. "Oh God, what did I do, what did I do?"

"You just grazed her shoulder, Pa, I don't think you even hit a bone," Nate said. "She'll be fine. We just need to get her to the hospital to get stitched up is all."

But Bud's eyes were filled with tears, and his nose was streaming.

Again, I said, "It's not your fault."

There was no official paperwork to be altered to erase her old identity. There was no record of Lillian Faust at all as far as the government was concerned—there never had been, and that was a bit of luck that had to do with her being brought to St. Catherine's, twenty years before. The man who'd brought her was a Dr. Faust. He didn't know who the mother or father was; he'd found the infant outside his office door that morning.

The orphanage named all foundlings after saints. Their first, middle, and last names were saints' names. We had a John Joseph Gregory and a Mary Catherine James at the home while I was there—they were foundlings too. But we'd learned, hearing the sisters talk over the years, that the nuns had argued about what to name the "Faust baby" for weeks. There were already too many Marys and Margarets and Joans in the home. Eventually, they agreed to name the Faust baby "Lillian," after a lesser known saint, but so much time had passed since her arrival, nobody remembered to register her birth with the city clerk. Somebody had scratched the name "Faust" into the orphanage logbook where all admissions were recorded, and at some point "Lillian" was penciled in front of the name, and she was Lillian Faust from that point on. The names Lillian Faust and Lillian Hennings were never on anything but institutional records, first at St. Catherine's and then at Nettleton State Village. Tom Hennings had their marriage annulled so soon after they wed, their marriage license was never filed. Now it never officially existed.

Olivia Moore's name is in the telephone directory and on federal income tax records. She was just mentioned in an item in the *New York Post*, praising her surprise recent appearance at a jazz club. And Olivia Moore would be the name on the passport that she'd applied for. When it arrived, she planned to take her niece to Paris to visit family they had waiting for them there. I asked Olivia, that day in the park, how long she and Rosemary were planning to stay abroad.

"Who knows?" she said. "Maybe a month. Maybe a year. Maybe forever. We might want to travel to other countries while we're there."

"Maybe you can go to Scandinavia and look for your parents," I said, giving her a playful nudge with my elbow.

"Maybe I'll meet my pop Rudy Valentino on the ship." She laughed. We watched Rosemary gleefully chasing another little girl around the swing set. Rosemary suddenly dodged one of the swings, tripped on the pavement, and fell. Before she'd had a chance to even cry out, Olivia and I had scurried over to help her.

"There, my poor baby," Olivia said. "It's just a little scrape on your knee. I'll kiss it and make it better."

"It's bleeding," Rosemary wailed.

"Bleeding? Is that what you call blood?" Olivia said. "Ask your aunt Mary what happened to our friend Deirdre, the little girl at our school who fell running like you were."

Rosemary stopped crying. She searched Olivia's face eagerly and then mine. "Did she break her leg bone right in half, Auntie Liv? Did she, Aunt Mary?"

"Oh, if only she'd just broken her leg," Olivia said woefully. "If only she had your luck, my sweet Rosemary."

Now Rosemary was searching Olivia's eyes hungrily and Olivia spun a tale so dreadful, our old ward matron would be astounded. It involved a leg that was lopped clean off and a wooden peg that replaced it, and if Rosemary didn't believe her, she could ask me. I chimed in with the sad news about termites and the peg leg, and Rosemary forgot all about her little skinned knee.

Sheriff Eckers had been quiet until we drove through the Village gate, that last day. When we were out on the main road, he glanced at me in his rearview mirror and said, "So, where to?"

"Excuse me?" I said.

"Doctor told me to escort you out of here. I can drop you in town someplace it you want."

"I thought you wanted to ask me some questions about the girl. Lillian. The one . . . who got shot last night." I wondered if I'd end up in prison for long. I wondered if Jake would come visit me there.

"Oh. No, the poor dead girl—she's in the morgue over in Northumberland County. Not my jurisdiction."

Charlie had told Dr. Vogel that Lillian was in that morgue. It was Charlie who'd come up with the idea of saying she'd been killed by the hunters. Nate was right: the injury to her shoulder wasn't serious. Dr. Vogel would send for her immediately if she knew we'd left her at the hospital with Jake. We talked about it all the way there. I said there would certainly be an investigation if we said she'd been killed. We'd have to explain. The police would want to speak to the hunters.

"Just play dumb," Charlie had said. That was his response to every objection I made. *Play dumb.*

"That poor dead girl's Northumberland County's problem, not mine," Eckers said as we drove away.

Lillian Faust had no family, no lineage to anchor her to this world. This was what allowed her to disappear so easily. Charlie had told Vogel that a coroner was coming from Northumberland County to go over details regarding Lillian's remains. If Vogel remembered that, she was probably relieved that the coroner never bothered. Dr. Vogel spent the next days and weeks meeting with the board and with attorneys; she wrote letters attacking the newspapers, attacking her board of trustees. She might have wondered why nobody even telephoned about the girl's body, but she was likely relieved that she had one less headache to deal with. Nobody ever contacted her because there was no body at any morgue. There was no investigation into how the Varnums killed Lillian because she wasn't dead.

Sister Rosemary used to tell us that foundlings are blessed with good luck. Lillian disputed this. Every time something bad happened to her, she'd say she was cursed; the nuns were mean to her; she'd broken her arm; she had no family.

"Luck always finds a foundling, Lillian," Sister reminded her. "It'll come around to you, yet."

I never saw Dr. Vogel again. I kept in touch with Charlie, Hal, and Betty, so I know a little about what happened. Vogel blamed Miss Hartley and Olga, the ward matron, for what happened in Building Five. She resigned in anger over lack of support from the board. In the end, she had the backing of not just Judge Filmore but the governor as well. I had thought that the illegal dealing of medicinal whiskey would be the thing that would sink her. It ended up being what saved her. The judge, the governor, the state attorney general, and others—they were all involved. They had to protect her, or they'd all go down. Within a few months of her resignation, she was appointed the first female head of the Pennsylvania Department of Health and Welfare.

What Betty, Hal, and some of the other workers did never appeared in any newspapers. They quietly reached out to the families of some of the girls who were out on "work parole." Those families hired a lawyer who met with the board of trustees and their lawyers. Dr. Vogel and Nettleton Village were never publicly sued or condemned for forcing so many women to work as unpaid laborers. The girls who'd been hired out were released to their families or friends, all of them. A monetary settlement was agreed upon behind closed doors. Their lawyer knew what he was up against. Later, I learned he was the youngest man to receive a Pennsylvania Supreme Court appointment.

Sometimes I wake up in the middle of the night and torment myself with regrets. If only Jake had been able to write the larger article, a true exposé, about not just Nettleton State Village but the many other, similar asylums, still being constructed and expanded all across the country. Institutions to warehouse the "unfit." He might have drawn more attention to the ideology celebrated and endorsed by legislators, scientists, and academics—the theory that future criminals should be removed from society before they actually commit crimes, before they're even conceived.

There hadn't been time. Everything had gone wrong that night we tried to get Lillian out, or at least it didn't go according to our plan. Bertie said everything that happened went according to God's plan. I never would have said a word about Building Five if everything had gone as we had planned. Now there's a new superintendent and the worst of the ward matrons at the Village are gone. It's a better place, everybody agrees about that.

There are nights, too, when I think of Sister Rosemary and how I wish I could ease her sorrow about Lillian. Then Jake will roll over. I'll feel his thigh against mine and its warmth has the effect of spring sun against skin that has finally shed the heavy wool of winter. I remember that I'm not alone, and neither is Sister Rosemary. She has her faith. I settle back into the arms of my husband and wonder why I'd come to think that Sister's ideas about fairies and angels were silly and superstitious. Now I don't think Sister was foolish. Now I think she's wiser than all of us, because she was the only one who knew, and what else could it have been but wisdom for her to know, that Lillian's luck would find her at last.

Acknowledgments

I WISH to thank the clerks and other staff who kindly offered assistance during my visits to the Pennsylvania State Archives building in Harrisburg, Pennsylvania; the Lewisburg, Pennsylvania, County Clerk's office; the Lackawanna County Clerk's Office in Scranton, Pennsylvania; and the Bucknell University Archives Library.

Thank you to my brilliant editor and publisher, Marysue Rucci, who asked to see this book when nobody was allowed to see it, and for making a new home for me at Simon & Schuster. Your endless patience and wisdom truly transformed this book. Thank you to Brittany Adames, Hana Park, Zachary Knoll, Sasha Kobylinski, Ashley Gilliam Rose, Brian Belfiglio, Michelle Chung, Georgia Brainard, Andy Tang, Stuart Smith, and the rest of the wonderful team at Scribner/Simon & Schuster. And many, many thanks to Dorian Karchmar, Margaret Riley King, Sylvie Rabineau, and Sophie Cudd at William Morris Endeavor.

Thank you to all of my friends who tolerated me during the years I spent researching and writing this book. I'm especially grateful to Julie Klam and Laura Zigman. I love you and would be lost without your friendship, support, and your uncanny ability, both of you, to make me laugh when I really don't want to laugh. Also, very kind of you to pretend that I'm right—the other person wrong, always. Speaking of friends, thank you, Kimberly Burns, for reading this novel's very flimsy first draft and helping me believe it was a book.

I'm very grateful to my mother, Judith Howe, who read every page of every draft and was this book's guardian and champion from beginning to end. I'm also indebted to my beloved children, Jack and Devin, who lived with me on and off during the years I worked on this book and endured my writer's fog, fluctuating moods, and overcooked or otherwise destroyed meals.

My deepest love and gratitude to my husband, Denis, whose unwavering encouragement, love, and support have buoyed me, as a writer and a person, for the past three decades.

About the Author

ANN LEARY is the *New York Times* bestselling author of a memoir and four novels, including *The Good House* (now a motion picture starring Sigourney Weaver and Kevin Kline). She has written for the *New York Times*, *Ploughshares*, NPR, *Redbook*, and *Real Simple*, among other publications. Ann lives with her husband in New York.

Visit her online at AnnLeary.com.

The Foundling

Ann Leary

This reading group guide for The Foundling *includes an introduction, discussion questions, and ideas for enhancing your book club. The suggested questions are intended to help your reading group find new and interesting angles and topics for your discussion. We hope that these ideas will enrich your conversation and increase your enjoyment of the book.*

Introduction

In 1927 Pennsylvania, Mary Engle's life changes forever when she lands a secretarial job with a pioneering institution, the Nettleton State Village for Feebleminded Women of Childbearing Age, under the employ of renowned psychologist Dr. Agnes Vogel. Orphaned at a young age, Mary finds a mentor and idol in Dr. Vogel and quickly adapts to life in the Village, making friends and even finding love in the surrounding town. Then one day, she recognizes a young woman, Lillian Faust, who she grew up with in her orphanage and is now an inmate at the Village. When Mary learns of the dark secrets of the Village and the eugenic ideology Dr. Vogel espouses, everything she has come to believe about Dr. Vogel and Nettleton is called into question—and she is forced to make a choice between rescuing Lillian and the future Dr. Vogel has promised her.

Topics & Questions for Discussion

1. When we first meet Dr. Vogel on page 6, she uses many dog whistles in her speech that alert the reader that she's talking about eugenics and that her practices and positions betray what modern readers understand to be a dehumanizing view of people with mental disabilities. What phrases did you pick up on as suspicious or concerning? What made them stick out to you? How do you pick up on language like this in everyday life?

2. On page 77, Dr. Vogel explains to Mary, "Wild antelope drive the genetically weak, aged, or inferior members away, for the health of the rest of the herd. . . . Of course, we're not animals. . . . We must look after our weak and our afflicted." How has eugenics historically couched racism, ableism, and sexism in compassion? What remnants can you find in everyday life and language?

3. On page 96, Jake and Mary talk about how women labeled "feeble-minded" aren't allowed to marry, and on page 123, Lillian mentions that if Vogel acknowledged that some women didn't have mental defects, she'd have to pay them or release them. Research laws in your state or county surrounding people with disabilities and marriage and labor laws, too. What parallels do you see between now and a century ago, when *The Foundling* is set?

4. On page 140, Mary grapples with the revelation that Lillian is not "feebleminded" and tries to reconcile what she sees as opposing truths. She tells Jake, "[Lillian] was so drunk one night that she was raped by one man. Another made her pregnant before she was married. Is that normal? I can't begin to imagine what might

happen to her if she were allowed back out on her own again." Discuss Mary's view of these events. Why does she work so hard to discredit her friend on behalf of Dr. Vogel? What role does Mary's guilt play in her journey to understand what's happening at Nettleton?

5. In the end, Lillian was "killed" in the midst of her escape, but her death led to a police investigation and the revelation of conditions at Nettleton. On page 308, a member of the board of trustees, Eloise Howell, says, "The condition in which we found the girls and women . . . Well it's something I'll never forget." Do you believe that Eloise Howell and others didn't know what was happening at Nettleton? Discuss the responsibility of those in power to ask questions of the institutions they support and profit from.

6. Dr. Vogel idolizes female suffragists like Elizabeth Cady Stanton, Lucretia Mott, and Susan B. Anthony. Do some research into their beliefs as well as other contemporaries, such as Anna Julia Cooper. Do you think they would have approved of Dr. Vogel's ideas regarding the rights of "morally defective" or otherwise "inferior" women? How do your opinions compare to theirs?

7. Some of the reasons women were imprisoned in Nettleton State Village and labeled "feebleminded" are very loose or ill-defined, like "insubordination" or "telling lies." Husbands and others could have them committed based on allegations regarding their behavior. What does this tell you about how they defined not only women with mental disabilities but those without? Could any of these traits of "feeblemindedness" be used against you today?

8. Nettleton State Village was funded by the government and yet also turned a profit selling dairy products as well as the labor of their inmates. It was also heavily funded by people, like Mr. Whitcomb,

who had a vested interest in keeping the institution going. How does this structure rely on exploitation and people in power turning a blind eye? Discuss the ongoing use of penitentiaries as profit systems.

Enhance Your Book Club

1. *The Foundling* is based in part on the author's true family history. Research your own local history and see if any similar institutions once existed in your area. Were there similar scandals there?

2. The IQ test issued to women to judge them "feebleminded" is still pervasive in the collective consciousness. Research the origins of the test and try some of the questions. Does this test seem like an adequate measure of your ability to make decisions for yourself? How does the persistence of the belief in such tests speak to the difficulty of changing public opinion, even after so much time?

3. Throughout *The Foundling*, the terms "idiot," "moron," and "imbecile" are used to describe mental disorders, as was the practice in medicine in the 1920s. Look into the history of other words that were once clinically used and have since fallen into the common vernacular. What trends do you notice?

4. Watch the PBS documentary *The Eugenics Crusade*. How does the plot of *The Foundling* fit into the history of eugenics in the United States? Discuss the continuing legacy of eugenics and how it has adapted over time.